Sunflower Lane Press

A Heart's Journey

Andie Young

Sunflower Lane Press

Visit Sunflower Lane Press at www.sunflowerlanepress.com

Visit Andie Young's website at: www.andieyoungwrites.com

Dedication

To my husband, Rod. My encourager and supporter in everything I do.

Chapter 1

Wrapping her arms around herself, Genny Jones stared out the passenger window and counted mile markers on Interstate Ninety-Five south. Poor sleep had sapped her energy, but she didn't dare sleep. The nightmare that had plagued her would come to life again. After fighting it for the past few minutes, she gave in. Leaning her head back against the headrest, her eyelids fell, and she drifted off to sleep.

Two weeks ago, she'd stood on the fight line at Pope Air Force Base in Fayetteville, North Carolina. The Air Force Honor Guard team, dressed in blue formal uniforms and wearing white gloves, had made slow purposeful movements in sequence as they carried the flag-draped casket of her brother Brandon down the ramp of a C-130 Hercules aircraft. She'd heard about fallen heroes that were flown home but never thought she'd witness her own brother as a fallen hero.

Her eyelids slowly opened when the U-Haul truck came to a stop. Glancing around, she realized they were at a rest area. He looked over at Paul as he shifted the truck into park.

"Welcome to South Carolina. Need a pit stop or want a snack?" Paul asked.

"I'm good." A yawn she attempted to hold back stretched her mouth wide open.

"Okay. Make sure you lock the doors."

Genny nodded and hit the lock button and watched him stroll up the sidewalk. Paul Thompson was her knight in shining armor. Her rescuer. He had gone to Fayetteville and helped her take care of Brandon's affairs and been an emotional support. Now he was moving her to Charleston, where he was stationed with the Air Force, to help her grieve and get on her feet.

A little girl and her mother walked down the sidewalk toward an RV parked in the oversized parking space beside them. The girl giggled and broke free from her mother's grasp, barreling toward the RV. A man stepped out of the driver's side and glanced at the back of the U-Haul. His mouth hung open a moment later.

Brandon's beloved Jeep Wrangler was strapped down on an auto transport trailer. Outfitted with the most popular off-road accessories, the Jeep frequently drew attention. Genny waited until the RV pulled away. She stepped down and walked back to the trailer. Reaching out, she ran her fingers over the treads of the tires. A fine layer of dirt covered the black paint, distorting her reflection. She brushed her hand across the door, wiping away the dirt, and stared at herself.

Brandon had struggled for two weeks debating over two-doors or four-doors. He had spread Jeep brochures across the coffee table one day. When she'd gotten home from class, she made a straight line to her bedroom, but he had other plans for her. "Come here, Genny. Help me decide." She had rolled her eyes and hunched over like the hunchback of Notre Dame and drug her feet like Frankenstein over to the couch. He hated her impersonations, especially when he wanted to show her something.

"Stop it, Genevieve. I'm serious."

"I don't know. Ask Paul."

After a weekend trip to Charleston, Brandon had decided. Paul had recently bought a four-door Toyota Tundra and had it converted for off-roading. Brandon came home and bought a four-door Jeep. The following week, the Jeep went into the shop for off-road conversion.

"Are you okay?" Paul said, touching Genny's arm.

She wiped tears from her cheeks. "Yeah. Just reminiscing."

Attempting to stuff the memory back through the hole it had escaped from was proving to be difficult. This used to be a time she would pray God would clear her mind. That wouldn't happen soon, or maybe ever. God had distanced himself from her. That explained why He'd let her brother die.

Paul's apartment was small, with one bedroom and one bathroom. A brown secondhand couch that had seen better days along with bare white walls was evidence of his bachelor life. The faint scent of cinnamon hung in the air. Genny's gaze fell on a bookshelf full of religious books with a nearly empty reed diffuser on top. She slipped her purse off her shoulder and dropped it to the couch. The thought of sharing such a confined space overwhelmed her.

"I'll sleep on the couch, and you can take the bed. My lease is up on March first, so we'll look for a two-bedroom apartment soon."

"Okay." Genny stared at the couch that was closer to the size of a loveseat. How his six-foot plus frame would fit on the couch was beyond her.

She stepped into the bedroom with her suitcase and slipped off her shoes. Paul's bedroom furniture took up most of the floor space. The same white paint adorned the sparse walls of the bedroom. Genny sat on the bed and laid back, wrapping a tress of hair tightly around her finger. Closing her eyes, she thought about her and Brandon's childhood. A drunk driver had interrupted their happy home, thrusting them into a new life in Tennessee.

The first Sunday Brandon and Genny went to church with their grandparents, a tall boy with black hair had come up to them before the service began wearing a wide grin. "Hi, my name is Paul Thompson. Come sit with us." He gestured to a group of boys a few pews up. Genny knew he had not included her in the invitation. That day, Brandon and Paul became best friends.

A year later, their grandparents believed it was best for Brandon and Genny to be around other kids and decided to sell their farm and move to the city. The house next door to the Thompsons went up for sale and they moved in a month later. Brandon and Paul's friendship strengthened, and they became inseparable. So much so, they joined the Air Force together.

⟫⟫⟫ ⟪⟪⟪

"Genny?" She opened her eyes to see Paul standing by the bed. "You've been asleep for over an hour."

Sitting up, she fought a yawn. "It seems I just closed my eyes."

"Too little sleep will do that." He smiled.

It was hard to sleep when nightmares tormented her every night.

"I'll shift things around to make room for your clothes."

Paul pulled open two dresser drawers and carefully arranged the clothes, so everything fit in one drawer. In the closet, he forced his uniforms onto the rod with his civilian clothes, leaving a rod free for Genny. Taking a few minutes to put away her clothes, she walked to the kitchen to see Paul's selection of beverages. Opening the fridge, she frowned. It was water or an energy drink.

"We'll go grocery shopping tomorrow," Paul said as he reached around her and grabbed the energy drink. He must be exhausted, too.

The next day, Paul pulled into the Piggly Wiggly parking lot and memories came flooding back. Genny's granny loved shopping at Piggly Wiggly. So did she, since her granny would buy her a Coke and a pack of Skittles at the checkout.rent At home, Paul brought in the bags as she put away the groceries. The lines on his forehead seemed to deepen with each load of groceries he brought inside. Brandon had joked about Paul's frugal nature. And being a single man, Genny was sure he'd never bought fourteen bags of groceries in his life.

Paul sat on the couch and searched for storage companies while Genny put away the last few bags of groceries. A few minutes later, he found a company down the road and suggested they go ahead and rent a unit straight away so they could unload the U-Haul. He feared the truck might be a target for thieves. Surprised, Genny didn't think Paul would live in a shady neighborhood. He assured her his neighborhood was safe, but thieves had been targeting moving trucks of military families moving in and out of the area. She was a little reassured.

She followed Paul out to the U-Haul and watched him back the Jeep off the trailer. Her body trembled when the realization hit her she was about to drive Brandon's Jeep. She hadn't driven it since the day she found out he died.

Take your time. Here's the address to the storage company." Genny willed her hand to stop trembling as she reached for the piece of paper. "It's a couple miles down the road on the left."

"Okay." She watched him drive away in the U-Haul. She stood looking at the Jeep as if it was a bull about to charge at her. She swallowed hard and walked toward the driver's side. Standing in a trance with her hand on the door handle, she heard a man's voice call out from the sidewalk.

"Nice Jeep."

She looked at him to make sure he was talking to her. There were no other Jeeps around and she forced herself to reply. "Thank you." Thank you? She had nothing to do with the Jeep. She didn't buy it or have it converted. Brandon's death was the only reason she possessed it now.

Opening the door, she stood for a moment as if she didn't know what to do next. She'd driven the Jeep for the past several months. Genny knew exactly what to do. She steadied her foot on the running board and grabbed the inside handle above the door frame. Afraid she was about to fall backward, she pulled with enough force that she almost propelled herself into the passenger seat.

Straightening, she sat quietly for a few moments and looked around. Why did everything seem so different? It was as if she'd never paid attention to what was inside. What she noticed first was that she hadn't taken care of the Jeep since Brandon had left for deployment. Crumbs, dirt, and debris she couldn't identify littered the floor. Fast food bags were tossed in the back. A Sonic cup that was empty, except for the fluid left after the ice melted, occupied a cup holder. She should be ashamed of herself.

Genny slid the key in the ignition switch and cranked the engine. Moisture filled her eyes when the mufflers growled to life. The steering wheel felt different now. How many times had Brandon wrapped his fingers around the steering wheel? How many times had his hand touched the gear shift? Lowered the window?

The *U.S. Air Force* sticker that stretched across the back window stared at Genny in the rearview mirror. Her eyes shifted down and she saw the safety belt that Brandon had worn when he worked on the flight line reflecting in the back window. Driving the Jeep was going to be harder than she imagined. Heat radiated throughout her chest. She had no idea how she was going to survive today, much less the rest of her life.

"Oh, Brandon..." She wiped the moisture from her eyes and shifted into drive.

Genny pulled out of the apartment complex and followed Paul's directions to the storage unit. If the temperature was higher, she'd take the top off and enjoy the sunshine. Four or five months until it was warm enough for her to visit her happy place—the beach. Her chest was light for the first time since December second, the day she found out Brandon died. But it wouldn't last.

Sunlight reflected off the windshields of oncoming vehicles as Genny drove to the storage unit. A U-Haul pulled up to a traffic light a few cars ahead and she wondered if she'd caught up with Paul. Maybe not. He said it was common to see U-Hauls since Charleston was a military town.

The weight of the responsibility she'd heaved onto Paul's shoulders was as heavy as a U-Haul. She was attending college full-time and worked part time when Brandon died. How could she support herself? Paul was all she had, and he wouldn't leave her to flounder.

Genny found the storage company and made her way to the area of the unit Paul had rented. When she pulled around the building, she saw Paul standing at the back of the truck. As she got closer, she realized he was leaning against the bumper and his face was as white as the walls in his apartment. She climbed down and jogged toward the truck. When she reached him, she noticed his red, puffy eyes.

"Are you okay?" Her own eyes burned with tears.

"Yeah. Just overwhelmed." He slipped his arm around her shoulders. They stood looking at Brandon's twenty-eight years of life crammed into nearly two dozen boxes that would soon be confined to the four walls of a storage unit. For as long as she lived, Genny would never forget the knock on the door the night of December second. Looking through the peephole, two men in dark blue military uniforms had stood on the doorstep. Genny had watched enough military themed movies to know the men were about to forever change her life. Nausea rose and hung in her throat as she grasped the doorknob. She didn't know if she should open the door or run down the hall and hide in her closet. Unfortunately, she chose the first option, making her nightmare a reality.

"Miss Genevieve Jones?" the taller man had asked.

Genny had recognized the other man as Brandon's sergeant at the shop. She braced herself on the door when a heavy black fog fell over her, threatening to bring her to her knees.

"Miss Jones, I'm Major Manning. I believe you know Master Sergeant Combs." Genny nodded when the man gestured to Brandon's sergeant. "I have an important message to deliver. May we come in?" he had asked. If she said no, Brandon would be home soon, and they could continue with their easy-going life. But that wasn't the reality. She didn't remember much after that. The major had handed her an envelope and talked, but she had no idea what he had said. She pulled out the letter and unfolded it. There were five words she read that she would never forget as long as she lived. "...*I regret to inform you...*" Inform her of what? She wished they had regretted to inform her that Brandon had lost a limb and not his life. They would have managed with a missing limb, but a missing life?

She and Paul pushed aside their emotions and focused on unloading the truck. Paul handed her a small box that contained her and Brandon's childhood pictures. When she's moved in with Brandon, they combined their pictures into one box. It was her plan to make a scrapbook album, but she soon discovered scrapbooking wasn't a hobby of hers.

The next box he handed her took her breath away. It was the box Brandon had been saving items he'd bought for his daughter. His ex-wife frequently moved and wouldn't give him her new addresses, and he wasn't able to send the package.

"Sarah's something else. How old is Zoe now? Eight?"

Genny peeked inside the box. "Nine. He loved that little girl. I hate she won't know her daddy. He hadn't seen her in nearly four years, and I have no idea where she is now."

"Mmm, that's so sad." Paul brought out Brandon's TV. "Let's put this close to the door. You can use it in your bedroom when we move."

"Okay." Genny fought a rush of emotion. It seemed wrong to take Brandon's TV. It seemed wrong for her to take possession of any of his belongings.

"The Air Force will find Sarah. Zoe is Brandon's next-of-kin and will get his life insurance."

"I forgot he had life insurance. Sarah will be happy. She always complained that the child support wasn't enough. How will they find her?"

"This is the military, Genny. They have Sarah's information, like her social security number or the British equivalent, from when she was Brandon's dependent. And I'm sure she keeps her address and bank account information up to date for the direct deposit of the child support."

"But she could be anywhere in England. They had such a nasty divorce. I think she moved around on purpose so he couldn't find her."

"It doesn't matter where she is. They'll find her."

"When they find her...maybe...I don't know."

"You could connect with Zoe?"

"Yeah. But I'm not holding my breath."

They moved the furniture into the storage unit on one side and the boxes on the other. Together, they had decided to use the living room and dining room furniture from the apartment in Fayetteville when they moved into a bigger apartment. Paul suggested Genny's boxes go in last, so they were easily accessible once they moved into the new apartment. Genny followed him to the U-Haul store to turn in the truck. He stared out the passenger window on the way to the apartment. What was he thinking?

Chapter 2

"**M**erry Christmas!" Paul grinned at Genny as she walked out of the bedroom, pulling her hair back in a high ponytail. She sat next to him on the couch and rubbed the sleep from her eyes. Grabbing a present from under the little Christmas tree, Paul handed it to Genny.

"Here." It was neatly wrapped in snowman wrapping paper. She must have rolled her eyes or something since the smile fell off his face. "I thought it would cheer you up."

"Oh, it does. I'm still half asleep. But…I didn't buy you anything." She glanced under the tree as if a present for him had appeared overnight.

"I didn't get you a get expecting to get something in return."

She took the present from his hand and unwrapped it, careful not to tear the paper. "Thank you!" She allowed a hint of a smile.

I know you like journals." He was right. She had enough journals to open her own journal bookstore.

"I've never had a fabric covered journal." She brushed her hand across the avocado-colored cover. Genny leaned over and hugged him. She thumbed through the pages and brought the journal to her nose and sniffed. Bible verses were at the bottom of the pages, and she read a few aloud. "Tears gathered in her eyes.

"Hey…" He draped his arm around her shoulders and pulled her close.

"I was saving money to buy Brandon the cover he wanted for the tire on the back of the Jeep."

"I'm so sorry, Genny." He rubbed her shoulder. "He talked about hiking part of the Appalachian trail this spring."

"I remember him talking about that. He was so excited." She looked down at the journal again and rubbed her finger over the appliqued teacup in the middle of the cover.

"Oh, my girlfriend is coming over this afternoon."

"Okay." Paul had a girlfriend, she knew as much. Since she'd found out that Brandon had died, Paul had been her comfort and her rock. She wasn't in the mood to socialize and hoped his girlfriend wouldn't stay for the rest of the day.

A knock at the front door tightened the knot in Genny's stomach. She'd been dreading this for the past two hours. She drew in a deep breath and rose from the couch when Paul opened the door. His deep voice greeted the woman. Genny averted her eyes when they exchanged a brief kiss.

Paul gestured to his girlfriend, "Genny, this is Brianna Javernick."

Genny rubbed her palms on her leggings and walked over to the couple. "Hello."

"Hi, Genny. Nice to meet you."

A real life Barbie doll was standing in front of Genny. Brianna's perfect long blonde hair, perfect makeup, and perfect body. Her hair happened to be the shade of blonde Genny had wanted as a teen. She'd begged her granny for months to let her dye her hair, but she always said no. "God gave you the most beautiful auburn hair, like your mother."

There was something about the way Brianna looked at her. Did she see her as a threat? Genny could almost see Brianna's claws protruding from her fingertips. But why? She was everything Genny wasn't. She and Paul made the perfect pair. They were both gorgeous and could grace the cover of magazines. She was little Genny Jones—a tall, skinny girl with the body of a twelve-year-old. And Paul saw Genny as nothing more than a sister anyway, so why was Brianna worried?

Paul guided Brianna to the couch and went into the bedroom for a moment. A trail of perfume assaulted Genny as Brianna passed by. When she sat down, she crossed her legs and stared at Genny like a bird of prey stared at a field mouse. She was right. Brianna saw her as a competitor. Genny allowed a slight smile. Brianna shifted her gaze to the patio doors in response.

Paul returned a few moments later with a small box and handed it to Brianna. Genny went to the kitchen for something to drink and watched the two exchange gifts. The gold cross necklace Paul gave Brianna would look perfect against her bronze skin. Brianna turned toward Genny and lifted her hair while Paul fastened the necklace around her neck. She proudly displayed a smirk on her face.

Brianna leaned over and kissed Paul full on the mouth. He pushed away, red tinting his tightened features. "Brianna."

"I'm thanking you for my gift." She pressed her lips tightly together and looked in Genny's direction. Brushing her hair over her shoulder, she handed a gift to Paul. She caressed his cheek as he opened the gift. He jerked his head away and glanced at Genny.

Genny fought hard to keep her lunch in her stomach. But it was a losing battle between Brianna's performance and the discomfited look on Paul's face. She guessed Brianna hadn't put on such a show before she came along.

"I'm going to rest for a little while." Genny headed to the bedroom.

"You don't have to, Genny," Paul said.

"No, it's okay. I have a headache." It was a lie, but she had to get out of there.

Genny closed the bedroom door and sat on the bed. The apartment walls were thinner than she had noticed before today.

"It's not right for you to sleep on the couch. It's your bed." Brianna's tone edged on hatred. Genny had done nothing to this woman except exist.

"Brianna, I will *not* make her sleep on the couch."

The words that drifted through the wall brought tears to her eyes. A walk would get her away from the tension in the living room. Genny slipped on her shoes and one of Brandon's sweatshirts. When she walked into the living room, Paul looked up at her. His eyebrows came together.

"I thought I'd go for a walk." She grabbed her coat from the back of the couch and slipped it on.

"It's too cold and you don't know the area," Paul said.

Brianna narrowed her eyes at Paul behind his back.

"I wanted to give you guys some privacy."

"Oh, that's nice of you." Brianna didn't hide her smirk.

"No, it's okay." Paul turned to Brianna. "Right?"

Red snuck up Brianna's neck. "Yea, that's fine. It's no problem, Genny. Paul and I can go out for coffee or something."

"Brianna, it's Christmas day," Paul said.

"I'll go into the bedroom then." Genny's statement broke the tension. When she turned, Brianna glared at her. She closed the bedroom door behind her and went into the bathroom. Staring at herself in the mirror, she'd cried every day for the past three weeks and it showed. The bags under her eyes puffed out like they were full of cotton. She'd gone through a bottle of artificial tears, but her eyes were still red, as if she'd been in a sandstorm.

Mumbled voices came through the wall. The front door slammed, rattling the door to the bedroom. Paul knocked a few moments later.

"Come in." Genny wiped her cheeks.

"Want to watch TV?" Paul tilted his head to the side and smiled.

Genny stared at him for a few moments. "Sure. I'll be there in a minute."

She'd been in Charleston for three days now and the walls of the tiny apartment had started slowly closing in on her. If she squeezed her eyes shut, she'd be back in Fayetteville when she opened them. She was still here. Still living in a nightmare. How long would it take for her to support herself? She couldn't rely on Paul forever. Now that she had a taste of Brianna, how long could she tolerate her presence and falling all over Paul at every opportunity?

So many questions. But the most baffling question of all? Why did Paul choose to spend the rest of the day with her and not Brianna?

A new year was a time for new beginnings, but 2010 flowed into 2011 like a raging river. Paul looked at his watch and softly sighed. Any other time, he'd have been on his way to church by now, but he had adjusted his schedule for Genny's sake. Paul looked up when he heard the bedroom door open.

Genny walked into the living room wearing a green long-sleeved dress and black leggings. Her long hair was in a single braid down her back. She slipped her purse over her shoulder and ran her hands down the front of her dress.

Paul had seen Genny a few times a year before Brandon died. The last time he'd seen her was before Brandon had deployed last May. Now that he had been with her every day since December third, he had seen a different side of her. She was no longer the awkward, skinny teenager.

At nearly six feet tall, with long auburn hair and green eyes, her presence drew attention when she walked into a room. Not only for her height but for her natural beauty, even if she didn't see it.

"You look very nice." For a moment, Paul's eyes lingered on her. Pink teased Genny's cheeks.

"Thank you. So do you."

Paul found a few friends in the foyer and stopped to catch up. Genny's arm bush against his and he looked at her. Her demeanor was like a small child afraid to leave her father's side. He lightly bumped her with his shoulder. A brief smile crossed her lips.

"I'm so sorry about your brother," one of Paul's friends said.

Paul had asked for prayer from his single's group, and he kept them up to date on Genny. She was shy by nature, and he didn't know how she would react to a condolence so soon, especially from a stranger.

"Thank you." She shifted her weight and leaned into Paul. "Excuse me." Her tearful eyes looked up at him, and she headed toward the restroom.

He watched her walk away. When she opened the restroom door, he caught a glimpse of Brianna primping in the mirror as the door closed. A moment later, Brianna emerged and headed straight to where he was standing. He'd never seen Brianna act toward anyone the way she acted toward Genny.

When Genny walked to where Paul and Brianna stood, Brianna draped herself over Paul like a cloak. An irritation he'd never felt for Brianna took root in his stomach. The worship band began playing, and Paul rested his hand at the small of Genny's back to usher her into the sanctuary. He glanced over his shoulder. Brianna trailed behind with her chin held high and jaw clenched.

After the worship band had finished, the pastor walked on stage and opened the service with a prayer. Paul heard the pew creak and looked over. Genny slipped past the family next to her and fled to the back of the sanctuary. The pastor ended the prayer and began the sermon. Ten minutes had passed, and Genny hadn't returned.

"I'll be right back," Paul whispered.

Brianna exhaled sharply as Paul rose and slipped past her. He walked into the foyer and glanced around. Maybe she was in the restroom. When he headed back to the sanctuary, he noticed her outside under the awning.

He pushed open the doors and walked toward her. "Gen?"

"I'm sorry. I couldn't breathe." Her eyes glistened.

"It's okay. We can go."

"No, I'll be okay. I'm going to stay here for a little while longer." She wrapped her arms around herself and shivered.

"It's cold out here. I'll be right back. I need to get my Bible."

"Paul." Genny's shoulders fell.

"It's okay, Genevieve. really." When Paul stepped inside the front door, Brianna walked up to him with his Bible in her hand.

"I guess you're leaving." She pinched her lips together so tight white peeked through her red lipstick. "You can take her home and we can meet for lunch."

Did she expect him to abandon Genny for lunch with her? "No, I won't leave her alone right now."

Brianna groaned. "So, when are we going out again? It's been over a month since we had a date."

"Brianna." Paul rubbed the back of his neck. Before him stood a woman he didn't recognize.

"I'm sorry. That was insensitive." She rested her hand on his arm. "Call me."

"I will." He kissed her cheek, grabbed his Bible, and walked out the door.

This past Labor Day weekend, one of the women in his singles group brought Brianna to the singles get together. There were about twenty people in total and a little over half were guys. Brianna singled him out from the start. He thought she was pretty, and they had easy conversation. By the end of the night, he'd asked her out and they had been dating ever since.

A few weeks before Brandon died, she had suggested that they get to know each other better. He didn't have to ask for clarification and reminded her of his feelings on the issue of intimacy, and she backed down. It was when he told her about Brandon and let her know he'd be going to Fayetteville, her behavior had changed. Paul had no idea she was so insecure.

She had called and texted him numerous times a day, wanting to know what he was doing and when he'd be back. On the day of the funeral, he had told her he would be unavailable for a while. By the time they got back to Brandon's apartment, he had two voicemails and a dozen texts.

Paul figured that once she met Genny, she would understand. He was wrong and, frankly, quite embarrassed by her behavior on Christmas Eve. He had a feeling she was showing her true colors and the woman he knew before Brandon died had hidden herself behind a mask.

On the drive home, Paul watched Genny out of the corner of his eye. She wiped her cheeks and caught him looking at her. She turned and said, "I didn't mean to ruin church."

He pulled into the parking lot of the complex and shifted the truck into park. "You didn't ruin anything."

"Brianna didn't look happy."

"She'll get over it." He grinned. "So, what do you want for lunch? I think there are still a few tomatoes. How about tomato sandwiches?"

"Yeah, that sounds good."

"Reminds you of summers in Tennessee, right?"

"Sure does." When they walked into the apartment, Genny headed to the kitchen and pulled down two paper plates and a bag of chips from the cabinet by the fridge. Paul sliced up the tomatoes and made two sandwiches.

They sat on the couch eating while a documentary on Area 51 played on the television. Well, mostly Paul. He doubted Genny was too interested in aliens.

"Hey, anytime you don't feel like going anywhere or doing anything, you don't have to, okay? Just let me know." He didn't want Genny to feel any pressure. She was going through enough.

Genny looked at him with a mouth full of sandwich. After swallowing, she nodded toward the television. "So, are you a conspiracy theorist?"

He looked at her and chuckled. "Not really. I'm educating myself." And a little curious, but he wasn't going to admit it.

"Oh, I see." Genny took a sip of water. "So, have you watched any bigfoot documentaries?" She grinned.

He couldn't lie. "Maybe one or two." She tossed her head back, closed her eyes, and let out a laugh that shook her shoulders. He couldn't help but laugh along with her. Today was the first day he'd seen her sweet smile and heard her lighthearted laughter since Brandon's death.

Chapter 3

Paul had been back at work for two full weeks now and had settled into his usual work routine. He had taken four weeks of leave to help Genny settle Brandon's affairs. Two weeks were initially scheduled to spend Christmas with his parents and two weeks his command had approved. God had given him all the time he needed to help Genny through the funeral, pack up the apartment, and settle into her new home.

Genny was depressed, but he was afraid to point it out. Nearly every day when he got home, she was either sleeping or still in her pajamas on the couch. Today was no exception. When he unlocked the deadbolt and walked in, Genny was lying on the couch, covered with the throw blanket.

She looked down at herself and grimaced. "I'm still in my pajamas. I was having a bad day." She sat up and readjusted her ponytail.

"You're entitled." He had bought a pizza on the way home since it was Friday, their unofficial pizza night. He sat on the couch next to her and opened the pizza box. "Want to talk about it?"

"Just what has been haunting me lately." She grabbed a slice and took a bite.

"I'm sorry, Genny."

She shrugged. "I know it will get better, but it's the journey to where he's not my every thought that I'm dreading. That didn't come out the way I meant it."

"I get it."

"I do have a question."

"Sure."

"Why did Brandon go to breakfast? You know he wasn't a breakfast person."

Paul had told Genny about the incident report. Brandon's shop superintendent was his superintendent when he was stationed in Colorado, so he had ways of finding out what had happened. An Iraqi contractor had opened fire in the dining room during breakfast. Brandon was among four people killed.

"I don't know, Gen. I'm not going to give you the standard answer that God needed him in Heaven. But Brandon knew when it was his time that only his life on earth would end, and he had eternal life in Heaven."

"God has my parents and grandparents. Why does He need Brandon too?"

"Gen, I'm as lost as you are. I take comfort in knowing that our answers are waiting for us in Heaven." Paul had to cling to God not only to help Genny, but for his own sake.

"Yeah, I guess." She went into the kitchen. "Are you and Brianna going out tonight?"

"Yep, I'm taking her to a nice restaurant."

"You're eating twice?"

"You know how those restaurants are. Hardly any food on the plate."

He grinned and went to shower and shave. When he came into the living room to head out, Genny was sitting on the couch channel surfing. She gave him a sly smile.

"Have fun."

"Thanks." He grabbed his jacket off the back of the couch and walked to the door. "I shouldn't be too late. Call or text if you need anything."

"Okay."

He locked the deadbolt and headed down the stairs to the parking lot. This was the first Friday night Genny was alone since moving to Charleston. Hopefully, it was a pleasant one.

Genny's stomach growled, and she went into the kitchen to search for something else to eat. There was nothing interesting in the cabinets or fridge, so she decided to go to Chick-fil-A for a milkshake. Changing into jeans and a shirt, she grabbed her purse and made her way out to the Jeep. While waiting in the drive-thru, she spotted a Chevy Silverado park and a group of guys poured out. They were laughing and joking with each other when she heard one of them make a comment about the Jeep. "Great," she mumbled under her breath. The guy walked up to the passenger window and tapped on the glass.

"Hey man, nice Jeep!" She lowered the window. "Oh. Pardon me, miss." He smiled and bowed. "Nice Jeep."

"Thanks." She raised the window and closed the gap between her and the car in front of her.

After dinner, she sat on the couch browsing through the guide to find something to watch on TV. Her mind drifted to Paul and Brianna. No matter how hard she tried to fight her feelings, Brianna came off as a two faced, self-absorbed snob. Brianna was nice to her in front of Paul but shot her flaming daggers behind his back. What did he see in her? They were polar opposites. He was nice; she was rude. He was genuine; she was fake. He was godly, and in her opinion, Brianna was not. And to think he met her through church.

Brianna was high maintenance, too. How much did she pay to keep her blonde hair blonde? Her wardrobe alone must cost a thousand dollars a year. Genny looked down. At least Brianna tried. Here she sat wearing five-year-old jeans and a white shirt with a stain on the bottom. An ensemble she had worn to Chick-Fil-A. She sighed. Thank goodness she went through the drive thru. She laid the remote on the coffee table and went into the bedroom.

Genny pulled a red dress off a hanger and slipped it on over her head. She'd worn the dress a few years ago to a club in Fayetteville with her friends. Mirrors didn't lie. The dress was too short and too clingy. She felt awkward then and awkward now.

The makeup tutorial Genny watched on YouTube was no help. A clown rocked red lipstick better, and her smoky eyes looked more like zombie eyes. She was no Brianna. Genny washed her face and took a step back. Why did she have to be so plain? She sighed and slipped into bed, pulling the covers up to her waist.

She decided to surf on her laptop and pulled it out from under the bed. She'd found herself going to Brandon's Facebook page more frequently lately. The day he died, he had updated his profile picture to Baby Jesus lying in the manger. Brandon loved shining his light at Christmastime. He'd said he hoped to reach his non-believing friends through Facebook.

Genny did something she probably shouldn't have done . Clicking on the photo album, she scrolled through the pictures. There were pictures of Zoe as a baby, and some of him and Paul. Only a few pictures of her, but that was her fault. She made him promise not to upload any pictures without her consent.

She came across a group of pictures that he had taken in Iraq. In every picture, he wore a smile that took up his entire face. That was Brandon. He was always happy. Her vision blurred, making it difficult to see. Closing the laptop, she slid it under the bed and turned off the light. Wiping tears from her cheeks, it was next to impossible to clear her mind.

⇢⇢⇢ ⇠⇠⇠

Paul walked Brianna to the door of her apartment and shifted his weight from foot to foot while she unlocked the deadbolt and stepped inside. "Aren't you coming in?" She brushed her long hair over her shoulder.

His heart pounded as he looked at her. She looked beautiful in black jeans and a fitted red sweater accentuating her curves. "I really should get back and check on Genny."

"A few minutes won't hurt. I can make coffee." Her eyes brightened.

Against his better judgment, he found himself across the threshold and standing in her living room.

"Have a seat. I'll put on the coffee."

While the coffee brewed, Brianna excused herself to her bedroom with a lighter in her hand. What was she doing? Better yet, what was she hoping would happen tonight? She made her way back into the living room and walked around the room lighting candles. Within a few minutes, a mixture of vanilla and cinnamon filled the air.

"How's Genny?"

"She's doing okay, considering her brother died six weeks ago."

"Does she have other family?" Brianna leaned against the door frame to the kitchen.

"No, Brandon was her last surviving family member."

"Oh, that's sad. So why does she have to stay with you? Doesn't she have friends?"

Where was this going? Paul's face burned hot. "No friends, and she is staying with me to keep her from being homeless. She's like family. I care about her and won't let anything happen to her."

"Oh, like a sister." The coffee maker beeped, giving him time enough for his blood pressure to fall out of the dangerous range.

Brianna grabbed two cups from the cabinet above the coffeemaker.

"There's no reason to be jealous, Brianna."

She looked at him with dark eyes—a look he'd never seen before. "I'm not jealous." The burner hissed when a drop of coffee fell as Brianna pulled out the carafe to fill the cups.

"Well, you said nothing to her about Brandon the two times you saw her. That's not like you."

Brianna sighed. "I wasn't thinking. I'll give her my condolences next time."

She walked into the living room with the two cups of coffee and sat down on the couch next to Paul. She handed him one cup and took a sip from the other cup and sat it on the coffee table.

"I had a nice time at dinner." A sultry smile played on her lips. She took the cup from his hand and sat it on the coffee table next to hers.

A jolt of electricity ran down his spine when she leaned over and raked her long, red nails through the hair on top and up the back of his head. "I've always loved the way your hair is shaved on the sides and back and longer on the top. It stands out with your black hair." Her warm breath caressed his neck.

"It's called a high and tight. A lot of military guys have the same style." Sensations stirred in him he'd fought to keep suppressed for years. Every ounce of his being screamed for him to leave, but he sat on the couch as if Brianna herself had glued him down. *God, give me strength to deny these urges.*

Brianna leaned over and slowly kissed him. Her perfume enveloped them. When he kissed her back, her fingers grasped his belt buckle. "Brianna!" He grabbed her hand and pushed it away. "Don't do that!"

"What's wrong, Paul?" Annoyed, she took a deep breath and pulled her sweater down over the waistband of her jeans. "We've been dating for over three months now. Don't you think it's time we get better acquainted?"

"Brianna, I've told you before that I'm abstinent and I'm tired of you pushing the boundaries." Pain seared through his jaw, and he realized he was clenching his teeth.

"Are you sure it's not because of Genny?"

"What?" Paul shot back. Her accusation brought a whole new level of anger.

"A pretty young thing like her? What is she, eighteen?"

"She's twenty-three and like a sister!"

"Are you sure about that?"

"You know what? This isn't going to work."

"So, you *are* sleeping with her?" Brianna scoffed.

"Wow, just wow." Paul grabbed his jacket and walked out her front door. He heard her throwing accusations at him he wouldn't repeat. He climbed in the truck and headed home, promising himself to never darken her doorstep again.

⤜⤜⤜ ⤛⤛⤛

Genny woke up thirsty and checked her phone. *Ten-thirty.* What was Paul doing? She went into the living room and turned on the lamp. Her scream pierced the silence when she caught sight of Paul sitting on the couch like an intruder.

"You scared me to death!" She pushed her fist against her chest to calm her pounding heart.

"I'm sorry. I turned off the lamp so I wouldn't wake you going into the bathroom."

"How long have you been home?"

"Half an hour." His jaw muscle tightened.

"Are you okay?"

"Brianna and I broke up."

"Oh, I'm sorry Paul. Want to talk about it?" An unexpected lightness filled her chest as tension left her shoulders. Paul's relationship with Brianna had affected her more than she realized.

"Not tonight. I'm going to get ready for bed."

"Okay." She grabbed a bottle of water from the fridge and gasped when Paul appeared around the corner.

"By the way, we need to find a new church."

"Okay." His eyes were red now. Who broke up with whom and was Paul that heartbroken? A rush of guilt hit her for her earlier thoughts about him and Brianna. The guilt didn't last long.

After Paul turned in for the night, she climbed back into bed and reached over to turn off the lamp. The journal Paul had given her for Christmas peeked out from a stack of papers on the nightstand. She grabbed it and ran her fingers over the fabric cover. A pen lay on the nightstand next to the water bottle. She picked it up and wrote the first entry.

January 15, 2011

I thought I'd write in this journal since Paul gave it to me for Christmas. 2010 ended horribly. I still feel like it's all a terrible nightmare and I'm going to wake up at any moment and be back in Fayetteville. I don't mind living with Paul. He's been great, but I want my old life back. Paul and Brianna broke up. I feel bad for Paul. I lied. I'm ashamed to admit that I'm glad she's out of the picture. I lied again. I'm not ashamed.

Chapter 4

"Genny?" Paul called out when he walked in the door from work. He had texted her a little before eleven to invite her to lunch, but never heard back. He turned the bedroom doorknob slowly and stuck his head through the crack. His eyes widened when he caught sight of her curled under the covers. He walked to the side of the bed. "Are you okay? You're pale." He reached down and touched her forehead.

"I'm hurting so bad." He sat on the side of the bed and softly touched her arm.

"I have endometriosis and it's getting bad."

Paul wrinkled his brow. "What's endumetresos?"

Genny let out a soft giggle. "Endometriosis. It's a girl thing. Uterine tissue grows outside the uterus and can cause lesions and scar tissue that can bind your organs together." She winced and groaned. "My doctor in Fayetteville said I will need surgery. It's a matter of when."

"Oh wow. Anything I can do for you?"

She drew in a deep breath. "Do you have a heating pad?"

"No, mine died on me, but I will run out and get one. Anything else?"

"I can't find my prescription medication and it always knocks out the pain." She inhaled sharply. "My prescription must be in a box in the storage unit."

"I'll go by the storage unit and search through the boxes."

Paul drove to Walmart for a heating pad, then stopped by the storage unit on his way home. He sifted through a few small boxes and ran across a box with *Important Documents* written on the top in Brandon's handwriting. Curious, he pulled off the top and scanned through the documents. At the bottom of the box was Brandon's will. He'd have to remember to give it to Genny once she was feeling better emotionally.

Putting the contents back in the box, he set it aside and continued to look for Genny's box. His phone vibrated and he pulled it out of his pants pocket. He guessed it was Genny requesting something else. He was wrong.

Paul, I'm sorry about what happened. Please call me so we can talk about our relationship.

He stared at the text from Brianna and gritted his teeth. He slipped his phone back in his pocket and continued going through the boxes. A few minutes later, he ran across a box labeled *Genny's extra bathroom stuff.* Opening the box, he moved around the items and discovered a bottle of prescription pain medication. He picked up the box and headed home.

Paul pushed the bedroom door open. Genny opened her eyes and rolled over to look at him. He pulled out the heating pad from its box, plugged it in, and handed it to her.

"Here's your medicine. Do you want me to heat a can of soup?" He sat the pill bottle on the nightstand.

"Sure, thank you so much."

"No problem."

After Genny ate dinner and settled down for the night, Paul sat on the couch looking at his checkbook. His cell phone vibrated. It had to be Brianna.

Paul?

He shook his head and laid the phone on the coffee table. It was the twenty-fifth of the month, and his checking account was well below his usual balance. Another week until payday. He'd have to talk to Genny about tightening the budget.

He sighed as he went through the stack of bills Genny had given him. There was a doctor's bill for over five hundred dollars, the Jeep insurance renewal, and to his disappointment, a bill for six hundred dollars on a maxed out credit card. How convenient that Genny had put that one at the bottom of the stack.

Genny also needed surgery. Judging by how bad off she was tonight, it would need to be soon. Without insurance, the surgery would be very expensive. He guessed at least a couple thousand dollars. He didn't have that kind of money lying around. He had some money saved but would prefer not to dip into it if he could help it.

The next day, Paul checked in at the dental clinic and took a seat in the waiting room. He laid his hat on the table next to his chair and noticed a Tricare pamphlet among the magazines that covered the tabletop. He picked it up and read about benefits for dependents. What caught his eye was health insurance. Genny didn't currently have health insurance and he guessed she hadn't in a while.

"Sergeant Thompson?" Paul looked up and followed the hygienist to an exam room.

He lowered himself onto the dental chair and got comfortable. The hygienist pressed the button to recline the chair and laid a disposable dental bib across the top of Paul's chest. Suddenly, thoughts pelted him from every angle. What if Genny had a dental emergency? Dental procedures were expensive. What about the flu? A car accident? Insurance would take care of a car accident with the policy he was paying for. Paul sighed.

"Are you okay, Sergeant Thompson?"

"Yeah." No, he wasn't. Paul swallowed hard. He was far from okay. On the way back to the shop, his mind raced from scenario to scenario. It wasn't just Genny's medical care that worried him; it was that he was paying for everything. He took in a deep breath and exhaled. And under no circumstances would he suggest she find a job. Brandon hadn't been gone two months yet. God would provide.

⟫⟫ ⟪⟪

Genny climbed into the Jeep and hit the main road close to the apartment. Paul had been covering all her expenses since she had moved in with him. The household account she shared with Brandon had a couple hundred dollars in it, but they used it for moving expenses. She brought up the idea of getting a job last night, but Paul was adamant that it was too soon for her to work. She had to do something to take the pressure off him.

As she drove down the road, nothing leaped out at her. Driving in the opposite direction, she ended up fifteen minutes past the apartment. A small coffee shop came into view. It was a perfect time for a break.

"The Roasted Bean. Cute name." Genny looked at the clock on the console. It was almost three, no wonder the drive thru was full. When she opened the front door, she was met with a mixture of freshly ground coffee beans and baking pastries. The restaurant was small and boasted a mom and pop feel. A few people sat at tables and stools here and there. When she approached the counter, the drive thru resembled a beehive with baristas darting in and out.

A frazzled woman wearing a headset looked her way and shouted over the coffee machines, "Be right with you!"

Genny nodded and looked around. A display of brightly painted mugs stood next to the counter. She walked up to another display that held small bags of fresh ground coffee. Picking up a bag, she closed her eyes and sighed. The coffee must be dark roast based on the strong aroma that seeped through the bag. According to the sign, the beans were ground on the premises. Genny continued to take in her surroundings. She'd love working at a place like this.

"Can I help you?" The woman the voice belonged to sounded like she'd rather be anywhere but here.

Genny stepped back to the register. The woman wore an expression that looked like she had eaten a pound of sour grapes. She glanced at the lopsided nametag pinned on the woman's apron. *Julie.*

"Julie! You made it!" The woman with the headset beamed from the drive thru.

"Yeah." Julie yawned. "What can I get you?"

"Medium caramel macchiato."

"Four seventy eight," Julie said after she pushed two buttons. Genny paid with a five dollar bill. Julie watched as she dropped the change into the tip jar. "Gee, thanks." Julie scoffed.

Genny wrinkled her brow and walked to the pickup counter. She continued to take in her surroundings as she waited for her coffee. A fireplace was tucked in the back corner and a row of tall tables lined the front windows, along with tables in the middle of the dining area.

"Sorry about the delay," the woman from the drive thru said. Before Genny could respond, she began slinging cups and pitchers around and frothing milk. Genny opened her mouth during a lull, but a blender cut her off. "One barista quit today, and the other was late," she shouted above the hum of the machines and shifted her eyes to the register, where Julie waited on another customer with her welcoming attitude.

"I don't guess you're looking for a job?" The woman grinned and flinched when the drive thru beeped again. "That thing's going to give me a complex."

She walked over to the pickup counter and slid Genny's coffee over to her. "I'm the manager and I'm serious about the job."

"Uh..." She'd love working at the coffee shop, but her only job experience was the month she worked at the bookstore before Brandon died and three months in a grocery store when she was eighteen. "I don't have any experience."

"I tell you what. Why don't you come back..." She looked up as if a calendar was attached to the ceiling. "Next Friday. We can sit down for an interview."

"Really?"

"Yep. By the way, I'm Renee."

"I'm Genny."

"Nice to meet you, Genny. I'll see you next week. Oh, enjoy your coffee."

"Thank you, Renee." On the way to the front door, Genny glanced at the register. Sour Grapes glowered at her. Maybe Renee's good mood would counteract Julie's bad one.

Genny climbed into the Jeep and pushed her favorite CD into the CD player. She sat at the exit, waiting for traffic to clear. When she pulled out, a Jeep was pulling in and the driver waved at her. She checked her mirrors to see if another vehicle was nearby, but she was alone. Why did the man wave at her? He must have mistaken her for someone else.

One of Genny's favorite songs played on the CD. She turned up the volume and was singing at the top of her lungs when a loud boom sounded throughout the cabin of the Jeep. The Jeep fishtailed and she fought the steering wheel to maintain control. When she was able to pull onto the shoulder of the road, she realized the Jeep was leaning to the right. Her heart slammed hard around in her chest, and she grabbed the steering wheel again to stop the world around her from spinning.

A vehicle pulled in behind the Jeep and an older man walked up to the passenger window. Genny hesitated but lowered the window enough where she could hear him better.

"Hey, you had a blowout. Are you okay?"

Genny's heart was still pounding hard. "Yes, sir, just scared me."

"You got someone you can call?"

"Yes sir, thank you."

Genny tapped on her contacts and tapped Paul's name. He was at work, and she prayed he was somewhere he could answer. It rang five times before he picked up.

"Hey, Genny. What's up?"

"I had a blowout."

"Are you okay?"

"Yeah, a couple pulled over to check on me. They were behind me when it happened."

Paul called a tow truck to take the Jeep to the auto center on the Air Force base. He pulled in front of the Jeep and Genny climbed into the truck. As the tow truck pulled up, they got out to meet the driver. That's when Paul noticed the other tire. Genny grimaced. Two new off-roading tires were bound to be expensive. They followed the tow truck to the automotive service center.

"Sir, all four tires are bad. You're lucky all of them didn't blow," the man behind the counter broke the news to Paul.

Another unexpected expense. What else could go wrong?

"Now for the bad news. Due to the size of the rims and the type of tires, you are looking at the very minimum two thousand for all four. That's for the tires only. By the time you add disposal and taxes, you're getting close to twenty-three hundred."

Paul's eyes widened when he looked at the tag from the new tire. He grabbed the back of his neck and squeezed.

"Well, we've got to have them."

The man looked at Paul. "So, it's a go?"

Paul nodded. "Come on, let's sit in the truck." Paul slumped as he headed to the door.

He was angry, Genny was sure. Who wouldn't be angry? She puffed out her cheeks and quietly blew out her breath as they walked to the truck. She climbed into the passenger seat and looked at Paul. He rested his wrists on the top of the steering wheel and stared off into nothing.

"I'm sorry, Paul." Tears blurred her vision. Paul sat for a few seconds, which was an eternity to Genny.

"It's not your fault. It's one of those things. The Jeep sat for a while before you started driving it. You're lucky it didn't happen before now."

In all the excitement, Genny forgot about the job interview. It couldn't have come at a better time. "I have a job interview for a part-time job at the coffee shop down the road. The Roasted Bean. It's three days a week for now."

Paul turned and stared at her. Her eyes widened.

"Genevieve—"

"I know what you said, but this way I can help. Especially now."

Paul exhaled and stared out the windshield again.

They sat in the truck for an hour while the Jeep was getting four new tires. Genny made small talk, but Paul wasn't very receptive.

She dreaded the rest of the day. She had never seen Paul in a foul mood. Anger was the only reason she could think of for his silence. She pulled into the apartment complex behind him and parked in a space next to the truck. Paul sat staring out the windshield. To soften the blow, she went to the driver's side to see if he needed any help to bring his stuff to the apartment.

"No, but thanks for asking." He grabbed his backpack and climbed down from the truck. "Does it drive better?"

"Huh?"

"The Jeep."

"Oh, yeah." It'd better after twenty-three hundred dollars. Genny bit her bottom lip as she followed Paul through the apartment complex. He unlocked the apartment door, and they walked inside. His demeanor was still quiet and withdrawn. He hung his hat up and draped his uniform overshirt on the arm of the couch. Sitting on the couch, he rubbed his hands over his face. Genny went into the kitchen to see what they could have for dinner. There was nothing interesting in the fridge and cereal didn't seem appetizing. She walked into the living room and eased down on the couch by Paul.

"What are we going to have for dinner?" Paul was quiet. Genny glanced at him. Silent tears flowed down his cheeks. She had weighed him down and he had reached his breaking point. "I'm sorry Paul. I'll do what I can to make things easier for you. I'll give you my paycheck."

"It's not that Genny. I keep waiting for him to text or call me and I've realized he never will." He took in a deep breath and exhaled. "I can't believe he's gone." More tears spilled down his cheeks. Genny moved closer to him and slipped her arm around his shoulders. She leaned her head against his as they both cried.

Chapter 5

Paul left for work early to run and go to the gym. During his run, Genny occupied his mind. She had been through so much in the past two months. The last thing she needed was to worry about her medical problems. And his financial situation was not what it used to be before Genny moved to Charleston. It had been a week since he dropped twenty-three hundred dollars for new tires on the Jeep. After his workout, he hit the showers. He stopped by the desk to return the locker key on his way out. Another stack of Tricare benefits pamphlets was on the front desk. What was the Lord telling him?

On his lunch break, Paul had researched the benefits of having a dependent. Genny would have insurance and the surgery would be free. And as a bonus, he would get the dependent rate housing allowance, which would make it easier to afford a two-bedroom apartment and he could put some money in savings. He did the only thing he knew to do. "Father, I feel lost. I feel there is no other way. Please open a door for financial blessings if it's Your will."

He wasn't in the frame of mind to go home right away, so he texted Genny and took a detour. Pulling up to Waterfront Park, Paul climbed out of the truck and found a free space on the grass. The air was chilly, but the temperature kept him focused on his prayers. No matter how quiet he was, he didn't have any other answer than what occupied his mind every second of the day and night. But he didn't know if it was from God or his desire to take care of Genny like he'd promised.

When Brandon and Genny's grandmother died, Brandon had had a talk with him during one of their visits. Brandon had taken care of Genny financially and emotionally since she moved in with him when she was twenty. He had told Paul that he worried about her. She was naïve and impressionable, which led to her making questionable decisions after she graduated from high school, and she ended up dropping out of college.

Paul had assured Brandon that he would do whatever he needed to do to help Genny. He couldn't let Brandon down. Pulling out of the parking lot, he headed home. With still no definitive answer from God, he didn't have a choice, but to do what he knew would help them.

Genny watched him from the bedroom when he strolled through the front door. He slipped off his uniform overshirt and walked toward the bedroom. "Hey Gen, I need to talk to you about something."

Genny dropped the shirt she was folding and headed to the living room. "Yep, what's up?"

Paul's heart raced. "Have a seat." He patted the couch beside him. "I know of a way you can have the surgery."

"Really?" Her shoulders relaxed.

"I can get you on Tricare insurance and your surgery would be free."

Genny arched her brows. "You can't get me on Tricare. Brandon looked into it since he was supporting me, but found out I had to be dependent on him. That wasn't the case since I could work."

Paul's mouth went dry, and he swallowed the best he could. "There is one way to guarantee you can have Tricare so you can have the surgery."

"How?" Genny crossed her arms.

"Well...we can get married." He tensed.

Her mouth hung open. "Married? You're like a brother." Disgust flashed across her face, but her reaction didn't surprise him.

"Hear me out, okay?" Genny nodded, parting her lips. "You would have insurance and I could get extra money for a dependent, which means we could get that bigger apartment. It would be in name only and you couldn't tell a soul. I mean no one. If anyone found out I could get in serious trouble; even kicked out of the Air Force."

"Can I think about it and let you know tomorrow?"

"Yes, of course." If she said no, he didn't know what he was going to do.

Paul wanted to get married. Well, not exactly *wanted*, he *suggested* marriage. Was there no other option? He had said he couldn't get a part-time job due to his work and deployment schedules. She could say no. But if she did, where would that leave her? Genny had much to think about. Pulling out her journal from the nightstand drawer, she drew a line down the middle of a page and began listing the pros and cons.

Extra money was at the top of the pros list as were insurance and a larger apartment. Paul was an all-around good guy. He was kind and often sacrificed himself for others. Was that what he was doing now? Did he view marriage as temporary until she could get on her feet? Surely, he didn't see them married for a lifetime. But then again, he didn't take marriage lightly, so why would he suggest marriage? Even she believed God ordained marriage and meant it for a lifetime. She rubbed her temples and exhaled hard.

She held the pen to the page for a minute. Finally, she wrote the only con she could think of:

Paul doesn't love me as a husband loves his wife.

Was that something she could live with for the foreseeable future?

The living room fell silent, and Paul appeared in the bedroom door-way. "I'm going to get ready for bed."

"Okay." Paul looked ten years older. Did the idea of marrying her have such an effect on him? If so, why would she even consider causing him more pain? Genny exhaled and turned to the next blank page.

February 11, 2011

Well, it looks like I might be Mrs. Paul Thompson soon. This is crazy. I remember writing Genny loves Paul *in my notebook when I was eleven. Never in a million years did I think I would marry him. I don't think I have a choice. Paul is going broke. He says our marriage would make life easier. What will other people think when I walk into a room on Paul's arm? "He could do better." I'm an average girl and he could be a model.*

Genny tapped the pen on the page and tilted her head. There was one thing she was sure Paul hadn't thought about. What if he fell in love with someone?

She laid the journal on the nightstand and turned off the lamp. Every time she closed her eyes, they flew open when another thought fought its way into her consciousness. How would they convince others they were a newlywed couple deeply in love? She forced her eyes closed and prayed for the first time in a long time. She prayed God would give her clarity about the life-changing decision she was about to make. After a few minutes, she got her answer. Silence.

Tossing and turning all night, she'd slept in until almost eleven. When she woke, she knew her answer. She prayed it was from God and not her fear for her future. Genny looked at the time on her phone. Paul was on his lunch break now. He usually brought his lunch but might be at lunch with his friend Peter. She tapped on his name and held her breath until he answered.

"Hey, Genny."

She swallowed the knot in her throat. "I've thought and prayed about it since we talked. I feel like I have no choice, but please don't think that's a bad thing. If I had to get married, I'd prefer it was to you."

Paul laughed. "Okay then. I'm going to ask for a few hours off this afternoon so we can get the license. I think it would be a good idea to get married on Monday so we can get you registered as a dependent as soon as possible."

"Okay." That soon? Shouldn't there be more time to get used to the idea?

"I'll be by to pick you up in an hour."

⇢⇢⇻ ⇺⇠⇠

Valentine's Day was the perfect day to get married. It was a day of romance. A day to celebrate love. Standing in front of the dresser, Genny studied herself in the mirror. Her long-sleeved, fitted cream-colored dress hit just below the knee. She had curled her hair and pinned the right side back with a sparkling silver barrette. A wooden jewelry box that belonged to her mother sat on top of the dresser. She wasn't one for jewelry and rarely looked at the contents. For today's special occasion, she pulled out her mother's silver necklace with a sapphire pendant. Both she and her mother were born in September, which gave her a special connection with her mom.

The weekend had passed in a blur. They talked about what to say and how to act when they were around people Paul knew from the Air Force. Her fear was that Paul's supervisors would find out about their marriage and kick him out of the Air Force. Where would that leave her? She'd be in the same predicament as she was before Paul brought her to Charleston.

Had Paul fully thought this through? It was out of character for him to do something so drastic as marrying for money. Was she such a burden he would set aside his goals for her? Her head spun. Too many questions, and she was afraid of the answers.

Genny slipped on her mother's necklace and gazed at her reflection in the mirror. The bathroom door opened, and Paul walked out without a shirt on. Scarlet heat caressed her cheeks. He was a far cry from the eighteen-year-old she remembered. He was a runner, but obviously worked out as well. As he passed by on his way to the living room, she was floored by the large tattoo of a cross prominently displayed in the middle of his back.

"You have a tattoo?" Wide-eyed, Genny's mouth hung open. The tattoo stretched from the base of his neck to his lower back and across his shoulders. It was an intricate design and reminded her of the cross hanging on the wall in her Catholic friend's living room back in Tennessee.

"Yep. I wanted something to remind me He is always with me. And a way to make my beliefs known and maybe start a life-changing conversation."

Faith had been important to Genny when she was younger, but she had fallen away over the years. "Well, it's nice."

Paul walked up to her, his blue-grey eyes shining. "You look beautiful, Genny."

The heat in her cheeks soared. "Thank you."

"Give me a minute and I'll be ready."

"Okay." She followed him into the living room, where he slipped on his shirt and shoes.

"Ready?"

"Yep." Genny grabbed the folder with the marriage license as they headed out the door.

They made small talk on the way to the courthouse. Genny took a quick peek at Paul. He looked handsome in his gray slacks and white button-down shirt.

"Oh." He slipped his hand in his pocket, pulled out two rings and held them in front of her. "I bought rings."

"When did you buy these?" She hadn't thought about rings. Paul was going all out to make their marriage look legit.

"Saturday. That was the errand I had to take care of."

Paul had stepped in the bedroom doorway as she looked through her dresses for a dress to wear for their courthouse ceremony. She remembered the determined look on his face. Now she knew why.

"Here." Holding his hand in front of her, she chose the smallest ring. "Wrong one."

She lowered her brows.

"You slip my ring on my finger, and I slip your ring on your finger."

She grinned. "Oh, yeah." She exchanged the rings and Paul slipped her ring in his pocket.

When they pulled up to the courthouse around ten-thirty, the parking lot was almost full. They stood in the long line with the other couples.

"Seems everyone wants to get married on Valentine's Day." Genny looked around.

"It's so us husbands don't forget the anniversary." Paul grinned and slipped his arm around Genny's shoulders.

He must be practicing.

"Are you nervous?"

"A little." She wiped her hands on her dress.

"Jones and Thompson."

A wave of nausea hit Genny. They followed the clerk into the room, and she showed them where to stand. The judge was nice and talked to them while the clerk prepared the paperwork.

"Are you ready to get married?" the judge asked with a smile.

Genny looked at Paul. "Yes," they said in unison.

"Do you have rings?"

"Yes, sir." Paul grinned at Genny.

She forced a grin in return. *What am I doing?*

The judge led Paul and Genny through their vows and pronounced them husband and wife after they exchanged rings. He turned to Paul. "You may kiss your bride."

Paul looked at Genny for a moment. When he bent down to kiss her, her stomach fluttered wildly at the chaste kiss. The clerk instructed Paul and Genny to sign the certificate and she signed as a witness. Paul asked the clerk if she'd take a picture and handed her his phone. He slipped his arm around Genny's waist and pulled her close. Her racing pulse was soon replaced by a hint of regret.

Once home, Genny changed out of her dress and relaxed on the bed. Paul knocked on the door. "Come in."

"Are you okay?" He sat on the bed next to her.

"I was thinking about Brandon. What would he say about us?" Genny twisted her new band, which was surprisingly a perfect fit, around her finger. She focused on Paul's left hand. The silver wedding band was still on his finger. She guessed he would have taken it off as soon as they walked into the apartment.

"I think he'd understand."

"Yeah." Genny's smile didn't quite reach her eyes.

Paul was right. Brandon wouldn't want her to struggle. Paul was the type of man who would step up and care for her. He was like a brother to her, after all. But now he was her husband.

On his way out of the bedroom, Paul passed by the dresser where a small wooden tray held a few pieces of his jewelry. It was odd that he didn't slip off the ring and put it on the tray. He must be trying to get used to wearing it for their sham of a marriage.

⋙ ⋘

Paul returned to work the following day. He had gotten a text from Peter checking on him because of the last-minute day off. He assured him they were okay. He could say one of them was sick, but didn't want to add to the lies that were piling up. Peter was perceptive, and Paul was afraid he'd see right through him. Lying to his friend turned his stomach, but he didn't have a choice and he knew Peter wouldn't understand.

As Paul strolled toward the flight line, he saw Peter standing at the open cargo bay of a plane with a clipboard in his hand. His mouth dried up like an arid desert and heart palpitations slowed his steps. Peter looked up and smiled.

"Hey Sergeant Thompson."

"Sergeant Parker."

"So, what's new?"

Paul's muscles twitched. This was the opportunity to break the news to Peter. Maybe he should wait. "I got married yesterday." Before Paul had the chance to think it through, the words flew out of his mouth.

Peter looked at Paul and lifted his chin. A tense smile spread across his face. "You and Brianna got back together?"

Paul ran his hand over the top of his head. "No."

Peter's eyebrows drew together. Paul watched the realization roll down his face.

"Genny?" Peter's eyes widened. Paul opened his mouth, but no words came. Peter took a long moment to speak. "You married Genny? Why?"

Paul hadn't thought of Peter asking him questions. His answer flew out of his mouth as fast as his marriage announcement. "Because I love her."

Peter scoffed. "Really, Paul? Are you sure it's not for the benefits?"

Paul's eyes narrowed. "Of course not! If you can't be happy for me, then I don't want to hear it."

Peter leaned in close to Paul and softly said, "You'd risk your career for her?"

"I'm not risking anything. Like I told you, we are in love." Paul turned and walked away. Tremendous guilt clung to his shoulders for lying.

"Paul!" Peter shouted. *"Paul!"*

Paul heard a commotion behind him and turned around. Out of nowhere, he was slammed to the pavement. An Air Force police officer pointed a gun at his back and demanded to see his ID badge. A few moments later, the police officer let Paul stand and handed the ID badge back to him. He sent Paul on his way with a warning. Against his nature, Paul avoided Peter for the rest of the day.

Looking in the rearview mirror, Paul rubbed the abrasion on his cheek. Ten years in the Air Force working on the flight line, he'd never wandered into a restricted area. In hindsight, he should have prepared better for the conversation with Peter. He climbed out of the truck and made his way to the apartment.

Genny was standing at the stove when he got home. When she turned to look at him, her lips parted. "What happened to you?" She walked up to him and brushed her fingers lightly across his cheek.

"I got jacked up."

"What?"

"Peter and I got into an argument about us, and I didn't pay attention to where I was going and broke red."

"Speak civilian, please."

"I crossed into a restricted area when I was heading back to the shop. I was upset and wasn't paying attention to where I was going. There is a red line painted around restricted areas and I crossed over it. It's called 'breaking red' for short."

"Oh. So, what did Peter say to get you so upset?"

"Accused us of getting married for the benefits."

"Well, it's true."

"Yeah, but I don't like lying to him."

"I know." She rested her hand on his arm.

Genny pulled down two bowls and sat them next to the stove. "Lasagna."

Paul rubbed his hand over his mouth to hide a grimace. He was tired of frozen food, but at least there was something on the stove most nights when he got home from work.

He spent a few minutes changing out of his uniform and headed to the living room. Genny had the tray tables set up in front of the couch. He sat down and bowed his head. Genny's fork clanked on the table a few seconds later. She'd started eating without praying again. He had his work cut out for him. He smiled to himself.

"What exactly do you do? All I remember Brandon talking about was the flight line."

"Air transportation is the career field. It's exactly how it sounds. The Air Force is the branch of the military that transports cargo.

For instance, troops, mail to overseas bases and deployment locations, baggage, special cargo, and even tanks. In deployment locations, we bring over the cargo to set up a forward operating base, the food for the military members, and ammunition for the weapons. Another job is working the counter as a ticket agent of sorts. Instead of tickets, military members have transportation orders. Air transportation is the military's version of an airport."

"Sounds interesting." Genny slightly nodded.

"We also bring home fallen heroes." He bit his bottom lip.

Genny lowered her head and was quiet for a moment. "So, what do you do?" She glanced at him.

"I work at the Air Terminal Operations Center. Better known as A-TOC. It's like flight line management. We meet incoming aircraft and make sure the cargo, whether it's baggage or people, is taken care of. So, we are always on the flight line."

"Cool. I'll clean up the kitchen, then get ready for bed."

"Okay, Gen." Paul picked up the remote and watched a few minutes of the news, then got ready for bed. Should he talk to Peter or let things lie low for a few days? Maybe it'd be best if he let Peter come to him.

Three days had passed since the incident with Peter on the flight line. He hadn't talked to him since then. Paul blinked back tears and closed his eyes. He thought he knew himself, but the decision he'd made to marry Genny was quickly turning him into someone he didn't recognize.

He rubbed his temples and sighed. Now that Genny was registered as a dependent, he was making a new budget. When they moved, the rent would increase, which would be a large part of the budget. He had checked in his current complex, but there wouldn't be any two-bedrooms available for at least six months. That was too far away.

Paul's phone rang, and Peter's name brightened the screen. For a second, he considered letting the call go to voicemail, but answered.

"Hey, brother." Paul's heart leaped into his throat.

"Are you looking for a bigger place?" Peter asked.

"Yeah, we can't stay here much longer."

"Anderson said he looked at a house, but it was too small for his family. He said the rent was reasonable. Are you interested?"

"Yeah, that would be awesome."

Paul jotted down the address and he and Genny made a quick trip to view the outside. Paul called the property manager and made an appointment to view the house the next day.

As Paul lay stretched out on the couch with his feet propped up on the arm, the exchange with Peter played in his head. He'd always tried to be an honest man, but within a week, he'd lied to everyone. Since when did lying come as natural as breathing? "I'm so sorry for lying, Lord. I've made a mess of things. Did I make a mistake?"

Paul desperately wanted to hear from God, but all he heard was silence.

When they pulled into the driveway of the house the next afternoon, the property manager was there to give a tour. The mid–1960s ranch featured three bedrooms and two baths. The smell of fresh paint filled the air when Genny walked into the house behind the property manager. The house had been upgraded with all the modern features. The dark grey granite was cool against her hand. She smiled at the new stainless–steel appliances and fireplace. They stepped out onto the large patio and looked out over the fenced backyard.

"I like it. What about you?" Genny asked and looked at Paul.

"I like it too."

Back inside, they filled out the application. Paul pulled away from the house and drove slowly around the neighborhood. It was older and all the houses seemed to be from the sixties and seventies but well maintained. When they pulled up to the stop sign at the entrance of the neighborhood, Paul looked at Genny.

"Let's say a prayer."

Her eyebrows drew together. "For what?"

"That we get the house. If it's God's will, that is. It'll be quick."

She watched Paul bow his head and close his eyes before he started praying. It was silly to pray for a house. She understood praying for a sick person, but a house? Was praying about marrying a friend silly too? That was one thing she was willing to pray about. Since moving in with Paul, her 'prayer life,' as he called it, had improved, although slightly. Before she moved in with him, she couldn't remember the last time she had prayed.

"Amen."

"Amen." She grimaced at her delay. She should practice focusing on an object so her mind wouldn't wander while Paul prayed. But wouldn't that be a sin?

Chapter 6

L ate morning, Genny walked into The Roasted Bean. There were a few customers in the dining room and one car in the drive thru, evidence that the morning rush was over. Julie was standing with her back to the counter. Hopefully, she hadn't eaten any sour grapes in the parking lot before she clocked in.

"Hi, I'm Genny. I'm here to see Renee."

Julie turned around. She must have eaten two pounds of sour grapes before clocking in. "Hey. Are you here to see Renee?"

"Yeah." Didn't she say that?

Julie said nothing before she stepped away from the counter. She came back a few moments later. "She'll be right up."

Did Genny want this job if she had to work with Sour Grapes?

"Hey Genny, follow me." Genny followed Renee to the back office. "So, you've met Julie."

"Yeah, she was here when I saw you last week."

"Oh, that's right."

Julie needed to refresh her people skills.

"Yes, she seems nice." Genny rolled her eyes as she followed Renee into the office.

"Have a seat and tell me about yourself."

Genny's mouth opened.

"Don't worry, this is casual."

"Thank goodness." Genny grinned. Ten minutes later, Renee informed Genny that she had the job.

Genny followed Julie around, learning how to use the register and brew all the different drinks. She was confident she could do her job and it would be a great place to work. If only Julie didn't wake up on the wrong side of the bed every morning.

Paul's truck was in the parking lot when she pulled up to the complex. She stopped by to check the mail before going to the apartment. When she came in the door, Paul was sitting on the couch.

"Guess what?" He grinned.

"What?" Genny handed Paul the mail.

"We got the house!"

Genny shrieked. "Yay!"

"You can have the master."

"Are you sure?" She arched her eyebrows. Paul had always been thoughtful, but she was surprised that he'd let her have the master since he was paying for everything.

"Of course, I'm sure."

"Guess what?" She grinned.

"What?" Paul raised a brow.

"I got the job!"

"Congratulations, Gen!"

"I'll give you my paycheck to help out."

"No, that's not necessary. We're good now that we are getting the extra money."

Genny headed to the bedroom to slip off her shoes and put away her purse. She grinned when she thought about what all she could buy. It had been a year since she'd bought new clothes and maybe she could get a new phone. In the bathroom, she brushed and braided her hair. When she looked at herself in the mirror, she frowned. No, she would save her money. Paul had made so many sacrifices for her.

They had a little over a week to pack up and move. Excited to have more room, Genny looked forward to decorating the house. In the closet, she went through her clothes to see what she could donate. She'd pushed Paul's clothes aside and noticed a small box on the floor against the back wall.

Feeling slightly guilty, she rested the box on her lap and opened it. Inside was filled with cards, letters, and pictures. She grabbed a small stack from the top and found a picture of Paul and a pretty young woman. She turned it over and read the back: *Paul and Staci 2003.*

A greeting card slid out of the pile when she gathered the contents to put back in the box. Curious, she read the front of the card and opened to read the inside. At the bottom was a handwritten note. *"I am so happy to have you in my life, Paul. I love you and want to spend the rest of my life with you. Love Staci."* Genny's eyes widened. She put the card in the box and put the box back in the corner of the closet. Who was Staci, and why wasn't she in his life now?

They moved the rest of the boxes to the new house by the end of February with the help of Peter and his wife Melissa. Melissa helped Genny clean the apartment and Paul had the final walk-thru and turned in the keys. Paul loaded the last of the boxes in the truck and Genny brought the fragile items in the Jeep. Boxes filled all the floor space in the new house.

"Oh, this will be fun," Genny rested her hands on her hips.

"When we get this put away, we can bring Brandon's stuff out of the storage unit."

"I'd like that." Genny smiled. Having Brandon's belongings close would be nice.

A knock sounded on the front door. Paul went over and pulled it open. Genny heard a soft feminine voice and walked up next to him. A slender elderly woman with short gray hair stood on the doorstep holding a pie.

"Hello. I'm Eloise Baker and I live next door. I wanted to welcome you two to the neighborhood." Genny took the pie from Mrs. Baker. "It's apple."

"Thank you." Genny added another item to the grocery list in her head: *vanilla ice cream.*

"Come in," Paul said.

"I can't stay but a minute. My daughter is on her way over."

"We're sorry we don't have anything for you to sit on. We are getting our furniture out of storage tomorrow." Paul had donated his old couch to a co-worker, much to Genny's delight.

"Oh, it's okay."

"By the way, we are Paul and Genny Thompson." Genny flinched when Paul clumsily slung his arm around her shoulders.

"It is so nice to meet you. I've lived in my house for over thirty years now. Let me know if you need anything or want to know about the area."

"We will, thank you," Paul said.

Mrs. Baker looked out the kitchen window when a car door shut. "Oh, that's my daughter, Susan." She walked to the front door. "Sue, come here for a moment. I have new neighbors. Paul and Genny."

A woman who appeared to be in her forties made her way to the door and smiled. She was slender and had short hair, like her mother. Susan was too far away to see if she had her mother's deep blue eyes.

"I have a son, Alan, as well."

"We need to run, Mom. It was nice meeting you."

"You too," Paul said. "See you soon, Mrs. Baker." She nodded and headed over to where her daughter's car was parked.

"She seems sweet." Genny stepped away from the door.

"She does. I think we'll like having her for our neighbor."

"Me too."

Genny opened the box in front of the stove and dug around until she found two glasses, two plates, and a frying pan. She pulled out a box of Hamburger Helper from the grocery bag and sat it on the counter. She dug around in the box and looked up.

Paul grimaced.

"What?"

"Again?"

Genny sighed. "You're in luck. I can't find the silverware or a spatula. Papa John's?"

"Sounds good to me."

As they waited for the delivery of the pizza, Genny went to her bedroom and opened her suitcase. Sitting on the floor, she surveyed her new bedroom and visualized where her furniture would go. Drawing in a long breath, she sighed and wiped the tears pooling in her eyes. She should be in Fayetteville, not here. Rubbing her eyes, she sat up straight and tried to clear the thoughts from her head. There was no use in thinking about Fayetteville. This was her new reality.

A few weeks passed before they had the house in order. Paul bought a charcoal grill, and they invited Peter and Melissa over for steak in appreciation for their help. They had practiced physical affection and using terms of endearment. Paul's toiletries had been moved to the master bath, and his personal items were moved into the closet in his room. An enlargement had been made of their wedding picture and was displayed on the mantel in a decorative frame.

They were ready to deceive their friends.

Genny headed to her room to change. On the way back to the living room, she glanced into Paul's room and saw him sitting on his bed looking out the window. She walked in and sat down next to him.

"You look deep in thought."

"Yeah. I'm afraid...well, worried that we..."

"Made a mistake?" She glanced out the window at the backyard. She shouldn't be surprised that Paul had regrets.

There was a knock at the front door and Genny pulled herself to her feet, hurrying to the living room before Paul could say anything. She opened the door and invited their guests inside.

Paul prepared the steaks and lit the grill while he and Peter spent some time catching up. There was a bit of tension between the two, but they were working on their relationship. Paul had said Peter still had his doubts about their marriage, but he had avoided the subject and so far, Peter did the same.

Genny and Melissa made a trip to Walmart to get some last-minute items. They stood in line behind two women who were unloading their cart onto the belt.

"How long have you and Peter been married?"

"Two years." Melissa glanced past Genny and smiled. Genny raised a brow when Melissa tilted her head toward the register.

Genny turned around and was met by Brianna's painted on smile. What were the odds? She braced herself on the shopping cart.

"Hi Genny. Melissa."

"Hi Brianna. How are you?" Genny watched as Brianna's eyes found her wedding band.

"Oh, did you get married?" Brianna's smile stayed in place despite the strain in her voice. Red flooded her upper chest and spread to her neck.

Genny looked down at her hand. "Yes."

"Do I know him?"

"Paul," Genny retorted.

Brianna's smile faded.

"Oh…well…congratulations." She turned around and followed her friend away from the register. Genny tightened her jaw muscle as she watched Brianna hurry out of the store. One mark for herself on her imaginary score board. Why was she trying to one up Brianna? Paul wasn't attracted to her. He was with her so he could help her.

When they arrived back at the house, Paul had set up camp chairs and his old tray tables on the patio. Genny's eyes widened, and she looked down at her shoes. She assumed they would eat inside since it was March, but she reminded herself that they lived in Charleston. She sighed. They needed patio furniture, and it would take forever to save the money. Paul's cash only policy was ridiculous.

"Paul, excellent steak." Melissa said, taking another bite.

Genny realized she'd been focusing on her steak as she vented her frustrations in her head. As she cut her steak, she almost knocked over the tray table. This wouldn't happen if they had a patio table.

"Thank you." Paul beamed.

The couples sat on the patio talking. Paul reached over and took Genny's hand in his. Her cheeks grew warm at his shy smile. She sensed the tension between Paul and Peter when she caught Peter staring at them.

"You guys want some coffee?" Genny asked, attempting to lighten the mood.

"I'd love some." Peter replied.

They moved inside, and Melissa offered to help with the coffee. Paul and Peter sat on the couch while Paul browsed on demand titles.

Genny would bet a hundred dollars that a documentary would soon play on the TV. Heat filled Genny's abdomen and radiated down her legs. She excused herself and went into her bathroom. Her period was starting, which meant endometriosis pain would soon follow. A few minutes later, a light tap sounded on the door.

"Is everything okay?" Paul called from the other side.

She opened the door and winced. "It's...that time of the month."

"Need your medicine and a heating pad?" Paul had gotten used to Genny's struggles since they'd lived together for the past few months.

"I can't go to bed, we have guests." She took a deep breath and sat down on the bed.

"Don't worry about us." Melissa and Peter stood in the doorway. "Whatever you need to do." Melissa crossed the room and rubbed Genny's back.

Paul grabbed the heating pad and plugged it into the outlet by the bed. He walked up to Peter and tilted his head toward the living room. A few moments later, Paul returned with a glass of water and her prescription bottle. He brushed his finger along her cheek and smiled. It must have been for Melissa's benefit. She watched him walk down the hall.

"What is it, if you don't mind me asking?" Melissa sat down on the bed next to Genny.

"I have endometriosis."

"Oh Genny, I'm sorry. My sister has endo and I know what she goes through."

Tears blurred Genny's vision. "I may have to have a hysterectomy if it gets worse. I'm only twenty-three."

Melissa slipped her arm around Genny and hugged her. Genny managed a smile and wiped the tears from her eyes.

After Peter and Melissa left, Paul cleaned up the kitchen. Genny attempted to read, even though she could barely keep her eyes open. Paul took the book from her hands and placed the bookmark between the pages.

"How can you concentrate on reading?" He laid the book on the nightstand. "Tonight was a success, huh?"

"Yes, Paul. Your steak was delicious." Genny's eyelids were half closed. "Do you think they believe us?"

"Time will tell."

"Guess who we saw at Walmart?" Genny rubbed her eyes and yawned.

"Who's that?"

"Brianna." Paul's face contorted. Or maybe it was the medication. She hoped it was the former. It meant he was over her.

"I'm going to get ready to turn in."

"Good night." Genny smiled and closed her eyes, but her thoughts refused to let her eyes close for more than a few moments at a time. Portraying themselves as a married couple was more difficult than she'd first thought. She hadn't known Peter and Melissa long, but lying to them was like a thousand-pound weight hanging over her head. How long could she maintain the charade before it crashed down on her?

⟫⟫ ⟪⟪

Flipping to the next blank page in his journal, Paul settled on his bed to read his Bible and take notes. An incoming text interrupted his reading, and he picked up his phone.

Why did you marry Genny? We were dating a month ago. I knew something was going on with you two.

Paul shook his head and deleted the text. The relationship had been heading downhill before Genny came along. Brianna had been pushing his well-defined boundaries but had eased back. Once Genny came into the picture, she was back to pushing like she did the night they broke up.

Chapter 7

"Genevieve, we are going to be late for church," Paul shouted from down the hall.

Genny took a step back and looked at her reflection in the mirror. "Why do I have to have a dimpled chin?" She rubbed her finger over the dimple. "I'll be right there."

"Finally." Paul shook his head and shifted his Bible from one hand to the other when she walked up to him. "It's our first visit. Do you want everyone to stare at us when we walk into the sanctuary fifteen minutes late?"

"Oh, it's not fifteen minutes." Genny rebuffed as they headed out the door.

"Close enough." Paul opened the truck door for her. "By the way, you look very nice." He shut the door and walked to the driver's side and climbed in.

"Thank you. You look nice, too." Genny turned and looked out the passenger window. She caught a glimpse ofsanctuary, herself in the side mirror and clenched her teeth to keep from smiling.

They hadn't gone to church for several weeks while Paul searched for a new church. Peter had invited them to his and Melissa's church this past week. Was it so Peter could keep tabs on them?

They arrived in time to hear the worship team's last song. Red crept up Paul's neck and his eyes darted around the sanctuary, searching for Peter and Melissa. Genny clutched her purse and held her breath.

"There they are," Paul said, taking a hold of Genny's arm. He gritted his teeth and hissed at her, "Come on."

"Chill out Paul Tyler," she mumbled.

After the service, Peter introduced Paul and Genny to several people, including the pastor, Ryan Hammonds. Genny stood quietly by Paul's side while the men talked about the sermon. She gasped when an arm looped through hers, and she turned around to see Melissa.

"Come on. Let me rescue you," Melissa whispered. Genny looked at Paul and smiled. He nodded and Melissa carted Genny off to introduce her to a few of the women. "I didn't mean to leave you hanging after the service, but I had to catch Selena before she left. We are starting a new Bible study next week. You should come."

"I'll check my work schedule." *Great.* Now she had Melissa talking about the Bible. What did she expect? They were standing in a church.

Paul and Genny stopped for lunch before going home. As they ate and talked, Genny noticed two women staring at Paul. A fire flickered in her chest. She'd yet to experience another woman's interest in Paul since they got married. Her mind raced, searching for a reason for her jealousy. Paul was her husband in name only. She had no right to be jealous.

"What are you looking at?"

Genny turned her gaze to Paul. "Nothing."

The two women smiled when Paul turned around to see what had caught Genny's attention. He shook his head when he turned back around.

"So, how do you handle that?"

"What?"

"Women falling all over you." Genny gulped and considered diving under the table. Paul raised his brow and looked down at his food. "I'm sorry, never mind."

"It's okay." Red swept across Paul's cheeks.

Genny popped a chip into her mouth to keep another embarrassing thought from slipping out. She swallowed and took a long drink of sweet tea. "We never talked about our dating relationship. You know, what led to us falling in love."

"You're right. Maybe something related to Brandon's death?"

"Like?" Genny arched her brows.

"We realized we love each other more than friends not long after we came home from North Carolina. You know, spending all that time together."

"Sounds good." What was one more lie added to the pile? If they weren't careful, the pile would ignite and spread like wildfire, scorching everything in its path.

"Are you ready to head home?" Paul laid his napkin on the table.

"Yep."

When they walked out to the truck, Genny noticed the two women from earlier watching Paul out the window. He escorted Genny to the passenger side and helped her get in. As she watched them fawn over him, she thought about sticking her tongue out but forced herself to behave.

On the drive home, Paul brought up the one subject she was afraid he would bring up. "Hey, what do you think about having a Bible study?"

Genny glanced out the window and rolled her eyes. "What do you mean? Hosting at the house?"

"No, with you and me. Maybe once a week?"

"Um...I guess." Genny winced at her reply, but having a Bible study with Paul or anyone else would be boring. She would force herself to read the Bible within the four walls of the church, but had no desire for Bible reading to trickle into her daily life.

"Don't sound so excited, Genevieve." Paul's tone was more hurt than angry. "Forget it."

"No, it's okay. I'd love to have a Bible study with you." Genny feigned a smile.

⤜⤜ ⤛⤛

"Good afternoon, sir. What can I get for you?" Genny smiled at the man in the business suit and rang up a hot mocha and blueberry scone.

Julie grabbed the order slip from the printer. "Genny, don't forget to ask the customer if he wants his scone heated," she snapped.

"Oh, I'm sorry." Genny sucked in her cheeks. She had been at her part-time job for less than a month and was still learning. Julie didn't seem to care. Genny was at the espresso machine making the mocha when she heard Julie gasp.

"Who is *that?*" Julie stared out the front windows wearing a wide grin. "Love me a man in uniform."

Genny looked up and saw Paul walking toward the door. She let out a chuckle, and Julie turned and wrinkled her brow. "That's my husband, Paul."

Julie's eyes widened. "What? Girl, you're lucky and I'm jealous."

Paul stepped up to the counter. "What are you two laughing at?"

"Nothing." Genny smiled at Julie's flaming red cheeks and introduced them. Amused, she watched Julie shift from foot to foot.

Paul handed Genny a copy of the house key. "Don't lose this one." He winked. "I'm going to the gym after work, so I'll be coming home a little later." He smiled, leaned over, and kissed her cheek. "I love you."

Genny held onto the counter to steady herself. It was the first time Paul said he loved her. He loved her as a friend, but he'd never said the words. Could it ever be more? No, she couldn't do that to herself. He was playing his part and she'd play her part too.

"Okay. I love you, too." She rubbed her hands down the front of her apron and watched him walk out to the truck.

"Does he have a brother?" Julie fanned herself.

"Nope, he's an only child."

Julie stuck out her bottom lip. "Where'd you find him, girl?"

Genny gave the customer his mocha and scone. "We grew up together. I've known Paul since I was five. He and my brother were best friends."

"Were?"

"My brother Brandon was killed in Iraq on December first." Genny faced reality once again. She should be in Fayetteville with Brandon, not on a stage playing a part with Paul.

"I'm so sorry, Genny."

"Thank you."

"Oh, listen. I want to apologize for my behavior the first time we met. My boyfriend had broken up with me the night before and I found out he has a new girlfriend two days ago. I promise not to be snippy again."

"I understand." Hopefully, Julie would keep her promise. One day, she'd tell Julie about the nickname she'd given her the first day they met. Genny smiled and walked over to the espresso machine.

As she waited for the cup to fill with dark roast coffee, she realized that talking about Brandon didn't bring a rush of emotions. Was that a good sign or a bad sign? She slipped her fingers under her braid and jerked out a few strands of hair. Flicking her fingers, she watched the hair float down to the terracotta tiled floor.

Paul sniffed the air when Genny came home from work.

"What are you doing?" She dropped her purse on the dining table.

"Now I want a cup of coffee." He headed to the kitchen and pulled down the container of coffee from the cabinet.

"Oh, stop." She grinned. "I'm going to take a shower and get ready for bed."

"Okay, goodnight."

She watched him put the canister back in the cabinet and shook her head. "Goodnight."

Genny sat down on her bed cross-legged with a towel wrapped around her head. Her emotions blindsided her. She opened her journal and grabbed the pen.

March 18, 2011

Julie and I became friends today. I'm glad. I don't think I could handle her attitude much longer. But now I know why she acted the way she did. I feel sorry for her. On the plus side, Paul brought Julie and I together. I think she has a crush on him! Haha!

She stared at the entry for a few moments. If she wrote what was on her mind, it would make it real, and she wasn't ready to admit it. But as if the pen had a mind of its own, the ink revealed her secret.

I pulled out my hair today.

Tears pooled in her eyes. Was she about to fight another uphill battle?

A mound of musty, wet towels laid limp on the bathroom floor, forcing Genny to do laundry. She scooped up the towels and stepped out of the bathroom into the bedroom. The front door opened, and Paul called out, "Hey, Gen. Where are you?" His strained voice echoed down the hall.

"In here."

Paul walked into her bedroom, playing with his hat. "Guess what we are doing Saturday?" His smile looked as if he'd worn it since he left the Air Force base.

"I don't know. What are we doing Saturday?"

"Having a wedding reception here at the house." His hat slipped out of his hands, and he bent down to pick it up off the floor.

"What? Absolutely not." Genny dropped the armload of towels. She'd rather eat dirt than have a party with a bunch of people she didn't know.

"Why not?"

"Why would you schedule a party without my input for one thing? And we have less than a week."

"I didn't plan it. Peter told the guys in the shop that we were having a party."

"Why would he do that?"

"I think it was a joke, but maybe he's testing us?"

Testing them? That seemed out of character for Peter but then again, she didn't know him very well.

"It will make our marriage more legit for others to see us in our everyday life."

He was right, and she took advantage of the opportunity. "Does this mean we get new patio furniture?" She gave him a sweet smile.

He groaned. "I guess."

"And a gas grill?"

"We'll see." Paul's features tightened.

Paul's expression knotted Genny's stomach. Patio furniture would wreak havoc on the budget, but camp chairs wouldn't do for their guests. She rarely wrote in her journal before bedtime, but she had to get her thoughts out on paper.

March 21, 2011

Paul and I are having a wedding reception here on Saturday. Why can't Peter leave things alone? I thought he was Paul's best friend. He must still be mad at Paul. I don't know how we are going to pull this off. Paul will probably suggest a lot of affection. It's weird and exciting at the same time. Paul's gorgeous and I admit I like having him as my husband even though it won't be forever. How long does he see us married for?

Well, I need to get back to work. I'm going to be really busy the next few days. I rarely clean my room so cleaning a whole house should be interesting. Oh, and we are getting patio furniture. I feel slightly guilty. Paul has spent so much money because of me.

She closed the journal and shoved it in the drawer of the nightstand. Thrusting herself off her bed, she scooped up the towels and trudged down the hall to the laundry room. It was going to be an interesting next few days.

⟫⟫⟫ ⟪⟪⟪

The days flew by in a blur. So many things to do to prepare the house, but by some miracle, every item was marked off the to do list by Saturday morning. Ten guests had arrived around noon. Paul had invited everyone in his shop and twenty out of twenty-six had responded.

Genny watched another couple stroll down the sidewalk and up to the steps. She took in a deep breath and slowly exhaled. Using every ounce of courage she could muster, Genny vowed to overcome her aversion to crowds for the day, so the reception—and proving their marriage wasn't a sham—was a success.

She prepared side dishes and desserts while Paul fired up the new grill on the patio. Peter and Melissa arrived, and Peter went out to the patio while Melissa helped Genny. Out the kitchen window, Genny saw Mrs. Baker on the sidewalk carrying a large present. She opened the door and smiled as Mrs. Baker walked up the steps.

"Let me take that."

Mrs. Baker handed the gift to Genny. "Can I help?"

"Sure, I'd appreciate it." Genny handed her a few tomatoes to slice for the burgers.

Genny was cutting fruit for the fruit salsa and looked towards the backdoor. A beautiful woman stood close to Paul with barely enough room for a gust of wind to pass between them. Heat flushed through her body. She put down the knife, rinsed her hands and stormed out the backdoor. As she approached Paul, the woman's perfect figure and long brown hair knotted her stomach. She was wearing leggings and a navy-blue jacket with the Air Force logo on the back. When Genny reached them, she slipped her arm around Paul's waist, something she'd never done before.

"Why don't you introduce me, babe?" Genny searched the woman's face for any signs of jealousy.

"This is my wife Genny. Sergeant Rogers works in the office."

"Nice to meet you, Genny. Call me Jennifer."

"Hi." Heat spread across Genny's chest.

Paul leaned down and whispered, "Don't be jealous, Genevieve."

"I'm not." She bit her bottom lip.

Paul smiled and winked. "If you say so."

Overwhelmed, Genny excused herself to her bedroom to recompose. Plain and simple, she *was* jealous. Her grandmother had always said the ugliness of jealousy could kill a relationship. Which relationship would it ruin? Their marriage or their friendship?

"Genny? You, ok?" She looked up and watched as Paul walked into her bedroom and sat next to her on the bed.

Her clenched fists rested on her lap. "Why was she all over you?" The words sprang from her mouth, surprising herself.

Paul sighed. "She wasn't 'all over' me."

"But why was she so close? I'm sure she could see the pores on your face."

"Genny...I give up." Paul tossed his hands in the air, rose to his feet, and disappeared down the hall.

He was right. Nothing inappropriate happened, and she had no reason to be jealous. But Paul was her husband, and the woman should respect the fact. She was at their wedding reception for crying out loud.

Genny waited until her breathing slowed and went to the kitchen to wash the platters Paul had brought in earlier. The backdoor opened and Genny turned around. She fought the scowl that tried to take over her face when she saw Jennifer Rogers walk in the backdoor.

"Congratulations again and the reception was very nice. I hope to see you at the squadron get-togethers."

"Thank you. I hope so, too." Genny watched Jennifer walk out the front door.

"'Congratulations.' blah blah blah." She rolled her eyes.

Peter and Melissa helped clean up and headed out. Genny and Paul sank onto the couch and put their feet up on the coffee table. Paul turned on the TV to catch the last of the news. A few minutes later, Genny's head rested on his shoulder. She opened her eyes, but drowsiness closed them again.

"Hey Sis…."

Her body jerked, rousing her.

"Are you okay?"

"I swear I heard Brandon's voice." Genny's pulse quickened.

"Maybe it's grief. I'm not trying to tell you what to do, but have you considered talking to someone? They can help you through the grief."

"I don't know. I don't like talking about personal stuff to people I don't know."

"Well, think about it, okay?"

"Okay." Genny stood and headed down the hall to her bedroom. She didn't have to think about it. She could handle it on her own.

Slipping under the covers, she grabbed her journal and turned to the next blank page. She stared at it, studying the faint blue lines that stretched across the paper. So many thoughts swirled around in her head like leaves caught up in a whirlwind.

March 26, 2011

Paul thinks I'm jealous. He's probably right. Every time a woman looks at him, it's like a fire starts in my stomach and shoots heat up to my head. Sometimes I feel like I'm going to explode. What if he thinks one of the women is beautiful and he wants to know her better? What would happen to me? Oh, and he wants me to go to therapy. Not going to happen.

Chapter 8

Genny sat in the middle of the living room floor looking through the boxes of Brandon's belongings from the garage. She grabbed the coffee cup on the end table and took a sip. "I love our new Keurig. Mrs. Baker's so sweet."

"Yes, she is. Here are a few more boxes." Paul set the boxes down in front of her. She opened the box of childhood pictures and held up one to show Paul.

"Wow, we sure were little, and you were so annoying."

Genny lightly smacked him on the hand. "Paul Tyler, that's mean."

"Here's a box that has *Journals* written on top. I bet there are some stories in there." Genny rolled her eyes and grabbed the box from his hands. Paul went into the garage for the last of the boxes.

A large box sat among a group of smaller ones. Genny dragged it over to where she was sitting and pulled back the flaps. She pulled out a few smaller boxes and found Brandon's letterman jacket on the bottom. Picking up the jacket, she slipped it around her shoulders, covering her nose, and inhaled deeply. A hint of Brandon's cologne drifted up her nose. Tears pooled in her eyes and spilled down her cheeks. Paul walked in from the garage with a box. He placed it next to her, then wrapped his arms around her shoulders.

"I can't believe he's gone."

"I know, Gen. Me either."

Later in the evening, Paul lugged a large green box into Genny's room.

"What's that?"

Paul sat the box down on the floor next to the bed. "This is Brandon's personal effects from Iraq. The airman who escorted Brandon home gave it to me after the funeral. His name is Sergeant Shawn Sullivan."

"Personal effects?"

"This is Brandon's personal items like pictures, cards, jewelry, clothes and other things that were with him in Iraq."

Genny stared at the box. What 'other things' were inside and what would happen when she opened it? Would Brandon's belongings spew out like a Jack in the Box? Jump out at her like a snake in a can?

"Do you want me to open it?"

No, but it would have to be opened, eventually. Might as well get it over with, like ripping off an adhesive bandage. She nodded and steadied herself.

Paul unhooked the latch and opened the box. A container on the top held Brandon's wallet, the cross necklace their grandmother had given him for graduation, greeting cards, and some pictures. On the bottom was his laptop and cell phone, as well as clothing and toiletry items. A few other items he had taken with him when he deployed were in the box as well. Genny pulled out his shaving kit.

"I'll give you some space. Let me know if you need me."

She nodded and picked up the pictures. A picture of Brandon with another airman in uniform was not far from the top of the stack of pictures. Flipping it over, Brandon's name and *Jon Quade* were written in Brandon's handwriting. The date was September first—three months before he died. She put the pictures back in the box and pushed it aside to go through the rest of Brandon's belongings.

Sifting through her brother's possessions seemed intrusive and wrong. Why did God find it necessary to end Brandon's life? She wrapped a thin section of hair around her finger and tugged, pulling out several strands. She looked at the hairs and flicked them to the floor. The secret she'd kept hidden was clawing its way up from her hiding place.

The personal effects box haunted Genny for several days. She had asked Paul to move it against the wall for easy access. Several times a day she'd opened the box and shuffled through the contents. The thought that the items were the last things Brandon touched gave Genny mixed feelings. She was happy to have the items but also sad that the last time he touched the items he had no idea he was about to die.

Sitting on the floor in front of the box, she picked up a picture of Brandon and another airman. She turned it over, but the back was blank. Paul had told her that Sergeant Sullivan was with Brandon when he was injured. Genny still struggled with thoughts of the details of the incident. Part of her wanted to know every detail, and part of her wanted to remain oblivious. Maybe she should contact Sergeant Sullivan. But how? She didn't know where he was stationed. She should leave it alone.

"Hey Genny, I'm going out for my run."

Paul was standing in Genny's doorway when she looked up. "Hey, do you know who this is?" She held out the picture.

Paul walked over and took the picture from her hand. "Yeah, that's Shawn Sullivan."

"Really?" She took the picture from Paul and stared at Shawn. She couldn't do this now. "Can I go with you?"

His brows lifted.

"I've been thinking. I want to start running again so I can get in shape."

"Uh, I thought it was so we could spend time together. But yes, you can run with me." Genny rolled her eyes. "There you go again."

"Stop it."

"I'm going to break you from that bad habit."

"Granny tried. I still remember what she said. 'You roll your eyes at me one more time Genevieve Marie and I'm going to set your rear on fire.'"

"It didn't stop you?"

"No, I didn't roll my eyes around her."

Paul chuckled.

Genny was able to keep up with Paul for the first few minutes, then she dropped behind. "Oh my gosh Paul, slow down!" Gasping for air, nausea drifted up from her stomach and a cramp stabbed at her side.

When they were back home, Genny collapsed on the couch with her hand on her heaving chest.

"Don't be so dramatic, Genevieve."

"I'm not. You tried to kill me." Genny's sweat drenched eyebrows lowered.

After dinner, Genny took a shower and laid down on the bed with her old journals. She picked up a journal from middle school. Genny thumbed through the pages and found the entry from when Brandon told her he had enlisted in the Air Force.

May 5, 2000

I'm so mad at Brandon. He's leaving me. He promised me it would always be us. 4 years is a long time. He said it's not like we won't see each other, but I know how that goes. At least Paul is going with him.

Hot tears fell from her eyes. Life was so unpredictable. She turned several pages and read another entry.

Sep 16, 2000

Granny and I went to San Antonio to see Brandon and Paul graduate from basic training. Paul's parents couldn't go because his grand-mother's sick. We watched the graduation ceremony. It was kind of neat. They got to go off base and we toured some of the parts of San Antonio. Granny was excited to see the Alamo. Brandon and Paul looked different with their shaved heads. Paul looked so cute, as usual. I want to marry him one day.

The flicker of a smile passed over her lips and she made her way to the living room. "Look at this." Genny pointed to the entry.

A slow smile spread across Paul's face. "How prophetic of you."

"I admit that I had a crush on you back then."

"I know."

Genny's cheeks grew hot. "How did you know?"

"Your cheeks looked like they were sunburned every time I saw you."

She tried to hide her grin but was unsuccessful.

Walking back to her bedroom, she thought it was ironic that she and Paul were married. She used to dream of him falling in love with her. He loved her as a sister, or he wouldn't be helping her. She cared about him but could never love him. God would see fit to take him too. But why was she suddenly jealous after they got married? It was part of the act; she had convinced herself.

Paul pulled into a parking space at The Roasted Bean. He'd dropped Genny off earlier to take the Jeep to be serviced. To kill time until her shift ended, he went in to get a coffee.

"Hello, Paul, what can I get you?" Red slowly filled Julie's cheeks.

"Hey, Julie. I'll take a medium cinnamon cappuccino."

"You got it."

He pulled out a chair at a table close to the fireplace and watched Genny walk up to the counter from the drive thru. She rested her elbows on the counter and smiled. When the drive thru beeped, she sighed and rolled her eyes.

"One cinnamon capp." Julie set Paul's drink in front of him.

"Thank you, Julie."

She grinned and went back behind the counter.

A silky feminine voice interrupted Paul's browsing the news on his phone.

"Hi there."

Paul watched a young woman sit down at the table next to him. She was petite, with short brown hair. "

"Hello."

"I'm Valerie." She tilted her head and smiled, her dark red lips stretching across her face.

Paul glanced toward the drive thru. "I'm Paul." He turned his attention back to his phone, but out of the corner of his eye he could tell that the woman was still looking at him.

"What are you having?"

Paul picked up his cup and took a sip. "Cinnamon cappuccino."

"Oh, that sounds yum." She lifted her brows.

Paul nodded and offered a slight smile. After a moment, he looked out the windows at the drive thru. The line was wrapped around the building. That was good. Genny would be busy for a while.

Another barista brought a cup on a saucer over to Valerie and returned to the espresso machines. "Caramel latte macchiato," she said and picked up the cup. She blew into the liquid before taking a sip. "I don't mean to assume things, but are you in the military?" She glanced up at Paul's short hair.

"Air Force."

"Ah, I knew it." Her gaze swept over him.

Valerie's attempt at a flirty conversation continued. Every brief response on Paul's part went unnoticed. He was not being rude; he was actually looking out for her wellbeing. Genny had developed a mean jealous streak. She'd overreacted to perceived advances of other women. She would be furious at Valerie.

"Hey, your *wife* asked me to let you know she will be off in fifteen minutes."

"Thanks, Julie." Paul looked up and smiled. Past Julie, he saw Genny in the drive thru looking at him with lips as thin as a twig. He fought a chuckle.

"Excuse me, can I get this to go?" Julie took the cup from Valerie and walked behind the counter.

Fifteen minutes later, Paul and Genny headed out to the Jeep. "Are you okay to drive?" She glared at him. "I guess that's a no." He walked her to the passenger side and opened the door. "Nothing to be jealous of, Genny."

"I'm not jealous."

"Coulda fooled me." Genny rolled her eyes. "You should enter a contest."

"What?"

"A contest for the best eye roller in the country." Paul chuckled. Genny rolled her eyes in dramatic fashion and shook her head. "Hey, why don't we start our Bible study tonight?"

Genny's eyes popped wide. "Okay."

"Good, I've got some passages written down."

"Can't wait." She crossed her arms over her chest.

Lord, this girl.

"It'll be good, Genny. You'll see."

Genny believed in God, but her life experiences had pushed her away from Him. Especially Brandon's death. At least she was attending church with him. Even if she felt compelled, it was a start. He was determined for his life to be a witness to her.

A screaming child a few rows behind Genny interrupted the word game she was playing on her phone. She guessed she'd scream too if she was wearing casts on both legs. Gritting her teeth, she fought to hold on to the little bit of compassion she'd mustered for the child.

"Mrs. Thompson?" She looked up and smiled. Not only was she getting away from the screaming child, but it was the first time she was called Mrs. Thompson. Following the ultrasound tech to a room, Genny's mind wandered. Having more lesions and scarring from endometriosis concerned her. It would mean surgery.

After the ultrasound, the tech said that the doctor would read the scans and be in to talk to her. A few moments later, Dr. Nichols entered the room and pulled the monitor over so she could see the screen. As he talked, he pointed to the lesions in her abdomen.

"Genevieve, I'd say the endometriosis is on the high end of stage three. I recommend a laparoscopic surgery to remove the lesions and hopefully keep it from becoming a stage four. We need to do something soon, or your fertility may be in danger."

She hadn't had more than a passing thought about children. At twenty-three, she wasn't ready for children, but maybe when she was twenty-five. What about twenty-eight or thirty? Would she and Paul still be married? If she was in danger of losing her fertility, would Paul have a baby with her now? It was too soon to talk about this with him.

She didn't feel like going home after her appointment and rode around for a bit. Pulling into a parking space at Sonic, she ordered a shake and thought about the future. What was going to happen with their marriage? What if she or Paul wanted kids one day? Would he want to have a baby with *her?* If so, how would that happen? Certainly not the old-fashioned way. Too many questions. Maybe she wasn't meant to be a mother.

On the way home, she remembered it was Wednesday. Paul had set aside Wednesdays for their Bible studies, but she wasn't feeling it today. Pain from endometriosis was a believable excuse. Tears dampened her lashes. Paul was so hopeful that she would feel the way he felt about God. Lying to get out of the Bible study would be a reason for God to strike her down. He'd already punished her for some unknown sin by taking everyone from her. Why not take *her* life too?

She shook herself from her thoughts when her eyes found Paul's truck in the driveway as she drove down the hill. He had told her in the past that she might not have the answers to her questions on earth. The thought of living the rest of her life with a gigantic question mark over her head overwhelmed her.

Genny stood on the patio with her hands on her hips, looking at the backyard. "We need a garden."

"Let me know if you need any help," Mrs. Baker said from her backyard next door.

Genny turned and waved. "Sure will Mrs. Baker."

She headed back inside and pulled out a notebook. She sketched a small garden and jotted down some plants she'd like. *Tomatoes, corn, okra, squash...* She tapped the eraser end of the pencil against her lips and continued writing. *Eggplant, peas, lettuce...* She was so caught up in planning the garden she didn't know Paul was home until he unlocked the front door.

She jumped up and darted toward him. Excited, she almost ran into him when he walked inside.

"Wow Genny, glad to see you too."

"I want a garden."

"You do?"

"Yes, can you ask if it's alright?" Genny grinned and batted her lashes.

"Well, why don't you start with a plant on the patio? Maybe tomato?"

Genny looked away. She wasn't sure why, but it hurt her feelings that Paul suggested a pot and not a garden. "Okay," she mumbled.

"We'll go to Lowe's this weekend," Paul said as he headed down the hall to change.

Genny went out onto the patio and flopped down in one of the chairs. Why was she upset? Paul was right. She should start small. Next year she could have an actual garden. A trickle of sweat ran down the middle of her back. The door opened and she watched Paul walk out and sit in the chair next to her.

"Warm out here." She raised her braid and fanned the back of her neck. Paul was staring at her with his hand on his chin. "What?"

"I can spray you with the water hose to cool you down."

Genny rolled her eyes.

"You don't think I will?"

Genny's eyes widened as she watched Paul walk over to the hose cart and turn the water on.

"You better not!" The hose unwound from the cart as he walked toward her. "Paul Tyler!" Genny jumped up and ran.

Paul turned the nozzle to the jet setting and chased Genny around the backyard. Screams mixed with laughter filled the air. By the time Paul disengaged the nozzle, her clothes were soaked. Grinning, she snuck up behind Paul as he dragged the hose back to the cart. When she was within reach, she jumped on his back and wrapped her arms around his neck and legs around his waist, soaking his t-shirt in the process.

Paul pulled Genny off his back. "I'll get my revenge." His smile warmed her cheeks.

"We'll see," Genny walked toward the house, water dripping from every part of her body. She made her way to her bedroom and took an early shower. Standing at the sink towel drying her hair, she studied her reflection in the mirror. She wished she had the ability to read minds. She was curious to know what Paul thought about their future.

Chapter 9

In less than seven months, Paul would be on a plane headed for his next six-month deployment. Feelings of dread, fear, and anticipation of Genny's reaction consumed his mind. Why had he waited so long to tell her? Brandon was killed two weeks before returning home. He was all Genny handle, and he didn't know how she would handle the deployment.

Paul pushed the food around on his plate and took a couple of bites.

"You, okay?" Genny asked.

Paul looked up. "Oh...yeah."

"I don't get off work until six tomorrow. Want me to bring home dinner?"

"As long as you go running with me in the morning."

"Fine," she murmured. Gathering their plates, she headed to the kitchen and opened the dishwasher.

"Why don't we get ready to settle in for the night and pick up where we left off with the Bible study?"

Genny put the last plate in the dishwasher and shut the door. She turned around and crossed her arms over her chest. "Okay. I'll go ahead and take my shower."

Paul nodded and was certain that there was an eye roll when Genny's back was turned to him. He let out a heavy sigh after she walked down the hall. He feared Genny was in the process of building walls around her heart. He had to reach her before it was too late. He went into his bedroom to grab his Bible, notebook, and something special he'd picked up for Genny.

She looked at him when she caught sight of the gift wrapped in white paper, prominently displayed on the coffee table next to his Bible and notebook. "What's that?" She asked as she sat down on the couch beside him.

"A gift for you."

Genny stared at him for a moment, then picked up the gift. Carefully unwrapping the paper, she pulled the top off the box and separated the gold tissue paper to reveal a maroon leather covered Bible.

"See, I had your name engraved." Paul pointed to her name, *Genevieve Thompson*. "And look at this." He pulled out the maroon ribbon bookmark with a small pewter cross tied to the end. Genny's lips parted as she stared at the Bible. He couldn't read her expression. She didn't look happy, but she didn't look disappointed either. He took the box from her, pulled out the Bible, and handed it to her. "It's a NIV women's study Bible."

"NIV?" She opened the Bible and turned a few of the pages. Paul watched her read a passage or two.

"New International Version."

"Granny and Granddaddy's Bible was different. It had old-fashioned language. You know, *thee* and *thou*."

"That's the King James Version. It was transcribed into Early Modern English."

"Oh." She closed the Bible and held it in both hands. "Thank you." She leaned over and hugged him.

"You're welcome. Now, let's continue in the Gospel of John." Paul heard her sigh under her breath. He picked up his Bible, removed the bookmark, and began reading, "Chapter one, verse thirty-five says, 'The next day John was there again...'"

Paul turned the page as he read. A little while later, he noticed Genny staring at the same page. She held her hand over her mouth to stifle a yawn. His body tensed, but before he could react, a knowing filled his heart that God was in control. He reminded himself that God was also in control of his upcoming deployment and would be there for Genny in his absence.

Genny climbed into bed and stared at the Bible next to her as if it was a snake waiting to strike. It was a book. The Good Book, actually. Not a book of spells and incantations. Why did she have such an aversion to reading the Bible? She grabbed her journal and pen and bit her bottom lip.

April 29, 2011

Paul gave me a Bible tonight. A Bible. I have a Bible. Yes, it's the Precious Moments Bible Granny gave me when I was baptized, but it still works. The Bible he gave me is a study Bible. How am I supposed to study the Bible? I hope he doesn't expect me to do a Bible study every night like he does. It's enough that I have to suffer through a weekly Bible study.

I almost lied about endo pain so he'd skip tonight's study, but I couldn't. I hate being coerced into doing something. He's my husband, not my daddy. I shouldn't say that. It's not coercion but I feel that he would be hurt if I didn't agree. I wish my faith was as strong as his. I think God hates me for some reason. I have a hard time worshiping someone who took everyone I love away from me.

She stared at the page for a minute. Glancing at the Bible again, she stretched out her hand and pulled it from the box. Tears stung her eyes when she opened the front cover. Earlier, she'd flipped through the pages so fast that she'd missed the presentation page.

Presented to my wife, Genevieve Marie Thompson

April 29, 2011

Your husband, Paul.

She looked up and stared at the back of her bedroom door. Holding the Bible up to her chest, a card slipped out from the back and rested on her lap. She tilted her head and opened the card.

Genevieve,

Never forget that you are a child of the one true King. God loves you with an everlasting love. We may never know the answers to our questions this side of Heaven, but rest assured, it will become clear once we are in His presence.

I care about you and only want the best for you.

Love,

Paul

Genny held her hands over her mouth as she sobbed. She'd been hard on Paul and all he wanted to do was minister to her. As touched as she was that he cared about her, there was a barrier between herself and God. One that she'd built.

⁘

Genny stretched out on the couch with her book. She opened to where the bookmark was placed and continued reading. When she was into a suspenseful part, she heard a vehicle slow down out front and realized it was Paul pulling into the drive. She stuffed the bookmark in the book, grabbed her lunch dishes from the coffee table, and hurried to the sink.

She peeked out the window. Paul was sitting in the truck talking on his phone. She sighed and hurried to finish washing the dirty dishes before he came inside. Drying her hands as he came in the door, she gave him a playful grin.

"I saw you talking on your phone when I was looking out the window." She almost gave herself away. He was always on her about leaving her dirty dishes around the house.

"Hey," he said as he hung up his hat and keys.

Genny didn't like the look he gave her. "What is it?"

"My parents are at Tybee Island and want to visit before they head back to Tennessee. It'll be for one night."

Genny's mouth fell open. "What? When?"

"Saturday." He winced.

Genny stared at him and looked around. "Today's Thursday. What are we supposed to do?"

"We need to move my stuff into your room so they can sleep in my room."

He was going to sleep in her room? And where would that be? The thought of passing themselves off as a married couple to Paul's parents terrified her.

Paul made a trip to the store Friday evening to pick up some last-minute items to host his parents. Genny spent the day cleaning her bedroom since Paul would be staying with her. She heard Paul pull into the drive from running errands. She blew out her breath and gritted her teeth while she struggled with a fitted sheet. It was as if the mattress came to life and refused to get dressed. A stifled laugh came from the doorway.

"It's not funny." Genny jerked the sheet off the mattress and glared at Paul.

"Want some help?" Paul walked over to the other side of the bed, and they slipped the sheet on the head of the bed at the same time and moved to the foot of the bed. "Now that wasn't so bad, was it?"

Genny shook her head and spread the top sheet across the mattress.

After dinner, they watched TV and talked about how to behave in front of his parents. Paul had moved his toiletries and personal items that were on his nightstand to the master bedroom and walked in with an armload of clothes from his closet.

"You never know," Paul said when Genny stared at him.

Genny showed him where to hang the clothes. "I'm going to take a shower and get ready for bed."

"Okay, Gen. Goodnight."

"Goodnight."

Exhausted, Genny climbed into bed and reached for her journal but found the dusted and polished top of the nightstand instead. Shuffling around in the drawer of the nightstand, she didn't find the journal. It was somewhere in her room. She only wrote in the journal sitting in bed.

The thought of losing all of her memories sent her heart into an erratic rhythm. Panicked, she peeked behind the nightstand. The journal was wedged between the back of the nightstand and the wall. She pulled out the nightstand, rescuing her journal from behind. She kissed the cover and climbed back into bed.

May 6, 2011

Paul's parents are coming tomorrow. Of all the people we are lying to, I never once thought about his parents. How are we going to do it? It doesn't help that his mom scares me. She reminds me of an angry librarian who shushes everyone all the time. Hopefully, it won't be too painful.

She closed the journal and turned off the lamp. As soon as she closed her eyes, panic welled up inside. What if they failed miserably and his parents saw right through them?

75

Chapter 10

Morning had arrived quicker than Genny had hoped. She stood at the kitchen counter sipping her second cup of coffee within an hour. Anxiety kept her tossing and turning all night. She wiped down the counter again and rearranged a few of the canisters.

Paul walked into the kitchen and sighed. "Chill Genevieve. They are my parents, not royalty."

"How much longer?" She wiped her hands on her shorts.

"Anytime now."

Nausea rose in her throat. She hadn't seen Paul's parents in years.

Mr. Thompson was over at her grandparents' house frequently, mostly due to Paul and Brandon's mischievous behavior. But she didn't see Mrs. Thompson outside of church much, although they were next door neighbors. Hopefully, Paul wouldn't leave her alone to entertain his mom.

Something caught Genny's attention from the kitchen window. A large black SUV slowed down and stopped in front of the house. "What kind of car do they drive?"

"Cadillac Escalade."

"What color?"

"Black."

She stepped back from the window. She could sneak out back. No, eventually she'd have to see her in-laws. She exhaled a shaky breath. When a knock sounded on the door, her pulse raced. Paul stepped over and opened the door.

"Hello, sweetheart!" His mom rushed in and hugged him. She released Paul and headed Genny's way with her arms open wide. "Give me a hug!"

"Hi, Mrs. Thompson." Genny's legs threatened to buckle.

"Call me Tricia." She wrapped her arms around Genny and squeezed. "I'm so sorry about Brandon. He was such a nice young man."

"Thank you." Tricia looked different. Genny's last memory of her was the pinched expression on her face at her granny's funeral. She looked like she'd taken a gulp of unsweetened tea. Today, her eyes were full of joy and a smile stretched across her face.

"The house is so cute." Tricia smiled.

"We like it." Genny slipped her hands in the back pockets of her shorts.

Paul's dad walked in and hugged Paul, then made his way to Genny. Her heart lurched. He was an older version of Paul. They both were attractive with the same tall, muscular build and blue-gray eyes. Although Mr. Thompson's hair was graying, his cut was similar to Paul's high and tight style. Genny had a preview of Paul in forty years, sending a tingle down her spine. She tried to keep her smile under control as he leaned in to hug her.

"Hi Mr.—"

He held up his hand before she could finish her greeting. "Brian."

Paul headed outside to help his dad unload the car while Genny and Tricia sat down in the living room. Genny was quiet for a moment, then offered Tricia a cup of coffee.

"No thank you, honey. I've already had two cups."

Genny gave an awkward laugh. "Me, too."

"Little Genny Jones. Who knew you would turn into such a beautiful young woman?"

Genny leaned back and focused on a coaster on the coffee table. When she looked up, Tricia was staring at her. "I must admit. I never imagined you and Paul married."

Genny tensed. What should she say? *"We are so in love."* She couldn't lie to Paul's mother. The pile of lies would surely explode like a truckload of dynamite. Her shoulders relaxed when Paul and Brian walked in.

"You ready?" Paul asked.

"For what?" Genny mouthed.

Paul leaned down and whispered, "To be a tour guide."

She bit her bottom lip. "As ready as I'll ever be."

"We'll drive." Tricia said as they walked into the living room after they settled into Paul's room.

Paul opened the car door for Genny. "I raised him right." Tricia said.

"That I'm thankful for." She looked at Paul and grinned.

To celebrate their marriage, Brian and Tricia wanted to treat Paul and Genny to dinner after the tour. The couples chose a quaint little restaurant in the heart of the city.

"Oh, this looks nice," Tricia said and slipped her purse strap over her shoulder.

Paul opened the door and stepped aside so Genny and his parents could walk inside. They were seated at a table in the middle of the dining room.

"This place is nice. The tablecloths are actual cloth." Paul said and ran his hand across the top of the table.

Everyone ordered their food and sipped their drinks while they waited. A knot formed in Genny's stomach when Tricia's eyes found hers. "So, how did this happen?" Tricia asked, pointing at Genny and Paul. Genny picked up her glass of sweet tea to quench her suddenly dry mouth.

"We never expected this to happen. We've kept in touch over the years," Paul said and paused a few moments. "As you know, I went to help Genny after Brandon died. We developed deeper feelings through his death." He turned and smiled at Genny.

"But Brandon died five months ago. That's such a short time frame for marriage." Tricia looked from Paul to Genny.

Genny's eyes widened. Paul parted his lips, but no words came.

"Trish, leave the kids alone. Can't you see they're in love?" Brian smiled.

Genny clenched her jaw to keep her mouth from hanging open. She and Paul should win an Academy Award for convincing his parents that they were in love. She wished she could read Paul's mind right now.

After they returned home from dinner, Paul and his dad moved out to the patio to visit, leaving Genny and his mom in the living room.

Genny picked up her phone and put it down again. It was rude to surf the internet when you have company. "Can I get you a cup of coffee, Tricia? I know it's late."

"You know what? I'd love a cup."

Genny brewed two cups of coffee and brought them into the living room. The tick of the mantel clock bounced off the walls. Genny wasn't one to make small talk, but the silence was killing her. "How's retirement?" She blew into her coffee and took a small sip.

"Oh, we love it. We spend more time traveling than we do at home."

"Where's your favorite place?"

"Hands down, the beach."

"I love the beach, too."

Back to silence. Now Genny knew where the phrase "silence is deafening" came from. She finished her coffee and considered another cup, but four cups of coffee in one day wasn't a good idea.

"I know you two haven't been married long, but I was wondering." Tricia gave Genny a smile that made her nervous. "We aren't getting any younger." Tricia raised her eyebrows.

Genny didn't know whether to blush or throw up at what Tricia was alluding to.

"You now, grandbabies." Tricia's smile brightened her eyes.

Genny's thoughts evaporated, leaving her mind blank. To prevent her throat from closing, she said the only thing she could think of, and it was the truth. "I'm not sure we can have a baby because I have endometriosis."

"Oh honey. I didn't know. Infertility is one of the worst things a couple can go through." Tricia ran her fingers through her shoulder length hair and looked at Genny. "It's obvious that Brian and I are older. Paul was born when I was thirty-eight. I had three miscarriages before I got pregnant with him. The doctor couldn't figure out what was the problem. Of course, that was almost thirty years ago. But I was so scared that I'd have another miscarriage."

"I didn't know about the miscarriages. I'm so sorry."

"Thank you. It was a rough time, but we had our miracle baby. Well, sweetheart, I think I'm going to go take a shower and get ready for bed. It's been a long day."

"Okay. I won't be far behind." Genny grinned.

Genny glanced out the backdoor on her way out of the living room. Paul and Brian were deep in conversation. Stopping, she quietly listened, but their voices were too low. She stepped closer and stood by the window, out of sight. She gasped when she heard what Brian said to Paul.

"You need to take care of that young lady, son. She's been through so much."

"I will, dad. Don't worry."

She took a step back and hurried down the hall to take a shower and get ready for bed.

When she came out of the bathroom, Paul walked in and shut the bedroom door.

"You and your dad were outside for a while."

"Yeah. We don't get to have good quality conversation often. What about you and Mom?"

"She asked me about grandchildren."

"I'm not surprised. They are in their late sixties, you know."

"Yeah, but…" Why didn't he seem concerned? Did he think that they'd have children one day?

"Don't worry about it. It'll pass. At least for now." Paul winked and went to the closet for a blanket.

"What are you doing?" Genny watched as he laid the blanket on the floor between the bed and the wall.

"I'm making my bed."

"What if your parents need something in the night?" Genny paused. "You have to sleep in the bed."

He looked at her for a few moments. "You're right."

Genny sat on the bed applying lotion and thought about what Paul and his dad had talked about. Paul's phone chimed. She picked it up and looked at the bathroom door. He'd gone in to take a shower and it would be a few minutes. When she laid it back on the bed, it chimed again. Curious, she picked up the phone. The screen wasn't locked, so she swiped and tapped on the message app. Her lips parted as she read the texts.

You owe me an explanation

DO NOT IGNORE ME

The shower turned off and Genny panicked. She deleted both texts and tossed the phone on the bed. Lava bubbled in her stomach when she looked at the phone. What was Brianna up to? The bathroom door opened, and Paul came out wearing only a pair of shorts. Genny's breath quickened, and she reluctantly averted her eyes, but not before he saw her.

"I get hot when I wear a shirt, but I'll wear one if you'd like."

The heat of a blush touched her cheeks. "No, it's fine."

Genny turned off the lamp and bit her bottom lip to keep a giggle inside. She was lying in bed next to Paul Thompson. Thinking about it gave her sharp palpitations. Biting her bottom lip again, she rolled over and ended up against Paul's side. She raised her head and quickly rolled over, mortified. He couldn't be asleep already. It'd only been ten minutes since she turned off the lamp. But he had to be. The Paul she knew would say something.

Drowsiness overtook Genny, and her eyelids drooped and closed. Thoughts of Brandon filled her mind as she felt herself falling asleep.

In a room that resembles a cafeteria, Genny wonders how she got here. She scans the room and spots Brandon sitting at a table with a group of men. They are talking and laughing as they eat. She catches a glimpse of a man as he stands up. There's something in his hand. Before she can warn Brandon, the man holds up a gun and begins shooting at people.

"Brandon!" Genny cried out. "Brandon!"

"Genny."

She opened her eyes and realized she was sitting up in bed and Paul had a hold of her shoulders. "I–I saw Brandon. He was in the dining hall about to be shot by that man." Tears flowed down her cheeks, and she sobbed.

"It's okay. It was a nightmare. I'm here. You'll be okay." He rubbed her back as she cried. "Want some water?"

"Okay."

After a sip of water, she laid back and closed her eyes, only for them to open again. She focused on the light fixture on the ceiling in the middle of the room. When would the nightmares stop?

When Genny woke the next morning, Paul was already up. She heard muffled voices down the hall and the smell of bacon drifted into the room. Glancing at the clock, she grimaced. It was nine-thirty, and she was the last one up.

As she brushed her teeth, Paul walked to the doorway of the bathroom and announced that his parents were ready to leave. Intimidation was a weak word for how Genny had felt about Tricia, but she'd seen a different side of her during their visit. It started out tense with Tricia questioning their marriage, but once they were home, she and Tricia had quality time together.

"Come on, Gen." Paul had walked back into the bedroom again.

"It's only been two minutes." Genny followed Paul down the hall to see his parents off.

"It's your turn to visit next time." Tricia leaned over and gave Genny a tight hug, followed by Brian's hug.

Genny and Paul waved as his parents drove off. She'd miss Brian and Tricia.

"Well, that visit was better than I expected." Paul said, smiling. Genny laced her fingers together behind her back and bit her bottom lip. "Fine, let's head out." She squealed and grabbed her purse.

Paul pulled into a parking space at Lowe's. Before he turned off the engine, Genny opened the door and stepped down. He hurried to catch up with her. "Give me your hand!" He grabbed her hand and pulled her back as a truck passed by. When they reached the garden center, she disappeared into the rows of vegetables and herbs.

Seeing and smelling the plants took Genny back to her grandparents' farm. She'd accompanied her grandfather when he'd bought seedlings for the garden. Wandering down an aisle of trees, she came across a flowering dogwood. Resting her hands on the pot, she smiled at the memory of the dogwood tree in the front yard.

"Okay, which planter do you want?" Paul asked. Genny pointed to a large red planter. "That's as big as the patio table."

"No, it's not." She sighed.

Paul picked up the planter and set it on a flat cart.

Along with the planter, they bought soil, a watering can, and a lone Beefsteak tomato seedling. Paul pushed the cart out to the truck and Genny held the cart still while he loaded the planter and soil.

"Admiring your husband?" Paul wiggled his eyebrows.

Genny realized her gaze was fixed on him and heat filled her face.

"Hot out here, huh?" Paul smiled. Genny rolled her eyes and walked toward the passenger door, holding the tomato seedling. "I see you're maintaining your professional status."

"What?"

Paul laughed. "You know."

Genny rolled her eyes and shook her head.

At home, Genny had Paul place the planter where she wanted it, and he filled it with the soil. Genny planted the seedling and walked over and filled the watering can. When she was watering the plant, a blast of water hit her in the rear, and she screamed. She turned around and saw Paul grinning and holding up the water hose.

"I told you I'd get you back." He lifted his chin and raised his brows.

"Paul! Where did you come from?" Genny gritted her teeth.

"I snuck out the front door." He walked up to her wearing a wide grin.

"Mission accomplished." She couldn't help but laugh.

June 7, 2011

The visit wasn't too bad. Maybe we will go visit them one day. I haven't been back to Murfreesboro since Granny died in 2008. I thought about something this evening. Did Brian and Tricia meet Brianna? I hope not.

Paul sprayed me on the butt with the water hose. If I was fast enough, I would have chased him down and sprayed him on the butt and see how he liked it. There's something about Paul. Is the crush coming back or is it more? It doesn't matter if the feelings aren't returned.

<h1 style="text-align:center">Chapter 11</h1>

S tanding to stretch, Genny bent back down to set a box on the closet floor with the others. A printer paper box that she had forgotten about was tucked in the back corner. Crawling under the lower rod that held her jeans, she dragged the box out and carried it to her bed.

The top of the box was labeled *Important documents* in Brandon's handwriting. She pulled the lid off. An accordion file lay on top. She grabbed it and pulled out the first group of papers and saw that they were financial documents. That was Paul's area of expertise. She walked down the hall and lightly knocked on the open door.

"What's up?"

"I found this in a box of important papers. I looked inside and it seems to be financial documents. When you get a chance, can you look through it? You can shred anything you think I shouldn't hold on to."

"Sure, I'll take a look as soon as I finish my Bible study."

"Thanks."

Genny headed back to her bedroom and gathered up her dirty laundry. She loathed doing laundry and it seemed to multiply overnight. She'd almost rather clean the toilet than do laundry. With an armload of towels and clothes, she made her way to the laundry room. If she threw everything into the washing machine together, she wouldn't spend all day doing laundry.

An hour had passed in what seemed like fifteen minutes. Genny carried her clean laundry into her room and dumped it onto her bed. She was proud of herself. Usually, her laundry stayed in the dryer until Paul yelled down the hall for her to come get it.

"Genny?" Paul stood in the doorway clutching the accordion file as if it was a treasured artifact that was unearthed after a thousand years.

He cleared his throat and walked up to where she was standing. "Got a minute?"

She'd gladly push the laundry aside for however long Paul wanted to talk. "Is it old bank statements?"

"Well, some. But there's more to it, Genevieve."

When he called her by her given name, it usually meant it was something serious or she had annoyed him. She hadn't annoyed him lately, so there must have been more than bank statements in the file.

"Let's sit." They settled on the bed, and he cradled the file for a few moments then pulled back the flap. "These are insurance papers."

"For the Jeep?"

"No, it's life insurance."

"Oh."

Paul pulled out a stack of documents. "There are three policies here. It appears that your dad had a policy for three hundred thousand dollars, but there isn't anything for your mom. I guess your dad was the only one that had life insurance. Your mom stayed home, right?"

"Yeah." Three hundred thousand dollars was a lot of money but where was the money now? Her heart rate picked up.

"Your grandmother had a spreadsheet accounting for the money. I added up the columns and it appears that your grandparents spent the majority of the money for your and Brandon's school. Private schools are expensive, you know. You went for thirteen years including kindergarten and Brandon went for eight years. They used the rest for your care. You know, food and clothing and extracurricular activities. Plus, the cars they bought for you and Brandon when you were teenagers.

"Your grandfather had a policy for fifty thousand dollars. She annotated that she used it to pay down the mortgage. Now, the last policy is for your grandmother. She had listed Brandon as the beneficiary. I'm not sure why your grandfather's policy was lower. Maybe it was his health. How old were you when he died?"

"Ten. How much is Granny's policy?" She sounded greedy, but she should know these things.

"It was a hundred thousand dollars."

"What? Where is it? She died three years ago." Genny clenched her jaw. *Calm down.* Brandon wouldn't waste the money. It was probably in some bank account somewhere.

"Brandon kept good records, too. Must run in the family." Paul's laugh sounded forced. "He split it in half so you each had fifty thousand dollars. He wrote down that he bought your Prius for almost nineteen grand after your old Camry died. And he paid your tuition for two years of college. Those two added up to around twenty-three thousand dollars."

"Why don't I know about this?"

"I don't know, Gen. My guess is because you were younger when your granny died."

"You mean I went crazy." She blew out her breath.

"Genny, you didn't go crazy. Yes, you made some bad decisions. We all do."

Not Paul Thompson. He was close to perfect.

"Staying out all the time drinking is close to crazy. Especially, since my parents were killed by a drunk driver. Not to mention flunking out of college. You know that's why she sent me to live with Brandon?"

"Yes."

"I figured he told you." She rasped.

He shuffled through the documents and pulled out a bank statement. "Here's what's left of your money. Looks like you are joint owner of the account."

Genny took the statement from Paul's hand. She had a little under twenty thousand dollars left of the life insurance money. That was a big amount but around seven thousand dollars was unaccounted for.

"I assume that the rest was living expenses."

"That's a lot for three years of living expenses." Genny laid the statement next to her and rested her clenched fists in her lap. "So, when he gave me money, he was giving me my own money? I paid for my own bedroom furniture? My own clothes? My own tuition?" Why was she surprised? It wasn't like Brandon was made of money. She narrowed her eyes. "And what did he spend his money on?"

"It's parked in the driveway."

"The Jeep?" Tears stung her eyes. She loved the Jeep and loved having a part of Brandon.

"I found the bill of sale and the receipts for the off-road conversion. It comes close to fifty grand."

"Wow." Genny's head spun. It was too much to take in. Why did Brandon keep it a secret? He must have thought she would blow the money.

"I need to turn in. We have squadron physical training at six in the morning. We'll figure out what you need to do to get the money, okay?"

"Okay. Goodnight."

"Goodnight."

Paul shut the door on the way out of the bedroom. She pulled open the nightstand drawer and grabbed her journal and a pen. Turning to the next blank page, Genny's heart flowed through the pen onto the paper as the tip danced across the page.

June 10, 2011

I'm mad that Brandon kept this from me, and I am so broken that he's gone. It's not about the money. The twenty grand can disappear for all I care. It's that my brother lied to me. How could he do that to me? I don't get it.

Genny lifted the pen from the paper. A tear rolled down her cheek and dropped onto the page. She grabbed a tissue and dabbed the smeared ink. Picking up the pen, she continued.

I'm a hypocrite. Brandon lied to me about the money, and Paul and I are lying about our marriage. Is Paul going to divorce me now that I have money?

Genny closed the journal and slid it and the pen into the drawer of the nightstand. It hit her that Brandon had planned to use the twenty thousand dollars to replace the Prius after it was totaled in an accident. Anger boiled inside her, but grief pushed it back down. Genny slowly exhaled. There was so much more to death than dying.

⇝⇝ ⇜⇜

Genny laid on her bed with her phone. She should be cleaning the kitchen, but it could wait until closer to when Paul was due home. As soon as she tapped on the Facebook app, a calendar reminder popped up on her phone: *Get Brandon's card and present.* Her heart dropped to her stomach like it was made of lead. Brandon's birthday was in ten days.

Climbing into the Jeep, she drove out of the neighborhood with no destination in mind. Dusk was settling over the city, and she crossed the bridge toward the ocean. She pulled off into a parking lot at the beach, climbed down, and headed toward the water. The crashing waves and smell of the salt in the air soothed her soul.

Near the water's edge, she sat down on the cool sand, pulled her knees to her chest, and wrapped her arms around her legs. Tears rolled down her cheeks and she swallowed hard. "Why did you leave me?" she whispered and lowered her head.

One of the few memories of her childhood was of the day their parents died. Mumbled voices from downstairs woke her early that morning. She'd made her way down, dragging her favorite blanket behind her. When she reached the bottom of the stairs, she saw her grandparents sitting on the couch and her grandmother was crying.

Even at the young age of five, she knew something was wrong. Their parents were nowhere in sight and their grandparents lived in Tennessee. They never came to Mississippi for a visit unannounced. She ran to the couch and into her grandmother's arms.

Brandon walked into the living room from the kitchen and sat next to Genny between their grandparents. He looked up at their grandmother and she nodded. Taking Genny's hand in his, he spoke softly while he rubbed the back of her hand.

"Sissy, there's something I need to tell you." Genny looked up at him. Tears streamed down his cheeks. His voice broke when he spoke, "Mommy and Daddy have been in an accident. They are in Heaven with God and Jesus now."

Her mother and father were in Heaven, her grandparents were in Heaven, and now Brandon was in Heaven. Why did God choose to leave her behind? He could have taken her, too. But He thought it was best to leave her to walk through life alone. She'd never forgive Him.

Genny looked up toward Heaven. She ran her fingers through the back of her hair and grabbed a fistful at the nape of her neck. The urge to pull her hair out had never been this powerful. She dropped her hands and shoved them under her thighs, restraining her compulsion this time.

Raising herself to her feet, Genny wrapped her arms around herself and walked to the water's edge. Strolling up and down the beach, she cried out to God. One moment she screamed at Him and the next she clung to Him. Was she being punished for some unknown sin or was He teaching her a lesson? A hundred years could pass, and she'd never understand why He took her family away from her.

Genny wasn't home when Paul pulled up. She probably had to work and forgot to tell him. He grabbed the pan he'd used to make a grilled cheese for dinner and washed it. As he dried the pan, Paul saw a man pass by on the sidewalk with his dog. Paul had noticed the man walked his dog like clockwork at the same time every day, whether it was raining or thirty degrees out. If Genny was an animal person, he'd suggest a dog to help her heal and keep her company during the upcoming deployment. He turned away and bagged up the garbage, including the empty milk jug on the floor next to the overflowing can.

He walked out the backdoor to put the bag in the bin and smiled. After work, he'd stopped by a co-worker's house and picked up something special he'd ordered for Genny. Peter met him at home and helped unload it and carry it to the backyard. Genny had been down recently, and he wanted to cheer her up.

Brandon's birthday was coming up, but Genny hadn't said anything. Paul planned to cook Brandon's favorite meal and watch his favorite movie to honor his memory. He grabbed the remote and lowered himself onto the couch. Browsing the channels, nothing seemed interesting and turned off the TV. There were times he sought the solace of silence. He ran his hand over the top of his head and down his face.

Paul had often thought about their marriage. If he had waited to hear a definitive answer from God, what would He have said? At the time, he had no choice but to use marriage as a means to support Genny. If it was a mistake, there was only one remedy and he'd promised himself years ago it would never happen. He sighed. But what if Genny fell in love with someone? The decision he'd made could prevent her from experiencing true happiness.

His phone chimed. Pulling it out of his pocket, Brianna's name showed on the screen, and he furrowed his brows. His first thought was to delete it without reading it, but he tapped on the message.

You can't ignore me. It's not fair to me. Why did you marry Genny so soon after we broke up? Were you cheating on me with her? Please call me so be can meet and talk.

There is nothing to talk about. I married Genny because I love her. I moved on and it is time for you to move on, too.

He scoffed and tossed his phone on the couch next to him. Picking it up, he deleted their conversation and blocked her number.

The mufflers on the Jeep sounded as Genny drove down the hill and pulled into the drive. She walked in the front door and hung her keys up on the keyholder. A flutter tickled Paul's stomach.

"Hey, I bought you a present." Paul grinned and slid his hands in his front pockets.

Genny's eyes were slightly red and puffy. "Why?"

"No reason. Can't I buy my wife a present? It's out back. You have to close your eyes." He motioned to the backdoor.

Genny's jaw muscles tightened, and she closed her eyes. Paul slowly led her outside and grabbed her when she tripped over the edge of the patio. She groaned and tensed. Stopping a few feet away, he let go of her.

"Open your eyes!" She opened her eyes and stared blankly for a moment. She wasn't impressed. His shoulders fell.

A moment later, surprise lifted his shoulders when Genny stepped up to the picnic table and ran her hand across the top. "Do you remember Granny and Granddaddy's picnic table? It was like this." Genny turned and hugged Paul. "Thank you."

"You're welcome. I think that's where your grandfather and my dad had most of their talks about mine and Brandon's shenanigans. One of my co-workers does woodworking on the side. He told us one day that he'd started making picnic tables and, I don't know, I thought it would remind you of a better time in your life."

"Oh, it does." She hugged him again.

Paul watched as she climbed on top of the picnic table and looked out over the backyard. He headed inside to wind down for the night. After his shower, he settled in to do his Bible study and glanced out the window.

Genny had been sitting on the picnic table for over an hour. She slid off the top of the table and strolled toward the backdoor. A few moments later, she stood in the doorway to his bedroom.

"Thanks again." She wore a faint smile.

"You're welcome, Genny." After she walked down the hall, he stood and pushed his door closed. Sitting on the side of his bed, he opened his prayer journal to the most recent prayer list. Genny was at the top, as usual. She was in a tug-of-war with God. He pulled her heart toward Him, and she pulled it back. He closed his eyes and began to pray that she would fully give her heart to God. He also prayed about their marriage. God couldn't remain silent forever.

⟫⟫⟫ ⟪⟪⟪

Genny guessed she'd be asking the same question for the rest of her life? Why did God take her family? She had to prepare herself for the answer or the continued silence. Everything happens for a reason, some would say. What reason could God possibly have? She couldn't ask herself any more questions today. She picked up her journal and pen. Turning to the last few pages, she started the entry for the day.

June 18, 2011

This evening started out horrible and ended a little better. I'm still mad at God, but my surprise made my anger less. Only by a tiny bit though. When I first saw the picnic table, I didn't know whether to laugh or scream at Paul, but the longer I looked at the table, the closer I felt to my family. I realized that I'm not walking through life alone. I have Paul. He truly is a blessing. What is going to happen between us? How long is he going to stay married to me?

With the journal and pen neatly tucked away in her nightstand drawer, Genny turned off the lamp and pulled the covers up to her chest. Paul inhabited her thoughts as she tried to fall asleep. They had settled into a comfortable routine. Besides for work, most of their time was spent together. She had become accustomed to seeing his truck in the driveway when she'd drive down the hill; his hat hanging on the keyring; his combat boots on the rug by the door to the garage.

She couldn't help but wonder what the rest of their lives together looked like. Would they still be married in five years? Ten? What if Paul found someone else and what would that mean for their marriage? She was too afraid to ask.

⤜⤛ ⟫⟫⟩ ⟨⟨⟨⟨

The personal effects box was still pushed against Genny's bedroom wall. She walked over and unhooked the latch. Although she'd had the box for several months, it was still emotional to see the items Brandon had with him in Iraq. There were a few pictures and cards she had sent him and even a card or two from Paul. She'd ask him later if he wanted them back.

There was a picture that had slid down the side of the box. Genny pulled it out and turned it over. *Shawn Sullivan*. Wrapping a lock of hair around her finger, she held it for a little while. Pulling her finger free, she watched the spiral curl straighten.

In the living room, Genny walked up to the backdoor and separated the slats in the blinds. The dark silhouette of the picnic table was illuminated by a sliver of moonlight that had broken through the clouds. She went out back and sat on the top of the table, looking at the woods on the other side of the back fence. The tops of the trees swayed in the light breeze. Childhood memories surfaced as they had been more frequently. It could be Brandon's upcoming birthday or that she missed her family. Probably both.

As thoughts darted in and out of her head, memories of her childhood on her grandparents' old farm played in front of her like a movie on a big screen. She and Brandon visited every summer before they moved in with their grandparents. There was a large oak tree next to the barn behind the old farmhouse. Genny and Brandon loved to play around the enormous trunk. One year, their grandfather hung a tire swing on a limb and she and Brandon took turns pushing each other. She smiled at the memory.

There was something familiar about the middle tree dancing in the breeze. She slid off the table and made her way to the back fence. Reaching over the fence as far as she could, she lightly ran the tips of her fingers over the rough bark. The tree was an oak and the size of the trunk, and the height reminded her of the old oak tree on the farm.

The massive limbs stretched out over her like protective arms. Why hadn't she noticed the tree before? The countless hours she had spent in the backyard, and she had never noticed the tree across the fence. And here she was, seeing it for the first time in the dark. *The picnic table.* Paul was the reason. The tree would still blend in with the other trees if it weren't for the picnic table.

Over the next few days, Genny couldn't get Sergeant Sullivan out of her mind. He had been with Brandon when he was injured. What did that mean? What did he see? Every time Genny tried to visualize what had happened that day, her mind came up blank. She didn't think she could grieve properly until she knew what had happened to Brandon. Contacting Sergeant Sullivan was next to impossible, since she didn't know where he was.

Genny heard Paul head out for his morning run around five-thirty. She hadn't felt well the past few days and told him the night before that she was going to skip the morning run. After Paul came home, Genny heard him getting ready for work and he was on his way out the door when she came into the kitchen.

"How are you feeling?"

"Okay. I'm getting a granola bar and going back to bed. I called into work, so I'll be home when you get home."

"Alright. Let me know if you need anything and I can pick it up on my way home," Paul said and opened the front door.

"I will."

Genny slept the rest of the morning and woke around noon. She was feeling a little better and made a sandwich for lunch and headed to the couch. Paul's laptop was on the coffee table, slightly open. She turned on the TV and channel surfed for a while. Glancing at the laptop, Shawn Sullivan came to mind. Paul had told her about a global address book in his work email. Maybe she could see if she could find Shawn. But that would be invading Paul's privacy. Paul would discourage her from contacting Shawn, anyway. But she couldn't let the opportunity pass. She opened the laptop and looked for the link to the email in his favorites.

Paul's login information was saved, so she didn't have to try to figure out his password and lock him out of his account. A lump formed in her throat. She pulled up the global address book and searched for Shawn Sullivan. "Eleven people named Shawn Sullivan in the Air Force." She huffed. Using rank, she eliminated eight people, which meant she would need to contact three.

Genny clicked on their names and wrote down their email addresses and put the piece of paper in her pocket. She closed out of the email and put Paul's laptop in the same position with the top slightly open and went down the hall. Neatly tucked inside her underwear drawer for safe keeping, she looked at the piece of paper for a few moments, then closed the drawer.

Chapter 12

As the weather grew warmer, Genny spent most of her free time at the beach. She headed to the beach in the early evening hours four days before Brandon's birthday. As she drove around the curve leading to her favorite spot, Genny's eyes narrowed. A feeling that her refuge had been invaded pushed through her veins.

Jeeps of all sizes and colors, old and new, occupied the parking lot where Genny would park and walk down to the beach. Anger turned to curiosity, and she pulled into the parking lot. Thanks to Brandon's love of his Jeep, she drew lots of attention. Genny had the top off and heard all the comments. Her first thought was to drive past the crowd to get to the other side and leave, but something inside urged her to pull onto the grass and park.

Climbing down from the Jeep, she saw a man approaching her. He was a few inches shorter than her and had an athletic build, like Paul. His hair was not much longer than Paul's and a light blonde that was almost white.

"I'm Trevor Simms, the president of the Jeep club." He offered his hand.

Genny accepted his hand with a smile. "Oh, this is a club? Is it okay for me to be here?"

"Sure. Come on and join us."

"Thank you. I'm Genny Thompson."

Genny walked with Trevor, and he introduced several of the club members. There were lots of questions about the Jeep that she answered the best she could. "It was my brother's, and I don't know much about the upgrades. He was killed in Iraq this past December."

"I'm sorry to hear that, Genny," Trevor said. "We are a group of active-duty military, veterans, and their families. I saw the Charleston Air Force Base sticker on your windshield."

"My husband's in the Air Force." She led a group of club members to the Jeep. She stepped back and watched while a few of them conducted a thorough inspection. They spouted off brand names of winches, roll bars, fog lights, and tires, to each other.

She followed Trevor as he showed her some of the Jeeps in the club. Although she was new to Jeep life, she had to admit that Brandon's Jeep was among the best-looking Jeeps there.

"Would you like to join?" Trevor asked.

"Join?"

"Yeah. The club. You qualify as a dependent of a military member."

"Oh, I don't know…"

"We'd love to have you, Genny."

Genny watched the growing crowd as they continued their assessment of the Jeep and smiled at Trevor. "Okay."

Trevor gave her a quick rundown of the bylaws and the yearly dues, along with activities that were held throughout the year. After an impromptu meeting of the club members who were present, Genny was accepted into the Veterans Jeep Club of North Charleston. Looking around, she instantly felt a connection with the people. For the first time in a long time, she was where she belonged.

Genny strolled through the front door. "Guess what?" She tossed her purse on the dining table and joined Paul on the couch.

"What?"

"I found a Jeep club. I went to the place at the beach where I usually go and there they were. The president invited me to join and now I'm a member."

"That's great, Genny. I'm sure you'll have a blast."

"Oh, they are active duty, veterans, and their families. You are why I could join."

"You're welcome." Paul grinned.

Genny headed to her room to wind down for the night. She propped up on her pillows, finding it hard to contain her excitement.

June 25, 2011

The coolest thing happened today. I went to my usual spot at the beach and a Jeep club was hanging out. I couldn't believe it. The members were so nice, and I joined the club. I haven't been this happy in a long time. I plan to go to every get-together I can. Trevor said they will go off-roading soon. I can't wait.

Brandon's birthday is in three days. June 28, 1982. The day the greatest brother in the world was born. I can't write anything else right now or my tears will smear the ink.

She closed her journal and laid it on the nightstand. Life made no sense. Most people walked through life with no bumps in the road and here she was walking through life with hills and valleys, detours, and roadblocks, on a road that seemed to go nowhere.

⋙ ⋘

Paul glanced at Genny's sand-covered feet as she came in the garage door. "Let me guess," he grinned, "you've been at the beach again?"

Genny let out a little laugh and hung up her keys. "How did you know?"

"Hey, any ideas for honoring Brandon on his birthday?"

"I don't know. Do you have any suggestions?" Celebrating Brandon's birthday without him seemed wrong. Grief tightened its grip around her throat.

"I could grill chicken and you can make your granny's potato salad? Then we can watch *Batman Begins* since it was his favorite movie. How does that sound?"

"Okay, I guess." What was the purpose of celebrating Brandon's birthday when he was dead? It was one more thing that made his death real. "I'm going to get out of these sandy clothes."

"Dinner will be ready soon."

Genny nodded and headed down the hall to her bedroom. Sitting on her bed, she reached over and opened the drawer in her nightstand. The picture of Brandon and Shawn lay on top of her journal. She grabbed it and closed the drawer. Sighing, she ran her thumb over Brandon's face. Those eyes. What did Brandon see right before he died? He was vigilant and told Genny to always keep her car doors locked and the apartment door locked. And be aware of her surroundings. Was Brandon aware of his surroundings right before he died? Knowing him, he was aware of what was about to happen, but she hoped he was taken by surprise this once.

After a fitful night, Genny laid on the bed looking at the ceiling. Streaks of sunlight peeked through the blinds and stretched across the ceiling like fingers. Last night, she'd discovered lightning bugs blinking outside the window. A peace filled her heart and pushed Brandon's birthday out of her mind for a little while. She had left the blinds open and fell asleep watching the insects dance in the dark. But the peace she had was gone when she woke up this morning. Tomorrow was Brandon's birthday.

Reaching over to her nightstand, Genny picked up Brandon's picture and studied it. She brushed her finger over the dimple in her chin—the same dimple in Brandon's chin. She drew in a deep breath. If she could get in the Jeep and drive until she ran out of gas, she would. But it wouldn't change anything.

She dragged herself out of bed and walked down the hall. It was almost ten and Paul had been at work for two and a half hours now. She had the whole day to herself. Normally, it wouldn't bother her, but she would give anything to have Paul at home. If she could make it through tomorrow, it would all be over. Her shoulders hunched and she sank onto the couch.

Brandon's birthday wasn't some terrible event, it was the celebration of his birth. But why did Paul want to celebrate? She'd never celebrated her parents' or grandparents' birthdays after they passed, so why would she want to celebrate Brandon's birthday? Her eyes filled with tears.

She pulled herself to her feet and made her way to her bedroom. In the closet, she reached for the box of childhood photos on the top shelf. She dropped her arms to her sides. Looking at the photos would intensify her pain. She staggered from the closet and lowered herself on the edge of her bed. With her spine straight, she rested her hands on her lap and balled them into fists. She drew in a deep breath and widened her mouth to let out a scream, but stopped short. What good would it do?

Lying back on the pillows, Genny closed her eyes and willed herself to fall asleep. Even if she could sleep for an hour, it was an hour she didn't have to think. A tremble rolled from her head to her feet and back up, settling in her stomach. Sleep would evade her once again. Why was this so hard? If she'd been the one that had died, Brandon would have no problem celebrating her birthday. But she wasn't the one who died.

The next morning, sunrays peeked around the edges of the blinds. Genny opened her eyes and sighed. Surprised she'd slept through the night, she yawned and ran her fingers through her hair. Paul had put the chicken in the fridge to marinate the night before and had asked her to turn it over. She rose from the bed and traipsed to the fridge to flip the chicken. It was a beautiful day and she decided to spend some time outside. As soon as she stepped out onto the patio, she noticed Mrs. Baker sitting at her patio table with her hands around a cup. Mrs. Baker looked over and smiled.

"Hi, Genny."

"Hello." Genny reluctantly stepped over to the fence. She was not in the mood to socialize.

"How are you?" Mrs. Baker took a sip from her cup.

"Okay. You?"

"I'm enjoying a cup of coffee with my Stanley." She smiled.

Mrs. Baker was a widow. Was she senile too?

"Today would have been our fifty-fifth wedding anniversary. He's been gone for ten years now."

Tears pooled in Genny's eyes. Mrs. Baker wasn't senile. She was heartbroken like her. "Today is my brother's birthday. Brandon would have been twenty-nine."

"I'm sorry, honey. So young."

As much as she liked Mrs. Baker, she couldn't handle someone else's grief right now. "Paul will be home soon, so I should start on dinner."

"Okay, honey. Hang in there." Mrs. Baker smiled.

"You, too." Genny offered a slight smile in return and headed back inside.

Paul was home right on time. Genny half-hoped he'd be late, so they'd have to push back the celebration. But that would add more anxiety. Genny sighed. She peeled potatoes and placed them in a pot of water.

Paul was on the patio getting the grill ready for the chicken breasts. An avalanche of emotions hit her when she woke up this morning. The day had finally come—Brandon's twenty-ninth birthday. Last year she'd sent him a care package to Iraq full of some of his favorites: four packs of Twizzlers, a new CD, some toiletries, and a silly birthday card. No presents this year. No card.

Paul pulled the chicken breasts off the grill and brought them inside, where Genny was spooning potato salad onto their plates. He smiled and poured two glasses of lemonade. They sat at the table, and Paul prayed over their food.

Genny took a bite of chicken and slowly chewed. Why did Paul insist on this dinner? She would have preferred to sleep through the day and wake up tomorrow when it was over.

Sorrow settled around her like a thick fog, threatening to smother her. Desperate to breathe, she took in a deep, cleansing breath, filling her lungs. Paul looked at her and laid his hand on top of hers. He gave her hand a gentle squeeze, but to her relief, said nothing.

They put the leftovers in the fridge and cleaned up the dishes. Paul turned on the TV and looked at her. "Hey, I thought we would watch the movie now."

"I'll be right back." To keep herself from screaming or falling to the floor in a heap of emotions, she needed to distance herself for a few minutes.

She headed down the hall to her bedroom. The curtains were pulled back, and the blinds were open. She walked over and stared out the window. Brandon was dead. He was never coming back. Her heart had shriveled and died along with him. Genny headed down the hall to the garage door, where they had some of their shoes lined up.

"Genny? What are you doing?" Paul rose to his feet and walked over to her.

"I can't do this." She shoved her shaky foot into a sandal. Her heart pounded in her ears.

I've got to get out of here.

Paul's mouth hung open. "But…I think you should stay home. You're not in the best frame of mind." He reached out and touched her shoulder.

"I can't. Please understand." She looped her purse strap over her shoulder and grabbed her keys.

"Genny..."

"I'm sorry Paul." She fought the rise in her voice. She opened the front door and walked out. After she climbed into the Jeep, she backed out of the drive and wiped the tears from her eyes as she drove out of the neighborhood. How could she go on without Brandon?

She drove around town and ended up at Waterfront Park and stayed in the Jeep for a while. Her mom crossed her mind. She missed her mom, or at least she thought she did. So many years had passed that she was at the point where she didn't remember that much about her. Or her dad. Tears pooled in Genny's eyes. What would their relationship have been like if her parents hadn't died? And, of course, Brandon. Were they together in Heaven and were her granny and granddaddy with them?

Genny climbed out of the Jeep and walked around the park. The sky was clearer than it had been in a while. She eased herself down and laid back against the soft, damp grass and stared at the stars. Right now, she should be in Fayetteville baking a cake. It would taste bad and look like a kindergartner decorated it, but Brandon would love it. She would have bought a nice button-down shirt that Brandon would be excited about but would hang in the back of his closet. One day, it would find its way into the donation bag for Goodwill.

She sang to him, her voice cracking as she began. "Happy birthday to you, happy birthday to you, happy birthday dear Brandon...happy birthday...to...you." Tears rolled down her cheeks. "Why God?"

It was past one in the morning when Genny made it home. The house was dark except for the lamp by the couch. She wanted to apologize to Paul for the way she acted and was disappointed that he was already in bed. Genny walked around the couch to turn off the lamp. Paul was asleep on the couch with a book in his hand. If she woke him, what would he say? For a moment, she stood watching him sleep. Slowly pulling the book from under his hand, she leaned over to take the throw her granny had made off the back of the couch to spread over him.

"Where have you been?" Paul raised up. His voice was gruff from sleep.

Genny gasped and pushed her hand against her chest to calm the pounding of her heart. "You scared me to death," she started. "I drove around and ended up at Waterfront Park."

"You've been gone for hours. I texted you but you never replied, so I called you. My mind was all over the place when the call immediately went to voicemail. I was worried something happened to you."

Genny looked down at her hands and twisted her wedding band. "I turned my phone off. I'm sorry. I just...I just couldn't handle it."

Paul stared at her, then moved over so she could sit down. "Please don't turn your phone off again."

"Okay." Her voice cracked. She eased down next to him with tears streaming down her cheeks. He slipped his arms around her, pulled her against his chest, and held her. The soft thump of his heart comforted her.

After a time, she raised up and looked at him. "It hurts so bad."

"It always will, to some extent. He left a huge hole in our hearts and our lives."

Genny rested her head on his shoulder. What would she do without Paul? He was the reason she'd made it this far.

Genny's journal entry for the day was the shortest entry she'd ever written in a journal. It was only four words, but those four words held so much pain and sorrow.

June 28, 2011

Happy birthday, big bro.

She placed her journal on the nightstand and picked up her phone.

Powering it on, a text and a voicemail notification popped up. As she listened to the voicemail, tears streamed down her cheeks at the fear in Paul's voice. Shaking her head, she made a promise not to intentionally hurt Paul again.

Chapter 13

"Sergeant Thompson. You got all your stuff together for November?" Master Sergeant Fields, the superintendent of the shop, asked as he flipped through the pages of a list of upcoming deployments.

It was early July and Paul hadn't told Genny that he was deploying. "I'm working on it." Paul cleared his throat.

"You better be. Don't wait until the last minute," Master Sergeant Fields said.

He shouldn't wait until the last minute to tell Genny, either. It wasn't something he'd do, but he needed to tell her soon, so she had time to process his absence. He grabbed a walkie talkie and headed out to the flight line.

"You look lost in thought." Peter said as he walked toward Paul.

"Master Sergeant Fields said something about me getting my stuff together for November and it reminded me I need to tell Genny soon."

"You haven't told her yet?"

Paul shook his head.

"I'm surprised Melissa hadn't said anything about the unit deployments."

"Oh, I didn't think about that." Paul rubbed the back of his neck.

Genny finding out before he could say anything would end in disaster.

"Buddy, you better tell Genny, or you'll regret it. She needs time to prepare."

"Yeah, that's what I told myself. I'll do it in the next few days. Keep me in prayer."

"I will."

On the drive home, Paul decided to tell Genny about the deployment the next day, so he had tonight to pray about how to tell her. His parents had been his only concern in the past. Genny was special, though. He had to take her emotions into consideration after losing Brandon.

Walking up the steps, he smelled something familiar and smiled. Genny had made chicken tenders and homemade French fries. It happened to be his favorite meal.

"Hey." Genny glanced at him and smiled.

"Hey, Genevieve." Regret tugged at his heart when he looked into her green eyes. She had no idea he would be on a plane headed to Qatar in November. He should have told her before now.

After dinner, Paul went into the office and thumbed through his personal document file. A notebook lay on his desk with a list of required documents. He needed to update his will and give Genny a power-of-attorney. And he wanted to make sure his life insurance was updated. His parents were the beneficiaries, but he considered changing the beneficiary to Genny. She would need the money more than they did since they were financially stable.

"Whatcha doing?" Genny asked from the doorway.

Fear clogged his throat. What should he say? The truth, that's what he should say. He looked up at her. "I'm updating my military related papers. Stuff like my life insurance." Paul slowly exhaled.

"So how much money do I get?" Genny's smile faded. "I'm sorry. I didn't mean to say that."

"It's okay." Paul rubbed his damp palms on his knees. "Well, I'm updating everything for my deployment. I will be going to Al Udeid in Qatar." He winced.

"Deployment?" Genny held her hand over her mouth and took a step back.

"Genny, with everything going on, I forgot about it. Master Sergeant Fields reminded me today that I need to have all my stuff in order."

"When?

"November."

Genny's mouth hung open, but no sound passed her lips. Trembling, she turned and ran down the hall to her bedroom.

"Genny, wait!"

Paul found her standing in her room, sobbing. She became hysterical and shouted at him.

"You can't leave! Tell them no!"

"I can't tell them no, Genny. This is the military." When he reached for her hand, she jerked it away.

"No, you can't leave me, Paul. Please don't leave me. *Please!*" Tears flooded down her cheeks. "If you leave, you won't come back. Please don't leave." Genny fell to the floor, sobbing.

He knelt down next to her and wrapped his arms around her, tightening his embrace when she resisted. She sobbed as she did when Brandon died. The thought of leaving her alone for six months left him feeling guilty. The guilt was unfounded—deployments were part of his military duty. But he feared for Genny's well-being. Somehow, he had to get her into counseling.

⋙ ⋘

Genny laid on her bed, staring at the picture of Brandon and Shawn. She glanced down the hall at Paul sitting on the couch. Tears spilled down her cheeks. "I can't lose you, too." She picked up her journal and made her entry for the day.

July 5, 2011

Paul is deploying, and I'm terrified. What am I going to do if he doesn't come home?

She looked at the entry. Praying may help. But her prayers had been pointless in the past. Maybe God would listen this time. Closing her eyes, she winced when twinges of pain twisted her abdomen. She went to the bathroom and grabbed her pain medication from the drawer in the cabinet. It could be regular cramps, but she had a feeling it was endometriosis.

Over the next few days, Genny's mind was consumed with thoughts of Paul never coming home. If that happened, she would truly be alone. She was putting her laundry away and opened her underwear drawer. Neatly tucked inside the front was the small piece of paper with the email addresses of the three men named Shawn Sullivan she'd found in Paul's email. On her bed, she picked up her laptop. Her hands shook as she drafted the same email for all three men.

Hi,

My name is Genny Jones Thompson. My brother Brandon Jones was deployed to Iraq with Shawn Sullivan from May to December of last year. I'm wondering if you are him. If so, I would love to talk to you about what happened to my brother. Please let me know.

Thank you,

Genny

She stared at the email and reread it several times. Did it sound okay? It was a long shot, but maybe one of the sergeants was deployed with Brandon. She read it one last time and clicked send. A snippet of regret passed through her head, but it was too late. All she could do now was wait.

Genny checked her email obsessively over the next two weeks. She hadn't received a reply to her email from any of the men that could have been with Brandon in Iraq. Maybe it was a sign. She'd give it two more weeks before giving up. To take her mind off of things, Genny decided to go on an outing with the Jeep club.

Looking at herself in the mirror, she braided her hair into two loose braids. The last time she'd worn two braids was at least fifteen years ago. She checked the back of her hair at her neck and sighed at the bare spot. Pulling off the hair bands, she re-braided her hair into a single braid down her back. She sat on her bed and slipped on her hiking boots.

Heading to the kitchen, she pulled out the insulated lunch bag from under the sink and grabbed an ice pack from the freezer. She'd made a sandwich earlier and slipped it into the lunch bag along with the ice pack. Rummaging through the cabinets, she pulled down a box of snack crackers and a bag of chips. She put the sandwich and snacks into a large, reusable shopping bag.

"What are you doing?"

She shrieked and turned around, narrowing her eyes. "You scared me!"

Paul leaned against the dining room wall and grinned. "I'm sorry. I was curious why a backwoods country girl was in the house."

"Paul Tyler!" Genny's cheeks warmed. She looked down at her clothes. How did he decide that a white button-down shirt tied at the waist, a tank top, a pair of denim shorts, and hiking boots were backwoods country?

"All you need is a cowboy hat."

"Hush." She couldn't help but smile. "I grew up in Tennessee, you know."

"But seriously, what are you doing?" He walked toward her.

"The club is meeting to go off-roading today."

"What?" Paul leaned his head back and let out a cackle.

"What's so funny?" She pinched her lips together.

"Do you even know what off-roading is, Genny?" He chuckled.

"Yeah, it's where you drive down dirt trails." She threw her hands on her hips. "And stop laughing at me."

Paul's lips turned white as he pressed them together. "I'm sorry. Off-roading is where you drive through rough terrain like hills and huge ditches. Oh, and mud."

Genny wrinkled her brow. "How do you know? You've never been trail riding."

"Yes, I have. Not in the Tundra. I don't want to scratch her pretty black paint, but I went trail riding in my old truck."

"Well, why do you have the new Tundra outfitted for off-roading if you don't want to drive it off the road?"

"Maybe one day when she's older." Paul wrinkled his brow. "Genny, are you sure you want to take the Jeep off-road? I'm not trying to offend you, but you don't have any experience and I'd hate for anything to happen to the Jeep."

Paul was right. Batting her eyelashes, she gave him a sweet smile. "Can you come and drive the Jeep?"

"Are you sure?"

"Yes, and you can meet everyone." She kept the smile on her lips.

"Okay. I'd like to meet this Trevor you keep talking about. Let me change clothes."

Genny made Paul a sandwich while he changed, and they loaded the Jeep and headed out.

Paul pulled up to the trailhead where the Jeep club was gathered. His eyes brightened. "That's a lot of Jeeps."

"The club's pretty big." They climbed out of the Jeep and weaved their way through the parking area towards the crowd. Trevor turned around and smiled as they walked up.

"I would like to introduce everyone to my husband, Paul."

Paul nodded and said hello. Not long after spending some time with introductions, Paul and Trevor were deep in conversation.

As they talked, a pretty woman walked up next to Trevor. Her tawny skin was flawless and her thick, wavy, black hair touched her shoulders. Her smile was warm and inviting. Genny noticed she was slightly taller than Trevor.

"This is my wife, Tamika," Trevor said. "Babe, this is Genny and her husband, Paul."

"Nice to meet you, Genny and Paul."

"You, too." Genny smiled, and Paul nodded.

After a few minutes, Trevor announced it was time to hit the trail.

"Don't get my Jeep stuck." She crossed her arms over her chest and gave Paul a stern look.

"I won't." He forced out a sigh. They climbed in the Jeep and prepared for the ride.

Her Jeep? The words surprised her. It was the first time she'd referred to the Jeep as hers. On paper it was, but in her heart, it still belonged to Brandon. She raised her hand to the back of her head, then dropped it to her lap. Slipping her hands under her legs would keep her from giving into her impulse. Why was this happening now? She'd been strong enough to control it in the past. She could be strong again. Paul couldn't find out. He'd make an appointment, drive her to the office, and sit in on her first therapy session.

On the trail for a mile or so, they hit a patch of mud. When it was their turn to drive through, the Jeep hit a rut and the tires spun. Genny's eyebrows came together. Paul did what he said he wouldn't do. So much for his experience. She crossed her arms over her chest.

"Don't say it." Paul set his jaw.

Genny glared at him and parted her lips, but he cut her off before she could speak.

"Genevieve. Don't.'"A light shade of red crept up his neck.

Genny pulled an invisible zipper across her lips and tossed the key over her shoulder. Paul's eyes narrowed. He shook his head at Trevor when he trudged through the mud to the driver's door of the Jeep. It had been a while since she'd seen Paul flustered.

Jumping down from the Jeep, Paul followed Trevor to the winch on the front bumper, and they planned to attach the cable to a nearby tree. Genny stayed in the Jeep while the winch pulled it out of the mud. Paul climbed back in and Genny looked at the floorboard where his shoes dragged in mud.

"Don't worry, I'll clean it." He grinned and pulled off his baseball cap and shades. "It's hot out here," he said as he ran his forearm across his brow and put his cap and shades back on.

Genny tried to look away, but her head wouldn't cooperate. There was something about Paul wearing a backward baseball cap and sunglasses that sent warmth to her cheeks.

"Is the sun getting to you?" He gave her a teasing grin. Reaching over, he touched her cheek with the back of his hand. She pushed his hand away and stifled a smile. Her cheeks had betrayed her, as usual.

Once the winch wound the cable back on the spindle, they followed the other Jeeps to the end of the trail where people were setting up picnics. Genny picked up the basket from the backseat and brought it, along with an old blanket, to where Tamika was setting up lunch for Trevor and herself.

"Trevor talks about you often," Tamika said as Genny and Paul spread out the blanket.

Paul looked at Genny. "She talks about the club a lot."

Trevor joined them. "Looks like you two will have a busy Sunday getting that Jeep back to normal." He grinned.

The couples talked while they ate. Paul and Trevor started a side conversation as if they were old friends. Genny and Tamika looked at them and laughed.

"Do you guys have any kids?" Genny opened a bottle of water and took a sip.

"We have a son named Zachary. He's fifteen."

"Paul and I got married on Valentine's Day, so no kids any time soon." Genny smiled. *More like never.* "You know? I haven't thought to ask, but what branch of the military was Trevor in?"

"Navy. He's been in eighteen years total. He was active duty for six years and has been in the reserves for twelve years now. He'd been in six months when I met him."

"Paul's been in almost eleven years." Genny remembered the day he and Brandon left Murfreesboro for the Air Force. It was one of the worst days of her life until Brandon was killed.

When they were ready to go, Paul pulled himself to his feet and held out his hand to help Genny to her feet. Taking her hand in his, he recounted the day's events as they walked to the Jeep. No matter how long she'd known Paul, she'd never tire of his deep voice.

"What are you smiling at?" Paul bumped shoulders with her.

Genny's eyes widened when she realized that she'd been daydreaming. "Oh, nothing." Heat filled her cheeks.

"Wow, those cheeks sure got some sun today." He laughed and brushed a finger over her cheek.

"Stop it." She pushed his hand away and turned her head to hide her smile. Paul opened the passenger door when they reached the Jeep. Her heart pounded when she caught a whiff of his cologne as she walked past him to climb in the seat.

Spending the day with Paul had both given her hope and left her confused. In the past, she'd justified his increase in physical affection as his caring nature, but today, it was different. He'd teased her repeatedly about her cheeks and had held her hand. She could attribute his actions to the Jeep club and all the military members that were present, but was there more to it?

It was close to dark when they arrived home. Genny climbed out of the Jeep and gave it a good once over and shook her head. Instead of an afternoon nap tomorrow after church, she'd be washing and cleaning out the Jeep with Paul's help whether or not he liked it. She grinned.

"What are you grinning at?"

"Imagining you scrubbing the floor mats." She raised her eyebrows.

Paul shook his head and took the basket from her hands as they headed for the steps. He was still wearing his cap backwards, adding warmth to her slightly sunburnt cheeks.

Settling in for the night, Genny flopped down on the couch and turned on the TV. Paul walked in and flopped down next to her, causing her to bounce. She looked at him and tried to hide her smile. Warmth seeped throughout her body when their legs touched. What was going on in his head? He reached over and grabbed the remote from her.

"Give that back." She reached for the remote, but he held it high above his head.

"There's a good documentary about annoying wives I want to watch."

"Paul Tyler." She turned to kneel on the couch to reach for the remote, but backed down. It was a losing battle.

"Just kidding." He smiled and handed her the remote.

She looked at him after she snatched the remote from his hand. His eyes reached into her soul. She handed the remote back to him and smiled.

A few minutes past eight, Genny's eyelids drooped. The reality show on prepping for the end of the world was boring, but it was too early to go to bed. She could go to her room and read, but she'd fall asleep in a minute. Opening her eyes wide, she rubbed them and refocused. It didn't help. Her eyelids fluttered and closed.

Rolling over, her head bumped Paul's shoulder and she roused slightly but didn't open her eyes. A man on the TV was talking about generators and emergency survival food kits. She should get up. There was nothing wrong with going to bed before nine.

The voices on the TV faded. She became vaguely aware that she was dreaming. Snuggling against Paul's shoulder, she slipped her arm across his chest and rested her legs on top of his. Her heart raced at his closeness. How embarrassing that she was dreaming about Paul while sitting on the couch next to him.

Paul's laugh reverberated in his chest, and Genny opened her eyes. It wasn't a dream. She gasped and sat up. "I'm sorry."

"It's okay, you don't have to move."

What?

"Well, I should get my clothes out of the dryer." She was on her feet before words came out of Paul's open mouth. Did his shoulders sag? No, she was still half asleep and dreaming.

"It's about time." A slow grin spread across his face.

She flashed a smile and headed to the laundry room. In her room, she sat on the bed and pulled a shirt out of the basket to fold. Looking at it for a few moments, she tossed it back into the basket and sat the basket on the floor. Picking up her journal, she smiled and turned to the next blank page.

July 16, 2011

Paul went with me today on a Jeep outing. We had fun and I think he was flirting with me. He kept touching my cheeks. He and Trevor spent a lot of time talking. Tamika is so nice. I'm glad I finally got to meet her. Trevor mentions her at least once during the get-togethers I've been to. Trevor and Tamika seem so in love. Tamika said they'd been married seventeen years.

I fell asleep on Paul tonight, and he looked a little hurt that I was freaked out when I woke up. It wasn't a bad freak out. It was a 12-year-old girl's fantasy freak out. He said that I could still sleep on him. My head is filling with all kinds of possibilities and I'm having a hard time keeping them under control. My heart hopes it is because he has feelings for me. We have gotten used to each other. We spend most of our time together when we aren't at work. And to be honest, I love being with him. Does he feel the same? I know the answer, but I'm still doubting myself.

Chapter 14

Paul and Peter were headed to the parking lot to go to lunch. Paul told him about the Jeep club and that he thought it was good for Genny to have more people to spend time with, especially with his upcoming deployment.

"How's Genny taking the deployment?"

Paul opened the driver's door of the truck. "I don't know. She hasn't really talked about it since she had the breakdown. I think she feels it won't happen if she ignores it."

Peter climbed into the passenger side. "You know what may help her?"

"What?"

"A dog."

Paul laughed. "Genny has never been around animals. I'm afraid it would starve to death."

Peter grinned and shook his head. "Think about it. Brown said he has a dog that roamed onto his property. He can't keep it because his Rottie and Pitt don't like it, and I think he said it's female."

Paul thought about what Peter said as he headed home after work. A dog could help, but it might be more of a burden to Genny. Lately, she had occupied more of his thoughts than usual. Something was changing within him. The more time they spent together, the stronger his feelings became. The way she felt in his arms the other night made his heartbeat triple. What about the promise he'd made to Brandon? What would Brandon think if he fell for Genny?

Slowing down to pull into the driveway, Paul stopped for the man who walked his dog around the neighborhood to pass by on the side-walk. Peter had brought up a dog. Was the Lord telling him something?

What would Genny think about getting a dog? Maybe it would be a good idea after all.

Paul was looking at dog supplies on Pet Smart's website when Genny came home from work. He placed his laptop on the coffee table and positioned it just right.

"Hey, how are you? How was your day?" Genny smiled and walked down the hall to change.

"It was good, you?" He grinned to himself.

"Same for me." She shouted from her bedroom. A few moments later, she came into the living room and sat down next to him. She glanced at his laptop. "Why are you looking at dog stuff?"

Paul smiled and raised an eyebrow.

"No. What would we do with a dog?"

"Genny, I think it would be a good idea to get a dog. They are intuitive and know how to comfort you, so I believe it would be good for the deployment." Genny leaned over and took a quick look at the webpage. "Plus, they love you unconditionally and get excited to see you when you come home."

Genny looked at Paul. "Well..."

"Great, I'll tell Brown." Paul patted Genny's knee and grinned.

The following Saturday, Paul and Genny headed to the country in Dorchester County.

"Wow, they live in the sticks," Genny said as they passed by fields and woods.

They found Brown's house and pulled down his long driveway. Brown met them outside and pointed to the doghouse where the dog was chained. As they walked toward the doghouse, the dog came out wagging her tail.

"Hey there, girl." Paul slowly reached his hand out for her to sniff. Genny reached down and patted the dog's head. "Genny, never reach to touch a dog without being invited." She giggled when the dog rolled over for a belly rub.

"Well, what do you think?" Paul asked. At first glance, Genny seemed interested.

"She's pretty." Genny scratched the dog's head. "Such pretty brown and tan colors."

The dog rolled over onto her back again, and Paul watched Genny as she rubbed the dog's stomach. "Yeah, she looks like she has some German Shepherd in her."

"I want her." Genny squatted and scratched the dog's neck with both hands.

Paul coaxed the dog into the kennel on the back seat. Genny stared at her and smiled. "She has soulful eyes and she's so pretty." She turned to Paul. "What are we going to name her?"

"Why don't you name her?"

The dog cocked her head to the side and lifted her ears when Genny looked at her. "You look like a Lucy."

"Lucy it is." Paul watched in the rearview mirror as Genny poked her fingers through the cage and scratched Lucy's head.

"So, what do we call each other?" She looked at him with a smile that reached her eyes.

"What do you mean?"

"Are we going to refer to each other as Genny and Paul when we are talking to Lucy?" Genny clicked her tongue and Lucy's ears perked up.

"How else would we refer to each other?" A slow smile spread across Paul's face. "Mommy and Daddy?" Paul eyed Genny and she grinned at him. "Okay, Mommy."

Genny turned back around and talked to Lucy until Paul pulled into the driveway at home. He was right. Lucy was going to be a special part of Genny's life, especially during his deployment.

⋙ ⋘

The Eatery on The Corner had a dozen cars scattered across the parking lot. Genny always laughed at the restaurant's sign when she drove by. Melissa was parked in a space near the front door. Genny climbed down from the Jeep and found the booth where Melissa was seated.

"Hey, how are you?" Genny placed her purse on the seat next to her.

"I'm good." Melissa's grin reminded Genny of a naughty child.

"Are you okay?" Genny's brows came together.

"Yes. I was going to wait until we finished our lunch to tell you, but I'm too excited. I'm pregnant!" Melissa did a little dance in her seat.

The news was like a punch in the stomach. Why? She didn't see herself having children. "Congratulations. Do you know the due date?"

The waitress stopped by to get Genny's drink order.

"The end of January. I'm ten weeks. We wanted to wait to share the news, just in case."

"Oh, I understand."

"It was our first time trying. Can you believe it?" The grin was back.

"That's great." The waitress placed Genny's drink on the table in front of her and she took a long drink to wet her dry mouth. Tears burned her eyes. What was going on? She needed to push it all down so she can be happy for her friends.

An hour later, Genny found herself zoning out on the way home. Melissa was a good friend, but if she was this excited now, the next however many months would be long and drawn out. She was coming up on The Roasted Bean and thought about stopping by to see what the crew was up to, but it was getting late, and she needed to plan dinner.

While Genny waited for the pizza to bake, she made her way to her bathroom. Looking at herself in the mirror, she turned sideways, raised her shirt, and pushed out her belly. She couldn't imagine herself pregnant. But Melissa's news today stung.

Melissa's excitement over babies, names, and nurseries, along with complaints of pregnancy hormones, almost forced Genny to make something up so she could leave. But she stayed. At least Melissa didn't ask when she and Paul were going to try for a baby. She stared at her belly in the mirror. What would it be like to have Paul's baby?

"Genny?" Paul called out from down the hall.

"Yeah?" Sucking in her belly, she lowered her shirt and walked into the living room.

"How was your lunch?" Paul asked. A natural extrovert, Paul was rarely down, so his reserved demeanor surprised her.

"Good. Melissa shared the good news."

"Exciting, huh?" He didn't look or sound excited.

"Yeah." Genny walked up to the sink to wash the few dishes from lunch to hide her tears. She lifted her shoulder to dab her eye, and Paul walked up next to her.

"Hey, are you okay?"

"Oh, yeah. Hormones, I guess."

"Do you need anything?"

Paul's cheeks no longer flamed red at the mention of "girl stuff" as he called it—just a light pink skimmed across his face now.

"No. Thank you, though." His hand rested on the small of her back. She managed to keep it together until later, when she was under the cover of darkness in her room. Lucy hopped on the bed and snuggled up to Genny as she cried. Why was she so upset? She was also curious why Paul seemed down. Peter was his best friend and best friends were happy for each other for good news.

⤜⟫⟫⟩ ⟨⟨⟨⟪

Genny went to the beach, hoping to clear her head. Two weeks had passed since Peter and Melissa's baby announcement, and her reaction still made little sense. Melissa texted Genny almost daily. Her excitement was the proverbial salt in Genny's wound, but she didn't have the heart to say anything. It was the sixth of August, which meant three more months and Paul would be leaving for his deployment. This deployment was another thing she needed to clear from her head.

Climbing out of the Jeep, she headed to where the group had claimed a section of the beach and passed by a black Jeep almost identical to Brandon's. The top was off, and she glimpsed the interior. The only difference was the lighter interior and off-road conversion.

"Genny," Trevor greeted her when she walked up to the crowd. "How are you?"

"I'm great." She looked around the area. "Is Tamika here?"

"No, Zach has football practice. How's Paul?"

"He's good. He volunteered to work for someone who was out sick today."

"He's such a great guy."

"Yes, I'm a lucky woman." She really was.

As she looked around the crowd to see who was there, her eyes found the face of a man she'd never seen before. He walked up to where she stood with Trevor.

"Oh, Genny. This is Michael." Trevor gestured.

"Hello, Genny." Michael offered his hand.

Genny smiled and accepted his hand. He was attractive and slightly taller than her, with a build like Paul. She'd guess he was Italian by his features and dark hair.

"I saw you drive up. My Jeep is the same model and color, but yours has more upgrades," Michael said.

"Yeah, I passed it in the parking lot. I did a double take." She laughed.

"But you got me beat. What do you have on it?" Genny noticed Michael's dimples when he smiled.

"I can't tell you much about the Jeep. It belonged to my brother, Brandon. He was killed in Iraq December last of last year." Genny watched Michael's smile fade.

"I'm so sorry."

"Thanks."

Michael stood next to Genny as she gazed out over the beach that was dotted with umbrellas and beach chairs. She watched the waves roll in and smiled at a group of children trying to jump over the waves.

"Well, I'm going to go say hi to the others."

"I'll join you." Michael walked with her to visit with some of the group members. He was personable and talked with everyone. A tiny red flag waved before her. But there was no reason to be wary of someone she just met.

Since driving the Jeep, Genny had noticed something odd. Every time she passed a Jeep in traffic, the driver would wave at her. At first, she figured the driver must have known Brandon, but the waving continued when she moved to Charleston.

One day, Paul had been with her when a Jeep driver waved. She made a comment and he explained that there was a camaraderie among Jeep owners like there was with active duty and veterans of the military, even bikers.

Talking among the group, she understood what Paul meant. She had a connection with these people she'd never experienced before. The feeling she'd had the day she became a member had lasted for days. And she experienced the same feeling every time they were together. Genny watched as the group included Michael in the conversation. One thing she had noticed was that the members treated everyone as if they'd been a member since the beginning of the club. She pulled her phone from her pocket to check the time. She had been there for close to two hours. Paul would be home in an hour or so, and she wanted to have dinner ready when he arrived home.

"I need to run. It was good seeing everyone."

"See you next time," Trevor said.

"Can I walk with you? I'd like to get a quick look at your Jeep," Michael said.

His smile brought warmth to her cheeks, surprising her.

"Sure." Genny opened the driver's door and Michael climbed into the passenger side. He looked around and made comments about the interior. Genny slid the key in the ignition and cranked the engine. Michael grinned when the mufflers roared to life.

"I'm jealous."

Genny giggled. "I hate to, but I've got to run."

"Okay. It was nice to meet you, Genny," Michael said.

"You, too."

"I hope to see you again."

"I'm sure you will. I come to about every get together." Genny brushed a few stray hairs away from her face.

"Good."

Genny had spent longer showing the Jeep to Michael than she'd planned and went through a drive-thru on the way home. When she drove down the hill, Paul's truck was in the driveway. Unexpected guilt stabbed at her heart. She hadn't realized until now that she'd been spending more time away from home than she meant to. It was either work or the Jeep club, and it wasn't fair to Paul. And she did miss spending time with him.

"I have chicken." She walked in the door with her arms wrapped around the warm container.

"Good. I was about to make a sandwich. I got home not long before you. I'm surprised we didn't see each other. How was the beach?" He put the lunch meat and mayo back in the fridge.

"It was good. Get this. There was a new guy, and his Jeep is like Brandon's. Same model, paint color, and—"

"Genny, it's not Brandon's Jeep anymore."

She looked at him for a moment. "It's still hard."

"I know, but it's time."

Paul offered to put away the leftovers and clean up the kitchen so Genny could get ready for bed. She pulled the covers up to her waist and stared at a blank page in her journal. She hadn't written an entry since mid-July and so much had happened since then. She sighed and picked up her pen.

August 6, 2011

It's been a while, and I need to catch up. We got Lucy on July 23. She is the sweetest dog. She has chosen me as her human. I pick on Paul about it all the time. Peter and Melissa are having a baby. It shocked me at first, but I'm happy for them. They've been married for over two years and that seems to be the time to try for a baby. I'm guessing it upset me because it is a reminder of what I probably can't have. I don't know. It doesn't help that I think the endometriosis is getting worse.

I went to the beach with the club today. There was a new guy named Michael, and he has the same Jeep. It's crazy. He said mine is better because it's off-road. He's the first new member we've had in a while. Maybe he'll be a regular.

She closed her journal and laid it on her nightstand. Paul walked from the bathroom to his bedroom across the hall and grinned.

"Goodnight, Gen."

"Goodnight."

They'd lived together long enough that she knew his Bible was on his bed, along with a notebook for him to do his nightly Bible study. Climbing out of bed, she walked into her closet and pulled down the box containing her new Bible from the top shelf. She returned to her bed with the Bible and browsed through the index. "Proverbs," she whispered. Melissa had talked about the Proverbs thirty-one wife, but she didn't understand what she meant. Turning to chapter thirty-one, the first few verses made little sense. When she turned the page, she found the verses that referred to the virtuous wife.

She skimmed over the verses and sighed. According to Proverbs thirty-one, faith was first in a virtuous wife's life. How could she have faith in someone who had let her down her whole life? She closed the Bible, put it back in the box, and walked into her closet. She didn't understand Paul's devotion to God. But then again, he'd walked through life untouched by tragedy.

Chapter 15

P aul sat on the couch browsing the internet. Genny's birthday was September ninth, four weeks away. She owned several jewelry items with sapphires, September's birthstone, and he wanted something different. Browsing birthstones, he noticed June had three: pearl, moonstone, and alexandrite. The blue with green undertones of the alexandrite gemstone caught his eye and he began a search for the perfect birthday present for Genny.

He'd spent almost three hours browsing the internet for the perfect piece of jewelry and came up empty-handed. During his search, he found a jewelry manufacturer in Charleston and planned to stop by after work tomorrow to in inquire about having something made for Genny.

A whimper came from the doorway to his bedroom. "Sorry, girl." Paul made his way out back with Lucy and stopped at the shriveled tomato plant on the patio. Since Genny found the club, she'd been neglecting the tomato plant she'd begged for. Dragging out the hose, he sprayed the plant for a while as he watched Lucy play with a ball in the backyard.

Genny had been distant. Surprisingly, her distance had caused a loneliness he hadn't felt before. Maybe it had to do with spending so much time together since Brandon's death and he'd gotten used to her presence.

"Hi, Paul."

Paul glanced over. Mrs. Baker stood on her patio watering her plants. "Hello. Seems like a good time to water."

"It's best in the early evening hours when it's a little cooler. Never water during the day. It can evaporate before it reaches the roots."

"I'll keep that in mind." Paul heard the Jeep drive down the hill and put the hose away. "Talk to you later." Mrs. Baker nodded, and Paul went inside with Lucy.

"Hey," Genny said when she walked in the door. Her mood was upbeat, which meant she probably had plans to go to the movies or out to eat with her friends.

"You look happy. Going somewhere?"

"No, not tonight." She smiled and walked down the hall to her bedroom. "What are we having for dinner?" she asked when she came into the kitchen a few moments later.

"I was going to make a sandwich."

"Sandwich sounds good."

They sat on the couch eating while Genny talked about work over the past few days. "I think I'm going to cut back to three days. Four days is too much. I want to do my share around the house. I kind of like taking care of things."

"The scraggly tomato plant on the patio would disagree with you." He tilted his head toward the backdoor.

"Oh, no." Genny grimaced. "I forgot about it. That's pretty sad since I'm in the yard with Lucy all the time."

"Yeah, that is sad." He smiled.

Genny sat her plate on the coffee table and stretched out her legs. Resting her head on Paul's shoulder, she drew in a deep breath and snuggled up to him. "I could fall asleep right here."

"Go ahead." He rested his cheek on the top of her head, awakening a thousand butterflies in his stomach. She'd laid her head on his shoulder several times since the night she fell asleep and stretched her arm across his chest. A time or two, she'd lay her legs on top of his. But this was the first time she'd been this close.

After dinner, Paul went to his bedroom. Picking up his Bible from the nightstand, he opened to where the bookmark held his place. He stared at the page. Closing his eyes tightly, he opened them and began reading, but his mind drifted to Genny again. Something that had been happening more often.

As planned, after work the next day, Paul stopped by the jewelry store and met with the jewelry designer. An hour later, he had an estimated date to pick up the bracelet he'd designed for Genny the week of her birthday. Just in time.

Genny had to work, so it was Paul and Lucy. After dinner, he took her out back for a while to get some exercise. He climbed on top of the picnic table and watched her race around the backyard. His thoughts went to Genny. They'd lived together for a while now and he'd noticed that his feelings for her had been slowly changing. He'd been her protector since Brandon died, but he was beginning to believe that it was more than the promise he'd made to Brandon.

Dusk turned into night, and Paul laid back on the table to watch the stars. It was something he'd done since he was a little boy. Tears dampened his eyes. It was also something he'd done with Brandon when they were kids. He stared into the heavens for a long moment. What would happen with Genny? He'd made a point of praying for their relationship and marriage a priority.

Deep in thought, he didn't hear Genny until she pulled into the driveway. He stayed on the table, knowing she'd walk out back. He was right.

"What are ya doing?" She climbed on top of the table and laid next to him. "Wow, lots of stars."

"I know. It's been a while since the sky was this clear." Her closeness stirred his senses.

"Sure has." Genny's head rested on his shoulder.

Paul inhaled deeply and caught a whiff of dark roast. "Now I want a cup of coffee."

"Will you stop." She giggled. "I can't help it if we have the best roasted beans in town. Oh, the club is hanging at the beach Saturday. Want to come? Trevor will be there."

Paul pushed down his disappointment. Genny had said she wanted to stay home more. She probably meant during the week. "You know, I'd love to, but I need to get some yard work done. The grass is so high Lucy is high stepping."

"Maybe after?"

"Maybe."

Lucy hopped up on the table and wedged herself between Paul and Genny, pushing Paul to the edge of the table. "She's telling you I'm hers, not yours." Genny laughed.

Unexpectedly, her statement nipped at his heart. What were God's plans?

The bright sun reflected off the windshields of oncoming traffic, causing Genny to squint. For a moment, the scene brought back the day they had loaded Brandon's belongings into the storage unit. She wiped tears from her cheeks. She couldn't believe that seven months had passed already.

In the parking lot at the beach were several Jeeps, including Michael's. Climbing down, she grabbed her beach bag and made her way to where the group had set up on the sand. She claimed a spot next to Trevor and spread out her towel. She'd always felt protected around him. He was older and like a father figure.

She looked out over the crowd for a moment and noticed Michael talking with a woman.

"Paul couldn't make it?" Trevor asked.

"He might. He has some yard work to do."

"I hope he can make it."

"Me, too." Genny stood alone for a few moments. All the women in the group walked around in their swimsuits.

Modest by nature, she rarely took off her coverup when she was in public, whether it was at the beach or a water park. She was wearing a tankini with boy shorts, but she was still uncomfortable. She glanced at where Michael stood earlier, and to her surprise, he was a few feet away from her now.

"There you are." He grinned.

"Hey, Michael. How are you?"

"I'm great...now." The last word was a mumble, but clear to her. "Why don't we walk toward the water?"

"Okay." They made their way to the water's edge and Genny stood where the icy-cold water washed over her feet. She turned and checked the parking lot, hoping to see Paul's truck. He'd been on her mind lately. Since she was a kid, she'd been fascinated by Paul. When she approached the pre-teen years, that fascination turned into a crush and continued until a few years ago. She smiled to herself. But she was sure what she felt now was more than a simple crush.

"So, you're married?"

Michael's words brought her out of her reverie. She noticed him glancing at her wedding band. Had he not noticed it last time? "Yes, I am."

"Where's your husband?"

"He's coming later." She hoped Paul would finish the yard work before everyone headed home.

"Is he active duty or a veteran?"

"He's in the Air Force. He's getting ready to deploy."

"Do you know where he's going?"

Genny tucked a few strands of hair that escaped from her braid behind her ear. "He's going to Al Udeid for six months."

"Oh, wow. Does he know when he's leaving?"

"Sometime in November." Why was he asking so many questions?

Another red flag was surfacing in Genny's mind. She wasn't quick to push this one down.

"So, tell me a little about yourself, Genny."

"Paul and I have been married since Valentine's Day. He said he'd never forget our anniversary." Genny laughed. "I'm hoping to start school in the spring. I quit when my brother died."

"It's great you're going back. Do you have a major yet?"

"I've thought about elementary education. My mom was a teacher before my brother and I came along." Genny held her breath when the cool water swept over her feet.

"Good choice. Teachers are under appreciated. So, how did you and your husband meet?"

"We grew up together. When my brother was killed, Paul came to help me sort things out. We realized we loved each other more than friends and, well, here we are." A feeling of guilt surprised her. Was it her lie, or standing on the beach with another man?

"I can't believe he is your childhood friend."

"Yeah, it's crazy how it all came about. Paul's a great guy. Not to sound cliché, but he would give you the shirt off his back." Genny laughed. "And he's athletic and loves to run. I'm not much of a fan of running, but he likes to drag me out with him every once in a while." She realized she was rambling. "So, what about you?" She gazed out over the ocean.

"I'm from Maine and I was in the Marines for five years."

"Oh really? How did you end up in Charleston?" She glanced at him, shading her eyes.

"That's a long story for another time."

"Oh, okay." She slowly nodded. "So, did you deploy when you were in the Marines?

"Afghanistan, Iraq , Africa, and a few others."

"Oh wow. This is my first deployment as a wife." Genny smiled. They were headed back toward the group when a loud vehicle pulled into the parking lot.

"Wow, that's a sharp truck. Tundra maybe." A wide grin spread across his face.

Genny's heartbeat picked up. She focused on the parking lot, and her eyes brightened. "That's my husband." Her steps turned into a sprint, and Michael jogged to catch up with her.

She made it to the parking lot and up to the truck as Paul was climbing down. "You made it." She threw her arms around his neck and pressed her lips against his in a lingering kiss. Pulling back, she tucked the strands of unruly hair behind her ear again. She kissed Paul. Where did that come from? Her heart pounded hard in her chest.

"Yeah, um." A blush swept across Paul's cheeks. "I had the lawn-mower in the backyard and cranked it, then decided it could wait." He smiled.

"I'm glad you did. This is Michael." Genny turned and found an empty space next to her. "Oh...hmm. There he is." Michael gave her a half smile as he walked away from a group of members he was talking with. It was odd that he stopped by the group when he was with her a moment ago. He slowly made his way to where she stood with Paul.

"Michael, this is my husband, Paul. Michael is the one that has the same Jeep as mine."

Paul smiled and offered his hand. "Nice to meet you."

"Hey, man. Nice to meet you, too." Michael shook Paul's hand and turned to Genny, motioning toward his Jeep.

"I'm sorry. I remembered something I'm supposed to do this afternoon. I've got to run. It was nice meeting you, Paul."

"You, too."

Michael disappeared between the parked vehicles. His Jeep cranked a few moments later, and they watched as he pulled out of the parking lot. Genny looked at Paul and shrugged.

After Michael left, Genny and Paul joined the others. Someone had brought out a portable sound system and cranked up the volume when "Sweet Child O' Mine" by Guns and Roses played. Genny cracked up when Paul sang along. After the song ended and he bowed at the applause, they stood around talking with the others.

A woman walked up between Paul and the man standing next to him. "Excuse me." The perky blonde ogled Paul.

Genny swallowed the lump in her throat. Heat filled her chest and climbed up her neck to her cheeks. She took a step closer to Paul, brushing up against him. It had been a while since he drew the attention of a woman in her presence. Why did it bother her? Paul was a humble man and would never relish the attention or disrespect Genny in any manner.

"Yes, ma'am?" Paul slipped his arm around Genny's waist, bringing a different kind of heat to her cheeks.

"Is that a tattoo on your back?"

How would she know Paul had a tattoo on his back unless she was sizing him up? Genny leaned back. The outline of the cross was visible through his white t-shirt.

"I'm curious to see what it looks like. Is it a cross?" The woman beamed.

"I'm not swimming, so I won't be taking my shirt off." Paul smiled and pulled Genny tight against him, causing her heart to beat in double time.

The red-faced woman took a step back with her mouth hanging open. Genny watched her walk to where her friend was standing and the two left the beach. The desire to do a cartwheel teased Genny, but she kept both feet on the ground.

Paul still had his arm around her waist. She had the sudden urge to break away from the group. "Want to go for a walk?"

"I'd love to," Paul said.

A lightness filled Genny's chest when he held her hand and laced his fingers between hers. She savored his closeness, and the clean scent of his cologne enveloped her as they walked shoulder to shoulder.

They strolled down the beach in silence for a few moments. Genny giggled when a little girl squealed as a wave chased her to the shore. She nudged Paul further up the beach where the sand met the grass and sat for a bit.

"Let's go for a swim."

"But my stuff is down by the group."

"It's okay." Paul rose and grabbed her hand, pulling her to her feet. He slipped his shirt off. "Take off your coverup."

"What? We can't leave our clothes here."

"Sure, we can. We'll come back."

Paul didn't give her a chance to rebuff, taking a step towards the water. She quickly slipped her coverup off over her head. He grabbed her hand again and sprinted toward the water. She had to take long strides to keep from stumbling.

"Paul Tyler!"

When they reached the water's edge, he didn't slow down. He led Genny into the water up to her thighs and pulled her down with him. She gasped and squealed.

"Paul!" Air left her lungs and her teeth started chattering.

Paul stood and pushed toward deeper water, but not before Genny jumped on his back. He lost his footing, and they went under. Genny forced herself upright, spitting and sputtering. Paul raised up and coughed. Taking her hand in his, he led her further out in the water.

"Paul, it's deep." A shiver ran through her body.

"It's okay. I got ya." He stopped when the water was at his chest. Genny reached out and grabbed his upper arms. With her fingers pressed into his muscles, she gazed into his eyes and found it hard to break away.

A shrill whistle sounded from the beach. Trevor was standing close to the water's edge, holding Genny's beach bag. Her shoulders drooped slightly. Why couldn't Trevor have shown up a minute later? Her breath hitched when Paul took her hand in his when they started toward the beach.

"Hey, man," Paul said.

"I'm heading out and thought you'd want this here."

"Yeah," Genny replied. "Thanks." She took the bag from Trevor's hand and walked to where her coverup and Paul's t-shirt lay on the sand. She heard Paul and Trevor talking as they walked up to where she stood. Paul bent down and grabbed his shirt.

"Paul, your tattoo is magnificent," Trevor said as he looked at Paul's back.

"Thanks. It's my walking testimony."

"It certainly draws attention. I see several ladies eyeing you." Genny's eyes narrowed. "You have nothing to worry about, Genny. This man loves you."

A shy smile spread across Genny's face, and she caught a quick glance of Paul's expression. He smiled and slipped on his shirt.

Trevor patted Paul's back. "We'll have to sit down and talk about it one day."

"I'd like that." Paul shook Trevor's hand.

They said goodbye and headed to the parking lot, holding hands. Paul walked Genny to the Jeep. When she was settled with her seatbelt fastened, he leaned in and kissed her softly on the lips.

"I'd like to talk when we get home," Paul said.

"Okay." Her heart thudded against her ribs, and she ran her hands over the top of her head to smooth down her wayward hair. She would ask herself what he could possibly want to talk about, but she knew. Today was a turning point in their relationship.

"See you at home." Paul held her gaze for a moment and smiled. He patted the door frame and walked to the truck at the other end of the parking lot. Genny paused, then cranked the Jeep.

As she drove, Genny thought about her relationship with Paul. He'd went to Fayetteville and did what she couldn't do due to her emotional state. She shuddered to think where she would be if he hadn't stepped up. As time went on, she'd realized she was developing feelings for him. Was it because he'd come to her rescue or were the feelings genuine?

Genny's eyes shifted to the rearview mirror, and she felt slightly dizzy. Paul managed to stay behind Genny during the drive home. Pulling into the driveway, she climbed down from the Jeep and stood at the front door until Paul pulled in the drive. Butterflies swirled in her stomach at the smile on his face as he climbed down from the truck.

"Let's go out to the picnic table," he said and unlocked the door.

"Okay." Why was she shaking? She'd known Paul for almost twenty years, and they'd been living together for eight months. It wasn't like they'd just met.

Opening the backdoor, Lucy slipped past them and bounded toward the back fence, where her favorite stick laid in the tall grass. Genny's stomach lurched, causing an unexpected sigh to slip out.

"You okay?" Paul rested his hand on her back as she sat down on the top of the picnic table.

"Yeah." She glanced at him and smiled, heat filing her cheeks. What was wrong with her? She was acting like a teenager whose crush looked at her for the first time. But wasn't that what was happening? Paul had been her crush for years and something changed in their relationship less than an hour earlier.

"Boy, you got some sun today." He laughed and brushed his fingers across her cheeks.

This time, she didn't pull away or deny it. She grinned and turned to watch Lucy playing with her stick and bit her bottom lip.

Paul took her hand in his and brushed his thumb across her knuckles. "Genevieve." He placed his finger under her chin and turned her face toward him. "There's something I want to tell you."

"Okay," she whispered. Her heartbeat doubled, making her head swim.

"I have feelings for you that go beyond friendship."

Closing her eyes, she drew in a deep breath and opened her eyes. He looked at her with a look she had never seen before. Was it love? Placing her hand on his cheek, she kissed him and eased back.

"Me, too." A smile spread across her face. If her heart beat any harder, she was certain to have a heart attack.

He kissed her this time. The stubble on his face rubbed against her chin. Drawing back, he ran his fingers along her jaw. "I want to court you."

"Court?" She wrinkled her brow. It sounded like something from the eighteen hundreds.

Paul laughed. "The modern-day definition is to date with the intention of marriage. We did it backwards." He winked. "I've felt differently for a while. I want it to be real and not because of Brandon. You know?"

"Yeah. It can be hard to know the difference sometimes." She played with the end of her braid. She'd struggled with her feelings as much as he had. But the truth was, if Brandon hadn't died, they wouldn't be having this conversation, much less living together. But he did die, and they were sitting on the picnic table talking about their feelings.

"Where do we go from here?"

"Do you work next Saturday?"

"Evening. Why?"

"Our first date."

She smiled. "I can ask Julie if she will switch."

"Good. I'm going to head inside to shower." Paul kissed her and slid off the table.

She followed him, her mind spinning from the day's events that started with a spontaneous kiss.

Sitting on her bed after a shower, Genny heard Paul talking to Lucy in the kitchen. Kissing Paul had felt natural, not like the kiss they'd performed on their wedding day. She picked up her journal and wrote an entry.

August 13, 2011

Paul has feelings for me. I never imagined I would write these words today. We've been friends since we were kids, and I can't expect that to change overnight. Our relationship is not the typical relationship, so we need to do what we can to make up for that. I feel like I'm dreaming. I've never been in love. This feeling is amazing. Paul is unlike any guy I've ever met. He has always been such a kind and considerate person. Well, not when we were kids, but boys are annoying.

Genny closed her journal and laid it on her nightstand. Paul walked in the doorway and gave the open door a light knock. She smiled as he walked up to the side of the bed and sat down.

"Goodnight." He leaned in and kissed her.

"Goodnight." She ran her hand down his arm and grasped his fingers.

Kissing her hand, he stood and walked to the door. Turning around, he smiled and pulled the door closed behind him. Climbing into bed and turning off the lamp, she rolled over and stretched her arm across the empty side of the bed. Butterflies fluttered in her stomach. One day soon, her husband would lay next to her every night.

Chapter 16

Genny was at work by the time Paul arrived home. He changed and took Lucy out back for a while. The tomato plant was thriving with tiny green tomatoes hanging from the branches. Genny must have made watering and fertilizing part of her routine. After sitting on the picnic table for a few minutes, an idea came to him. He called Lucy, and she followed him inside. He gathered his wallet and keys and hooked Lucy's leash to her collar.

"Want to go for a ride?" Her ears perked up and she wagged her tail.

A week had passed since the day at the beach. Before, their relationship was similar to a married couple. They spent much of their free time together and physical affection had become a regular part of their relationship. More so on Genny's part. Spending time watching TV with Genny had become one of his favorite activities because of their closeness.

Paul glanced in the rearview mirror and smiled at Lucy stretched out across the backseat. Pulling into the drive thru at The Roasted Bean, Paul hoped Genny wasn't looking out the window. Julie recognized his voice when he placed his order.

"Well, hello Paul."

"Shh." He laughed.

"Okay," she whispered through the speaker. When he pulled up to the window, he was greeted by Julie's mischievous smile. "I switched with your wife for Saturday night after making her beg for a while. I hope you two have fun." Julie winked.

Because of the height of the truck, Paul could see Genny cleaning tables in the dining room.

"You have a visitor, Genny," Julie called out over the hum of the machines. Genny looked up and met his eyes. She grinned and hurried around the counter.

"What a surprise!" Paul lowered the back driver's side window and Lucy poked her head out. "Aww. hey sweet girl." Lucy whined and trembled at Genny's attention.

"We missed you." Paul smiled.

"I missed you guys, too."

"You two are so sweet," Julie said.

Genny was still beaming at the window when Julie handed her Paul's coffee. She took a swig, then handed the cup to him.

"Sure, you can have some." He grinned. "See you at home."

"Wait!" Genny hung out the window and puckered her lips. Paul unbuckled his seatbelt, opened the door, and gave her a tender kiss.

"See you two later." Her eyes sparkled.

When he pulled up to the exit out of the parking lot, he looked in his side mirror. Genny was still leaning out the window, watching them. He waved when he pulled off, and she waved back. Every day that passed, his love for her grew deeper.

As he drove home, Paul went through Saturday's schedule in his head. Dinner at Genny's favorite restaurant, Red Lobster, and a walk at Waterfront Park. Possibly a movie. Five more days until their official first date.

⤛⤜ ⤚⤙

Stirring a large bowl of her granny's potato salad, Genny sighed. Why did she sign up to bring a side dish to the squadron's picnic? Paul said she didn't have to, but she wanted to do her part. She rolled her eyes. Her afternoon would be better spent in a dental chair getting a root canal than with a bunch of military wives.

After she packed her dish and headed to the door, she heard the click of Lucy's nails on the hardwood floor. "I'm sorry, girl, but you can't go." Lucy's ears fell, and she lowered her head. Genny let out a heavy sigh and quickly opened the front door and headed to the Jeep.

Digging around in her purse, she didn't see her phone. She blew out her breath and went back inside. !t wasn't in the living room, so she headed down the hall to her bedroom. !t was on her bed, nestled with the covers. She had an email notification and she tapped on the app. The email was from Shawn Sullivan. Her heart pounded as she opened it.

Hello Genny, I'm sorry but it wasn't me. I hope you find him.

Genny slumped. Maybe it was a sign. She hadn't had a nightmare in a while, so she must be better. She opened the drawer of her nightstand and picked up the picture that was on top of her journal. Brandon and Shawn were wearing flak vests and Kevlar helmets with smiles on their faces. She ran her thumb over Brandon's face. "Big bro, what happened to you?" She put the picture back in the drawer and headed out to the Jeep.

Feeling awkward at a place where she didn't know anyone, Genny sat in the Jeep waiting for Paul. Sweat beaded on her forehead despite the full blast of the AC. The end of August still produced blistering heat, although fall was around the corner. Genny caught a glimpse of Paul in the side mirror and killed the engine. Paul opened the door and kissed her. "Hey, you," she said.

They strolled to a group of airmen, and Paul introduced her to everyone. Now would be a good time for the earth to open up and swallow her. She stood quietly by his side as the guys talked about work. The wives had formed a clique and a few of them looked from Paul to her and back to Paul. !t was like she was back in high school when one woman leaned over and whispered to another woman. They made it obvious that they were talking about her and Paul.

Genny turned around. Melissa was standing behind her with her arms open. She stepped away and gave her a hug. "Look at that bump."

Melissa smiled and rubbed her stomach.

"We've been here less than ten minutes and I'm already the subject of gossip."

"Ignore them," Melissa said. "They have nothing better to do. They are the military's version of Mean Girls. But you need to meet Kari and Jessica. Kari is Aaron Anderson's wife and Jessica is Will Brown's wife. They are at the dessert table." Melissa led the way. "Hey, didn't you and Paul get your dog from Will and Jessica?"

"Yes, Lucy. But I didn't meet Jessica that day and I didn't know Will's First name until you said it. Paul calls him Brown." A heaviness settled in Genny's chest. Will was her dad's name.

"So does Peter. You gotta love the military."

Melissa left soon after they ate lunch, and Genny once again found herself next to Paul at the picnic table with a bunch of strangers. The majority of their conversation was about work. She'd been around the military for a few years now, but it was still new to her.

A little while later, she excused herself to the restroom. When she was headed back to the table, the Mean Girls were sitting at the next table over. *Great.* Paul rose to his feet and smiled when she walked up to the table.

"I've got to head back to the shop. Are you ready?"

She turned her head to the table of wives and back to Paul. "That's a silly question." He laughed and gestured toward the parking lot.

Paul opened the driver's door, and Genny climbed into the Jeep. "See you at home." He kissed her and pushed the door closed.

She watched him in the side mirror as he walked to the truck. Brushing her fingers across her lips, she smiled. Kissing Paul was quickly becoming one of her favorite things to do. She smiled and warmth flowed through her body. The women at the picnic table were watching them. The old Genny threatened to take over and stick out her tongue, but she managed to keep her inside.

Later in the evening, after getting ready for bed, Genny held her pen to the next blank page in her journal. She looked up when Paul knocked on the open door.

"You left your phone in the kitchen. It chimed, so you have a text or email." He walked over to the side of the bed.

"Thank you."

"Sure. Goodnight." He leaned down and kissed her.

"Goodnight." She smiled and watched him close the door on the way out of the bedroom.

Tapping on the email app, an email from another Shawn Sullivan was in her inbox. With a shaky finger, she opened it and prepared for another dead end to protect her heart.

Hi Genny,

It was me. I'll talk to you about Brandon, but I want to make sure you are prepared to hear what happened. Please think about it and let me know what you want to do one way or the other.

Shawn

Genny stared at the screen, willing the letters to rearrange themselves to read that there had been some mistake. Brandon's deployment had been extended, and he would come home soon. But it didn't matter how long she stared at the screen. The truth remained; Brandon was gone.

Genny's stomach flipped, and she fought to keep the nausea down. She picked up her journal again and wrote today's entry.

August 26, 2011

I found Shawn Sullivan. I don't know if I can do this. I don't want regrets either way. If I talk to him, I won't keep wondering what happened, but if I don't talk to him, I'll wonder for the rest of my life. I should talk to Paul, but I'm scared of what he will say. He might tell me it's not a good idea. But I'll never know unless I ask.

She swung her legs over the side of the bed. Sitting still for a few moments, she changed her mind and slipped under the covers again. She'd have to admit to Paul that she used his laptop. She'd pray about what to do. Hopefully, God would listen. She turned the lamp off and settled under the covers. "No," she whispered. "No." But she was too weak. The email from Shawn Sullivan had pushed her to the edge, and she jumped off. Reaching to the back of her neck, she grabbed a handful of hair and held it tight. "No, no, no. Don't do it." She gave in and pulled out several strands of hair. Tears flowed down her cheeks and onto her pillow. Brandon's smiling face shone brightly in her mind. Why did life have to be so cruel?

Paul took Genny's hand in his as they strolled along the waterfront. She loved the feel of his strong hand protecting hers. Memories of their childhood filled her thoughts. She was still amazed that she was married to Paul Thompson and that they cared for each other. As a twelve-year-old, she never would have dreamed they would be anything more than friends.

Shawn Sullivan pushed her thoughts away. What was she going to do? She should talk to Paul. The words rolled to the tip of her tongue, but she swallowed them down. He might discourage her from contacting Shawn. "It's for your own good," he would say.

"You've been a million miles away tonight. Want to talk about it?" Paul brought her hand up to his lips and kissed the back. A warm feeling started in the middle of her chest and spread to her stomach.

Genny shook the thoughts from her head. "Just tired."

"Mmm." He kissed the back of her hand again.

They continued their walk, and Genny's mind wandered. How long until they were married in every sense of the word?

"Whatcha thinking about?"

"Nothing." She would keep it to herself.

"You were smiling."

She was smiling? Heat filled her face. "Well, I was asking myself a question."

"What's that?" He stopped and turned to face her.

Having his undivided attention, she lost her voice. But she had to be honest with her husband. "When...when will we be a regular couple? You know. When we are like our friends." She grimaced. "It's not coming out how I thought it would."

"I know what you're trying to say."

Had he been thinking the same thing?

"I think about it often. I don't want to rush into it, you know?"

She softly sighed. "I know." She trusted Paul and knew he would follow what God had laid on his heart. He took her hands in his, pulled her close and kissed her—a kiss that took her breath away. Restrained passion was how she would describe it.

"We should probably get to the theater." He caressed her cheek.

"Okay." They made their way back to the truck and headed to the theater.

Genny woke up when Paul pulled into the driveway. It was past midnight, according to the clock on the console. He climbed down from the truck and opened her door. She followed him to the steps. Unlocking the door, Paul stepped aside so Genny could walk into the house. She headed to take a shower while Paul took Lucy outside.

Returning her toothbrush to the holder, she studied herself in the bathroom mirror. No doubt she was tired. Dark circles appeared under her eyes anytime she was up late. She turned her head upside down, dropping the towel wrapped around her hair to the floor. Running her fingers through her damp hair a few times, she opened the door and walked into her room.

The shower was on in Paul's bathroom. A few seconds later, she heard the shower handle squeak and the water stopped. Lucy was stretched out on the bed with her head on Genny's pillow. "You know you aren't a person, right?" Genny grinned when Lucy's wagging tail slapped against the mattress. She sat on the side of the bed to apply lotion. The bathroom door opened and Paul appeared in her doorway.

He walked up to her. "Goodnight."

She stood and slipped her arms around his neck. "Goodnight."

Giving him a quick kiss, she stepped back and watched him walk toward the doorway and close the door behind him.

There was no doubt in her mind that she was in love with Paul Thompson.

Chapter 17

Genny pressed the button on the espresso machine and watched the dark brown liquid flow into the cup. Three days ago, she'd received the email she'd been waiting for, but she hadn't decided yet. The nightmares were back and worse than they'd ever been. She'd woken in the middle of the night last night standing by the window. Never had she gotten out of bed when she was dreaming.

"Genny, are you okay?" Julie asked.

Genny had been staring at the full cup of espresso. "I found the guy who was with Brandon when he was hurt. He said he would tell me what happened."

"Oh, wow. I don't think I could do that myself."

"I have to know what happened to Brandon. I feel stuck and I think it will help the nightmares go away. But a part of me is scared of what he'll say."

"I bet. What does Paul think?"

Genny handed the customer his coffee and looked at Julie. "I haven't talked to him yet."

"Why not? He seems like he'd understand."

"I'm afraid he will tell me I shouldn't."

"Really?" The drive-thru beeped and Julie tapped her headset to answer.

Genny heard the front door, and she approached the counter. She smiled when she saw Michael. "What a surprise."

"I didn't know you worked here." His eyes brightened.

"Over six months now." She straightened her apron and grinned. "What can I get you?"

"What do you recommend?"

"Caramel Macchiato is my favorite." Michael acted more like himself today. His behavior at the beach when Paul showed up was odd.

"Then that's what I'll have. Make it cold, since it's a hundred and fifty degrees out today."

Genny smiled. She rang up his order and walked over to the espresso machine. What were the odds of Michael coming into The Roasted Bean? She'd seen him twice at the beach now. The caution she felt was baseless. He seemed like a likable person.

At the pickup counter, he smiled when she walked over. He looked different today. When he leaned over to pick up his cup, Genny noticed the stubble on his face. A five o'clock shadow added to his attractiveness.

"Thank you, ma'am. I'd stay, but I've got to head to work."

"Okay, it was nice to see you again."

"You, too. I hope to see you at the beach soon."

She smiled as he headed to the door. When he backed up and drove around the building, a hint of guilt flowed through her veins. She brushed it off. Michael was a friend. Actually, that wasn't true. She didn't know him well enough to consider him a friend. He was an acquaintance and there wasn't anything wrong with having a conversation with him.

Genny took off her apron and climbed into the Jeep and headed home. What to do about Shawn Sullivan was eating at her. It was time to do something she should have done three days ago. She'd wait until she was home, though. After changing her clothes, she took Lucy outside and climbed on top of the picnic table. She sat quietly for a while. Why was this so difficult? She took in a deep breath and exhaled.

Embarrassed to admit, her so-called prayer life was close to non-existent. She didn't know the proper way to pray. She'd say quick prayers here or there, but not the way most people prayed. That had to be why her prayers weren't working. Her grandmother had said talk to Him like He was a good friend. Genny would give it a shot.

"Okay, here we go. Hey...I mean dear Lord. No, He's a friend, Genny. Okay...well, it's been a long time since I sent up serious prayers. I know most of the time I yell at You, but I need help. Should I talk to Shawn? Will it help me move on?" She sat quietly, watching Lucy. "Give me a sign." She gazed at the oak tree over the fence. A bird flew from the top of the tree. "Is that a sign?" She sighed. "Should I talk to Paul about Shawn? You've given him wisdom."

God was everywhere, according to Paul. He spoke to people in different ways, so always pay attention. How was He speaking to her, or was He choosing not to speak to her like she had chosen not to speak to Him? Sweat rolled down her back but she couldn't go inside. She had to do this.

Focus, Genny.

"Should I talk to Paul? Please send me a sign?" The words barely passed her lips when she heard Paul's truck coming down the hill. Glancing at her phone, he was thirty minutes early. Was Paul her sign?

In five minutes, he'd be on top of the picnic table next to her. It was something he did if she was outside when he came home from work. Sure enough, she heard the backdoor and the creak of his combat boots as he walked. Her pulse picked up speed.

"Hey." He sat on top of the table next to her and kissed her.

"Hey." Genny's voice cracked. She cleared her throat and took a second try at her greeting. "Hey."

"Something wrong?"

"Um, I have a dilemma."

"Okay."

"I found Shawn Sullivan." She bit her lip. Reaching under the table, she pulled up a long blade of grass and wrapped it around her finger.

Paul turned to face her and raised a brow. "Really? How did you manage that?"

That was not what she expected him to say. How would she explain she snooped? "Well, I...um...I looked in your work email one day when you left your laptop on the coffee table." She bit the inside of her cheek. He stared at her. His brows came together, forming a deep crease between them. "I'm sorry."

He sat quietly, watching Lucy play. His silence was too long and too silent. She couldn't take it any longer.

"I emailed him. Actually, three sergeants named Shawn Sullivan. The first one said it wasn't him and now the Shawn that was with

Brandon emailed me back. He said he will talk to me about what happened. Should I talk to him?"

Another long, silent moment.

"I'm sorry, Paul. I shouldn't have used your laptop."

"I also thought about looking for him. I searched for his name but didn't pursue it any further. Genny, I can't tell you what to do. But you need to consider the pros and cons and pray."

"I was praying when you came home. I asked God for a sign, and you drove down the hill a second later."

He smiled. "Whatever you decide to do, I'll support you."

"Thank you. It means a lot."

"Of course, you're my wife." He leaned over and kissed her on the temple.

Genny went inside and emailed Shawn. He responded a half-hour later. They planned to Skype on September first, three days away. Laying her laptop on the bed next to her, she slipped her hands under her thighs. It didn't help. She spent a few minutes easing her fears, one strand of hair at a time.

⋙ ⋘

The next three days went by quicker than Genny expected. She sat on her bed with her laptop. To keep her head from spinning and the nausea down, she'd been taking slow, deep breaths the past few minutes. She wasn't ready to hear about what happened to Brandon, but she also felt it was now or never and she couldn't bear not knowing.

"Hey." Paul walked in and climbed into bed next to her. "How much longer?"

Genny glanced at the clock on her laptop. "Less than five minutes."

Nausea watered her mouth, and a few deep breaths did the trick. Paul slipped his arm around her shoulders. Genny swallowed hard when a message notification popped up on Skype. As if it was a balloon taut with too much air, her heart felt like it was about to burst. This was it.

The Skype melody that drifted from the laptop speakers knotted her stomach. She clicked the answer button with a shaky finger. The face of the man in so many of Brandon's pictures emerged before her on the screen. He looked different, as if he'd aged twenty years since those pictures were taken. His face was thinner and pale, his eyes hollow.

"Hey," he said in a shaky voice.

"Hi." Heat radiated through Genny's shoulders and ran down her arms into her fingers.

"Hey, Shawn," Paul said.

"Hey." Shawn ran his hand over the top of his head. "Are you sure you want to hear what happened?" He looked at Genny.

"Yeah, I think it will help." She prayed she was right.

Shawn looked at Paul, and Paul nodded.

"Okay." He paused and drew in a deep breath. "Well, after a long, hard shift me, Brandon, and Quade decided to go to breakfast. We went through the line at the chow hall and found a table. We hung our weapons on the back of our chairs and laid our helmets on the table next to us and sat down to eat."

Shawn let out a little laugh and smiled. "Brandon had a huge stack of pancakes on his plate. I rarely saw him eat breakfast, so it was weird to see that much food on his plate." His smile faded and he was quiet for a moment.

Paul withdrew his arm from around Genny's shoulders and held her hand, slipping his fingers between hers.

"We talked about the deployment. Me and Quade were joking with Brandon about him leaving soon. We were jealous. But he had been there seven months. That was Brandon, always putting others first."

"Yeah, he went a month early to cover for that sergeant so he could go home on emergency leave." Genny wiped tears from her cheeks. Would that have changed anything with what had happened? It happened and there was no point in wondering. Paul gave her hand a light squeeze.

Shawn nodded and sucked in a quick breath. "A group of marines sitting at a table not far away from us started shouting, and Quade yelled for everyone to hit the floor. A loud popping sound filled the room and lots of yelling and you could hear scuffling. It was dead quiet for a few seconds. Me and Quade raised our heads up over the tabletop to make sure it was safe. I didn't know it, but a bullet had grazed my arm and Quade saw my arm bleeding. He asked where Brandon was.

I looked under the table and saw him lying on the floor and blood was everywhere.

"I screamed for help and kept yelling at him and slapping his face to wake him up. A medic ran up and ducked under the table to assess Jones, I mean Brandon. He said his pulse was weak and he was losing a lot of blood. Another medic knelt down by Brandon and said he had a chest wound. They came over with a stretcher and took him to the hospital. I don't know what happened between then and the time he died, but I heard he died on the table as they were preparing him for surgery." Red blotches surfaced on Shawn's face, and he pressed his lips into a thin line. "We found out later that the shooter was an Iraqi contractor."

Genny clenched her jaw to keep from sobbing, but she couldn't stop the flood of tears.

"I wanted to be the one to escort him home. I really liked Brandon and considered him a good friend." Shawn's lips curved into a faint smile. "I can still see his smile." He cleared his throat and ran his hands down his face. "I've struggled a lot. I was sitting next to him. Why not me, you know? Maybe I could have pushed him out of the way. I'm in therapy and attending a PTSD support group at the VA. It's helping some."

"I'm glad you are getting help. And thank you for talking to me." Genny tightened her grip on Paul's hand.

"Yeah, thanks Shawn," Paul added.

Shawn nodded.

Genny moved the cursor over the disconnect button. When she glanced up, she saw silent tears streaming down Shawn's cheeks. She gave him a half smile and he gave her one in return. She clicked the button and ended the call.

Shawn's words had painted a picture in Genny's mind as vivid as if she had been sitting at the table with the men. Brandon's bright smile as he talked with his co-workers eating the breakfast he never should have been eating. She reached over and took the picture of Brandon from the nightstand drawer. Her heart burned with devastation for her brother and abhorrence for the man who tore him away from her.

Paul closed her laptop and placed it on the bed beside him. Everything Genny had been holding back while Shawn talked spewed out of her.

Paul pulled her close and held her while she sobbed. He said nothing and let her grieve. After a while, Genny sat up and wiped her damp cheeks. "I soaked your shirt." She ran her hand over the damp fabric of his t-shirt.

"It's okay." He took her hand in his and kissed it. "I'm going to let you get ready for bed."

"Okay." She watched him get out of bed and head down the hall.

Walking into the bathroom, she reached into the shower and turned on the water. While she waited for the water to warm, she stared at herself in the mirror. A year ago, Brandon was in Iraq serving his country with no idea what would happen to him. She stepped into the shower and wet her hair. Rubbing her hands over her face, she slid down the shower wall, sat on the floor, and sobbed.

After she was ready to turn in, she sat on the bed and pulled out her journal.

September 1, 2011

I talked to Shawn Sullivan tonight. I keep imagining Brandon laying in blood. I don't understand why he went to breakfast. He NEVER ate breakfast. Why did God choose to end his life by murder? Paul has been wonderful in all this. I'm blessed to have Paul. I love him.

The backdoor closed, and Lucy bolted down the hall and jumped onto Genny's bed. Talking to Shawn had brought back the devastation of Brandon's death. A night with images flashing in her mind was daunting.

The only way she felt safe and calm was to have Paul by her side, but how would that work now? They'd slept in the same bed when his parents visited, but that was before their relationship turned romantic. Once that changed, they had set firm boundaries while they dated, or courted, as Paul called it.

Genny sighed. She'd suck it up. Laying her journal on her nightstand, she reached to turn off the lamp, but stopped. The kitchen light went out and Paul walked around to the lamp on the end table in the living room. Swinging her legs over the side of the bed, she stood and walked to the doorway of her room. Paul turned off the lamp and made his way down the hall. He tilted his head when he walked up to her.

"Goodnight."

"I–I was wondering if..." She tucked her long hair behind her ears. "Um...Goodnight." She stepped back and grabbed the door to close it.

"Wait." Paul put his hand on the door.

Tears filled Genny's eyes and spilled down her cheeks. "All the pictures in my head are of Brandon and the horror and...I don't know how you feel about this with courting."

He took her by the hand and led her to the bed. Flipping back the covers for her, she laid down and he pulled the covers up to her shoulders. He turned off the lamp and disappeared into the darkness. The covers pulled and the mattress sag slightly on the other side of the bed.

"Come here."

Genny grabbed one of her pillows and pushed it toward Paul. She moved over and laid her head on his chest. Sleep would come easier now that she was safe in his arms. Soon, the images that flashed through her mind slowed enough for her to fall asleep.

Opening her eyes, it was morning, and Paul was already at work. She didn't remember him getting up, but it must have been not long after she fell asleep. She grabbed her phone from the nightstand to check the time. The phone rang and Paul's name appeared on the screen.

"Hey." Genny ran her fingers through her hair.

"Good morning. Just checking on you. How are you?"

"Okay."

"You tossed and turned most of the night. The last time I looked at my clock, it was a quarter to five. Thought I'd get up and get to the gym early."

Genny glanced at the other nightstand where Paul's alarm clock sat. He stayed with her the entire night.

"Sorry." Genny let out a little laugh.

"I'm always here for you. Let me know if you need me, okay?"

A lightness filled Genny's chest. "Okay."

"I've got to run. I'll bring home a pizza, okay?"

"Sounds good."

After they hung up, Genny laid in bed thinking. The feeling of Paul's arms around her was difficult to describe, but it was a feeling that she wanted to experience for the rest of her life. She couldn't wait until she could spend every night in his arms.

She grabbed the picture of Brandon from the nightstand and held it for a while. Since he had died, it was as if she'd been trying to catch her breath. Inhaling deeply, but never filling her lungs. She slipped her hand behind her head and pulled out several strands of hair. Looking at the strands, she closed her eyes. There was nothing she could have done to change what had happened to Brandon. Learning to live without her big brother would be impossible.

$$Chapter\ 18$$

G enny requested the day off, since she knew she'd be emotional after talking to Shawn Sullivan. She was right. The daily routine would hopefully keep her mind occupied. As she washed the dishes, wiped down the counter, and folded her laundry, it was as if she was watching someone else's hands. It was the shock of losing Brandon all over again.

In the bedroom, Genny spent a few minutes putting away her laundry. Sinking into bed, she picked up the picture of Brandon and brushed her finger over his face. It was as if the photo was of Brandon himself. Lucy hopped up on the bed next to Genny and wagged her tail as Genny stroked her back.

Lucy shot off the bed and down the hall when she heard Paul's truck. Genny followed and grabbed a few paper plates from the cabinet. When Paul came in the door, he placed the pizza box on the counter and walked up to her. He kissed her and pulled her into his arms.

"How are you?" He eased her back and smiled.

"I'm okay. I cleaned and tried to keep busy."

He looked around the kitchen and living room. "I see that."

They both grabbed a couple slices of pizza and sat on the couch, and Paul talked about work. He avoided the topic of talking with Shawn for her sake; she figured. That was how considerate Paul was.

After a few minutes, Paul picked up the remote and clicked on the TV. He browsed the guide and found a channel with classic TV shows. Once they were finished eating, Genny rested her head on Paul's shoulder, slipped her arm over his chest and her legs over his.

A while later, Genny opened her eyes. She'd fallen asleep on him, as usual. Sitting up, she smiled and pulled away from him.

"You probably need to get ready for bed, huh?"

"Need to? Yes. Want to? No." He raised his brows.

Paul grabbed their paper plates and headed to the kitchen. Genny decided to get ready for bed herself. When she came out of her bathroom, Paul stepped in her doorway and walked up to her. Giving her a soft kiss, he eased back. "Goodnight."

"Goodnight." She ran her hand down his arm and held onto his fingers.

Paul lingered. Maybe he was conflicted. He wanted to comfort her and support her, but he also wanted to protect their growing relationship. He kissed her again and shut the door when he stepped into the hall. She picked up her journal and held it in her hands for a while. Not tonight. She laid it back on the nightstand and turned off the lamp. She stared at the ceiling, thinking about Brandon. Was he horrified when he saw the shooter, or did he thank God that he was on his way to Heaven?

She rolled over and faced the windows. Brandon was on temporary duty and would walk through the door any minute or he'd gone out for a gallon of milk. She'd always forget milk when she went grocery shopping. But he wasn't on temporary duty or at the grocery store. He was dead. She peeked at the clock. It was almost midnight and thoughts of Brandon's last moments ruminated, stealing her sleep. Sighing, she closed her eyes and after a moment, drifted off to sleep.

⤜⤛⤜⤛

A sound opened Genny's eyes, and she squinted to focus on the figure in the doorway. She sat up and blinked.

"Paul?"

The figure didn't move or make a sound. The hairs on her arms stood on end. "Paul?" her voice squeaked out his name.

"Gen."

The familiar voice didn't belong to Paul but sounded like...

"Brandon?"

"Hey, sis." He stepped into the room, and she could make out his face.

Excitement thrusted her out of bed. She rushed to him and pulled him into her arms. His body was cold and stiff, as if he'd come inside from being out in freezing weather. What was happening?

"I thought you were dead!" her words muffled against his frigid shoulder.

He laughed. "I am."

"What?" Something warm and moist covered her pajama top. She leaned back and rubbed her hand over her chest. When she pulled her hand away, it was covered with blood. A gaping hole had appeared in Brandon's chest, with blood spewing down his front. She stepped away, screaming.

"Genny? Genny? Shh, it's okay. You're having a nightmare."

She opened her eyes at Paul's warm embrace. "I'm dreaming?"

"Yes. You were screaming and woke me."

"It was Brandon. He came. I thought it was a mistake and he wasn't dead, but he was and so cold. Blood was everywhere." Trembling took over her body.

"Shh, it's okay. I'm here." Paul walked her to the bed and eased her down. I'll go get a glass of water."

"*No!* Don't leave me." She clung to his arms.

"Okay. I'm here." He sat down next to her and held her as she sobbed. He pulled away and she started violently trembling. "I'll be right back."

"No, please."

"I'm getting my pillows. I promise I'll be right back."

Genny watched him jog down the hall and appear in her room a few seconds later. He helped her get settled and slid under the covers on the other side of the bed. Her body relaxed when he slipped his arm around her waist and pulled her against him. His scent and the feeling of his breath in her hair calmed her fears. The warmth of his body soothed her to sleep. She had never felt safer.

The next morning, Paul had plans with Peter and another friend but canceled so he could be home with Genny. She'd told him to go, but he refused. They watched TV all day, and Paul made lunch and dinner. When it came time to go to bed, both left their bedroom doors open, and Paul urged her to wake him if she was scared or couldn't sleep. She longed to spend another night in his arms, but she was unsure of how he felt. Did he see it as comfort only, or maybe more? He may not be ready for more.

She sat up in bed for a while, trying to read. She gave up and put the book on the nightstand and picked up her journal.

Sep 3, 2011

I had a horrible nightmare last night. I thought I saw Brandon in my room. He was bleeding and told me he was dead. Paul said I was screaming and standing by my bedroom door. To help calm me, he slept in the bed with me. I can still feel his arms around me. I wish I could feel his arms around me every night. One day soon, I hope. I'm still scared something will happen to him, but I'm trying to work through my fears with God's help.

She laid in bed, staring down the hall. Paul had moved the night light from his bathroom into the hall. It shone bright enough that she could see his open door. Tears pooled in her eyes. No amount of laying on her hands or praying would stop the compulsion tonight. She plucked hairs from her lower scalp until the impulse eased. She rolled the strands into a ball. It was the most hair she'd pulled out yet. Tears slid down the sides of her face, and she closed her eyes. By some miracle, she slept through the night.

⟿⟫ ⟪⟵

Genny stood staring at her reflection in the bathroom mirror. She held a cool, damp washcloth over her eyes for a while. Removing the washcloth, she sighed at the dark bags still hanging under her eyes. Shuffling around in the drawer in the bathroom cabinet, she found a small container of concealer and applied a light coat under her eyes. It helped some, but the bags peeked through, reminding her of her misery.

Paul had said they could stay home today but despite the images of Brandon's last moments seared into her head, tormenting her, she felt the urge to go to church. She'd gone with Paul to church every Sunday since they started going with Peter and Melissa, but this was the first time she *wanted* to go. Could she finally be at a place where she could run to God instead of run from him?

Paul was very attentive and kept her close. He draped his arm over her shoulders and brushed his fingers over the top of her hand during the sermon. He was worried about her and had suggested counseling several times. She should probably go to therapy. This was too much for her to handle on her own.

After the service was over, they made their way to the back of the sanctuary, where Pastor Hammonds was greeting people as they left. They were among the last few members leaving. Desperation gave her the strength to ask Pastor Hammonds a question.

"Hello, Pastor Hammonds." Genny swallowed the knot in her throat.

"Call me Ryan." Although he was a few years older than Paul, Ryan's wisdom was of someone much older. "How are the Thompsons?"

"Well..." Paul looked at Genny.

A sense of vulnerability swept through Genny. "I was wondering if you could recommend a counselor. I'm having some problems. I talked to the man who was with Brandon when he died this past Thursday and I'm not doing well." Paul's hand rested on her back.

"Of course. I know someone who would be perfect. Her name is Lizbeth Reynolds. Let me get her number for you." He pulled out his phone and Genny added Lizbeth's number to her contacts.

"Thank you."

"You're welcome. Let me know if there's anything else you need."

Genny nodded and they headed for the door. She smiled when Paul held the door for her. "Can we go home to eat?"

"You bet."

Paul cleaned the kitchen after lunch and suggested that Genny rest. She loosened her braid and ran her fingers through her thick, auburn hair. She picked up a small mirror. With her back to the bathroom mirror, she lifted her hair high and pulled it to the side. A bald spot the size of a small egg rested at the nape of her neck where her braid veiled her secret.

"Genny?" Paul's strained voice sounded an octave higher.

She turned and saw him standing in the doorway. Ashamed, she let go of her hair and her gaze fell to the floor. Moisture filled her eyes at the look of shock on Paul's face. His gentle touch spilled the tears down her cheeks.

"What's going on?" He took the mirror from her hand and laid it on the bathroom counter. They walked to her bed and sat down.

Sitting quietly for a few moments, she finally spoke. "I have trichotillomania. It's an impulse control disorder. When my emotions are out of control, I pull out my hair. It started when Granddaddy died. I pulled it out in random places over my head. I would roll the hair I pulled out into a ball and hide them. Granny found one of the balls of hair and took me to the doctor. That's when I was diagnosed. I saw a counselor for a few months, and I learned how to control it.

"It started again when Granny died and lasted about a year. I focused on the hair at my lower neck and that's when I started wearing my hair in a braid. Most of it grew back except for a thin line." Her focus fell to her hands, and she twisted her wedding band. "It started again when Brandon died. This is the worst it's been."

"Genny, I'm so sorry." He took her hand in his. His tone was soft. "Please make sure you talk to the counselor about this."

Tears filled her eyes. "I will, I promise." The warmth from his hand calmed her. "This is so hard. He shouldn't be dead."

"I know." Paul wrapped his arms around her and gently rocked her as she cried.

Sep 4, 2011

Paul was so sweet to me today in church. Well, not just church. Every time I turn around, he's there. I'm going to go to counseling. Pastor Ryan said the counselor is nice. I hope so. I forgot to close the bathroom door this afternoon and Paul came in to check on me when I was looking at my neck. I'll never forget the look on his face as long as I live. I haven't slept well since the night Paul stayed with me. I feel protected when he's next to me, but I don't know how to talk to him about it. It may be too tempting for him.

Paul flipped the hamburger patties on the grill and continued his conversation with Peter. "I'm glad we didn't go to the beach."

"Yeah. Labor Day is as bad as the Fourth of July." Peter took a few chips from the open bag and tossed them to Lucy. "How's Genny?"

"Not good, brother. But she has an appointment Thursday with a counselor Ryan recommended."

"That's great. We'll be praying."

After they finished eating, Genny brought out graham crackers, marshmallows, and chocolate bars to make S'mores. Paul started a fire in the fire pit while Genny handed out the skewers.

"So, what are you going to do while Paul's gone?" Peter brought his marshmallow to his lips and blew out the flames.

"I'm thinking about taking some classes in the spring and I'm still working at the coffee shop."

"You know we are here. You can call or come over anytime," Melissa said.

"Thank you. I really appreciate it." Genny slid two marshmallows onto her skewer and held them over the fire.

Paul watched her as she stared into the dancing flames. What was she thinking? A small flame flickered at the bottom of a marshmallow, but Genny didn't seem to notice. Soon, both marshmallows were engulfed.

"Genevieve." He grabbed the skewer from her hand and blew out the flames.

"Oh, I'm sorry," she mumbled.

"Genevieve?" Melissa raised her eyebrows.

"Yeah, my name is Genevieve, but I go by Genny. Paul calls me Genevieve sometimes."

"Genevieve is such a pretty name."

Genny crossed her arms. "He used to call me Genevieve as a way to pick on me when we were kids. I hated the name when I was little."

"What'd he do?" Melissa looked at Paul.

"Tell her what you did."

"When we were kids, I told her that old ladies are named Genevieve, so I called her an old lady all the time." Paul pressed his lips together to stifle a grin.

"You did not." Melissa rolled her eyes and shook her head. It seemed she'd picked up Genny's bad habit.

Paul dragged Genny's chair over to him. Heat spread over his body when their legs touched. "You are definitely not an old lady." He leaned close and kissed her cheek, then stretched his arm across the back of her chair. The fragrance floating in the air around Genny sent a shiver down his spine.

"Are you sniffing me?" she whispered.

"I noticed your body wash. Is it new?"

She giggled. "It's sunblock."

"Oh." He grinned and kissed her. Glancing in Peter and Melissa's direction, Paul saw Peter smiling at them, something he'd never done. Had Peter finally stopped questioning their marriage?

At work the next day, Paul headed out to his truck for his lunch break and saw a voicemail from the jeweler designing Genny's bracelet. The bracelet was ready, and the timing was perfect, with three days until her birthday. He stopped by after work and waited for the designer to bring the bracelet up from the back. A case of engagement rings drew him in, and he walked over.

"Mr. Thompson?" Paul turned toward the sound of the voice and saw the designer carrying a small box to where he was standing. "Nice to see you again."

"You, too."

The man opened the box to reveal a beautiful bracelet of alexandrite gemstones set in silver. Paul's breath caught in his throat. He could see the bracelet encircling Genny's slender wrist. "It's beautiful."

Later at home, he sat on the picnic table attempting to clear his thoughts so he could come up with a plan to give Genny the bracelet on her birthday. She was going to the beach for a few hours after work to see some of the club members. Although he didn't say it, he was hurt that she would consider spending time at the beach instead of coming straight home from work. Lucy walked up with her bone and laid on the ground at his feet, gnawing. Watching her as she gnawed, the jingling of her collar gave him an idea.

Paul finished eating dinner and turned on the TV. He needed to think of something else to eat on the nights Genny had to work late. Sandwiches were getting old. Lucy's ears perked up, and she tilted her head. She'd gotten used to the sounds of their vehicles and could often hear the truck or the Jeep approach before he or Genny heard. Lucy jumped off the couch and met Genny at the front door.

She walked in and flopped down on the couch next to him. He leaned over close to her, and she pushed him away. "Don't sniff me and say you want a cup of coffee. I can't help that we have the best roasted beans in town." She grinned. "I'm so tired. We were super busy tonight."

"Makes your shift go by faster."

"I guess." She frowned. "Not another documentary."

"That's an advertisement for a reality TV show." He shook his head and smiled.

"Thank goodness!" Genny rolled her eyes.

Paul playfully elbowed her in the ribs. She talked a few moments about work, then quieted. A second later, her head rested against his shoulder. The closeness of her sent a rush of warmth to his stomach. He brushed his finger across the top of her hand and leaned his cheek against her head. Soon, her breaths came in a slow, steady rhythm. He loved this woman and savored her closeness. Nearly every thought he had was about her. She consumed him.

Chapter 19

Genny drove around a group of offices searching for numbers on the outside of the buildings. She pulled into a parking space in front of the building number she was provided and sat in the Jeep, waiting for time to pass. The name of the counselor she was seeing was on the outside of the building, near the front door.

She had five minutes before her appointment time and said a quick prayer. "Lord, please calm my nerves. I know this is difficult, but necessary." She drew in a deep breath and climbed down from the Jeep.

As she waited, she had second thoughts. Melissa said she went to counseling after her dad died and the first session was gathering your history from childhood to the present. Therapists liked to dig deep. It was their job. A door opened down the hall, causing Genny to tense. *Please, Lord...*

"Genevieve?" The woman gestured down the hall.

Genny pulled herself to her feet and followed the woman into a small office. The small, black couch was comfortable, and the office was lit with lamps instead of the fluorescent lights overhead. The cool, sweet scent of peppermint hung in the air.

"My name is Lizbeth. Unfortunately, people call me Elizabeth." Lizbeth smiled. She was older and wore a pair of jeans and a nice pullover top. At least she wasn't wearing a pantsuit.

"I go by Genny." Inhaling deeply, Genny willed herself to stop shaking.

"Have you been to therapy before, Genny?"

"No." She shifted on the sofa. "Well, as a child." Genny twisted her wedding band around her finger.

"Oh, ok. We'll get into that later. Ryan Hammonds referred you?"

"Yeah. He's our pastor."

"Very nice man."

Genny smiled.

"Okay, let's get started."

Genny's heart pounded, and her throat tightened.

"So, Genny, what brings you into therapy?"

"My husband thinks I need counseling."

"Oh? Why is that?" Lizbeth raised a brow.

"My brother was killed in Iraq on December first of last year and I have been having nightmares. My last one was the worst one I've had."

"Oh, Genny. I'm sorry to hear about your brother."

"Thank you." Genny fidgeted a little and crossed her legs.

"Grief can be a tough thing to get through."

"And, I have trichotillomania." Why did she blurt it out? She twisted her wedding band. "That's why I went to a counselor when I was young."

"Oh, okay."

Genny watched Lizbeth take notes as they went along. Lizbeth talked about grief and how there were stages Genny would go through. Listening to Lizbeth talk about depression, impulse control disorders and grief, Genny realized she'd been twisting her wedding band the entire time they'd been talking. She separated her hands and rested her arm on the arm of the couch. Several times she fought the urge to twist her wedding band again.

Lizbeth grabbed a pamphlet from the edge of the desk and handed it to Genny. The word *Depression* was at the top in large bold letters. She gave Genny a printout from a website on impulse control disorders and a grief workbook.

By the end of the session, Genny was emotionally exhausted but comfortable with Lizbeth. Ryan was right. She was down to earth and compassionate. Genny had a feeling she would soon be comfortable enough to talk about everything she'd been struggling with. In the Jeep, she looked at the workbook on the passenger seat. She thought of something that might help her get through the workbook.

At home, she dug through the stack of pictures in her nightstand drawer. The picture of Brandon in his blue suit was close to the bottom of the stack. He had called it a service dress uniform, but to her, it looked like a suit a man would wear to church except for all the little colored ribbons over one of the upper pockets. Grabbing a roll of clear tape, she opened the workbook and taped Brandon's picture to the title page. This book full of words and worksheets was going to cause her much pain, but she hoped it would help her process through her brother's death.

Sep 8, 2011

Counseling wasn't too bad. I'm a little scared of the workbook, but I know it will help. At least I hope so. I can't stop thinking about Paul. Neither one of us has said I love you. I know he loves me, but it would be nice to hear him say it. Maybe I should say it first.

P.S. Tomorrow's my birthday!!!

⟫⟫ ⟪⟪

The beep of the time clock as Genny scanned her badge sent a jolt of excitement through her body. She pulled off her apron and made her way to the door.

"Happy birthday, Genny!" Julie shouted, turning every customer's head toward Genny. She narrowed her eyes at Julie and got a lopsided grin in return.

"Happy birthday," an elderly man said.

"Thank you, Mr. Ed." Genny waved and darted out to the Jeep.

The sun was bright on the way to the beach, lifting her spirits. She thought about her birthday last year. Brandon had sent her the latest Papa Roach CD and a gift card. What was Paul up to? One day when she got home from work, she noticed her jewelry box open. She rarely wore jewelry except her wedding band and was certain Paul was snooping. Smiling, Genny's mind raced as she tried to guess what he had planned. She promised herself she wouldn't be late getting home today. When she pulled up to the beach, she saw a few group members. Michael eyed her and strolled over.

"How's it going? I didn't think you'd be here today. Isn't it your birthday?"

"Yeah. I thought I'd stop by for a little while."

"I'm glad you did. Happy birthday." He smiled. "Any news on when Paul's leaving?"

"Thanks, and not yet." Genny twisted her wedding band. Michael's unsettling gaze left her feeling exposed.

"Let's go for a walk." Michael gestured for Genny to go ahead of him. She hesitated, then stepped forward.

Down the beach, Genny noticed that Michael's eyes were fixed on her. How had he not tripped yet?

"Missed you last weekend."

"Oh...um...I wasn't feeling well." It wasn't a lie. Her world was falling apart all over again.

"I'm glad you're better." Michael's shoulder bumped into hers as they strolled down the beach. A feeling deep down inside urged Genny to go home. "What are you going to do while he's gone?"

"I'll still be working and hopefully take a class or two at the community college."

"Do you and Paul want kids?"

"Not sure on that one. But, speaking of Paul, I need to head home." Michael's interest in her and Paul's future children caught Genny off guard. *Why am I here?* She'd been at the beach for less than an hour. It was time to go home to her husband.

"Oh, okay." Michael's slightly furrowed brows and tight jaw muscle surprised Genny. They headed back toward the parking lot. "It was nice to see you today." He relaxed and smiled.

"You, too." Genny stiffened when Michael gave her a hug. His attention was unsettling.

He opened the driver's door after Genny hit the remote. She slid in and he shut the door. Pulling out of the parking lot, she glanced in the side mirror and saw him leaning against his Jeep, watching her. She pushed him out of her mind and focused on what Paul had planned.

The sun was low in the sky as Genny drove down the hill and she held her hand just below the visor to shade her eyes. Paul's truck came into view, waking the butterflies in her stomach. Maybe he didn't have anything planned but the standard cake and card. She frowned. When she opened the front door, Lucy came trotting up to her with something stuck in her collar. She pulled out the white paper and unrolled it. Genny smiled as she read.

Daddy has something special for you out back.

She looked out the window and saw Paul sitting on the picnic table. Controlling herself was difficult as she darted to the back door and made her way out to him. He grinned at her. She noticed the small box wrapped in pastel floral paper next to him.

"Happy birthday, Genevieve." We handed her the gift.

She carefully opened it with a smile spread across her face. When she pulled off the top, the smile fell. "Paul..." She swallowed hard.

"You have several sapphire pieces of jewelry, so I did something different. It's alexandrite."

"It's beautiful." Tears pooled in her eyes as she studied the bracelet. The many stones reflected the sunlight as Paul removed the bracelet from the box. The feel of his fingers brushing against her skin as he looped the bracelet around her wrist sent chills up her arm.

"I thought it would help you feel closer to Brandon since it's one of June's birthstones."

She sat quietly while she ran her finger over the gems. Tears spilled down her cheeks. He slipped his arm around her shoulder and pulled her close.

"It will. Thank you so much." She brushed her finger over the gems once more.

"You're welcome, Genny." He kissed her, stirring the butterflies in her stomach.

They went inside, where Paul brought out a small cake from the fridge and cut two pieces. They sat in the living room talking and eating. She looked at him as he told the story of having the bracelet made. No one else in the world had the same bracelet.

For the rest of the evening, they sat on the couch and watched TV. Genny laid her head on Paul's shoulder and intertwined her legs with his. She loved being close to him. A thought drifted through her mind. The same thought that'd stayed with her since Valentine's Day.

"Mmm." Genny traced the neckline of Paul's t-shirt with her finger.

"What is it?" His voice vibrated in his chest.

"I can't believe we're married."

"Me either," he whispered.

Genny ran her finger over Paul's jawline and raised her head. Their faces were close enough that the heat from his skin touched hers. Brushing her thumb across his lips, she kissed him. He returned her kiss, but like at the waterfront, she felt his restraint.

The ringtone of Genny's phone interrupted their intimacy. Genny pulled back and steadied her breathing. Reaching over to the side table, she picked up her phone and saw Tricia's name on the screen. It was her birthday. Of course, her mother-in-law would call. She softly sighed and smiled at Paul.

While talking to Tricia, Genny watched Paul walk down the hall to his bedroom. What would have happened if Tricia hadn't called? Getting married and then falling in love had given their relationship a different, and at times confusing, dynamic. Being intimate seemed wrong, but she reminded herself often that they were already married, and there was nothing wrong with desiring her husband.

Genny hung up with Tricia and headed to her bedroom to get ready to turn in. Sitting on her bed, she turned the bracelet at different angles and watched the lamp's light reflect in the gems. Never had she received such a precious gift. Before taking a shower, she slipped the bracelet off and laid it on her nightstand. As soon as she was in her pajamas, she fastened the bracelet around her wrist. For tonight, she'd sleep with it on. Rubbing her finger across the gemstones, she pulled out her journal and picked up her pen.

Sep 9, 2011

Today was the best birthday I've ever had. Paul is the sweetest man. I can't stop thinking about him. I have never felt this way about a guy before. Love is such a wonderful feeling. I'm trying to be patient, but it's hard. Kissing him takes my breath away. I can only imagine what it will be like to give myself to him. I can't wait until we spend every night together. I feel safe when he's next to me...

Paul sat on his bed, finishing his Bible study. Putting away his Bible and journal, he looked at his closed bedroom door for a while. He and

Genny had been courting for almost a month. They'd gone out each weekend. Sometimes they'd have dinner and see a movie and other times, they'd spend the day out and about. Last Saturday, they spent the day at Middleton Place. He smiled. A day somewhere like Middleton Place was his favorite way to spend time with Genny.

He breathed in deep. Kissing Genny had stirred sensations he'd kept hidden for years. How much longer did God want them to be patient? By Genny's kiss, she was struggling as well. Glancing at his alarm clock, it was close to ten. He had fitness with his unit in the morning and needed to get to bed.

Opening his door, Paul stepped into the hall and saw Genny sitting on her bed with her journal. She looked up and smiled. He made his way to her room to tell her goodnight. She stood and walked up to him. Slipping her arms around his waist, she rested her head on his shoulder, and they held each other for a while. There was a time years ago he thought he was in love, but he was wrong. The feelings he had for Genny he'd never had for anyone. He would love her until his last breath.

"Goodnight, Genevieve." He ran his fingers through her hair that flowed down her back.

"Goodnight," she whispered.

He eased her back and kissed her softly. "Sweet dreams." He winked and smiled as pink filled her cheeks. Releasing her, Paul made his way to his room, closing her door behind him.

He went down on his knees and prayed. "Father, I pray for our marriage, that we continue to keep You at the center. It is easy to lose focus with daily life, but we know we won't make it without You. I pray for Genny that she keeps her eyes on You and that You protect over her." Paul got ready for bed and climbed under the covers.

Prior to taking responsibility for Genny, Paul had always kept God first in his life. But when he discovered how much Genny needed him, he had struggled and felt pulled in opposite directions. Now, she was at a place where she could stand on her own and her relationship with God was growing. Paul realized something. God was where he'd always been—the center of Paul's life.

There were exactly three weeks until Paul's birthday. Genny stopped by the store on the Air Force base to look around. "I don't think Paul would be happy getting a witch." She giggled and put the witch back on the shelf. While children made their way around neighborhoods in Murfreesboro, Tennessee, collecting bags full of candy on Halloween in 1982, Paul's mom was in the hospital giving birth to him. When they were kids, he joked his birthday was extra special because he got presents and a bag full of candy.

She made her way to the men's clothing section and browsed the shirts, but nothing jumped out at her. A shirt would probably end up in the back of the closet like Brandon did with the shirts she bought for him. She sighed. A belt? No. Tie? No. Socks? Definitely not. Paul was a hard man to shop for. He bought his wants and needs throughout the year.

She went to the cosmetics counter and picked up a tester bottle of men's cologne. Taking a big sniff, she grimaced and put the bottle back. A flier for the Christian bookstore came in the mail yesterday. Maybe she should go check it out. She frowned. Paul had so many theology-related books and she'd probably buy something he already had. She'd have to look for a present later. Paul would be home in an hour, and she wanted to start dinner.

Gathering ingredients from the cabinet, Genny pulled out a frying pan to brown ground beef for the pot of chili simmering on the stove. As she pushed around the meat in the frying pan, tears gathered in her eyes. Brandon died, so she and Paul would fall in love. Why would God do that? She loved Paul with all of her heart, but at times she missed Brandon so badly that she couldn't catch her breath.

Genny swiped her fingers over her cheeks and cleared her throat when she heard Paul pull into the driveway. She continued to push around the beef as Paul walked in the door. Tears filled her eyes again.

"Hello, my beautiful wife." Paul walked up behind her and slipped his arms around her waist. Putting it off as long as she could, she sniffed. "What's wrong, baby?" He turned her around to face him.

She closed her eyes, pushing fresh tears down her cheeks. "I was thinking about Brandon." She covered her mouth and held back a sob.

Paul reached around her and turned off the burner under the frying pan, and led her into the living room. They sat down on the couch and Paul wrapped his arms around her and held her as she cried. "What is it, my love?" he whispered in her ear.

"We are the reason Brandon is dead."

"No, sweetheart. Why would you say that?"

"He died so we could be together." She sniffed and fingered the buttons on his uniform overshirt.

"I don't think that's what happened."

"Then what?" It made sense to her. If Brandon hadn't died, Genny would still be in Fayetteville and Paul would still be with Brianna.

"We are together *because* he died. He didn't die, so we would fall in love. God brought us together through our grief."

"So, we didn't lie to everyone after all?"

"At first, maybe, but you know it didn't take long for feelings to grow."

He tipped her chin and gave her a slow, gentle kiss. Brushing his nose against hers, he leaned back and smiled. "Why don't you call in?"

"I'll be okay. It's four hours."

"If you insist. I'll take care of dinner so you can relax some before you have to head to work."

"Thank you, handsome husband."

"You're welcome, beautiful wife."

Genny's cheeks warmed. She went to the bedroom to get ready for work. Two months had passed since their relationship changed. Everything was in God's timing. Thankfully, God brought them together before Paul deployed. Their time apart would have been long and painful while both of them wrestled with their feelings.

Genny groaned when she pulled into the parking lot at The Roasted Bean. The drive-thru was wrapped around the building and the parking lot was full. She had to park in the back next to the dumpster, which creeped her out. She'd ask a co-worker to walk her to the Jeep after her shift.

The evening rush lulled once everyone had their mochas and lattes. Genny walked to the dining room to wipe down the tables. She looked up and saw Michael pulling into the parking lot. She noticed him looking at her through the window. He smiled the smile that had once warmed her stomach, but it no longer had the same effect. He walked up to her when he came in the door.

"Hey, how are you?"

"Good, you?" Genny pushed in a chair and wiped down a tabletop.

"Hanging in here. I missed you Saturday."

"I was asked to take a shift. One of our baristas was out with the flu and we all took turns working her shifts for the week. But I'm spending all my free time with Paul before the deployment."

"I understand." He shifted his weight. "As long as you're not mad at me." His lips parted into a grin.

An unsettling heat slowly filled Genny's chest. "Oh, no. Not mad. Sometimes adulthood takes precedence. At times, it's hard for me to remember that I'm an adult." She laughed.

"How about a caramel macchiato?"

"Coming right up." Genny walked behind the counter and rang up his coffee. His fingers brushed against hers as he handed her his debit card, knotting her stomach. It wasn't an accident.

Michael sat in the dining room, sipping his coffee for a long while. A time or two, she caught him watching her.

"I'll catch you later," Michael said as he stood.

"Okay. I'm not sure when I'll be at another club get-together. It might be a while since Paul's leaving soon."

Michael's lower lip protruded like a pouting child. "I'll miss you." He looked at her for a few seconds and smiled.

"Bye." Genny smiled.

Michael gave her a little wave and walked out to his Jeep.

"Who's that?" Bridget, a fellow barista, asked as she walked up next to Genny.

"Michael. He's a member of the Jeep club I'm in."

"He's cute." She bit her bottom lip.

"Want me to put in a good word?" Bridget raised her brows and grinned. Genny laughed. Maybe another woman would turn his attention away from her.

Michael backed out and sat looking into the restaurant for a few moments. Genny took a step back and moved behind the espresso machines. He seemed too interested in her as a married woman. She should tell Paul. No, she was overreacting.

Once her shift ended, Genny swiped her badge and made her way to the parking lot. Taking a quick glance around, she climbed into the Jeep and headed home. As she drove, her thoughts settled on Paul. He was leaving in a month. She was still trying to wrap her head around being without him for six months. He'd been by her side for close to a year. How was she going to survive?

Genny hung up her keys and made her way down the hall. She noticed the light under Paul's bedroom door as she walked by. She took a quick shower and got ready for bed. With her journal open and pen in her hand, she contemplated where to begin with her entry for the day. Paul's bedroom door opened, and he headed down the hall to her room with a gentle smile that reached the depths of her heart.

"How was work?" He sat on the side of her bed.

"Not bad. It went by quickly." She laid her journal and pen aside and rested her hand on top of his. Her shift was fine, except for Michael's attention. She'd keep it to herself for now.

"Good." He laid his other hand on top of hers and gave it a gentle squeeze. "Goodnight." Leaning over, he kissed her, letting his kiss linger.

Weakness flowed from Genny's shoulders, down her arms, and into her fingers. "Goodnight," she whispered when he eased back.

His gaze held hers for a long moment. "I love you, Genevieve." As he caressed her cheek, tears glistened in his eyes.

"I love you, too." Genny's heart soared. In all her life, she had never felt about anyone the way she felt about Paul.

Brushing his fingers over her cheek and along her jaw, he kissed her again. And in that moment, they fully gave themselves to each other, becoming husband and wife the way God intended.

October 10, 2011

I'm wide awake and in the living room writing in my journal while Paul's asleep. My mind is so full of thoughts I'm finding it hard to think.

But the one thing that keeps coming back to me is that my love for Paul has grown more than I ever thought possible.

Since we got married, husband has meant friend to me. But being with our married friends and seeing the love they had for each other had put a longing in my heart for a real marriage. I'm so thankful God joined us together.

Genny picked up her Bible from the side table and thumbed through Song of Solomon. She smiled when she saw the verse that she was searching for. Chapter two, verse sixteen: "My beloved is mine and I am his..." She glanced down the hall, then returned to her journal.

God, please don't let anything happen to Paul.

Chapter 20

P aul had moved most of his theology-related books and journals into the office after he moved into the master bedroom with Genny. He smiled to himself. Their relationship had changed so much in the past few weeks. Falling asleep each night with his arms wrapped around Genny filled a void in his heart he didn't know he had.

Grabbing the box of journals from the top shelf in the now guest room, the box slipped out of his hands and landed upside down, spilling half the contents. He groaned and started piling the journals back into the box. Picking up the last journal, he turned it over and his heart lurched. He was holding the journal from 2003—the hardest year of his life.

He sat on the bed and gripped it tightly, whitening his knuckles. Why had he kept it all these years? As a reminder of redemption. That was why. With shaking hands, he opened the cover and thumbed through the first few pages. He came across the entry for early February that had hurled him down a slippery slope.

February 4, 2003

I met a woman today. I've seen her in the laundry room of the dorm a time or two, but today I saw her in the dining hall. It was the lunch rush and there weren't any free seats. I saw her wandering around with her tray and invited her to sit with me. Her name is Staci. She has big brown eyes and the brightest smile I've ever seen. She's beautiful. I have never felt this way after meeting a woman for the first time. Of course, I don't have that much experience. I've only dated a few women that I met through the chapel.

I started off our conversation with my faith. I always let people know where I stand. She didn't seem put off, so that's good. I can't help wondering if she is the one God has chosen for me. Time will tell.

Paul swallowed hard and fought back tears. He flipped through the pages and read more entries.

February 23, 2003

Staci and I spend almost every day together. I don't know how love feels, but I think I love her. We are officially in a relationship now. I've been talking to her about God, and she went to church with me today. She doesn't seem interested, but I'm not giving up on her. God uses us to bring others into His flock. Maybe that's why she is in my life...

March 1, 2003

I am so ashamed of myself. I have broken my promise to God...

Paul looked out the window and wiped the tears from his cheeks. He thumbed through the journal to the last half and found the entry he was looking for.

September 18, 2003

I am devastated by my own sin...

He stared at the page. The words had been hidden in the journal in a box for years, but he would never forget. Through tears, he flipped to the last few pages.

December 3, 2003

Pastor Mike noticed I've been down. He took me aside after the singles' Thanksgiving get together and I fell apart. He talked to me with love and compassion and prayed over me. I have a renewed faith and I promise to never make the same mistake again. I have an appointment Friday to start the process of a different kind of outward expression of my faith. I am getting a tattoo of the cross on my back. I love the Lord and I'm not afraid to show it.

Paul sat on the bed and sobbed. If he could go back in time and do things differently, he would, but that wasn't how life worked. The stitches God had used to mend his broken heart were slowly coming undone. He raised himself to his feet and walked into the bathroom, and slipped off his shirt. Turning his back to the bathroom mirror, he looked over his shoulder at the reflection of the tattoo of the cross. "I am redeemed." Tears flowed down his cheeks.

He was redeemed and he refused to let the enemy tell him otherwise. With the stitches in his heart pulled tight once again, he knew it wasn't the right time to tell Genny about his past. Two, maybe three weeks until he deployed. It wouldn't be fair to tell her and leave. He'd use the six months to pray that God would give him the right words and show him the right time to tell Genny. And he'd also pray that she would forgive him.

⫻⫻

Genny clocked out and hurried to the Jeep. She'd left early for work today and stopped by the Christian bookstore to pick up the engraved leather journals she bought for them to use during the deployment. The clerk had helped her think of clever sayings or verses for the front cover. "While we're apart," he had suggested. It was perfect.

When she pulled into the driveway, Paul opened the front door and grinned. "What did you buy me?"

"You'll see. Come grab the cake. I can get everything else."

Genny put the ice cream in the freezer and pulled the present and card from the shopping bag. Paul grinned and rubbed his hands together.

"You're like a little kid." Paul pulled her into his arms and dipped her as if they were dancing and kissed her. "What's gotten into you?"

"It's my birthday. When are we going trick or treating?" He laughed. She rested her hands on her hips.

"If we aren't going trick or treating, then I want to open my present and eat cake and ice cream before dinner." He crossed an arm over his middle and touched his chin.

"Really?" She shook her head.

"Yeah." He grinned. Pulling down two bowls, he sat them on the counter and grabbed a knife to cut the cake. Genny gave up and got the ice cream from the freezer and the ice cream scoop from the drawer.

They sat on the couch, enjoying dessert before dinner. Paul kept his eye on his present displayed on the coffee table and grinned between spoonfuls of cake and ice cream. Genny looked at her bowl and shook her head. She hadn't seen him on his birthday in years. This could be how he acted every year. Hopefully not. She giggled to herself.

With empty bowls on the side table and a wide grin on Paul's face, she handed him his present and watched wide-eyed as he ripped the paper off the box in all of a second. He pulled the top off the box and stared at the journal. Pulling it out, he saw the second journal on the bottom. Genny slid closer and explained her idea of each writing their feelings during the deployment and exchanging journals when he was back home.

"I love this idea, sweetheart." Paul leaned over and kissed Genny, letting his kiss linger. When he eased back, his expression had changed.

"What is it?"

"I got my deployment orders today. I leave on the tenth."

"But that's less than two weeks." She blinked back tears.

"I know."

She leaned against him and slipped her arm over his chest. It had been less than three months since their relationship had changed. November tenth was technically early November, but she'd hoped the military would have changed its mind. But she'd learned it wasn't how the military worked. Tears pooled in her eyes and spilled down her face, dampening his t-shirt. She'd hoped she could have more time to get control over her fears, but she had no choice. Ready or not, he was leaving in ten days.

⇶ ⇷

Anxiety hung over Genny like a rain cloud, dumping massive amounts of rain, and she had no umbrella. In the morning, Paul would board a plane to the Middle East for six months. Genny had shed so many tears she was sure she had none left. She was wrong. Watching herself in the mirror as she braided her hair, she had to stop every few moments to wipe her cheeks. She tried to hold back her tears in front of Paul. He didn't need added stress or guilt for leaving her.

"Gen?" Paul appeared in the bathroom doorway. "Ready?"

"Why do we have to do this? Brandon already taught me some moves."

"Yes, but that was a while ago. It's my job to make sure my wife's safe."

She let out a long, exaggerated sigh and followed Paul out to the backyard.

"Okay, if someone comes up behind you and wraps their arms around yours, rendering you immobile..." He demonstrated and kissed her neck.

"Paul!"

He laughed. "Throw your head back as hard as you can. That is, if the person is around your height. You are tall enough that it will work on most men."

"Gee, thanks." Genny rolled her eyes.

"More than likely, you'd break his nose. Now try this." He turned her around to face him. "Oh, wait." He turned her back around.

"You're making me dizzy."

"Sorry." He wrapped his arms around her again. "You can lean over, and thanks to gravity, you can flip the person over your head. They will most likely land on their back, which will give you a chance to get away. Now try on me."

"What?" Paul was six two and two hundred pounds of pure muscle. "Go ahead."

To her surprise, Genny easily flipped Paul over her head, laying him flat on his back with a loud *thud.* She gasped. "I'm so sorry!"

"Don't apologize to an attacker." He groaned.

With a few more moves down, Paul wanted to teach her one last move. "Okay, this one will work with both men and women, but mostly men."

Genny didn't have to ask what he meant.

"If you can get your foot between his, you have it made. You bring your knee up fast and hard. Remember—knee 'em where it counts. Now try to shove your foot between mine, but don't raise your knee." He gave an awkward laugh. Genny complied. "I think you got it, love."

They walked over to the picnic table to take a break. "I'm going to miss you so much." Genny sat on the picnic table next to Paul. Tears rolled down her cheeks.

He slipped his arms around her shoulders and pulled her close. "I'm going to miss you too, my love."

"Hello, you two," Mrs. Baker said, standing on her patio.

"Hi, Mrs. Baker." Genny waived. They stepped off the picnic table and walked to the fence.

"When are you leaving again, Paul?"

"Tomorrow morning bright and early," he answered.

"Safe travels and I'll be praying for you. Genny, I'm here for you if you ever get lonely or want to come over for dinner or tea."

"Thank you, Mrs. Baker."

"Yes, thank you," Paul added.

Paul and Genny went back inside and settled on the couch. Paul turned the TV to the music channel and slipped his arm around Genny, pulling her against his chest.

"I wish we had more time," Paul said.

"Forever would be nice." She made a sound that was more a cry than a laugh.

"It doesn't work that way."

"Unfortunately. Hey, maybe you can hide me in your duffle bag." Genny raised her head and grinned.

"Or I could go AWOL." He kissed the side of her head.

"Hmm, as much as I hate to say it, that probably wouldn't be a good idea." Genny clung to Paul to memorize his scent and the feel of his body in her arms. She prayed it was enough to last until he was in her arms again.

⇢⇢⇢ ⇠⇠⇠

"Genny?" She opened her eyes when Paul softly called her name. Sitting up, she picked up her phone. It was a little after four. She couldn't remember waking at such an early hour in the past. Paul sat on the edge of the bed and caressed her cheek.

"Aaron's on his way."

Genny nodded and rubbed her eyes. A slight feeling of nausea filled her throat. She slipped out of bed and followed Paul down the hall. He took her hand and led her to the couch. It didn't take long for the tears to fall. God had a plan in everything, Paul would say. A vehicle slowed and pulled into the driveway.

"There's Aaron."

"Already?" Genny's eyes burned.

"Yeah." We've got to be there by five."

"Where's he going?"

"Afghanistan."

"Oh." At least Paul was going somewhere relatively safe. He rose to his feet and Genny followed him to the front door, where his bags were neatly arranged.

"Hey Paul, you ready?" Aaron asked when Paul opened the front door.

"Nope." He looked back at Genny standing behind him. She gave Aaron a faint smile.

"Yeah, Kari's not doing well. But she never does with deployments."

Genny leaned against the doorjamb and watched them load Paul's bags into the back of Aaron's truck. Paul walked up to her and lightly brushed his fingers across her cheek. Fighting back tears, she leaned her forehead against his shoulder. He eased her back and gave her a slow kiss.

"I love you, Genevieve. I'm going to miss you so much," Paul's voice grew thick. The light by the front door revealed his damp cheeks.

"I'm going to miss you, too. I love you." Warm tears trickled down her face. Lucy walked up next to her, and Paul leaned down to scratch her neck with both hands.

"You take care of Mommy, okay?"

Genny smiled and watched him walk down the steps and climb into the passenger seat of Aaron's truck.

The truck backed out and disappeared over the hill. She shut the front door before her knees buckled. Bracing herself on the back of the door, she slid to the floor, sobbing. Several minutes passed before she could stand. She made it down the hall to the bed. Grabbing the journal she'd bought for the deployment. Genny wrote her first entry.

Nov 10, 2011

You are gone now. You left less than ten minutes ago. I literally feel like my heart is split in half, and you took a half with you. I feel so lost and scared. I don't know what I'm going to do if something happens to you. I'm putting you on every prayer list I can find. I should start a countdown calendar and mark off each day that passes until you are in my arms again.

Pulling the covers up to her neck, Genny laid in bed, staring down the hall. The house was too quiet. She was alone for the first time since Brandon died. Her mind was too alive with thoughts to sleep, and she threw the covers back and headed down the hall. Lowering herself on the couch, she picked up the remote and browsed through channels.

She spent the day in her pajamas, watching TV to distract her thoughts. Paul said he'd try to call during his layovers, but she may not hear from him until he was in Qatar, which could be a few days.

The day dragged on, and the evening was winding down. Genny figured Paul wasn't calling today, but she would make sure the volume was up on her phone in case he called during the night. Exhausted, Genny decided it was time for bed, even though she knew she wouldn't be able to sleep.

Stopping in the kitchen, she opened the drawer they used for odds and ends and pulled out a large black marker. She drew a big X over November tenth on the calendar hanging in the kitchen. The remaining white squares for the month begged to hold a black X but she couldn't do it. She had no choice but to take it one day at a time. The next six months might as well be six years.

⟫⟫ ⟪⟪

The C-17 Globemaster III cargo plane touched down on the runway at Al Udeid Air Base, Qatar, at almost four in the morning local time. Passengers shuffled off the plane and Paul waited with the others to collect his bags. He scanned the different buildings. Which one was the chapel? Beads of sweat formed on his forehead and trickled down his back in the fifteen minutes since they'd disembarked. It was at least eighty-five degrees outside.

The quarters seemed adequate. Paul saw a variety of deployment quarters throughout his Air Force career, and Al Udeid was not the best, but certainly not the worst. He found the dormitory and the room he was assigned to and put his belongings away. He heard the door open and turned around. A tall, thin young man with brown hair bent down and picked up something off the floor. Paul remembered seeing him on the flight over.

"Is this yours?" he asked, holding a photo of Genny.

"Yeah, it must have fallen off the bed when I was putting my stuff away.

"Wife?" He flung his duffle bag on the other bed.

"Yep."

"She's beautiful. Lucky man."

Paul smiled. "I think so."

"Damien Tucker. I guess we're roommates." Damien offered his hand.

"Paul Thompson. Nice to meet you." Paul reached over and shook Damien's hand.

Paul had the remainder of the day to rest before his first day of work. The group he flew over with had occupied all the computers and phones at the cybercafé, so Paul would ask if he could call Genny from the shop.

Standing in line for a coffee, Paul fingered his wedding band. He'd left Genny three days ago. She'd been on his mind constantly since then. It didn't matter if he was awake or asleep, she had taken up residence in his head. At least one hundred and seventy-seven days until he could hold her. Walking away from her for six months was one of the hardest things he'd ever had to do.

As Paul walked around, he found the chapel next to the base shopping center. A chaplain preparing for the Sunday service looked up. "Anything I can do for you, Sergeant?"

Paul noticed *Our Daily Bread* booklets in his hand. "I was looking for the chapel."

"Glad you found us. I'm Chaplain Ford."

"Paul Thompson." Chaplain Ford gave Paul a list of service times and another handout on the upcoming holiday season events.

"Do you have any prayer needs?"

"Yes, sir, I do. My wife. This is our first deployment and I know it's going to be hard, but my main concern is the upcoming anniversary of her brother's death. He was killed in Iraq last year on December first, so it's going to be tough with me not there to support her.

"I'm sorry to hear about your brother-in-law, and I understand. What's your wife's name?"

"Genevieve."

"Let's have a seat over here." Chaplain Ford led Paul to a pew, and they sat down to pray.

After he left the chapel, he grabbed a bite to eat and headed to his shop, where he met some of his co-workers. He went into the office and saw a master sergeant sitting at the desk.

"Sir. Paul Thompson." Paul offered his hand.

"Matt Gibson. Nice to meet you, Sergeant Thompson." He shook Paul's hand.

"You, too, sir. Would it be okay if I called my wife to let her know I made it? The cybercafe was busy."

"Of course, just call...aw, you know how to do it." Master Sergeant Gibson chuckled.

"Yes, sir." Paul dialed Charleston Air Force Base and asked to be connected to Genny's number. His heart pounded as he waited. As the phone rang for the fifth time, he prepared himself to leave a voicemail. Exhaustion brought tears to his eyes. Before the sixth ring, Genny's groggy voice greeted him. "Paul?"

"Yes, it's me. You asleep already?"

"I worked a long shift today. I guess I fell asleep watching TV. Are you finally there?"

"Yeah, the plane landed a few hours ago, but I was just now able to call."

"I miss you." Her voice trembled.

"I miss you too, my love. I'll let you get ready for bed. I should have my internet hooked up in a few days. I can't wait until I can see your beautiful face. I love you."

"I love you, too. Hopefully, we can Skype next Saturday."

"Yes, hopefully. Goodnight, sweetheart."

"Goodnight."

Paul exhaled slowly. He made his way to his room to see if he could get some sleep. Before turning off the lamp, he pulled out his new journal and made his first entry.

November 13, 2011

My sweet Genevieve,

I am finally here. I miss you so much. My roommate seems nice, and I met the chaplain. I wish you could sit next to me at each chapel service. I cannot wait to have you in my arms again. I pray for you each time you cross my mind, which is often. I can't wait to Skype. I love you more than you will ever know.

Chapter 21

Genny stood on the front steps for a moment and walked to the Jeep. Paul had left for Qatar five days earlier. Since he'd called to let her know he made it, they'd emailed at least once a day, but with twelve-hour shifts six days a week, he said communication may be limited. They planned to Skype each Saturday, schedule permitting, and Genny couldn't wait to see his face, even if it was through a poor video connection.

Genny pulled into a parking space at The Roasted Bean and grabbed her backpack, slinging it over her shoulder.

"Hey, Gen," Julie said when Genny walked in the door. "What are you doing here?"

Genny smiled as she approached the counter. "I came to study. It's too quiet at home."

"Aww, how's Paul?"

"Busy. We're having our first Skype date this Saturday, and I can't wait." Warmth spread across her chest.

"I bet. Caramel Macchiato?"

"Yep." Genny claimed a table in the back corner and pulled out her study materials. Julie brought her coffee over and chatted for a few moments.

Genny stared at her notebook full of incorrect algebra problems. She'd worked and reworked several problems, but the answers always came out the same. They were the wrong answers, but at least she was consistent. Checking the time on her phone, she'd been working on the algebra problems for close to thirty minutes.

She propped her elbow on the table and rested her head on her hands. Closing her eyes, she rubbed her temple and forehead for a few minutes.

"Headache?"

She opened her eyes at the familiar voice. "Michael. Hey. I was taking a moment to clear these crazy algebra problems from my head." She laughed. "I'm studying for my upcoming CLEP test for college algebra. I can't bear another semester in a classroom. I failed the first time and had to drop out the second time when my brother died."

He smiled and stood quietly with his hand on the back of the empty chair across the table. Certainly, he wouldn't want to socialize when he saw her notebook, papers, and *Algebra for Dummies* book scattered across the table. Without asking, he pulled out the chair and sat down.

"Has Paul left yet?" He leaned forward and crossed his arms on the table.

A feeling of caution bubbled in Genny's stomach, but she let it go. "He left on the tenth." Soon, it would be obvious that Paul was gone, so there was no reason to lie. But why would she consider lying to begin with? Behind Michael's deep brown eyes, dimpled cheeks, and chiseled jaw, was a man she couldn't read.

"Hey, girl." Both Genny and Michael turned their heads. Bridget looked from Genny to Michael and shifted her weight.

"Oh, Michael. This is Bridget, one of my co-workers." Bridget pointed at her apron. "But you probably figured that out." Genny laughed.

"Nice to meet you, Michael." Bridget looked at Michael like a high school girl with a crush on the star football player.

"You, too."

To Genny's surprise, pink washed over Michael's cheeks. Maybe she overreacted about his intentions towards her. Bridget smiled and headed behind the counter.

Five minutes of small talk and it was obvious Michael didn't—or wouldn't—take the hint. Genny pulled her backpack off the chair and slipped her study materials inside.

"Are you working tomorrow?" Michael asked.

"No, I'll be studying." She smirked, but it didn't faze him.

"Walk you out?" He tilted his head towards the door and smiled.

Genny hesitated. "Sure." Michael opened the Jeep door after Genny pressed the remote. She climbed in and reached for the door handle, but he took a step forward, blocking her attempt. A feeling of panic flashed through her stomach.

"The holidays are coming up. Are you going to be at the Jeep club's Christmas party?"

"No. My in-laws have invited me to spend Christmas with them."

"Oh, I don't blame you. It's not fun being alone during the holidays." Michael cocked his head to the side and smiled. His gaze penetrated her personal space, forcing her to look away.

"I'm sorry, but I really need to get going."

Michael remained for a moment and stepped back. "No problem. Hope to see you soon." He pushed the door closed.

Genny backed out and made her way toward the exit. She glanced in the rearview mirror and saw Michael watching her until she drove around the building. Her stomach tightened once more.

As she drove, her mind wrestled with thoughts of Michael's unsolicited attention. She'd seen him at the beach three times, and today was his third time at The Roasted Bean. To be fair, their first encounter at the beach and The Roasted Bean didn't count. She didn't know him until meeting him at the beach, and the day he walked into The Roasted Bean was a coincidence.

At home, Genny sat on the couch and unpacked her backpack. With a cup of tea on the side table and eyes fixed on an algebra problem, a soft knock sounded at the door, thrusting her heart to her throat. Lucy barked and bolted off the couch. Genny's heart settled back down in her chest, and she walked over to the kitchen window and saw Mrs. Baker standing on the steps. She opened the front door with a smile on her face.

"Hi, Mrs. Baker. Come in."

"Thank you."

Genny led Mrs. Baker to the living room. "Would you like a cup of coffee or tea?"

"I'd love some tea if it's not too much trouble."

"No problem at all." Genny headed into the kitchen while Mrs. Baker sat on the couch. Lucy hopped up next to her and stared at her with her tongue hanging out of the side of her mouth. "Down, Lucy," Genny commanded when she walked back into the living room.

"She's okay, honey. Thank you." Mrs. Baker took the cup of tea from Genny's hand. "How's Paul?"

"He's keeping busy. We email back and forth, and we will have our first video call on Saturday."

"That's great. Technology has come a long way. No more waiting for letters." Mrs. Baker glanced at the coffee table.

"I'm taking a CLEP test for college algebra on December first.

"Good luck, honey."

"Thank you." They sat quietly for a few moments. Genny and Paul had gotten to know Mrs. Baker through conversations over the fence in the backyard. It was the third time she'd come over to visit.

"Do you have plans for Thanksgiving?" Mrs. Baker asked, her voice wavered.

"Actually, I don't. Are you spending it with your family?"

Mrs. Baker rubbed her hands together, and her gaze fell to the coffee table. "No, both Susan and Alan are busy with their spouse's families. Most of my friends are visiting with their families and I'd rather not spend the day with the ones who aren't."

Genny let out an unexpected laugh. Her eyes widened, and she held her hand over her mouth. "I'm so sorry." Mrs. Baker grinned and shook her head. "Why don't we have our own Thanksgiving dinner?"

"I would love that. We could have chicken instead of turkey, since it's the two of us."

"Sounds perfect." Genny straightened her algebra papers and book, shoving the stack to the side of the coffee table. As they visited, it became obvious that Mrs. Baker was lonely. Both of her children lived an hour away, yet Genny rarely saw them over for a visit. She decided then that she would adopt Mrs. Baker as her grandmother.

⇛⋙ ⋘⇚

Paul slipped into the back of the chapel for the Saturday evening service. It was his first opportunity to attend services since he'd been in the country for a week. The worship band was playing a praise song while he made his way down the aisle towards a free chair. He was surprised that so many people were attending service and was happy to see how God was working.

Before long, Paul realized that the service was a concert, but he didn't mind. The worship band played a variety of songs, from hymns to contemporary Christian. After the service was over, several people stood around and talked for a moment. Paul chose not to stay behind and made his way to the doors.

"Hello, Sergeant Thompson. I hope you enjoyed our concert tonight."

"Chaplain Ford." Paul reached out and they shook hands. "I did. I'll see you at the small group Wednesday night."

"Good, see you then." Chaplain Ford patted Paul on the back.

On the way to the dining hall, butterflies woke from their slumber as thoughts of Genny filled Paul's mind. Tonight was their first Skype date, and he couldn't wait to see Genny. Grabbing a ready-made to-go box from the sandwich section, he made his way to his room.

Paul sat at the desk and finished his dinner. As of now, Saturdays were his days off and he and Genny planned to Skype every Saturday at two in the afternoon east coast time. He had 'hit the ground running,' as the saying goes, when he arrived in Qatar after three days of travel. The long hours and time difference had extended the jet lag, but after six days in-country, he was finally falling into a routine.

"I'm heading out. See you in the morning," Damien said. He and Paul both worked night shift but had different days off.

"See you tomorrow." Paul dropped the carryout container in the trash can and chugged down a bottle of water. He stretched out on his bed with his laptop and counted down the minutes until his love's beautiful face graced the screen of his laptop. Butterflies danced a slow dance in his stomach when he saw Genny come online. He clicked the call button and drew in a breath as the familiar melody sounded off the walls of his room.

When Genny picked up, she was lying in bed propped up on all four pillows. Before he said a word, her chin trembled, and she burst into tears. "What's wrong, sweetheart?" If anything serious had happened, he would have heard by now.

"I miss you," she said and covered her face with her hands, sobbing.

Paul caught a glimpse of Lucy as she lay next to Genny. "I miss you, too." A lump formed in his throat. He sat quietly until Genny gained her composure.

"I'm sorry. I didn't know I was going to do that." She grabbed a tissue and wiped her face.

"It's perfectly fine, my love." Paul smiled and Genny managed a smile in return.

"Just as I've gotten used to being close to you, you're gone. I miss snuggling with you."

"I miss our snuggles, too." Paul winked. "Distraction helps. You can pick up a hobby."

"Maybe." She gave him a slight smile.

"Hey, at least you don't have to deal with my annoying documentaries." He smiled.

Genny smiled and shook her head. "I'd gladly suffer to have you by my side." Paul watched Genny stroke Lucy's back. "How was the chapel service?"

"Tonight, the praise and worship team put on a concert. It was nice. I like that there are several services throughout the week. It helps with everyone working crazy shifts.

"That's awesome. I'm glad you enjoyed the concert."

"Chaplain Ford runs the Saturday evening chapel. I met him the day I arrived. He's a nice guy."

"I'm so happy."

They were quite a moment; gazing into each other's eyes.

"How's the studying going? Do you still think it will be okay for you to test on the first since it's the first anniversary of Brandon...?"

"Yeah, it'll be fine. I think it will help distract me."

"Okay."

"Oh! Mrs. Baker and I are spending Thanksgiving together. Her family has plans and so do her friends. She came over the other day. We had a nice visit." She smiled.

"I think that's wonderful. She's a sweet lady."

"Yes, she is."

They fixed their gaze on each other. Genny's chin trembled. She pulled another tissue from the box next to her. "I want you to hold me. I wish I could reach through the screen." Tears flowed down her cheeks, and she blotted them away with the tissue.

"Me too, Genevieve." Tears stung Paul's eyes. "I love you."

"I love you, too." Genny glanced at the bottom of the screen.

"Do you need to get ready for work?"

"Unfortunately."

"Okay, my love. I'll see you next Saturday, but I'll email you as soon as we hang up.

"Okay." Genny smiled and blew him a kiss.

She would be emotional, but he was caught off guard by her outburst at then beginning of the call. It worried him. He sent her a quick email, then closed his laptop. Picking up his Bible and journal, he settled back and wrote an entry in the deployment journal.

November 19, 2011

My sweet love,

Seeing your pain today broke my heart. I wish someone else could have gone in my place, but unfortunately, that's not how it works. I can't wait to hold you in my arms again. I miss you so much. I've been busy with long shifts, but when I get back to my room and try to get some sleep, my thoughts of you keep my mind too active. Like you said today, it doesn't seem fair that the deployment happened so soon, but then again, if we hadn't discovered our love for each other before I left, we would have gone six months without knowing how we feel about each other. That's probably the one positive from this deployment. I love you, my sweet Genevieve.

⇝⇝ ⇜⇜

At work, Genny stood in a bathroom stall with her hands over her mouth. After a few moments of silent sobs, she tore off a strip of toilet paper and blotted her eyes. The bathroom door creaked open, and Genny held her breath.

"Genny?" Renee called out. "Are you okay?"

She slid back the lock and walked out of the stall. "I talked with Paul on video for the first time right before I left for work, and seeing his face reminded me of how much I miss him." She took in a sharp breath and exhaled.

"You can go home, if you'd like."

"No, I think it would make it worse. You know. Being by myself."

"Okay, well, take a few minutes and splash some cool water on your face. If you can't handle the front and don't feel like going home, you can help me in the office."

"Really?"

"Sure. I'm prepping the supply orders for the season. Oh, that's right. You haven't experienced the holidays yet. Hold on to your hat!" Renee laughed.

Genny followed Renee through the front to the back office. Julie patted her on the back and whispered words of encouragement. Genny didn't step inside Renee's office often, but she couldn't help but gasp when she saw the papers spread over every surface.

"See what I mean?" Renee grabbed a haphazard stack of papers and handed them to Genny. "You can separate these by product types. Like baked goods and mugs for the shelves by the register."

"Sure." Genny grabbed the stack and began separating the orders.

"Hey," Julie said, poking her head in the door.

Genny flinched and held her hand on her chest.

"Sorry. That guy is in the drive thru."

"What guy?" Genny's brows came together.

"The one that comes in all the time that drives a Jeep like yours."

Genny's stomach tightened. Michael had been in four days earlier. She was overeating. He probably lived close by and liked their coffee better than the big chains. No need to worry.

"Did he ask about me?" Genny laid the stack of order forms on Renee's desk.

"No, but it looked like he was trying to look around through the window. Bridget is drooling all over him. Does he have the hots for you or something? I only see him come in when you're here."

"I'd like to say no, but I have to admit, it's kind of weird." Genny had tried to avoid thinking about Michael's attention in the past, but when he came in, he approached her as opposed to her co-workers.

"He better be glad he hasn't had a run-in with Paul."

"He met Paul at the beach one day." Genny wrapped a lock of hair around her finger, then tucked it behind her ear.

"Oh?"

"Yeah, and he seemed, I don't know, intimidated is a good word I guess." Genny picked up the stack of order forms again.

"He should be. I'll go see if he's gone."

"Okay." Genny finished separating the orders and focused her attention on her wedding band. She pulled it up to her knuckle and pushed it back down. "I wish you were here, my love," she whispered. Now that Paul was thousands of miles away, she wouldn't bother him with her suspicions. She had a tendency of overreacting, as evident by her past jealousy, and she was overreacting to Michael's attention.

Opening the driver's door, Genny tossed her apron and purse onto the passenger seat and climbed into the Jeep. She did what Paul had reminded her to do—immediately lock the doors. The parking lot was sparsely occupied in late evening. Her schedule had recently changed to three o'clock until nine o'clock. She didn't mind since she wasn't much of a morning person.

The Roasted Bean was perched on top of a slight hill in front of a small shopping center. Before backing out, Genny quickly scanned both parking lots. Easygoing most of the time, she'd found herself paranoid lately. How many times in the past few months had she told herself she was overreacting about Michael's attention?

As she exited the parking lot and made her way home, she checked the mirrors for Michael's Jeep. If what Julie said was true, Michael only came in when he saw her Jeep in the parking lot. Genny shuddered at the idea of Michael following her home. That was far-fetched, even for Michael. At least that was what she had convinced herself.

Chapter 22

The line at the dining facility featured the traditional Thanksgiving entrees, side dishes, and desserts. Paul grabbed a tray and made his way down the line, ordering a variety of food. By the time he made it to the dining room, he was performing a balancing act to keep everything on the tray.

"Sergeant Thompson."

Paul looked toward the sound of the voice and saw Chaplain Ford waving. He headed to the table where several others were sitting and took the seat across from Chaplain Ford. "How are you, Chaplain?"

"Full." He laughed and patted his stomach.

"I soon will be." Paul grinned.

"How's your wife?" Chaplain Ford cut a piece off a slice of ham.

"Well...she's doing the best she can. We Skyped this past Saturday. She was a mess, unfortunately."

"I hate to hear that."

Paul slowly nodded and took a bite of turkey and washed it down with sweet tea. "I wish I could be with her. A week until the anniversary of her brother's death. She has a college test on that day, and she believes it is a good distraction. I sure hope so."

"It's tough to lose a sibling."

"He's not the only one she's lost. Her parents died when she was a child and both her grandparents passed away over the years."

"Oh, my goodness. That's hard. But God is walking beside her."

"Yes, He is." Paul spooned off a section of pumpkin pie and slipped it into his mouth.

After finishing their meals, the men talked for a while before going their separate ways. Walking towards the dorms in the warm evening air, Paul would never get used to the difference in climate on the other side of the world. Summer temperatures in November were odd. He headed up the stairs to his room to get ready for his shift. Picking up his deployment journal, he wrote the entry for the day.

November 24, 2011

Today is Thanksgiving and I wish we were together. I'm thankful for you, my love. So thankful. I don't know what I would do without you. These past few weeks have been some of the hardest weeks of my life. I promise you that next Thanksgiving will be different because we will be together.

I pray for you constantly. I hate I had to leave you alone, but we will make it through this. Too bad you can't come for a visit. I love you so much and I can't wait to hold you in my arms again.

Armed with an oven mitt on each hand, Genny was ready to pull the dinner rolls from the oven when the timer buzzed. A billow of heat mixed with the smell of fresh-baked bread teased her senses when she opened the oven door.

"On my goodness, this smells heavenly."

"I've been making dinner rolls for as long as I can remember. No store bought here." Mrs. Baker smiled.

"I'm glad." Genny laughed.

Mrs. Baker handed a dish of melted butter and a pastry brush to Genny. She gingerly brushed butter over the top of the rolls and arranged them on a serving platter. Mrs. Baker followed Genny to the dining room and sat at the head of the table as Genny placed the platter of rolls on the table. Genny joined Mrs. Baker at the table.

"Before Stanley passed, we had a tradition of going around the table and saying what we are thankful for throughout the year." Mrs. Baker cleared her throat and rearranged the napkin on her lap.

"We did that. Would you like to?"

"If you don't mind."

"I'd love to, Mrs. Baker. I'll go first if that's okay." Mrs. Baker nodded. "I'm thankful for the love of the Lord, my wonderful husband, and for you, Mrs. Baker." She reached over and patted Mrs. Baker's hand.

"I'm thankful for you, too. And Paul, of course. I'm thankful for my Savior and my children and grandchildren."

Mrs. Baker's eyes glistened, and Genny heard the sorrow in her voice. Genny had met her daughter once but had never met her son. She fought her burgeoning anger. People were busy with their own lives, she understood, but Mrs. Baker was their mother.

An idea came to Genny, and she hoped Mrs. Baker would agree. "Mrs. Baker?" Genny attempted to contain her excitement.

"Yes, honey?"

"When do you usually put up your Christmas tree? I don't know if I'm going to put one up since I'll be spending Christmas with my in-laws. I thought if you put up a tree, I could help you decorate. No pressure, though."

"I would love that. We can put it up tonight if that's okay with you."

"Yes! I love decorating." Genny bubbled with excitement.

Bing Crosby's "White Christmas" played as Genny and Mrs. Baker put the finishing touches on the four-foot tree. Taking a step back, they inspected their work. Genny turned toward Mrs. Baker and grinned.

"Another cup of hot cocoa?" Mrs. Baker asked.

Genny contemplated for a moment. She was tired but loved spending time with Mrs. Baker. "Sounds good."

"Great, I'll put on the milk." Mrs. Baker followed Genny to the kitchen and grabbed the milk from the fridge. The more time Genny spent with Mrs. Baker, the more she reminded her of her own grandmother.

After they finished their cocoa, Genny headed home. She waddled down the hall, straight to the bathroom. Shuffling around in the drawer, Genny found the bottle of antacid tablets. She'd eaten too much, as usual. Something she'd done since she was a child. Reclining on the bed with her laptop, she opened her email and saw a new email from Paul. She sighed, squeezed her eyes shut, and wiped the tears that trickled down her cheeks.

Happy Thanksgiving, my love. I'm so sorry but I won't be able to call. Three planes are coming in and I'll be on the flight line for most of my shift. I will see you on Saturday, two days away. I love you so much.

Closing the laptop, she slipped it under the edge of the bed and slid down under the covers. Since Paul had deployed, she felt as if she was climbing a wall desperate to get to him, but the wall was under construction. Every time she reached the top, a new layer of bricks was laid.

Genny hadn't written in her personal journal in a while and decided to write in both journals.

November 24, 2011

My dearest husband,

I'm so sad that we didn't get to talk today. I was looking forward to hearing your voice tonight, but I understand you are busy with work. Thanksgiving with Mrs. Baker was the best. She taught me how to make some of her side dishes and desserts. We ended up decorating her Christmas tree as we listened to classic Christmas songs and drank hot chocolate. I love spending time with her. I love you so much. I can't wait to feel your strong arms around me and your lips against mine. Yes, my cheeks are turning pink. Haha.

Genny closed the deployment journal and pulled out her personal journal.

November 24, 2011

Sometimes I hate the military. Supposedly, they care about family, but the military always comes first. Paul's been in eleven years now, but we haven't talked about his career goals. He mentioned finishing his accounting degree, but I don't know when that will happen. I am so afraid he will want to stay for twenty years. I wonder how many more deployments will interrupt our lives.

⇢⇢⇢ ⇠⇠⇠

Genny sat at a computer the testing proctor had assigned for the algebra CLEP exam. She held her breath and glanced around the room, then pressed her fist into her abdomen. An hour before her alarm was set, she woke up with severe abdominal pain that extended down her legs. The pain had been getting worse over the past few months, but she had never experienced such severe pain. Since her medication caused drowsiness, she had taken acetaminophen, but it might as well have been a sugar pill.

After the proctor gave her the go-ahead, Genny said a quick prayer and began scribbling down algebra problems. Thirty minutes later, she leaned back in the chair and winced. The rest of the answers were chosen at random in between deep breaths. She submitted the test and left the room with tears streaming down her cheeks. She accepted she had failed the test and she hurt so badly she wanted to curl into a ball and die. It was time to make an appointment with Dr. Nichols.

On the way home, she realized not once had Brandon crossed her mind. What kind of sister was she? She had gone through the worst year of her life due to Brandon's death, and she didn't remember the day that started it all. At a stoplight, she reached to the back of her neck and plucked out a few hairs. "Please, Lord," she whispered. She'd had the impulse under control until now.

Crawling into bed, Genny pulled the covers over her head and cried. The mattress sagged slightly as Lucy jumped up on the bed. Genny heard Lucy's loud sniffing by her head and flung the covers back. Lucy laid down next to her and Genny caressed her side. She and Lizbeth had talked about the benefits of having a pet to regulate emotions. Lucy proved perfect for the job.

Genny's eyes flew open when she was startled by her ringtone. The screen showed an unknown number, but she knew exactly who was on the other end. "Paul?"

"Hey, sweetheart. How are you?"

She clenched her teeth for a quick moment to stifle a sob. "Sad."

"I know. I wish I was there to hold you."

"Me, too. I forgot it was the anniversary until I was on my way home from taking my test, which I probably failed."

"Why's that?"

"Endometriosis." Genny squeezed her eyes shut.

"Did you make an appointment?"

"Yeah, it's on the fourteenth." Genny blew out her breath. She was still a little drowsy from the medication she took after she got home.

Paul would end the call so she could get some rest if she told him and kept it to herself. "I don't think I'm going to do anything to celebrate today. It's weird to celebrate someone's death."

"It's not really celebrating his death, but more of a remembrance. But if you don't feel comfortable doing anything special, then don't. Okay, sweetheart?" Genny heard the concern in his voice.

"Okay." She wrapped a lock of hair around her finger and tugged. Releasing the hair, she stroked Lucy's side for a moment. Like Lizbeth said, she was stronger than she imagined.

"I love you, Genevieve."

"I love you, too."

Genny laid her phone on the nightstand, then opened the drawer and picked up Brandon's picture. She had learned about the stages of grief in counseling. She'd been angry, depressed, and in denial, but she was unsure she'd make it through the last stage—acceptance. There was nothing about Brandon's death she could accept.

December 1, 2011

I forgot that today is the first anniversary of Brandon's death. How could I forget that? There are times that I feel like it's all been a dream and I'll wake up in Fayetteville on the morning that Brandon's flight is arriving. But if that was my reality, Paul and I wouldn't be together, and I don't know if I'm willing to sacrifice our relationship to have Brandon back. I know that sounds heartless, but it's how I feel. I love Paul that much.

I miss Paul so much. I feel like he's never coming home, and he's only been gone for three weeks. Six months is going to last forever. It's weird. The last time I was alone like this was when Brandon was deployed.

Paul had made more trips to the shop than usual during his shift. He checked his email every fifteen minutes or so for news from Genny. Her appointment with Dr. Nichols was at three, east coast time. It was now close to four-thirty, and he had yet to hear from her. He walked into the shop and saw Master Sergeant Gibson raise a brow.

"Back again?"

"Yes, sir. My wife has a doctor's appointment today and I'm waiting to hear from her."

"Oh. I hope everything is okay."

"Thank you, sir." Relieved that Master Sergeant Gibson didn't react negatively, Paul pulled up his email. An email from Genny was waiting for him. He held his breath and clicked to read.

It's not good news. He said I need a hysterectomy. I'm sorry.

Paul's mouth went dry. "Sir, is it okay if I call my wife? I'll be quick."

"Is it bad news?" Master Sergeant Gibson sat straight in his chair.

"It seems that way."

"Go ahead." Master Sergeant Gibson left the room and Paul was thankful. The conversation would be difficult. The operator at Charleston Air Force Base connected Paul to Genny's number. A knot formed in his throat as he counted the rings.

"Paul?" She asked.

"Yes, my love. What did the doctor say?"

Genny took a deep breath and exhaled. "It's between stage three and stage four. Stage four is the worst. And now I have PCOS, which is cysts on my ovaries. He said that's why I've gained weight, especially in my belly. There's lots of scarring and one ovary is adhered to my uterus and the other is covered in cysts."

The shop door opened, and Paul saw a young airman step over the threshold. Master Sergeant Gibson mumbled something, and the airman stepped back, closing the door behind him. It wasn't the first time that he saw the compassionate side of Master Sergeant Gibson.

"He thinks you need a hysterectomy?" Paul steadied his voice. Genny was emotional and he was afraid she would break down.

"Yes, to alleviate the pain, and he feels I probably can't carry a baby, anyway. Paul, I'm so sorry."

"Why are you apologizing?"

"I want to give you a baby." Genny sobbed.

"Oh, sweetheart." He would love to have a baby with Genny, but if she couldn't bear children, they would find another way to be parents. "Did he say when you would need a hysterectomy?"

"He feels it can wait until you get home, but not much longer." Genny sniffed.

"We'll talk about it when I'm home. Please don't let it upset you, okay?"

"Okay," her voice was above a whisper.

"I need to get back to work. Let's say a prayer." Paul prayed for God to comfort Genny and to clear her mind of her fears.

He propped his elbows on the desk and rested his head in his hands. Tears burned his eyes. He wanted to hold and comfort Genny. All his previous deployments had gone smoothly. This deployment was different. Genny was already dealing with a lot. Between grief, taking care of the household, and working, she had a full plate. Now with a new diagnosis and upcoming hysterectomy, it was enough to suffer a setback.

The door creaked open, and Paul raised his head. Master Sergeant Gibson walked in and sat at the desk next to him. Paul rubbed his eyes and sighed.

"Is everything all right?"

"She needs a hysterectomy." Paul sighed.

"I'm sorry to hear that."

"Thank you. I know we will be parents one day, but I understand why she's upset."

"It's hard. My wife had a hysterectomy before we met. She was twenty, which is very young. She had cancer."

"That is young."

"When I was a recruiter in San Antonio, we adopted our three kids through foster care. They are siblings—two boys and a girl."

"Really? I didn't know that was an option."

"Yeah. It's not for everyone, but if you two find yourselves headed toward adoption, I encourage you to look into foster to adopt."

"I'll keep that in mind. Well, sir, it's time for me to get back to work."

Master Sergeant Gibson patted Paul on the back and stood. Paul headed back out to the flight line and spent the rest of his shift thinking about Genny. He wiped an errant tear from his cheek and went back to checking flight manifests.

After a shower, he laid on his bed with his personal journal. He was consumed with thoughts of Genny and guilt from his past.

December 14, 2011

It was difficult to hear Genny's grief tonight. We knew this was a possibility, but now it's a reality. I don't know how I'm going to tell her about Staci. It will cause her tremendous pain. I pray she can forgive me. All those years ago, I never thought about how my actions would affect my future wife. All I was concerned about was my own selfish desires.

Chapter 23

G enny sat in the front seat with Tricia as they drove through the old neighborhood. She hadn't been in Murfreesboro since her grandmother's funeral. The house her grandparents had once owned came into view as Tricia slowed to turn into their driveway. When Genny stepped out of the car, she looked at her childhood home next door with tears pooled in her eyes.

"The neighbors are good people. I'll introduce you before you leave."

"Okay." She smiled, but her heart was hurting.

Genny pulled her small suitcase off the backseat and followed Tricia inside. She showed Genny to the guest room, which used to be Paul's room. After spending a few moments unpacking, she took her toiletries to the bathroom and returned to the bedroom. She sat on the bed and looked around. She hadn't seen the inside of the room since she was eight. Once Paul and Brandon turned thirteen, she was no longer allowed in Paul's bedroom. She was too young, according to Paul. Now she would sleep in his old bed.

Standing in front of the enormous Christmas tree, Genny spent a few minutes examining all of Paul's handmade decorations from his childhood that reached all the way to the top.

"It's twelve feet," Tricia said as she walked into the living room.

"Wow. It fits perfectly in the cathedral ceiling."

"That's Brian's doing." Tricia laughed. "You should see him on the ladder stretching to put the angel on top. My nerves are so frazzled that I have to stay in the kitchen with my phone in my hand in case he falls." Trisha shook her head. "We bought this tree not long after Paul left home."

"Oh, yeah?"

"The child leaves and the parents go all out." She laughed.

Genny grinned. "It's beautiful." The flocked tree had at least four strings of blue lights laying across the branches.

"Coffee?"

"Yes, thanks." Genny walked around the room looking at the photos on display. Even as a newborn, Paul was beautiful. All his school photos were displayed in order, and he seemed to grow before her eyes. Making her way toward the fireplace, she saw Brian and Tricia's wedding photo on the mantel. If she didn't know better, she would think that Paul was the man in the picture. It amazed her how much Paul looked like his father.

"Ready?"

Genny turned around and saw Tricia holding two cups of coffee. "Yep."

"There is a tray of sugar and some of those little individual creamers in the sunroom."

"Okay." Genny took one cup from Tricia and followed her to the sunroom. She eased down on the oversized chair and added creamer and sugar to her cup.

They spent some time catching up. Genny assumed Paul had told his parents about their fertility challenges, but Tricia hadn't brought it up. Maybe she was waiting for Genny.

"Is everything alright, honey?"

Genny realized that she'd been staring into her coffee cup. "Well...did Paul tell you about my doctor appointment?"

"No, he didn't."

"Oh. Um, my doctor says I need a hysterectomy. I've been having pretty severe pain more frequently and he says my uterus is too scarred to carry a baby."

"Oh, honey. I'm sorry. I know it's hard since you two are so young. Have you considered adoption?"

At the mention of adoption, Genny broke down.

"I'm so sorry. I didn't mean—"

"It's okay. A hysterectomy is so final, you know?" She wiped tears from her cheeks.

"I know. I had one after Paul was born. He was our only baby, but there were times I felt the pull for another child. But it wasn't meant to be." Tricia took a sip of coffee. "I want you to know that we will love and spoil any grandchild you give us. It doesn't matter if the child comes from you two or through an adoption agency."

Genny managed a faint smile.

Tricia reached over to pat Genny's knee. "Since we are having a serious conversation, there's something I've been wanting to talk to you about."

Genny's stomach twisted. Something serious? "Okay."

"Brian and I want to let you know that, if you feel comfortable, you can call us Mom and Dad. But only if you feel comfortable. We won't be mad if you choose not to."

Genny hadn't considered calling her in-laws Mom and Dad. She had gone all her life without calling anyone Mom or Dad as far as she could remember. "I would like that, but it might take me a little while to ease into it." Genny smiled and took a sip of coffee.

"We understand, honey."

The front door opened, and Brian walked inside. He noticed Genny and Tricia in the sunroom and walked straight to Genny. She gave him a hug when he leaned down.

"How was your flight?" he asked.

"Actually, it wasn't bad." Genny tugged on the hem of her shirt.

"Good." He walked over to Tricia and leaned down to give her a kiss. "I'm going to change."

"Okay, sweetheart." Tricia's phone rang. She excused herself and walked into the living room.

Genny turned around and looked out the windows. The Thompson's backyard had always looked like it could be featured in *Southern Living* magazine. Even in the winter, the yard was beautiful. Genny smiled at the memories of playing in the birdbath during the summer. Once, Tricia scolded Genny and sent her home. She feared Tricia after that, but here she was fifteen years later, sipping coffee in her house and married to her son. Tricia was a different person now, and so was Genny.

The next three days slipped by. Genny sat at the foot of the Christmas tree with Tricia. Brian walked over and placed his laptop on the coffee table with Skype up on the screen. All three stared at Paul's profile until he came online. The speakers sang the Skype melody and Genny clicked the answer icon.

"Hello, family!" Paul grinned.

"Hi, sweetheart," Tricia replied.

"Son," Brian said and smiled.

"There's my love." Paul winked at Genny.

Tricia talked about the Christmas Eve service the night before and what they had planned for the rest of the day. Paul wished his parents a Merry Christmas and asked to speak to his wife alone. Genny carried the laptop into Brian's office and sat on the sofa.

"I love you so much, baby," Paul said.

"I love you, too and miss you bunches. Christmas isn't the same without you here."

"I feel the same way. I wanted to talk to you alone to let you know you will get your present once I'm home. It's very special and I have to give it to you in person."

Genny raised her eyebrows. "Oh?" Usually, when Paul said he had a surprise, she'd start a guessing game, but not this time. It would drive her nuts until he came home, but she'd manage. "You'll have to wait for your present, too. Don't be caught off guard when I show up at the airport with a big red bow on my head."

"I couldn't ask for a better present." He winked.

Genny and Paul made plans to Skype the next weekend. Later, as Genny laid looking at the ceiling in Paul's old bedroom, she thought about the future. Soon, it would be 2012. Paul would be home in May and life would go back to normal. After the hysterectomy, that is. She sighed and closed her eyes.

Curiosity opened her eyes. Turning on the lamp, she pulled open the drawer of the nightstand and frowned. A tube of lip balm, a small jar of hand cream, a pen and pad of paper were the only items in the drawer. Climbing out of bed, she went to the closet and opened the door. A few boxes were stacked in the corner. Grabbing her phone, she used the light from the screen to read the labels. None of them referred to

Paul. She sighed, climbed back into bed, and closed her eyes. She should have known that Paul would have taken everything with him when he moved out. It would have been interesting to see personal belongings from his teenage years—the years he'd denied her entry into his private life.

Genny's flight was scheduled to leave Nashville at ten in the morning and land in Charleston a little before three in the afternoon. She'd already made plans for New Year's Eve. Lucy would lounge on the couch beside her as they rang in the new year, watching the ball drop in Times Square. Not much different from last New Year's Eve, except this year, she didn't wish she'd died along with Brandon.

Brian loaded Genny's bags into the car. Both he and Tricia insisted on driving Genny to the airport. They chatted about the new year and future visits. Tricia told stories of shy, little Genny Jones, causing Genny to giggle a time or two. Spending time with Brian and Tricia alone had strengthened her relationship with her in-laws. Genny enjoyed her visit and looked forward to future visits. She and Tricia could make plans for a girls' day out.

Parking in the short-term parking lot, Brian and Tricia walked Genny to the check-in and the three stood at the entrance for passengers. Genny's eyes burned, and she swallowed hard.

"I should find my gate. I loved spending Christmas with you two." She blinked back tears.

"We did too, sweetheart." Tricia wiped her eyes.

"Sure did." Brian smiled.

Genny hugged Brian and Tricia. Any intimidation she'd had for Paul's parents disappeared. She couldn't wait to see them again.

"We love you, Genny." Tricia wiped her eyes again.

"I love you too, Mom and Dad." She wiped the tears from her cheeks. Smiling, she waved and headed toward her gate.

Genny grabbed her shopping list and headed to the front door. Reaching for the Jeep keys, she changed her mind and grabbed the truck keys.

Paul had asked her to drive it at least once a week. He'd been gone for over a month and a half, and the truck hadn't moved since Paul left.

Slowly pushing her cart up and down the aisles, Genny checked items off her list as she went. She made her way to the pet area and heaved a large bag of dog food into the cart and headed to the checkout. As usual, she couldn't fight the temptation of a soda and a pack of candy at the checkout. Tossing a handful of candy in her mouth, she headed to the exit.

The sky had darkened, and a light drizzle turned into a downpour as Genny hurried to the truck. She managed to get the bag of dog food onto the back seat and quickly loaded the bags of groceries. After rolling the cart to the corral, she climbed into the truck and wiped the drops of rain off of her face.

Sliding the key into the ignition, she looked up and noticed a white piece of paper under the wiper on the driver's side. She wrinkled her brow, climbed down, and pulled it out from under the wiper. It was a note written on the back of a fast-food restaurant receipt. The rain had soaked the paper and caused the ink to run, but it was legible. Genny's jaw dropped as she read.

Paul,

I know you blocked me, but I need to talk to you. I can't stop thinking about you. Genny doesn't love you like I do and will never make you happy. Please call me so we can talk.

Love,

Brianna

She read the note again and gritted her teeth. Lowering the window, she wadded the note and threw it out into the rain. Gripping the steering wheel, her knuckles whitened, and her chest heaved with each breath. Brianna didn't know that Paul was deployed. By chance, Genny had driven the truck. She could imagine Brianna as she crept up to the truck, slid the note under the wiper, and slithered off like the snake she was.

A few minutes had passed before Genny calmed down. She glanced around and slid down from the driver's seat. The paper was under the rear of the car in the next parking space. She hurried and reached under the car, grabbed the note, and climbed back into the truck. Still fuming, on the way out of the parking lot, she punched the gas pedal, causing the rear of the truck to fishtail. After her pounding heart calmed, she drove home in a daze.

Once the groceries were put away, Genny sat on the couch staring at her phone. She'd typed the phone number at the bottom of the note into her phone repeatedly since she'd been home, but couldn't bring herself to tap the call icon. What would she say to Brianna? Whatever it was, it wouldn't be Christ-like. Saturday was New Year's Eve and her Skype date with Paul. She was tempted to keep the note to herself, but it would haunt her, and Paul would know that something was wrong.

December 29, 2011

I H.A.T.E. Brianna! I know we aren't supposed to hate, but why does she keep showing up? God must be testing me but why with her? Ugg. Paul would be mad at me if I didn't tell him, and he found out. Brianna's been thinking about Paul all this time? Great, now I'm not going to be able to sleep tonight.

The next afternoon, Genny was at work preparing drinks when she looked up and saw Michael walk in. Julie had said he hadn't been in during any of her shifts since they had talked about him in Renee's office weeks ago. That wasn't the actions of a man who was obsessed with her. Once again, Genny doubted her thoughts of Michael's behavior. If he was obsessed, he would have been in at least once a week.

A caramel macchiato was on the order slip Genny plucked from the printer and she knew who had ordered the drink. After filling a cup with the steaming hot liquid and milk, Genny sprayed a swirl of whipped cream on top and drizzled caramel sauce across the whipped cream. When she walked over to the pickup counter, she was greeted by Michael's charismatic smile.

"Hey, Genny. How have you been?"

"Good. Working all the time." She grinned. Maybe she shouldn't have. Michael might take it as interest.

"How's Paul?"

He always asked about Paul. Was it genuine? She honestly didn't know. "Good. Working a lot—twelve-hour shifts, six days a week." The printer spit out another order. "I need to get this." He nodded. Genny watched him walk over to a table close to the counter.

"I see your stalker came for a visit," Julie whispered and wiggled her eyebrows.

"Stop." Genny sighed and handed Julie a drink for a customer in the drive thru.

"Hey, me and Bridget are going to Freddy's tomorrow night. Why don't you come along? I bet you have no plans to ring in the new year," Julie said, raising her voice above the hiss of the coffee machines and the whirl of the blenders.

"I'll have you know I'll be partying it up with a friend."

"Lucy doesn't count. Come on, Gen."

"I need to talk to Paul about it."

"You don't need his permission." Julie jerked her head back.

Genny fought the heat filling her face. "It's not about permission; it's about respect. I'd be mad if he told me after the fact that he went out."

"I'd be worried about Paul going out, too. Not because of him, but there's too many s—"

"Julie," Genny chastised.

"Sorry."

Genny stepped out from behind the espresso machine to hand a customer her drink, but found Michael standing at the counter.

"Hey, can I get this to go?"

"Sure." Michael's fingers brushed against Genny's when she took the cup from his hand, raising the hairs on her arms. She poured the coffee into a to-go cup and handed it to Michael.

"Have a good one." He smiled and headed toward the door.

"You too, Michael." A feeling of vulnerability seeped into Genny's bones. There was something about how he looked at her. He had a way of invading her personal space with his gaze.

At the end of her shift, Genny headed out to the Jeep. She hit the remote and Chad, a co-worker, hurried and opened the door before she could get to the Jeep. "Thank you, Chad."

Chad was a high school student that had been working at the coffee shop for three weeks. After Genny had mentioned feeling nervous walking out to the Jeep at night, he had assigned himself as her protector and walked her out to the Jeep each time they worked together.

"You're welcome." He grinned and pushed the door closed.

Genny locked the doors and took a quick glance around the parking lot before she headed to the exit. As she sat at a stoplight waiting for the light to turn green, narrow headlights rolled to a stop behind her—the tell-tale sign of a Jeep. The light turned green, and she accelerated faster than usual. She watched the Jeep change lanes and drive up beside her. She maintained her focus ahead until the other driver honk the horn. Her heart jumped into her throat and every muscle in her body tensed. She slowly turned her head and could make out that the Jeep was lime green and recognized it as one that she'd seen at group meetings. She blew out her breath and waved.

At home, Genny sat on her bed with her laptop, staring at an email she'd written to Paul but had yet to send. Giving him a heads up about New Year's Eve was the right thing to do, but it would also give him time to weigh the pros and cons. He wouldn't tell her no, but he would probably tell her he'd prefer that she not go. She forced out a sigh. Part of her wanted to go, but most of her wanted to stay home. She let out a little laugh and deleted the draft email. She'd bring it up when they Skyped next.

Chapter 24

Paul headed to the shop from the flight line. Before he reached the shop door, he heard a variety of noisemakers ringing in the new year. To his surprise, when he walked in, he saw Master Sergeant Gibson with a blowout noise maker in his mouth. Master Sergeant Gibson was personable, but he also demanded respect which usually meant lower ranking airmen were intimidated by him. It was nice to see him letting his hair down.

Paul looked at his watch and calculated the time difference. It was a few minutes after five in the evening in Charleston. Pulling up his email account, he saw an email from Genny wishing him a happy new year. A kiss would start the new year off right. He sat up straight and glanced out the window at the flight line. Genny had told him about Julie inviting her to go to a club for New Year's Eve. The idea of some drunk man trying to kiss Genny at midnight hadn't crossed his mind. Closing his eyes, he said a prayer that God would put a hedge of protection around her.

The sun peeked over the horizon as Paul headed to the dorms with a to-go box for breakfast. He'd been in Qatar for almost two months and this morning was the first time that he'd thought about Brandon as he walked through the line at the dining facility. Guilt soon followed. As time progressed, Paul's thoughts of Brandon's death decreased, which was normal, but a year seemed too soon.

He unlocked the door to the room and sat his breakfast box on his bed. Damien was asleep, and he did his best to change clothes and eat as quietly as possible. After Paul ate his breakfast, he eased the box into the garbage can and picked up his laptop to use for light. He grabbed his journal from the nightstand and pulled out the index card with Brianna's phone number.

Since Genny had told him about Brianna when they'd Skyped earlier, he'd attempted to wrap his head around Brianna's reappearance. Why now? Holding the index card in his hand, he had considered calling Brianna but as Genny had admitted;Some dresses she he was afraid he'd lose his composure and say something he'd regret. Paul softly sighed. Was the enemy using Brianna to wage a war on their marriage?

⋙ ⋘

Genny arrived at the club a little before ten. Sitting in the Jeep, she second guessed her decision. She cranked the Jeep and shifted into reverse to go home. Sighing, she shifted back into park. She'd promised her friends she'd go and who knows? She might have a good time. Shutting off the engine, she climbed down and headed to the entrance. Some of the dresses she saw on her walk to the doors left nothing to the imagination. Genny chose a red loose-fitting dress that hit at the knee and flats instead of her usual wardrobe of jeans and a sweater.

"Hey Gen! You look hot, girl. What do you want to drink?" Julie asked, moving her hips to the beat of the music.

Hot? Genny looked down at her dress and rolled her eyes. "Coke."

"A Coke?" Julie giggled.

"Yes, a Coke."

Julie looked as if she'd already had two or three drinks.

"Where's Bridget?" Julie pointed to the dance floor. Genny grimaced when she saw Bridget sandwiched between two guys. Genny sighed. She'd made a mistake by agreeing to go to the club and should have stayed home. She looked at her watch. A little less than two hours until she could run out of the club like Cinderella running out of the castle.

If Julie wasn't attached to her side, Genny would gladly be a wallflower. Better yet, she'd be at home on the couch in her pajamas with Lucy by her side like she'd planned. But if she wasn't at the club, Julie wouldn't have anyone to hold her upright. Thank goodness Julie and Bridget had taken a cab.

Genny managed to get Julie to a free table and sat with her until a few minutes before midnight. To her surprise and annoyance, she had to fend off several admirers since she'd walked in the door. Why couldn't Paul be home? Not that he'd be in a club, but they would be on the couch ringing in the new year together.

Julie insisted they head to the dance floor for the countdown and was able to stand on both feet again. She grabbed Genny's hand and led the way. The dance floor was packed, and the crowd grew louder and more energetic as midnight approached. Someone's hand brushed against her thigh and Genny suspected it wasn't an accident. Midnight needed to hurry.

A large digital clock hung on the wall, and the crowd counted each second that passed. As the clock struck midnight, everyone in the crowd found someone to kiss. Genny looked at the floor as if she had dropped something to avoid a stranger's lips. Someone tapped her shoulder, but she maintained her focus on her shoes. Another tap piqued her curiosity. She turned around and saw Michael standing behind her. His eyes caressed her, spreading caution through her veins.

Music pushed through the speakers again, and everyone moved to the rhythm. Genny searched for Julie on the dance floor, but the crowd was too thick to see. Michael leaned in and suggested they dance, but Genny pretended she couldn't hear him over the thundering bass. She turned to push her way through the crowd, but Michael grabbed her hand. Pulling her back, her body bumped against his chest. Panic grabbed at her throat, and she jerked her hand free from his grip and pushed her way off the dance floor. Glancing over her shoulder, she saw Michael was a few steps away.

Julie and Bridget sat on stools at the bar. Julie gave Genny an odd look when Michael appeared from the crowd behind her.

"Well, hey there Michael. Mmm, you made my night. Let's go dance," Bridget said, slurring her words. Before he could get a word out, Bridget hopped off the barstool, slightly stumbling, and clung to him. Relieved, Genny headed for the door.

"Wait." Julie caught up with her and followed her outside. Her eyebrows came together. "What's he doing here?"

"I don't know." Genny drew in a breath of cool, fresh air. The cigarette smoke had burned her eyes and tightened her chest. Her heart leaped to her throat when a man that resembled Michael walked out the door.

"Genny..." Julie's voice held a tone of concern.

"I'm sure it's a coincidence. He probably lives nearby and comes here often." Genny barely believed her own words. Maybe he did and maybe he didn't. If it was the latter... She didn't want to think about it. "I'm going to head home."

"Are you sure?"

"Yeah." Genny crossed her arms over her middle and shivered in the cool night air.

"Goodnight." Julie hugged her and headed back inside.

Genny climbed into the Jeep and sat for a few minutes. Cranking the engine, she backed out of the parking space. When she drove toward the exit, she saw Michael sitting in his Jeep and she shuddered. He must have broken away from Bridget and left the building a few minutes after she did. Pulling out of the parking lot, her heart pounded when he pulled out behind her. It was probably his route home, too. Just in case, Genny quickly turned onto a side road, hoping he didn't follow her. When no one was behind her, she drove back to the main road and made her way home.

After a shower, she had finally rid herself of the smell of cigarettes. She sat on her bed and opened her journal.

January 1, 2012

Michael showed up at the club. How did he know we were there? Is he stalking me? What kind of behavior is considered stalking? I have no idea. I haven't been to a Jeep club meeting or get-together in a long time, so maybe he wants to see how I'm doing since Paul left. He's nice and never inappropriate when he sees me, except for tonight. He acts like he is interested in me romantically. Maybe I'm seeing things that aren't there. I don't know. I'm clueless about people's intentions. I can't wait until May when Paul's back home and I don't have to worry about all this.

Genny picked up her phone. It was almost two in the morning. She turned off the lamp and laid back against the pillows, pulling the covers up to her neck. Michael probably lived down the road from Freddy's and was a regular there. Heat settled in Genny's shoulders when she remembered Michael was at The Roasted Bean when she and Julie talked about going to the club. It might not be a coincidence after all. There was no need to upset Paul since he could do nothing about it from seven thousand miles away.

⟫⟫⟫ ⟪⟪⟪

Paul closed his laptop and laid it on the desk next to his bed. Genny didn't seem like herself. Everything had been fine; she had told him. She and the women from work had a good time ringing in the new year last weekend and she seemed excited when she showed him the brochure she'd picked up at the college when she'd talked to an advisor. But Paul had known Genny long enough to know something was off.

Glancing at his watch, he sighed and changed into his sweatpants. One good thing about a deployment, everything was open twenty-four hours a day, seven days a week. As he headed to the rec center, the conversation with Genny played in his head. She'd worked an early morning shift due to a scheduling error. Never a morning person, he understood Genny was tired, but some things she couldn't blame on exhaustion.

The smell of fresh-brewed coffee and baking cookies hit Paul when he pulled open the door to the rec center. To his surprise, there were a good many people inside. He walked up to the counter of the coffee shop and ordered a coffee and two cookies once they came out of the oven. As he looked around the room for a free table, he heard someone call his name. Damien was sitting at a table by himself and waved him over.

"Hey, brother. What are you doing here?"

"It's my dinner break." Damien raised his coffee cup and pointed to a half-eaten scone.

"Dinner of champions." Paul grinned.

The men sat quietly for a few moments, sipping their coffee. Damien seemed withdrawn, but it wasn't the time or place to say anything.

"I never thought to ask. How long have you and Genny been married?"

213

"It will be a year on Valentine's Day."

"Way to go, my man." Damien held up his hand for a high-five. "You'll never forget your anniversary."

"That's what I told her." A woman walked up to the table and handed Paul a pastry bag with two warm chocolate chip cookies inside. He pulled out a cookie and took a bite.

"Aren't you going to pray?"

"Huh?" Paul wrinkled his brow.

"Don't Christians pray before they eat?"

"Well, at meals, but not for a snack. I suppose someone out there may pray over everything they put in their mouth, but most don't."

"What about a piece of gum?" Damien grinned and pulled a pack of gum from the pocket of his uniform pants.

Paul laughed. "Maybe." He didn't take Damien's question as sarcasm, but as an honest question that was cloaked in humor. They had been roommates for three months, and Damien had never asked him about his faith. Paul had a few faith-based items displayed in their room and listened to Christian music. But God could use anything or anyone to draw someone close to him, including a piece of gum.

"Have you always been a Christian?" Damien asked.

"I grew up in church. I gave my life to Christ when I was ten, but made some poor choices in my early twenties. Because of one of those choices, I rededicated my life to Christ. I even got a tattoo." Damien glanced at Paul's arms. "It's on my back and pretty big."

"Oh, yeah?" Damien drank the rest of his coffee and popped the remainder of his scone into his mouth.

"It's about a foot and a half long and a foot wide."

"Wow, man. You weren't kidding."

"I call it my walking testimony."

Damien slowly nodded. "I've got to run. A plane is coming in soon and I've got to run maintenance." He pushed his chair back and stood.

"All right. Enjoy the rest of your shift."

"And you enjoy your evening." Damien smiled and walked away, stopping at the garbage can to throw away his trash. He turned and looked at Paul, then headed to the door.

On the way back to his room, Paul's thoughts centered on Damien's expression. He appeared lost. Damien had been in the room while Paul studied his Bible and had walked in on his prayer time more than once. He was always respectful, but Paul couldn't help but feel Damien was searching.

Changing back into his shorts, Paul pulled out his journals and made entries for the day.

January 7, 2012

My love,

I love you so much. I want you to know that you can talk to me about anything. If you are sad, scared, upset, or annoyed, I'm here for you. I can't wait to wake up beside you. I miss you so much it hurts.

He closed the deployment journal and opened his personal journal. He closed his eyes and opened them.

January 7, 2012

Father, I pray that you use me to reach Damien. I feel he is seeking the truth and I know I'm in the perfect position to bring Your truth into his life. Please give me wisdom to know what to say and when, and open Damien's heart to hear Your words through me.

⇒⇒⇒ ⇐⇐⇐

Genny sat on the couch with her sociology book and notebook spread out on the coffee table. Sociology was her only class for the semester. Algebra was finally behind her when she passed the CLEP test. She was shocked, since she had chosen answers at random. Easing back into school was her advisor's suggestion, and she had reluctantly agreed. If she had stuck with her initial plan after she had graduated from high school, she would already be a teacher. But instead of going to college, she had developed a wild streak and derailed her plans. Now that it was the end of January and she was into her second week of college, she understood why her advisor suggested taking it slow.

While reviewing the answers in the back of the book, Genny's phone rang. She picked it up and saw Melissa's name on the screen. They'd texted several times a week, but she hadn't talked to her in three weeks, and it had been longer since she last saw her.

"Hey, girl."

Peter laughed. "Just calling to let you know that Asher Philip Parker came into the world at six twenty-eight this evening. He weighs six pounds and two ounces and is twenty inches long. Both he and Melissa are doing great."

Genny looked at the mantel clock. Asher was born less than an hour ago. Melissa wanted her to be one of the first people to know. "Oh, my goodness! Congratulations!"

"We should be home mid-morning tomorrow, and Melissa wants you to come over in the afternoon."

"So soon?"

"Yep, you know Melissa."

"Okay. I'll text before I come over." A sweet, soft cry sounded in the background. She was truly happy for her friends, but why did she still feel the sting of jealousy?

After a sleepless night, Genny pulled up to the drive-thru window at The Roasted Bean and was greeted by Julie's perky disposition.

"Girl, I have never seen you get a large double shot, and by the way, you look terrible."

"Hence the large double shot. I didn't sleep well last night." Genny held her hand over her mouth as she yawned.

"What's up?"

"Oh, it happens from time to time since Paul left."

"Gen, I'd have sleepless nights too if that sexy man wasn't sleeping beside me."

Genny rolled her eyes and took the cup from Julie with both hands. "So much for an afternoon nap." The sleepless night had nothing to do with Paul and everything to do with the baby. She hadn't held a baby in years, and she was afraid of how she would react with a hysterectomy looming over her.

Julie laughed. "Bye, girl."

On the way to Peter and Melissa's, Genny came up with reasons she shouldn't visit. She woke with a sore throat and didn't want the baby to get sick. Or maybe she had an upset stomach. Ridiculous thoughts. Her friends wanted her to meet their new baby and she shouldn't deny their wishes.

Sitting on the couch waiting for Melissa to bring the baby from the nursery, Genny noted all the baby items and gadgets around the living room. Why did babies need so much stuff? She saw the portable crib that she and Paul bought in the corner. The day of the baby shower, Genny had stopped by to drop off the crib on her way to work. Earlier in the week, she had volunteered to take a shift for a co-worker who wanted to go out of town last minute. That shift was the day of the shower.

Dread had plagued her for weeks before the shower. Ashamed, she knew Melissa would be disappointed, but Genny was not in a place emotionally where she could sit for two hours listening to women gush about their pregnancies and babies.

The front door opened, and Peter walked into the foyer with plastic shopping bags hanging from his arms. Genny heard Melissa's slippers scrape the hardwood floor as she walked into the living room.

"Here, let me help you." Genny sprang to her feet. She met Peter, taking the bags off one of his arms. She noticed the hurt flash across Melissa's face.

Peter thanked Genny and assured her he could put the groceries away. Genny eased down on the couch and raised her arms when Melissa leaned down.

"Have you held a baby before? You're shaking," Melissa said.

"It's been a while." Genny let out a soft laugh that she hoped hid her uneasiness.

"You'll do fine."

Asher was a beautiful baby. Wisps of light blonde hair the color of Peter's covered his head, and his lips were the shape of Melissa's lips. The babies Genny had watched in the church nursery when she was in her early teens were usually swaddled in a blanket, but Asher's blanket was loose and Genny glimpsed his slender legs. He opened his eyes and looked at her. Amazed, Genny watched Asher's mouth move as if he were sucking a bottle.

"I think he's hungry. He's sucking. Do you have a bottle?" Genny wrinkled her brow when Melissa looked at Peter and giggled. "What?"

"I nurse him."

"Oh." Genny's face flushed with heat. Why? It was perfectly natural for a mother to breastfeed.

"He ate not long ago. The sucking motion is a natural reflex. You can hold him for a while if you want."

Genny looked down at Asher and bit the inside of her cheek.

"Hey, I'm going to work on getting the garage organized," Peter said and walked out the front door.

Melissa shook her head. "He was supposed to do it weeks ago so I could get the van in the garage."

Genny looked at Melissa and smiled. Asher made a soft noise, and she looked down at him. His movements amazed Genny. She'd imagined him laying still and quiet, but he wasn't a doll. She ran her finger over his soft, new skin. As she gazed at his pudgy cheeks, a dull pain swelled in her lower abdomen. The precious new life she held in her arms was a sudden reminder of the baby she could never give Paul. The avalanche of tears she'd been holding back surfaced.

"Genny, are you okay?" Melissa scooted to the edge of her seat.

Genny held Asher out and Melissa walked over to take him in her arms. "I have to have a hysterectomy."

"Oh, honey. I'm sorry." Melissa laid Asher in his bassinet and sat down on the couch next to Genny. "I will not say the standard reply. You already know what your options are."

Genny looked at her.

"I will be here for you if you ever need to talk. I can sit here and be silent for hours while you talk. Ask Peter." Melissa grinned.

Genny smiled. "Thanks. It means a lot. Paul said from the beginning that we can adopt but, I don't know, I want to have a biological child with him. Is that so bad?"

"Not at all." Melissa leaned over and gave Genny a tight hug.

Genny stayed for a cup of coffee. By the time she left, she was keyed up from all the caffeine. At home, she hooked Lucy's leash to her collar, and they set out to walk around the neighborhood. It was cooler than Genny expected, and she considered turning back, but Lucy needed the exercise and she needed to bring down her caffeine high.

As they walked, Genny's thoughts circled around adoption applications, social workers, lawyers, and waiting. She'd read an article recently about an adoptive family that had to relinquish custody to the biological father three years after the adoption. It would be yet another loss. They could remain childless. If that was God's plan, why was the desire to be a mother strengthening?

January 25, 2012

I went to see Peter and Melissa's baby today. He is so sweet and tiny. I felt like I was holding a doll. I can't help but be a little angry with God. Why do I have to have all these reproductive problems? Why can't Paul and I have a baby like everyone else? Doesn't God say, 'be fruitful and multiply?' What if I can't multiply? I guess Paul and I'll have a serious talk about babies when he gets home. Why doesn't anything work out for me? I feel like I'm finally on the right track in my life. I am married to a man who loves me and I'm finally back in school. But for whatever reason, God has placed a huge speed bump on our road to parenthood.

Chapter 25

Almost a month had passed since the night at the rec center when Paul and Damien had the conversation about prayer before eating. Paul had around three months left on the deployment, and time was slipping away. He had to minister to Damien before the deployment was over. The problem was, when Damian was in the room, he listened to music through earbuds. It was something he'd started since they talked about faith that night at the rec center and Paul didn't feel right interrupting him.

Turning the delicate pages of his Bible as he read, Paul looked up when he heard Damien toss something onto his nightstand. He had pulled the earbuds from his ears and laid his iPod beside them and picked up a magazine. Paul returned to reading his Bible.

"You know? I went to church when I was little. At least, that's what my parents said."

Surprised, Paul looked up and watched Damien flip through the magazine. "Oh?"

Damien laid aside the magazine and met Paul's gaze. "I've heard over the years that my dad had a disagreement with the pastor of the church we attended and was asked to leave the congregation. My family never went to church again. As a matter of fact, we have never practiced any type of religion since then."

"Really? And you don't know why?"

Damien shook his head and picked up the magazine again. "I've never met anyone like you, Paul." His eyes met Paul's again.

"What do you mean?"

"You're not all preachy and condemning or try to beat people over the head with your Bible. You're such a humble guy and it's clear that you love God."

Did Damien believe in God? Most of the time when a non-believer talked about God, it was in a general nature—even mocking.

"I know something's out there, but I'm not sure who or what. My dad has been anti-religious for as long as I can remember. He classifies himself as an atheist. Whatever went on between him and the pastor did a number on him. I guess most people would have moved on to another church, but not my dad."

"I'm not going to pretend I know everything because I don't. But if you ever have questions or want to talk, I'm here for you." Paul smiled slightly.

Damien looked at the magazine, then tossed it on his nightstand with the rest of the magazines. He sat quietly for a while, staring at his hands. Without a doubt, God had opened the door for Paul to minister to Damien.

"Well, let me drag myself off this bed and get ready for work," Damien said as he sat on the edge of his bed.

"All right, man." Paul returned to reading his Bible. Inside, he was shouting for joy. He planned to take full advantage of the opportunity laid out before him.

As soon as Damien left the room, Paul raised his hands to Heaven and praised God. He pulled out his journal and made the entry for the day.

February 4, 2012

Praise God! I pray God gives me more opportunities to lead Damien to Christ. I haven't had the opportunity to minister in a long while. I'm on fire, Lord!

Paul laid his pen in the spine of his journal and focused on the picture of him and Genny on his nightstand. Genny's journey back to the Lord had been bumpy at best. He loved his wife, but there were times he found himself overwhelmed at the idea of holding her hand through her faith journey for the rest of his life. He had encouraged her to read her Bible daily and gently urged her to join the women's small group. He didn't understand her reluctance, especially since Melissa attended the group.

A sting of guilt pierced his heart. If holding her hand was what she needed, then that was what he'd do. It was his responsibility to lead her and guide her. Setting his personal journal on his nightstand, he picked up the deployment journal and wrote an entry for the day.

February 4, 2012

My sweet Genevieve,

I miss you so much. I wish I could wrap my arms around you and protect you from the world. I'm so honored that God has blessed me with you. Sometimes I think about how God has brought us to the place we are in life. I still remember seeing you for the first time. You were so young, yet your spirit was already broken. It was as if you'd lived a long, hard life in your five short years.

Seeing you grow into the woman you are today has been both rewarding and heartbreaking. So much loss, but so much gained. I have a feeling God will use you for something great in the future.

I love you so much, Genevieve. I can't wait to see where God takes us.

⟫⟫⟫ ⟪⟪⟪

Genny had settled into a routine with work and school. The women at church had invited her to a Wednesday night bible study and she had decided to start the next week. Two weeks had passed since she had visited Asher for the first time. She was finally at a place where she didn't want to cry every time she saw him or another baby.

This evening, she was meeting Julie and Bridget at the movie theater to see the latest *Twilight* movie. Genny wasn't into vampires, but it was nice to get out of the house. Applying a thin layer of light red lipstick, Genny stepped back and rubbed her lips together. She rarely wore makeup, but felt like dressing up. She walked into the living room and sat on the couch to lace her boots. When she stood, she sighed and brushed Lucy's hair off her black jeans.

Standing in line at the concession stand, Genny gasped when someone wrapped their arms around her from behind. She turned her head and saw Bridget standing behind her.

"Thank you, thank you, thank you!" Bridget said, barely able to contain her excitement.

"For what?" Genny thumbed through her memories for something she'd done for Bridget. The only thing she could think of was working a shift for Bridget, and that hadn't happened in a while.

"Introducing me to Michael." Bridget giggled.

Tension Genny didn't know she had left her shoulders. "Oh, you're welcome. When are you going out?"

"Tonight!"

"Tonight?" They must be getting together after the movie.

"Yes, silly." Bridget grabbed Genny by the shoulders and turned her to face the doors. Michael was not far from the entrance talking to someone. Why was he joining them for the movie? It was supposed to be a girls' night.

"I told him we were seeing a movie tonight and he said he could meet me at Logan's after. I didn't want to wait that long so I told him he could see the movie with us, if he wanted. Then we could go to the restaurant. He said yes before I got the whole sentence out."

I bet he did. She needed to stop and be happy that Michael had turned his attention to someone else.

Julie was running late and asked Genny to save her a seat. The three of them made their way to the theater and found vacant seats toward the middle. Michael stepped aside for Bridget to walk in first, which meant Genny would be sitting next to him. As she walked down the row behind Michael, she considered leaving a chair between them for Julie. It would look odd, so she sat next to him.

Michael's cologne drifted past Genny's nose. There was something familiar about the scent. Her stomach knotted. Paul wore the same cologne. She had to sit through a two-hour movie next to a man who smelled like her husband and was possibly stalking her. Julie slid past the other movie goers in their row and sat next to Genny. She raised her brows when she saw Michael.

"Why's he here?" Julie whispered.

"He came with Bridget." Genny shrugged.

During the first half hour, Michael's arm brushed against Genny's arm every time he took a sip from his cup. After the last time, she gave up her arm rest and rested her hands in her lap. During the rest of the movie, she'd lost count of how many times he'd looked at her. Wasn't he supposed to be looking at his date? By the time the movie was over, Genny felt like she had sat next to Michael for an eternity as she tried to avoid his gaze and physical contact.

As they left the theater and said their goodbyes, Genny and Julie were making their way to their cars when Bridget called out to them. They stopped and watched Bridget sprint to where they were standing. Michael remained in the background and Genny felt his gaze on her.

"We talked, and we want you two to come to Logan's with us. We'll make it a night. What do you say?"

Julie looked at Genny and bit her lip.

"You Know? I'm tired, so I'm going to head home." Genny yawned for effect.

Bridget walked up to her and grabbed her arm, playfully shaking her. "Come on, Gen."

"Bridget, this is supposed to be your first date. You don't want me and Julie crashing it for you."

"Michael said he wanted you and Julie to come."

"No, you two need to get to know each other, and what better way than having dinner?" How odd Bridget was giving in to Michael's wish that Genny and Julie join them on their first date.

Bridget scoffed and walked away. When Genny turned to walk to the Jeep, she saw Michael staring at her with an expression that raised the hair on her arms. She climbed into the Jeep and headed home.

After she was settled in bed, she picked up her journals. She opened the deployment journal and wiped her eyes.

February 8, 2012

I miss you so much that I feel like I can't breathe. All throughout the day, I wonder what you are doing. Are you getting enough rest and enough to eat? I'm sure you're eating better since I'm not cooking for you. You laughed, didn't you?

Lucy misses you too. Every time we go outside, she looks at the truck like she's waiting for you to open the door. When she's on your side of the bed, she lays her head on your pillow like she's a human. I know it's because she smells you. I try my best to be mommy and daddy, but it's hard. I never knew I could love an animal so much and that an animal could love me in return.

What I miss most is your love. The way you love me with your gentle words and everything you do for me, especially washing the dishes. I bet you laughed again. But what I miss the most right now is the way you love me with your body. Not just being intimate, but your hugs, the times you let me sleep on you when we are watching TV, and the times I feel you touch my back when we are out and about. I feel protected when you do that. I'm sorry if I never told you.

I can't wait until you are home. You are my love, my soulmate, and my best friend. I love you Paul Tyler Thompson!

She closed the deployment journal and rested her hand on the cover. Three more months.

February 8, 2012

Michael showed up at our girls' night out. Lucky for me, it was because he had asked Bridget out. It was weird sitting next to him in the theater. I've never been that close to him for that long. Not even the times on the beach. He seemed too touchy, feely. No, he was too touchy, feely. He's dating Bridget now, but I can't help but wonder why.

⇶ ⇇

Genny walked in the house after class and grimaced when she saw the line of dirty dishes on the counter waiting to be washed. She'd get to it later tonight—or not. She took Lucy out back for a little while and sat on the picnic table while Lucy played. A year had passed since she and Paul had gotten married. A year. She could hardly believe it. They'd been through a lot in the past year. Thunder in the distance interrupted Genny's reminiscing. Lucy slicked her ears back and bolted to the back door.

The living room was no longer the ideal study area. Genny's sociology book lay open on the coffee table, but instead of a pencil in her hand, she held the remote, browsing the channel guide. A knock at the door brought out a single bark from Lucy. Genny looked out the kitchen window and saw a florist van in the driveway.

Opening the door, a man stood on the doorstep with a large bouquet of beautiful red roses. He handed her the vase and smiled. Genny pulled out the card and opened it.

Happy Anniversary, Genevieve. I love you. P.S. I told you it would be easy to remember!

Genny held the vase to her chest as if it was Paul himself. She added more water to the vase and sat it in the middle of the dining table.

Five o'clock came quicker than Genny had hoped. The past few hours were spent cleaning the kitchen as rock music pumped from the stereo speakers. To break up the housework, she'd step over to the table periodically to inhale the sweet smell of the roses, reminding her of the man she loved on the other side of the world. Genny changed into her navy polo and khaki pants. She was scheduled for a five-hour shift and was closing with Renee so she could show her part of the closing routine.

When Genny pulled into the parking lot of The Roasted Bean, she saw Michael's Jeep in a parking space, something that'd been happening more frequently since he and Bridget had started dating. Annoyance and dread no longer plagued her every time she saw him. Only occasionally now.

Most of the time, Genny started her shift in the dining room. To her surprise, the tables were clean, and the floor was swept. All she had to do was restock the condiments. She caught sight of Michael in the corner, and he smiled. After she clocked in, she walked back out to the dining room and went to work refilling the condiment station.

"Hey," Michael said.

Genny turned her head and saw Michael walking toward her. She gave him a half-smile. "Hey, yourself." Bridget's car had been in the shop and Michael had been dropping her off and picking her up, but she remembered that Bridget wasn't on the schedule for the day. "What are you doing here?"

He raised his hands and took a step back.

"I'm sorry. I didn't mean it like that." Genny laughed. "Bridget is off today."

"I know. I wanted to talk to you about something."

"Oh?" What could he possibly want to talk to her about? He should be concerned with Bridget, not her.

"I know it's short notice, but there's a concert Friday night, Battle of the Covers. Have you heard of it?"

"No." Why was he talking about a concert?

"It's actually a competition. Anyway, it's where cover bands compete for the title of the best cover band in the southeast."

Genny grimaced.

Michael smiled and shook his head. "It's not cheesy covers. These are professional cover bands. Some have top selling albums. They cover bands anywhere from Def Leppard to Incubus."

Incubus was one of her favorite bands. She probably wouldn't see the real band, but a cover would be the next best thing. "What does this have to do with me?" A customer walked up to the condiment station and Genny stepped aside.

"I want to take Bridget, and I figured she'd be willing to go if you went. Don't tell her though. It's a surprise."

Something didn't add up. "Why would she be reluctant? Aren't you two dating?"

Michael sighed. "The truth is, I did something stupid, and I want to get back on her good side by taking her to the concert. I figured she'd be willing to go if you went with us."

If Bridget was going, what was the harm?

No Genny.

She stared out the front windows for a moment. "I guess."

Michael exhaled and grinned. "Good. It's at the coliseum. I'll meet you at the door at six forty-five. I'll have your ticket."

"Okay, see you then."

For the rest of her shift, Genny had an uneasy feeling about the concert. What did Michael do that angered Bridget to the point that she had stopped speaking to him until recently? And why hadn't she said anything to her and Julie about their fight? Bridget tended to over share. Did Michael ask Julie? But Julie was out of town the upcoming weekend, leaving Genny as his only option.

Three days later, Genny studied her image in the bathroom mirror. The new hair growth was long enough she could pull all her hair back into a ponytail. She'd dreaded the concert since Michael talked her into going, but she had no way of contacting him, and he had asked her not to tell Bridget. She could stay home, but she didn't want Bridget to be angry with her.

Sitting on the couch, she slipped on her boots and sat looking at Lucy in her bed. She trotted over to Genny and laid on the floor between her feet. Genny leaned down and scratched Lucy's back. She should stay home; nothing felt right about tonight.

Twenty minutes had passed, and Genny was still sitting on the couch stroking Lucy. Pulling herself to her feet, she grabbed her purse and keys, and headed out to the Jeep.

Michael was standing by the entrance doors, but he was by himself. When Genny was closer, she saw his set jaw and dark eyes.

"Sorry I'm late. Where's Bridget?"

"She can't make it." His voice held an edge.

Leave, Genny.

"Oh, that's too bad." A lump formed in her throat, and she fought to swallow it before it choked her. "You Know? I think it's best if I go back home."

"Is it wrong for two friends seeing a concert together?" His voice was calm, but Genny noticed his clenched fists.

Genny froze. "Well, no—"

"Good. Shall we find our seats?" Michael's features softened and he gestured to the line with a smile.

Leave now, Genny. No more giving him the benefit of the doubt.

He took a step toward the back of the line and stopped when she didn't follow. He hung his head and sighed. "At least let me walk you to your Jeep." His smile appeared forced.

Michael's arm brushed against hers as they walked. Genny stepped away and headed down the row where she was parked. His hand touched the small of her back, turning her stomach. Panic seized her chest when he followed her in between the Jeep and the car in the next space. Genny clicked the remote to unlock the Jeep.

Before Genny had a chance to reach for the door handle, Michael grabbed her arm and turned her around to face him. The next few moments went by in slow motion as Michael leaned in and kissed her, pulling her tight against his chest. When her senses returned, she pushed him away and took a step back. Too stunned to speak, she stared at Michael as he extended an invitation.

"Come home with me, Genny." The two dimples that'd caught Genny's attention before now repulsed her. Michael reached out to caress her cheek, but she stepped back before he could touch her.

"If I've said or done anything that led you to believe I'd cheat on Paul, then I'm sorry. I love him and would never do anything to hurt him." She steadied her voice the best she could. Did he think she wanted to commit adultery with him because they attended club meetings on the beach?

"Well, the thing is, I've fallen for you." Her skin crawled at the sincerity in his voice. "Paul doesn't have to Know. I've been with married women before."

"I've got to go." Genny yanked the door open and almost lost her footing as she stepped on the running board. As soon as she shut the door, she hit the lock button in time to lock Michael out. He jerked the door handle and pounded his fist on the window, yelling at her to unlock the door. Genny flinched and fought the rising panic. People passed by staring, but no one stepped in to defend her.

Nausea burned Genny's throat, and she began violently trembling. Her eye caught a group of men and women wearing black leather jackets covered in patches walking between the rows of parked cars. An older man stepped away from the group and headed their way.

"Are you okay, miss?" he asked through the closed window when he stopped a few feet away from the driver's side door and Michael.

Genny gasped for air and shook her head.

The man intimidated Genny and she prayed Michael was intimidated as well. He was a big man—taller than Paul and bulky. When he crossed his arms and cocked his head to the side, Genny noticed the tattoos on his neck and hands. She assumed by his appearance he was a biker. Michael looked at Genny and clenched his jaw. Without saying a word, he walked away, shaking his head and balled his hands into fists.

She looked at the man. Tears pooled in her eyes and rolled down her cheeks. She tapped the button to lower the window, but stopped when he held up his hand.

"Don't roll down your window. I'm a stranger to you." Taken aback at first, what he said was true. "Do you Know him?"

"We're in the same Jeep club." Genny exhaled slowly to push the nausea down.

"I suggest you talk to your president, and miss, I also suggest you go to the police and file a restraining order. There's something disturbing about that man. I saw it in his eyes."

Genny's throat tightened as if a hand slipped around her neck and squeezed the life from her. "Okay."

"We'll stand here until you are on your way. What does his Jeep look like?"

Not noticing before, she saw that the rest of the group had moved to where she was parked. "Like mine, except it's not lifted, and it doesn't have mud grips."

"All right. We'll keep an eye out."

"Thank you, sir." He nodded, and Genny backed out, making her way to the exit. Taking a different way home, she checked her mirrors often to make sure Michael wasn't following her. What should she do? Tell Trevor or go to the police? Or, most importantly, should she tell Paul?

February 17, 2012

What am I going to do? I hate to think what would have happened if the bikers hadn't been there to help me. I should probably tell Paul, but what can he do? He'd have to suffer for another two months. I want to throw up. Michael kissed me. I mean, kissed me like Paul kisses me. I brushed my teeth four times and used the rest of Paul's mouthwash. I'm so disgusted and scared. What if he comes to The Roasted Bean? And where was Bridget? If she had been there, none of this would have happened. God, did I do or say anything to make him think I liked him? And why did You let this happen? It's not like I wanted it. Please let me sleep. It's almost four and I'm laying here freaking out at every sound the house makes. Sounds that I've been used to for almost a year now. Poor Lucy. I keep waking her up so she can listen for noises outside. I have to work tomorrow, but I think I'll call in.

Chapter 26

Leap year had interrupted Paul's monthly countdown. If it wasn't February twenty-ninth, he would have already announced he had two more months until he was home. One day made a world of difference. Paul slipped on his boots, grabbed his Bible, and headed for the chapel. He'd invited Damien to the Wednesday night Bible study, but he was called in early to cover for someone who was sick.

Paul found a seat and laid his Bible and journal on the chair next to him so he could tie the laces on one of his boots.

"Is this seat taken?"

Paul looked up and saw Damien with his hand on the back of the chair where he laid his Bible and journal. He froze for a second, then regained his senses. "No brother, it's yours." Paul grabbed his hat and Bible.

Damien pulled back the chair and sat down. The only thing in his hand was his hat.

"Did your co-worker feel better?"

"Yes. Um, no. I-I lied. I didn't have to go in early."

Paul raised his brows and kept himself from shouting his praises to the Lord. It was a big step for Damien.

"I was nervous, so I hung out at the rec center."

"I understand, but I think you'll like Chaplain Ford. He's very down to earth and he won't beat you over the head with his Bible." Paul chuckled and saw Damien crack a smile.

Damien glanced around the circle of attendees and shifted in his seat. He was the only one without a Bible. Paul stood and found Chaplain Ford. When he returned, he handed Damien one of the chapel's Bibles. Damien smiled and thumbed through the pages.

Chaplain Ford led the study like they were a group of friends getting together. He had a way of setting people at ease and reminded Paul of an older Pastor Ryan from their church back home. Damien's attention alternated between Chaplain Ford and following along in the Bible. Paul had led people to Christ in the past, but Damien was different.

Paul's shop was a little further away from the chapel than Damien's shop, so he had to cut out a few minutes early. But he left Damien in good hands with Chaplain Ford. Paul couldn't wait to talk with Damien in the morning.

As he walked, he thought about Genny. She hadn't seemed like herself for a while now. He had asked a time or two if she was okay, and she always said she was fine. Since he wasn't there to see for himself, he had to take her at her word.

With more aircraft coming in than usual, Paul's shift seemed to pass by quickly. When he opened the door to the dorm room, his shoulders sagged when the light was off, and Damien was asleep. His shift must have ended earlier than scheduled. Disappointed, Paul opened his laptop for light and changed into his t-shirt and shorts.

Sitting on his bed checking his email, the rising sun peeked around the blinds, shedding light on Damien's nightstand. Paul smiled when he saw the Bible Damien had borrowed from the chapel on top of his stack of magazines. From Paul's side of the room, he thought he saw a bookmark somewhere in the New Testament. A seed had been planted and was taking root.

Paul picked up his deployment journal and wrote an entry for the day.

March 1, 2012,

Two more months, my love! I can't wait to wrap my arms around you and plant a huge kiss on your soft lips. I have seen growth in Damien. When I came home this morning, I saw the Bible he borrowed from Chaplain Ford on his nightstand. Can you believe it? I assumed that he'd use it during the study and give it back to Chaplain Ford, but he kept it. I pray God uses me in the time we have left together.

I have missed you more than I ever imagined. I didn't fully understand what God meant when He said that two shall become one until I fell in love with you. This deployment has shown me that not having you by my side physically hurts. It's like I have been torn in half and the half that is missing is you.

⋙ ⋘

The past two weeks since the concert were hard for Genny. She'd convinced Paul that everything was fine. At least she'd hoped she had. He never said anything, so she figured she was successful at hiding her feelings. She hated lying to him, but didn't want him upset so far away.

Michael had come to The Roasted Bean at least eight times since the concert. She'd driven the truck a time or two, but it didn't matter since Michael had seen the truck the day Paul came to the get together at the beach. Bridget had told her she had no idea about the concert. She was furious that Michael used her to get to Genny. Michael had made the whole thing up to get Genny to the concert, hoping she'd go home with him.

Genny would go to the back office or the bathroom each time Michael pulled into the parking lot. Julie had said that he'd gotten visibly angry the last few times she'd hid from him. Julie had tried to convince her several times to at least tell Trevor, but if she told Trevor, he would send Paul an email and that could never happen.

Renee was happy with Genny's progress over the past year and had given her more responsibilities with the goal of promoting her to shift manager. It was a full-time position which meant a significant raise. Genny turned off the lights in the dining room and made sure all the coffee equipment was turned off before heading to the back office. The closing crew would forget to turn off a machine or two on occasion. She laid the money bag in the safe and closed the door.

Three seconds later, the electronic lock engaged. Turning off the office light, she made one last round before she locked up for the night.

The parking lot was full when she arrived for her shift, and she had to park in the back of the building by the dumpsters. Chad had been walking her out to the Jeep, but he went home early due to not feeling well. Since she was alone, Genny surveyed the parking lot as she made her way to the Jeep.

233

The Jeep's alarm chirped twice, and the lights flashed after Genny hit the remote. When she climbed into the driver's seat, she shut the door and slid the key in the ignition. She checked her phone and saw an email notification. A smile spread across her face when she saw the email was from Paul. She couldn't wait to get home to read his love note in email form, as he called it, on her laptop. Reading on the tiny screen of her phone blurred her vision.

Distracted by the email, Genny screamed when the driver's door flung open. Michael stared at her with an expression that shook her body from head to toe. Fear climbed on her shoulders, weighing her down. Her eyes shifted to the shopping center parking lot below, but at almost eleven at night, it was empty.

He held up his hands. "I just want to talk."

"I..." Every beat of her heart grew louder than the last. Tears welled in her eyes, but she refused to let them fall, giving Michael the power.

"I've tried to catch you at work, but when I come by, I'm told that you're busy."

Genny's words jumbled together in her throat and remained there.

"Genny, why don't you want to be with me? We can meet at my place. I love you, so it doesn't matter that you are married."

Genny shook her head. "Michael, I don't love you. I love my husband. Please leave me alone."

"I can't do that, Genny." Reaching in, he grabbed her arm and dragged her out of the Jeep. What was he about to do to her? Whatever it was, it would be bad. She screamed and he shoved her back against the Jeep, knocking the wind out of her. He leaned in and tried to kiss her while his hand traveled over her body. His hot breath reeked of alcohol, and he backhanded her hard across the face when she turned her head to avoid his second attempt at a kiss.

Gasping for air, she tried to push him away. Slamming his hand against her throat, he forced a kiss on her. His fingers dug into the delicate flesh of her neck and squeezed out her breath. Terrified, she grabbed at his fingers, trying to loosen his grip. *Please God, help me!*

He reached for the handle on the back door. Panic jabbed hard at Genny's stomach. She knew what would happen if he got her onto the backseat. His grip tightened around her throat. Black spots danced in front of her eyes, and Paul's face flashed before her. *"...knee 'em where it counts..."*

She managed to get her foot between his and brought her knee up as fast and as hard as she could. He released his grip and fell backwards, hitting the pavement, groaning. Coughing and gasping for air, she climbed into the driver's seat and locked the doors.

After she cranked the engine, she slammed the gear shift into drive and stomped on the accelerator. The Jeep jumped the curb and tore down the hill. She didn't stop until blue lights appeared in her rearview mirror.

Pulling onto the shoulder, she realized she was on the highway. She didn't remember anything after driving down the hill. Genny saw the officer approach in the side mirror, and she lowered the window. When he walked up to the door, he shined his flashlight at her and grimaced.

"Ma'am, are you okay?"

"I was..." Genny coughed. "I was attacked when I left work," she rasped.

"Where do you work?"

"The Roasted Bean."

"Ma'am. That's at least two miles from here. I clocked you going sixty-six in a fifty-five and you ran a red light."

"I'm so sorry, sir. I had to get away as fast as I could." She coughed again.

The officer stepped away and clicked the walkie talkie on his shoulder. Genny heard him call for an ambulance and gave information about The Roasted Bean. The blue lights bouncing off the surrounding trees made her head spin. Her chest burned like fire with each breath.

The officer stepped back to her window and informed her that an ambulance would transport her to the hospital for evaluation. Tears filled her eyes. She could no longer keep her concerns from Paul. Michael had left her no choice.

Paul stood in the cargo bay of a plane counting passengers on an outgoing flight bound for Iraq. His walkie talkie squelched, and Master Sergeant Gibson's voice came through the speaker.

"Sergeant Thompson, please come to my office ASAP."

"On my way," he replied. An airman probably made an error and he'd have to clean up the mess. He stepped in the doorway of the office where Master Sergeant Gibson sat with the commander. His heart sank to his feet. Something had happened to Genny. He felt it in his gut.

"Have a seat." Master Sergeant Gibson motioned to the chair next to the commander. Paul complied and tried his best to calm his pounding heart. "We received a Red Cross notification about your wife."

Paul stopped breathing and the room began to spin.

"Sergeant Thompson, she's okay, but we are sending you home."

"What happened?" Countless possibilities raced through his head, and he swallowed the knot in his throat.

"She was assaulted as she left work a couple of hours ago," the commander answered.

"Go to your room and pack up. You're leaving on the plane departing at twelve hundred hours," Master Sergeant Gibson said.

Two overstuffed duffle bags and a backpack sat on Paul's bed, along with a box of items to be mailed home that wouldn't fit in his bags. Slipping on his backpack, he reached down and picked up a duffle bag in each hand, and glanced at Damien's bed. He sat the bags down and slipped off his backpack.

Pulling out a pen and a pad of paper, he wrote Damien a quick note explaining what had happened and added his personal email address at the bottom. He prayed that what he'd shared with Damien was enough to nurture the seed that'd been planted. He slipped on his backpack, grabbed the bags, and headed to the passenger terminal to wait for his flight.

After three days of travel, Paul was on the last leg of his journey home, and he was physically and emotionally exhausted. Genny had spent the first night in the hospital and second night with Trevor and Tamika. His parents had flown in and were at home with Genny. He had talked to her, but it was a one-sided conversation due to the injuries from strangulation. Not hearing her voice had added to his distress.

The captain turned on the fasten seatbelt sign and a flight attendant instructed the passengers to prepare for landing. Time dragged out as the plane descended and landed at Charleston International Airport. He grabbed his backpack from under the seat in front of him and made his way down the aisle. A flight attendant grinned when he approached the exit.

"Thank you for your service," she said.

"Thank you for your support." Paul walked through the door and up the jetway toward the gate. Normally he didn't mind wearing his uniform when he traveled, but this trip, his mind was somewhere else and being thanked for his service was the last thing he wanted to hear.

He pulled his phone from his uniform pants pocket and powered it on. His dad had sent a text letting him know that he would meet him in the baggage claim area. Strolling toward baggage claim, Paul spotted him standing by the carousel for his flight. Seeing the look on his dad's face knotted Paul's stomach.

On the drive home, he told Paul what he knew about the assault. Heat filled Paul's veins when his dad said that Michael was the man who assaulted Genny. He had never told Genny, but there was something about Michael that he didn't like after meeting him on the beach.

As they approached the house, Paul saw the Jeep. Michael dragging Genny out of the driver's side played in his mind as if he were watching it in real time. Paul's mom met them at the door and held her finger over her lips. Genny was asleep on the couch with a blanket spread over her.

"Genny hasn't left my sight," his mom whispered. "She tried to stay up, but as you can imagine, she hasn't been sleeping well."

Paul nodded and walked up to the side of the couch. Genny's bruised and battered face brought a rush of heat to his face. The blanket was pulled up under her chin, but he could see the finger shaped bruises that the blanket didn't hide. He reached down and brushed his fingers along her hairline. She gasped and sat up. When she realized who he was, she sprang from the couch and into his arms. After several moments, she leaned back, revealing the full extent of her injuries.

Paul could no longer be strong for her. Tears flowed down his cheeks, and he gave her a gentle kiss, careful to avoid the split on her swollen lower lip. Tears continued to flow as he brushed his fingers across the red, swollen skin around her right eye and cheek. He cupped the back of her head and pulled her close to him. They held each other as they cried.

After talking with his parents, he walked Genny to their bedroom and helped her into bed. She grabbed his hand and pulled him down as she scooted over.

"My combat boots—"

"It's okay," she whispered.

Paul stretched out on his back next to her and she moved over close to him, laying half her body on his. "Let me take a shower."

"Not now," her voice was hoarse.

"I've been traveling for three days. I smell."

"You smell good to me. Please lay here with me until I fall asleep." She cleared her throat and coughed.

"Okay, my love."

Genny's breath slowed to a steady rhythm within minutes. Paul ran his fingers up and down her arm as she slept. For the first time since he had enlisted in the Air Force, he considered ending his military career once his enlistment was up. He should have been home to protect Genny. The assault would haunt both of them for the rest of their lives.

Chapter 27

S tudying her face in the mirror, Genny sighed. An ugly light yel-low-brown hue that stretched across her cheekbone and circled her eye, had refused to go away. At least her face was no longer black and blue. The swelling of her bottom lip had gone down, and the split had healed except for a slight discoloration. Four weeks ago, Michael had turned their world upside down.

The first few days after Paul arrived home on emergency leave were hard for them both. The physical side-effects were difficult, but Genny had experienced emotional side-effects as well. Paul had learned to announce himself before getting near Genny if her back was turned to him. On several occasions, she'd screamed and flailed her arms if she was caught off guard. Once, he walked up behind her and touched her arm. She whirled around and hit him in the face.

The Monday after the assault, Genny and Paul received shocking in-formation. Michael had recently been released from The United States Disciplinary Barracks in Fort Leavenworth, Kansas before arriving in Charleston. He had been tried by a military court-martial for the rape of two women and had served five years in prison. He was also a registered sex offender. The self-defense refresher she'd balked at had saved Genny from becoming his next victim. She was told by the detective that Michael had disappeared. It was her and Paul's prayer that he'd left the area, but Paul had made sure she could take care of herself if he wasn't around to protect her.

Paul was back at work for the first day after three weeks of emer-gency leave. He had been scheduled to work nights until May, when he was originally due to return from the deployment. Genny had made it clear that if he worked nights, she and Lucy would camp out in the truck in the parking lot while he was working. She refused to stay home alone at night. He'd talked to his supervisor and was switched to day shift.

Genny looked at the mantel clock. It was after two in the afternoon, which meant she had three hours to knock out her to-do list. She'd wanted to tackle the closets for a while. Paul had moved most of his religious books into the office before he deployed, leaving a couple boxes behind in the guest room. She spent a few minutes carrying the boxes to the dining table.

One by one, she opened the boxes to inspect the contents. Maybe she could downsize from three boxes to two, or possibly one. The first box held important documents like their marriage license, bank statements, and tax forms. Another held the cards and notes Genny had sent Paul while he was deployed. She smiled as she sifted through the memories.

She went through the last box, pulling out some of Paul's military records. In the bottom was a smaller box. When she opened it, a picture of Paul and a young woman lay on top. She remembered seeing the box at the apartment while getting ready to move into the house. Back then, she had gone through the box but only read one card that had fallen from the stack as she returned it to the box. Guilt had kept her from reading the rest of the cards at that time.

After the Keurig warmed up, Genny popped in a K-cup and made a cup of hot cocoa. She sat crossed legged on the couch and held the box on her lap. Before pulling out the first stack of cards, she hesitated for a moment. Was it a good idea to go through the box? Was it okay since she was Paul's wife? Were they entitled to privacy, or should a husband and wife share everything? She hadn't kept anything from her time with her old boyfriend, so why was he holding onto the box? Genny frowned and shoved her hands in the box.

The empty mug sat on the end table next to Genny. An hour had passed as she slowly looked through all the items in the box—greeting cards, letters, love notes and more pictures—all from a woman named Staci. The dates spanned a six-month period, as far as she could tell.

Gathering a handful of cards, she reached over to drop them in the box but paused when the corner of a white piece of paper peeked from under one of the bottom flaps. Unfolding the piece of paper, her throat closed, cutting off the air to her lungs.

⤜⤛ ⤙⤚

Genny was usually in the middle of making dinner when Paul arrived home from work, but she was nowhere to be found. It was evident she'd been cleaning by the boxes on the table. He strode down the hall calling out for her. When she wasn't in the closet, he headed back into the living room. His heart dropped when his eyes found the familiar box and its contents spread over the coffee table. Pulling back the curtain, he saw Genny sitting on the picnic table with Lucy. He braced himself for the hardest conversation of his life.

The picnic table seemed a mile away. The walk would give him time to organize his thoughts. But that wasn't fair to Genny. She had no idea her world was about to change by an image in a box that should have been disposed of years ago. As painful as the conversation and its consequences would be, God was at work. God would tell him when the time was right, and that time was now.

Genny looked at him with red and puffy eyes when he walked around the end of the picnic table. She held the image in her trembling hand. He sat next to her, keeping some distance between them.

"You have a child?" She took in a shaky breath.

He would never forget the pain in her voice when she asked him the question. Paul shook his head, not knowing how to answer. *Please, God.*

"Then who is this?" she asked, holding up an ultrasound picture. "You were obviously in a relationship with someone named Staci. You have a box full of love notes and cards." She looked down at the picture. "And apparently a baby."

"No, s–she had an abortion." His breath came in quick bursts, drying his mouth. *Stay strong.*

Her lips parted. She looked down at the ultrasound picture and back at him. "I'm sorry. I..." She looked at the picture again. "I don't know what to say."

"You don't have to say anything, Genevieve." She needed him; he couldn't fall apart. She had a difficult time handling her emotions. That was evident in how she dealt with Bandon's death.

She kept her distance, but he didn't blame her. He'd dropped a bomb on their marriage. God would help them through. They'd fought hard to get to where they were. Something like this couldn't tear them apart. He should have told her. It wasn't right for her to find out this way.

"So," Genny handed the ultrasound picture to him, "why did she have an ultrasound before she had an abortion? Was she going to have the baby?" She rubbed her hands over her face.

He no longer had the will to stay strong. The pain released a torrent of tears. "Yes. We were going to raise the baby together. She wanted to get married, but I couldn't marry her since she wasn't a Christian and I always wanted a Christian wife."

"You knew she wasn't a Christian, but slept with her anyway?"

Paul's mind betrayed him, wiping his thoughts away as if they were scribbled on a chalkboard and swiped with an eraser.

"I thought I could convert her."

Genny let out a sad laugh.

"Genny, I was twenty. I was immature and naive." Frustrated, he clenched his jaw.

Genny was processing the best she could. He couldn't blame her for her reaction. His confession had changed the way she viewed him as a man and a Christian. She'd never look at him the same way again—a consequence of his actions.

"When I told her I wouldn't marry her, she said she was having an abortion, and she did."

Quiet tears rolled down Genny's cheeks. Lucy hopped on top of the table between them, and Genny stroked her back. "Why didn't you tell me before now?"

"I..." Paul rested his elbows on his knees and ran his hands over his face.

"So, let me get this straight. Would it be better for me to believe that you have been abstinent all these years? You flat out lied to me to keep your secret."

Paul sighed. She had every right to be angry. "I'm sorry."

"You're sorry? You let me go on and on about how special it was that *we* were able to give each other *our* virginity. I'm such a fool."

"No, I–I'm sorry."

"How many times have you said you're sorry? You should have told me." Genny scoffed.

"When was I supposed to tell you? With the way our relationship started, it was not something I would have told you. At least not at first. And when things changed, I didn't think it was the right time since it was so close to the deployment." He prayed God would keep him from falling into the depths of despair he was in the first time.

"Don't you dare turn this on me."

"I'm not." A sick feeling bubbled in his stomach.

"And a baby on top of it all? Do you know how bad I want to have your baby? Struggling with why God keeps saying no? All this time, you had fathered a child and kept it to yourself. I feel like I've been punched in the stomach twice by my own husband."

"Genny..." Tears pooled in his eyes.

Pushing herself off the table, Genny sprinted to the back door.

"Where are you going?"

"I've got to get out of here. I need to think without you around."

"What?"

"I'm sorry, but I can't look at you right now."

"Genny?" Her coping mechanism was to flee. He had to stop her from leaving.

Paul hopped off the table and went after her. He couldn't let her leave. By the time he made it inside the back door, she was grabbing the keys to the Jeep off the keyholder by the front door. He ran up behind her and slammed the door shut when she opened it. Genny jerked on the knob, but Paul held the door closed at the top. She looked at him like she wanted to rip him to shreds.

"Please don't leave. You are too upset."

"I can't...I can't be here. Can't you understand that?" Tears streamed down her cheeks.

"I know I've hurt you and I'm sorry. If you need time to think, you can sit on the picnic table. I'll stay inside, I promise. Please don't leave." Paul feared Genny would run for the back door, but she didn't. Lowering her head, she nodded and started to cry, but he stopped himself from comforting her. She hung up the keys, grabbed her phone, and went outside to the picnic table.

Paul went to the office and closed the door. Genny would be upset, but he didn't know that she would be disgusted by the sight of him. Tears filled his eyes. The stitches in his heart were threatening to pull loose again. This time it wasn't only because of what happened years ago, but he had broken his wife's heart.

He walked to the window and separated the blinds. Genny was sitting on the picnic table with her head in her hands. He had made such a mess of his life when he was in his early twenties. Because of his weakness, he lost his child. Memories of the talk he had with his pastor brought him comfort. God had forgiven him, but would Genny?

❧ ❧

The moon cast light over the oak tree, emphasizing the new leaves sprouting from the branches. Genny had been alone on the picnic table for over two hours. She couldn't wrap her head around how a woman Paul barely knew could influence his beliefs. What bothered her the most was that Paul hid it from her.

Not only had her husband been with another woman, but he had also fathered a child—a child she could never give him. A cool breeze seeped through her skin, deep into her bones. Once again, God had punished her for some egregious sin she had no idea she'd committed.

Returning to the Lord hadn't been easy for her. He'd let her down all her life, taking every person she'd loved. Now He tried to take her husband from her by causing strife in their marriage. No. It wasn't fair to blame God for Paul's sin. Paul knew the risks of what he was doing. Not only physical risks, but emotional and spiritual risks. Paul was a strong Christian for as long as she'd known him. He would have struggled with the choices he'd made.

Picking up her phone, she typed a message.

You can come out.

Are you sure?

Yes.

The hinges creaked when the back door opened. Paul stepped around the end of the table and sat next to Genny. They sat quietly, watching the soft breeze ruffle the leaves on the oak tree.

"I'm sorry for how I acted. But...you're not who I thought you were."

Paul sighed. "I never imagined I'd have a physical relationship with a woman I wasn't married to. I was disappointed with myself, but never considered that the physical part of the relationship didn't have to continue after the first time. Like I said, I was young and naive."

"You made it known that you were waiting for marriage. I guess...I'm...just..."

"I'm human and humans sin. The pedestal you put me on was so high I was bound to fall."

Was he turning this on her again? If she put him on a pedestal, it was because of his own words. She chose to remain silent, as did he. Genny glanced over her shoulder when she heard something and saw Lucy looking at them from the living room window.

"I better let her out." Genny braced herself to stand.

"I'll do it." Paul was up and halfway to the backdoor before she could respond.

Lucy bounded toward the back fence and grabbed a long, white stick glowing in the moonlight. Paul rejoined Genny on the picnic table. Both sat quietly watching Lucy play.

"What hurts the most is that she had two things that should have been mine: you and your baby."

"If I could go back in time, I would choose a different path. Not just because of my faith and the vow I made, but because of you. It kills me that I hurt you."

He laid his hand on top of hers. For the first time since hearing his secret, she didn't want to get as far away from him as possible. He was right. Only Jesus was without sin.

"Any other secrets?" She glanced at Paul.

"Nope."

"So you didn't sleep with Brianna?"

He looked at her with wide eyes. "That was why we broke up. I wouldn't sleep with her."

"Really?" Now she knew the reason she didn't like Brianna.

"Yeah. That night, actually. She'd tried in the past, but I refused to give in. She was jealous of you."

"Her. Jealous of me?" She almost laughed. Brianna was the last person she'd expect to be jealous of her.

"You're a beautiful woman, Genevieve." He leaned toward her, then hesitated.

She met him halfway and kissed him. Resting her head on his shoulder, she poured out her heart to him.

"I am very hurt so it might take some time for me to get over it. I feel like she was blessed with my baby and, I don't know…"

"I don't expect you to get over it. My past hurt you and I hurt you by lying about it. I never thought I'd lie. I felt like dirt as the words left my mouth."

She remembered Paul's tattoo. He had said that he got it after he rededicated his life to Christ.

"Is this where did the tattoo come from?"

"Yes."

"I want you to know that I do trust you. I know you'd never intentionally hurt me. Like you said, our marriage is different, and it would have been strange for you to confide such things in me in the beginning. But please never lie to me again."

"I won't, I promise."

March 29, 2012

This is my first journal entry since the night of the concert (Feb 17). So much has happened. Michael showed up at work one night as I was getting ready to leave and attacked me. Chad was sick and wasn't there to help me close or walk me to the Jeep. I know Michael's plan was to rape me (he's a convicted rapist), but I prayed, and God gave me the memory of Paul teaching me moves to protect myself. Michael is still out there somewhere, which scares me. Detective Carter thinks he's moved on now since he knows he is a wanted man. I hope so. But just in case, Paul took me to the range to target practice. I'm a pretty good shot.

It's been rough. My larynx was fractured, and I was hoarse for over a week. I also had bad headaches and was dizzy all the time. The doctor said that I was seconds from severe injury and possible death. I also had bruises all over my body. Paul cried when he saw the bruises down my spine from where Michael slammed me against the door frame of the Jeep.

I hate Michael. I wish I was never nice to him. Better yet, I wish I'd never met him. The thought has crossed my mind that he would have done far worse to me even if he hadn't choked me. I probably would have ended up in a ditch somewhere.

I had bad nightmares every night at first. I stayed with Trevor and Tamika the night after I was discharged from the hospital. Trevor feels responsible for what happened since he allowed Michael into the Jeep club. I stayed in Zach's room and when I went to the bathroom, I heard Trevor and Tamika talking and Trevor was crying. I cried too. I told him that I don't blame him, but he still feels it's his fault. Tamika caught me sleeping in the corner that morning. She did what I would have done. She knelt in front of me and touched me to wake me so she could check on me like the doctor said. I came out of the corner and knocked her backwards. I feel so bad. She brushed it off, but I still feel bad.

Mom and Dad came and stayed until a few days after Paul came home. Mom found me the first morning like Tamika, but she didn't get close, so I didn't knock her down. After that, she was with me except when I was in the bathroom. She even slept with me.

Tonight, my world changed all over again. Paul had a girlfriend back when he was 20 or 21. Their relationship became physical, and she got pregnant. The worst part is that she had an abortion. Why would God give her the miracle of conceiving Paul's baby only for her to have an abortion? I want nothing more than to have Paul's baby, yet God denies me. I'm trying not to be angry with God but it's hard.

Chapter 28

Genny slipped on a long-sleeved shirt over her t-shirt. The temperature was in the high fifties most mornings. By late afternoon, the temperature would be in the low seventies—usual weather for mid-April. Lucy trotted out the backdoor ahead of Genny.

Climbing onto the picnic table, Genny focused on the trunk of the oak tree and smiled. Brandon's childhood voice echoed through the branches. Pumping his legs back and forth, she could almost see him flying through the air on the swing at their grandparents' farm.

Thinking of her own childhood, she couldn't remember a time that she played with dolls and pretended that they were her children like most girls. As she got older, children weren't something she had desired. Tears filled her eyes. Why was she desiring motherhood now?

Genny heard Mrs. Baker's backdoor and watched her walk out onto her patio with a watering can. Genny wiped her cheeks and gave her a weak smile. Pulling her overshirt tight, she blew out her breath to calm herself. Slipping off the picnic table, she made her way towards the fence, hoping that she'd rid herself of a red nose and eyes.

"Are you alright, Genny?"

"Yeah. Just my allergies." Her smile was weak. Biting her bottom lip to keep it from trembling, Genny couldn't hold back the tears.

Mrs. Baker reached out and brushed a tear from Genny's cheek.

"I was told by my doctor that I needed a hysterectomy soon. In December he told me that it needed to happen soon after Paul came home but, you know, with everything that's happened, I forgot. I realized this morning that May is next month and...and it's hit me that my chances will be gone soon."

"Oh, honey. I'm sorry." Mrs. Baker rubbed Genny's arm.

Genny's phone rang, and she pulled it out of her back pocket. Glancing at the phone, her school advisor's name appeared on the screen. She had dropped her class after Michael assaulted her and she wanted to talk to him about her transcript.

"I need to take this call. I'll talk to you soon."

"Okay. Take care."

Genny smiled and waved as she headed inside.

In the afternoon, Genny went to the kitchen to make a cup of coffee before sitting down to read her latest book. Spinning the K-cup carousel, she groaned. She was out of her favorite coffee. Opening the cabinet, she moved a few items around until she found the tea bags. Her phone chimed and she stepped into the living room to check her messages. She smiled when she saw a text from Mrs. Baker.

Would you like to come over for tea and cookies?

I'd love to. I'll be right over.

Genny grabbed the box of tea and shoved it in the cabinet. Heading out the backdoor, she walked over to Mrs. Baker's and knocked. She smiled when Mrs. Baker opened the door. Following her through the dining room into the living room, Genny's eyes brightened when she saw what resembled a setting for an English tea party on the coffee table.

A large silver tray sat in the middle of the coffee table holding a white porcelain teapot covered with small pink flowers. Matching teacups with saucers were next to the teapot. A small white porcelain plate held several kinds of cookies and a small porcelain covered sugar dish sat next to the teapot. A small silver tin sat off to the side.

Genny was touched that Mrs. Baker had prepared something special for their afternoon tea. She'd expected two mugs with the standard tea bags. Instead, she found much more.

"The pot is full of hot water, and these are Earl Grey tea bags," Mrs. Baker said as she touched the silver tin.

"Okay. This looks wonderful. I feel like Queen Elizabeth." Genny reached for the tin of tea bags and noticed the pink in Mrs. Baker's cheeks. Her heart was full of love for Mrs. Baker.

Mrs. Baker filled Genny's cup with hot water. Genny dunked a tea bag up and down then laid the string over the rim of the cup.

"Cookies?" Mrs. Baker asked with a smile.

"Yes, please."

Mrs. Baker used a pair of silver tongs to put a few cookies on a saucer and handed it to Genny. They sat for a while talking and enjoying their tea and cookies. Mrs. Baker reached out and patted Genny's knee.

"How are you feeling?"

"Actually, pretty good. I haven't felt this good in a while. And I really mean that."

"That's good to hear." Mrs. Baker smiled and took a sip of tea. She sat her cup down and looked at Genny. "I know how you feel."

Genny raised her brows.

"I gave birth to two stillborn babies in a row."

Genny gasped. "Oh no. I'm sorry." Not once would Genny have guessed that Mrs. Baker lost two children.

"It is not something I talk about often."

Genny was grasping at each thought that floated by in her head. Her heart went out to Mrs. Baker, but it wasn't the same. She went on to have two children.

As if she read Genny's mind, she continued. "I am blessed but not in the way you think." Genny's eyebrows came together. "Alan and Susan are adopted."

"I had no idea. Susan looks like you."

"Yes, we've heard that a lot. After our second baby passed, I had to have a hysterectomy."

They had more in common than Genny had imagined.

"The adoption came about in a strange way." Mrs. Baker put a few more cookies on Genny's saucer. "My sister's husband's niece was pregnant and unmarried. In my time it was frowned upon for a young girl to have a baby out of wedlock. She would be shunned by society."

Genny sipped her tea and pushed the saucer of cookies away.

"It had been two years since the hysterectomy. We had already accepted the fact that we were to never have children, so babies were not on our minds."

Genny heard Paul's truck come down the hill and glanced at her phone. She'd been at Mrs. Baker's for almost two hours. Usually, she'd start dinner around the time he came home from work. Dinner would be late. Her time with Mrs. Baker was too precious to interrupt.

"When we were contacted by my sister, the girl was nine months pregnant, and she went into labor three days later. Stanley and I were shocked when we arrived at the hospital and found out it was not one baby, but two."

Genny grinned. "I bet that was a shock. I didn't know they were twins."

Mrs. Baker reached out and took Genny's hand in hers. "I'm not telling you that you two should adopt. I'm simply telling you that you are not alone."

"Thank you." Genny hugged Mrs. Baker. God had put her in Genny's life for a reason.

Genny took one last sip of tea. "I need to head home and get dinner started."

"Okay, honey. I hope we can do this again."

"Definitely." Genny said and gave Mrs. Baker another hug.

She made her way to the backdoor and strolled through the gate that separated their yards. A grateful smile warmed her heart. Mrs. Baker was a very special woman and Genny was glad that God had brought them together.

⤛⤜ ⟫⟪

Genny pulled into a parking space at The Roasted Bean. She breathed in deep and looked around before exhaling. Opening the door with a shaky hand, she stepped down from the Jeep and took her time walking to the door. It was the first time she'd been back since the night Michael assaulted her almost three months ago.

The week after Paul came home, Renee and Julie had stopped by the house to visit. Renee burst into tears when she saw Genny's face and Julie seethed with each breath. Both women, along with Bridget, provided statements to the police. By the time they prepared to leave after the visit, Renee had accepted that Genny wouldn't be returning to work.

Genny chose a time when it wasn't busy to get a cup of coffee. As she approached the counter, Julie walked around and gave her a hug. Renee saw her and came over to greet her. Nausea burned her chest, and she blew out her breath. Renee took her hand and led her to the back office. Genny took slow, deep breaths until the nausea passed.

While Genny talked with Renee, Julie brought her a cup of her favorite brew and talked for a few moments then returned to the front. Genny blew into the cup and took a sip. She immediately sat it on Renee's desk and ran to the bathroom to vomit. Pushing open the bathroom door, she heard Renee behind her asking if she was okay. As Genny bent over, she vowed that she'd never drink a caramel macchiato again. She'd introduced Michael to the drink and now it was tainted with his memory and what he had done to her. The memories at The Roasted Bean were too strong. Genny said goodbye, went out to the Jeep, and headed to the Air Force Base.

Genny had an appointment with Dr. Nichols for a follow up and a referral to a fertility clinic. She and Paul had talked not long ago about looking into IVF. He agreed to a consult but was still on the fence. It was quite expensive, even at a military hospital, and Paul said that their savings would take a hit. She reminded him about the money that was left from her grandmother's life insurance, but he still had reservations. The success rate was around fifty percent for Genny's age. Paul didn't like the odds.

The pain had been intense for the past two months or so and it worried Genny. There was just over a week left in May, which meant a hysterectomy would be scheduled in the next couple of weeks unless the fertility clinic believed there was a chance she could conceive through IVF and carry a baby to term.

An ultrasound tech led Genny to a room and prepared her for the ultrasound. Dr. Nichols wanted to perform the ultrasound himself since her appointment was for a referral to the fertility clinic. He entered the room shortly after she had slipped on a hospital gown. His smile lit up the room.

"Hello, Genevieve. How have you been?"

"I'm great."

Dr. Nichols was an older man in his sixties with salt and pepper hair. He was personable and Genny was always at ease around him. She talked about the increase in pain and irregularities of her cycles as well as bloating from PCOS. As Dr. Nichols performed the ultrasound, he asked Genny about life in general. Paul's deployment was the main topic of their conversation. Genny left out the part where he came home early due to the assault. She liked Dr. Nichols but thought it best to maintain their professional relationship. After several keystrokes to collect images, Dr. Nichols leaned back in the chair and laced his fingers behind his head.

"Genevieve?" He sat up in the chair again and turned the monitor to where Genny could see. He pointed to an odd-shaped mass in her uterus. "Do you know what that is?"

Tears pooled in her eyes. "Cancer?" She'd never known Dr. Nichols to be nonchalant. quizzing her about the contents of her uterus was a horrible way of telling her that she had a cancerous growth inside of her.

He chuckled.

Now he was laughing at her.

"No, Genevieve. See that?" He pointed to the largest end of the mass.

"Yes." Her heart pounded in her ears. How would she tell Paul that she had cancer? Did this mean she would have to have chemo? She prayed it hadn't spread to other organs. Did endometriosis cause cancer?

"That's the head."

"Head?" Masses had heads?

"You won't need a referral to a fertility clinic. Genevieve, you are pregnant."

"What? I can't get pregnant. Are you sure?"

"I've been doing this for over thirty-five years, and I know a baby when I see one." He smiled and winked. "See that? That's the baby's torso." He spent a few moments pointing out the rest of the baby on the ultrasound. Since her periods were irregular and based on the size of the baby, he estimated her to be around ten weeks pregnant.

Genny sat in the Jeep for a while studying the ultrasound picture. She had been rolling around in her own sorrow about not being able to have Paul's baby when she was already pregnant. Cranking the Jeep, she pulled out of the parking lot and headed to Paul's shop.

Genny planned to take the pregnancy day by day. She was already in love with the baby and wanted to do everything she could to make sure they had a healthy baby come December. No exercise and only organic food. She'd plant a garden, but Paul would take care of it. She couldn't overexert herself in the heat of summer. Fresh tomatoes, corn, and squash would be healthy. Not that they ate red meat often, but now she would eat white meat only until the baby was born.

Nausea hit Genny as she turned onto the road that led to Paul's shop. The closer she drove to the shop, the higher the nausea rose in her throat. Pulling into the parking lot by Paul's truck, Genny opened the Jeep door and vomited. After she sent a text to Paul, she pulled up the calendar on her phone. Counting back ten weeks, she estimated conception shortly after Paul came home on emergency leave. God had given them a gift after the turmoil Michael had caused. She rested her hand on her swollen abdomen and waited for Paul's reply.

⟫⟫⟩ ⟨⟨⟨⟨

Paul looked out the wall of windows waiting for the aircraft due to land in a few minutes. His phone vibrated but he ignored it. A moment later, God urged him to check his phone. Retrieving it from his pocket, he tapped to read the text from Genny.

Are you busy?

Yes, love.

Do you have five minutes? I'm in the parking lot.

A plane is coming in.

It's important. I'll be quick. I promise.

Ok, but I only have a few minutes. Be right out.

As Paul strode up to the Jeep, Genny's expression concerned him. Holding her hand over her mouth didn't hide her pain.

"What is it? Did something happen at your appointment?"

She nodded and held out a piece of white paper. He turned it over and realized it was an ultrasound picture. The ultrasound from the child he lost came to mind but why would Genny bring the picture to him and why was she crying? Holding the picture, he looked at the top and saw Genny's name and the date.

Genny was pregnant.

"What? Is Dr. Nichols sure?" His stomach twisted in a knot, and he feared he was dreaming.

"I asked him the same thing and he said yes. When he showed me the ultrasound screen, I knew what I saw was cancerous mass until he pointed out the head and body. He said the pain I've been having is my uterus stretching and the bloating isn't bloating after all. It's our growing baby."

"Wow." Paul rested his hand on the door frame of the Jeep. The walkie talkie clipped to his pants pocket chirped and announced the approach of the aircraft he'd been waiting on. Torn, he kissed Genny and grinned. "I can't believe it. What a blessing."

"Yes, it is."

"Okay, my love. Drive carefully," he said and headed back to the shop.

While checking cargo against the manifest, he could think of nothing but the new life growing inside of Genny. After everything they'd been through and the odds against them, God had given them a miracle. The rest of Paul's shift flew by and somehow, he made it through shift change.

On the drive home, thoughts flooded Paul's mind. He wanted nothing more than to share the news of their miracle, but he and Genny needed to talk and process what had happened.

They talked throughout dinner about their child. Neither could believe that they were having a baby. Genny had told him she would be closely monitored since in some women, endometriosis could worsen during pregnancy. The doctor would deliver the baby by a cesarean section, followed by a hysterectomy. Instead of preparing for a hysterectomy in a few weeks, they were preparing for the upcoming birth of their child. Genny's estimated due date was December seventeenth, the week before Jesus' birthday.

Paul cleaned the kitchen while Genny relaxed on the couch watching TV. A cloud of panic drifted over him. The house was small—barely eleven hundred square feet. Would that be enough for the three of them? The bedrooms were small, and the living room wasn't much bigger. Babies were expensive. They'd need a crib and many other things he had no idea a baby would need. Setting up a nursery could cost... He didn't know but was sure it was expensive.

Finding a bigger house was on the list of possibilities. No, they should stay. Any day he could receive notice that he would be transferred to another base. Looking around, his eyes fell on Lucy laying in her bed. Would they need to rehome her? The baby might be allergic to her or maybe she wouldn't like the baby. But in the past, he'd read articles where dogs and babies had a special bond. Besides, they loved Lucy, and she was a part of their Family.

What about college? Paul's stomach twisted in a knot.

"Are you okay?"

"Oh, yeah." Paul's focus moved to Genny as she reached down to scratch Lucy's head.

"You look a few shades lighter than usual." She laughed.

"Just thinking about how everything is about to change."

"It's overwhelming." Genny closed the space between them and wrapped her arms around him. Resting her head on his shoulder, he felt her growing belly press against him. God was good.

⟫⟫⟩ ⟨⟨⟨

Genny grabbed a pillow off the bed, folded it in half and stuffed it under her shirt. Checking her profile in the bathroom mirror, she had a preview of what she would look like come December. Pregnancy had been foreign to Genny. Maybe God was blessing her with the baby due to all the loss in her life.

Tossing the pillow back on the bed, she picked up her journal and made an entry she never thought she'd write.

May 21, 2012

I can't believe I'm writing this, but I'm pregnant. If I didn't see the ultrasound, I wouldn't believe it. Here I was grasping at my last chance at having a baby and God had already answered our prayers. I'm so scared that the baby will die. I've already been to the bathroom at least ten times checking for signs of a miscarriage since I've been home. I think Paul noticed. I have to put my trust in God that our little Genny or Paul will be here in December.

I wish my mom was here. Paul will be great, but I hear there's nothing like having your mother with you to help along the way. And after, of course. I bet she would have been an awesome grandmother.

Genny braced herself on the bathroom counter and wiped a cool, damp washcloth over her face. Asher's shrill screams floated down the hall into the bedroom, adding to the pounding in her head. Drawing in a deep breath, Genny slowly exhaled and closed her eyes. Two weeks had passed since they found out that they were having a baby. This evening, they had invited their friends over for dinner and had shared their news. Genny had excused herself for a quick break.

"Pregnancy headache," Tamika said from the bathroom doorway. "I got them like crazy when I was pregnant with Zach."

"I'm learning all kinds of things here lately. It's weird. I felt no different until I found out that I'm pregnant. Now all this stuff is happening." Genny laughed.

"That's how it goes. Zach is almost sixteen, but I remember it all like it was yesterday."

Genny ran her hands over her growing abdomen. "I'm scared something will happen. You know?" Fear had become as much a part of her as breathing. Stepping out in faith had always been difficult for Genny, but she would put her faith in God that He would see her through her pregnancy, and she would deliver a healthy baby.

"I was the same way. Anytime I felt something was off—which was often—I was in the bathroom."

Genny laughed. "Me, too." She squeezed the water from the washcloth, wiped her face again, and laid it on the bathroom counter. She and Tamika headed into the living room where everyone was gathered.

Every muscle went rigid when Genny saw Melissa's weary expression as she attempted to console Asher. Melissa looked up, picked up Asher, and held him out to Genny. Eyes-wide, Genny glanced over her shoulder to see who Melissa was looking at. Lucy looked up at her from her bed and wagged her tail. Sweat dampened Genny's palms. Melissa wanted her to hold Asher.

"You need practice." Melissa's plea was veiled by a grin.

Practice was good. Genny drew in a quick breath and slipped her hands under Asher's arms as Melissa pulled her hands away. His wailing quieted as his blue eyes studied her face. She hadn't held him since he was a newborn over four months earlier. Flailing his arms and legs, he squirmed, and Genny tightened her grip. Melissa would kill her if she dropped her baby. Her back stiffened when she brought him against her chest.

Paul strolled up to her and caressed the back of Asher's head. Leaning close, he whispered, "He's not an UXO."

"A what?"

"Unexploded ordnance. You know, a bomb."

Genny rolled her eyes. Asher cooed and pushed his hand into her hair, grabbing a fistful. "Ouch!" Genny winced and held him out with her hair still wrapped around his fingers. "*Oww!*"

Paul laughed and untangled Genny's hair from around Asher's fingers. He took Asher from her and sat on the couch. Paul was a natural. As if he'd interacted with babies all his life. Where did that leave her? She'd always been uncomfortable around babies.

Once their guests had left and the house was in order, Genny took a shower and sat in bed writing in her journal. Laying the journal aside, she rested her hands on her middle. "Hi," she whispered. "I'm your mommy." Mommy. She'd come to terms a long time ago that she would never have the opportunity for a child to call her mommy. But here she was, laying on her bed with her and Paul's child inside of her.

The backdoor closed and Lucy ran down the hall and launched herself onto the bed. She walked up to Genny and laid down next to her. Genny raised her brows when Lucy moved toward her belly and sniffed. Did she know she had a little sister or brother inside Genny? She scratched the top of Lucy's head for a few moments. Paul walked into bathroom to get ready for bed. A few moments later, he came out and slipped under the covers on his side.

"Oh, time for bed?" Genny smiled and placed her journal and pen on the nightstand. She turned off the lamp and got comfortable. Closing her eyes, her mouth curved into a smile when Paul rolled over and lay his warm hand on her belly.

"Babe?"

"Hmm?" She rested her hand on her chest and took a deep breath.

He moved his hand from her middle and turned her head to face him. "God told me something."

"What's that?"

"This baby is the blood relative you've longed for since losing your family." He ran his thumb down her jaw.

The words that came from his mouth brought tears to her eyes. Why hadn't she thought of this before? She'd struggled over the years with anger toward God for taking her family from her and now He had blessed her with her heart's desire. Not just to have Paul's baby, but to have a connection to someone by blood. Paul, Brian, and Tricia were her family, but now she had a child with whom she shared the same DNA.

Fear trickled in and her thoughts ran away with her. *God, please don't let anything happen to this baby.* Tears burned her eyes. A mustard seed. Jesus said all she needed was faith the size of a mustard seed. She feared it wasn't enough. *It's so scary to feel I have no control over my life. Faith is so hard. Please Lord, I want faith the size of a mustard seed that this baby will live.*

Chapter 29

The hanging rod groaned each time Genny shoved a hanger across the bar on Paul's end of the closet. She'd been wearing his running pants and t-shirts since she'd outgrown her clothes. Saturdays were usually spent on the couch all day, but not this Saturday. Paul had said that they'd spend the afternoon at the mall.

She was almost half-way through her pregnancy, and it was time to set up the nursery. Peter had helped Paul move the furniture around. They had crammed Paul's desk and two of the four bookshelves into the guest room with the remaining bookshelves moved to their bedroom. The former office was the perfect size for a nursery. They would wait until they found out the gender to pick a theme. Genny had an appointment earlier in the week, but the baby wasn't cooperating. The ultrasound tech was going to try again at her twenty-week ultrasound in a little less than two weeks.

The pants she'd selected were snug. Paul laughed from the doorway of the bathroom. Genny shook her head and sighed. Standing behind her, he slipped his arms around her waist and rested his hands on her belly. Leaning her head back against his shoulder, they gazed at themselves in the mirror.

"This must be bittersweet for you," Genny rested her hands on top of Paul's.

"Yes, it is."

It had taken Genny some time to come to terms with Paul's past. To help her heal, Paul had sat the box full of pain and hurt on the gas grill and lit the burner. Together they watched as the flames crawled up the sides of the cardboard box. Remorse moved Genny to snatch the ultrasound picture from certain death. She had held it in her hands before handing it to Paul. No matter how painful it was to find out about Paul's past, the baby was a blessing from God and his or her short life had meaning and purpose.

Genny and Paul walked into a department store at the mall and Genny found the baby section right away. She stopped to gawk until Paul grabbed her hand and led her to the women's section against her will. After trying on two outfits and pouting, Genny accepted her fate and picked out several items of maternity clothing.

In the baby section, they picked out a crib and a chest of drawers. Paul didn't understand why they needed a changing table but gave in. He promised he would find a way to fit it in the nursery. With delivery of the furniture scheduled for the following week, Genny led the way to the food court. She handed Paul the shopping bags and headed to the restroom.

When Genny came back to the food court, she found Paul standing against the wall talking to a blonde woman. A familiar heat that she hadn't experienced in a while rose from her stomach. She had finally reached a place where she was secure in her relationship with Paul and now God was testing her.

When Genny was within a few feet of Paul and the woman, Paul looked at her with an apprehensive smile. Genny stopped when the woman turned around. She was none other than Brianna Javernick. Why did she keep showing up in their lives?

"Hi, Genny."

Bye, Brianna. "Hello." Genny took her place beside Paul. She rested her hand on top of her protruding belly. Mostly out of habit but she also wanted to draw attention to the baby she created with Paul.

"Congratulations." Brianna looked from Genny to Paul and back to Genny. "When are you due?"

"December seventeenth." Paul softly bumped shoulders with Genny and the scowl fell from her face.

Brianna needed to fall into a pit and never come out. She hadn't changed. Always the shallow self-absorbed snob. At least she wasn't wearing a skin-tight dress. It was odd seeing her in Levi's and a pullover with her long blonde hair pulled into a high ponytail. Caked-on makeup was also missing.

"Do you know what you are having?" Brianna's bright smile lit the space around them.

Wouldn't she love to know? Odd how no one was talking about the gigantic elephant in the middle of the food court. Did Brianna still think Genny could never love Paul like she did?

"We don't know yet. At the last appointment, the baby wasn't cooperating. Genny has another appointment the week after next. Hopefully the baby is more cooperative."

Paul volunteered too much information. Brianna didn't deserve to know anything about their baby.

"I have my own good news. I'm engaged!" Brianna held up her left hand displaying a rather large diamond solitaire. Genny didn't have an engagement ring and her wedding band no longer fit. "We haven't set a date, but it will be sometime next spring after I finish nursing school in December."

"Congratulations on both, Brianna," Paul said with an enthusiastic tone.

Genny rolled her eyes. She didn't care about Brianna's good news and felt sorry for the guy. "Congrats Brianna. Paul, I don't feel well. Can we get going?" Her congratulations were more obligatory than genuine, and she felt fine, but she'd say anything to get rid of Brianna. She couldn't stand one more second in Brianna's presence.

"Sure." Paul said.

"I wish you well and congratulations again on the baby." Brianna tilted her head to the side and smiled.

Genny smirked and looped her arm through Paul's arm, pulling him away from Brianna.

"Thank you. Congratulations to you, too," Paul replied.

Genny imagined Brianna falling off a cliff. God convicted her heart, but everything that Brianna had done to them prevented her from saying anything.

Brianna waved as she walked off. Paul turned to Genny and raised his brow.

"I've got to be honest. I hope this is the last time we see her."

"There's some reason she keeps popping up."

"To torture me."

Paul laughed. "Remember, God has a plan for everything."

"I guess." Genny rubbed her belly and glanced around the food court. She'd ask Paul later what he and Brianna talked about before she joined the conversation. It was sure to be interesting.

July 21, 2012

Brianna is like a wad of gum stuck to the bottom of my shoe. She's always hanging around. I don't know why God keeps her in my life. Paul said there's a reason, but I can't think of one reason why Brianna keeps popping up.

We have the furniture picked out and Paul made me buy maternity clothes. They look decent, I guess. I can't wait to hold this baby.

⟫⟫⟫ ⟪⟪⟪

Paul sat next to Genny in the waiting room. She was twenty weeks now and they were going to try again to find out the gender of the baby. They'd prayed the night before that their little one was cooperative. The names they'd picked out were Brandon Jacob and Katherine Kelly. When picking out a name for a boy, they both wanted Brandon, and Jacob was Paul's paternal grandfather's name. Katherine was his maternal grandmother's name and Kelly was Genny's mother's name. They were honoring their loved ones whether their baby was a girl or a boy.

"Genevieve." Genny looked up and smiled at the woman standing in the doorway. She had told Paul about Brenda, the ultrasound technician, who had performed all her ultrasounds.

Genny slipped her phone into her purse and Paul helped her to her feet. They followed Brenda back to one of the ultrasound rooms. Genny was used to the routine. She'd been having ultrasounds on a regular basis to check endometriosis lesions and scarring and to detect any potential problems with her pregnancy. So far, Dr. Nichols was happy with Genny's progression.

Reclining on the table, Genny rolled down the waistband of her pants to expose her abdomen. Paul brushed his fingers along her arm. She looked at him and smiled. Genny gasped when Brenda squeezed a blob of cold jelly on her skin.

"Sorry, the warmer is broken." She laughed.

As soon as Brenda spread the jelly over Genny's abdomen and pushed down, Paul saw it. At least, he believed he did. He glanced at Genny as she focused on the monitor.

"What is it?" Genny looked at Paul and grabbed his hand.

"If I'm right, she's Katherine." Paul smiled.

"You are right. You have yourself a little girl. She decided to cooperate today." Brenda smiled.

"Katherine." Genny's eyes glistened. He leaned down and kissed her. "Can we go buy a bunch of pink stuff now?" She grinned and pulled down her shirt after Brenda wiped away the jelly.

"Not too much. That's what baby showers are for." Paul helped Genny sit up and they headed out of the room.

Once they left the clinic, Genny had sweet talked Paul into stopping by a baby store. Heading home, he watched as she pulled out each piece of clothing from the shopping bag and held it up as she talked. A moment later, she dropped the last piece on her lap and glanced out the window.

"I'm scared I won't be a good mother."

"Why would you say that?" Where did that come from?

"I didn't have a mother."

"Yeah, but you had Granny. You and Brandon turned out pretty good." She looked at him. He smiled and propped his elbow on the arm rest. "Besides, she raised your mom. You will be an awesome mother, Gen." He reached over and brushed his finger across her cheek.

Pulling into the drive, Paul helped Genny down from the truck and grabbed the shopping bags. On the way to the front door, his eyes found the Jeep. He followed Genny inside, where she laid her purse on the dining table.

"I've been thinking." Paul turned her around to face him. "Don't you...maybe we should..."

"What?" Genny rested her hand on her belly.

"Get a family friendly vehicle. Maybe a minivan."

Genny's brows drew together.

Paul held up his hands. "I'm not saying to get rid of the Jeep. I'd never suggest that. I thought it might be hard to climb in and out of the Jeep with a baby."

"I'll be fine."

"Sweetheart…"

"If I find it's hard, then we'll look."

"All right." He kissed her and carried the bags into the nursery. Genny would learn soon enough that the Jeep wouldn't work. Especially the closer to her due date and she had to drag herself up into the driver's seat. It was inevitable so he'd start looking at minivans and SUVs.

⇝⟫ ⟪⇜

A minivan? Genny sat on the bed and clipped off the tags on Katherine's new clothes to put them in the wash. Paul wanted to buy a minivan. She bit her bottom lip. She was a Jeep girl, not a minivan girl. Resting her hands on her belly, as much as she hated to admit it, Paul was right. But no minivan. She grinned. They'd stay in the Jeep family and look for a SUV. Grand Cherokees were nice.

"Hey."

Genny looked up and saw Paul in the doorway. She sighed. "Fine."

"Huh?"

"We can look at SUVs."

Paul stepped over to her and took her hands in his. "We can wait a little while. It might not be as hard as I think it will be." He kissed her hands. "Has Melissa said anything about a baby shower?"

"She asked if we had plans in the near future. So, maybe she is planning something." She hadn't been to many baby showers. One or two at the most. To be the guest of honor was exciting. A flutter danced in her stomach. It wasn't like her usual butterflies. Her lips parted.

"What?"

"I think I felt her move."

"Really?" Paul's eyes brightened and he knelt down in front of Genny. She took his hands and rested them on either side of her abdomen.

"It might be too early for you to feel."

He stuck out his bottom lip and rested his head on her belly. Running her hand over his head, bristles of hair brushed across her hand from his recent haircut. She smiled. Paul was going to be a good daddy.

July 31, 2012

We are having a girl!! Katherine Kelly Thompson is healthy and right on schedule. I felt her move today and it was an amazing feeling. I'm so happy! A part of me is still a little paranoid that something will happen but I'm putting my faith in God. We bought a few cute outfits today and Paul thinks we need a bigger car. The thought of getting rid of the Jeep seems like getting rid of Brandon. But I know he wants to keep the Jeep as much as I do. I think Melissa is planning a shower. I can't believe all this is happening to me.

Three boxes of baby furniture leaned against a wall in the nursery. Paul exhaled and grabbed the crib box. Second guessing his previous decision, he should have paid the extra money to have the furniture assembled. Pulling out the parts and instruction booklet, he scanned the instructions and sighed. There had to be over a hundred parts.

"Can Peter help?"

Paul looked up and saw Genny standing in the doorway with her hands resting on top of her belly. She was twenty-eight weeks and more beautiful with each passing day. Seeing his baby grow and feel her movements was something he couldn't describe.

"Good idea. I'll call him. Maybe he can come over after church tomorrow. This crib is going to keep me busy all day today." Paul looked down at the open instruction booklet. The sketch of the assembled crib took his breath away. The feeling wasn't due to Katherine but to his surprise, his first child. Tears dampened his lashes. "I–I don't know why, but I just thought of my child that died." He took in a shaky breath.

Genny walked up to him and slipped her arms around his waist, her belly pushing against his abdomen. "I'm so sorry, honey." They held each other for a few moments. "Do you ever wonder if the baby was a girl or boy?"

Genny's question caught him off guard. He'd thought about it over the years. "I've always felt that he was a boy."

"Maybe so. A son and a daughter. Brandon and I used to say that our parents were lucky to have one of each. We said it was 'fair and square.'" She laughed. "I'm sure it was hard for your parents to lose their first grandchild."

Paul's chest tightened, squeezing his heart. "They don't know."

Genny eased back and raised her eyebrows. "You didn't tell them about the baby?"

"I never told anyone."

"Not Brandon?" Genny lips parted then closed.

"No. I talked to him when, you know, it turned physical. He told me it didn't mean it had to continue. So, when it did and she got pregnant, I didn't tell him. I was too ashamed. I thought he'd end our friendship when she had the abortion."

"He would have been there for you."

"I know that now." He leaned his head against Genny's.

She eased back and wiped the tears off his cheeks. "I'm here for you.

He smiled and kissed her. Katherine's movements pushed against him. Stepping back, he rested his hands on Genny's swollen middle. Twelve weeks until he could hold his daughter.

Genny went next door to visit with Mrs. Baker. Paul turned to the first page of the instruction booklet and got to work. In a little over two hours, he had the crib assembled. Placing the mattress in the crib, he ran his hand over the top. Imagining Katherine sleeping in the crib brought a smile to his face.

Paul sat on the couch and picked up the remote. The guide listed one of his favorite shows and he clicked to watch. A few minutes in, his phone rang, and he grabbed it from the side table. His mom's name showed on the screen.

"Hey, Mom."

"Hi, honey. How are you? How's Genny?"

"We are well. Genny's glowing as usual." Paul laughed.

"I can't wait to see her. I received the invitation for the shower. Dad and I want to come. You know I can't come for a visit without him." She laughed. "Do you have room for us?"

"Yeah. Peter helped me move things around for the nursery. It's kind of tight in the guest room, but the bed is usable."

"Good. We bought a present and I'm having it sent directly to you. It will be early for the shower. It's due to be delivered by next weekend."

"Okay, Mom. Can I guess?"

"No, you may not." The backdoor opened, and Genny headed into the living room.

"It's Mom." Paul held the phone out to her.

"Hi, Mom."

The two talked for a few minutes and Genny headed down the hall to take a nap. Paul made his way back to the nursery and sighed. Pulling out his phone, he dialed Peter's number. Plans were made for the Parkers to come over after church and have dinner with Paul and Genny after the men assembled the rest of Katherine's furniture.

Paul went to the office and opened the closet doors. He spotted the three-ring binder on the shelf and grabbed it. A document protector toward the back held the ultrasound picture of his oldest child. He ran his finger over the black oval in the middle of the picture. One day he may tell his parents about the baby, but for now, the picture would remain in the closet.

Chapter 30

The chill in the air pushed Genny to stop by The Roasted Bean. Rarely did she go since Michael had attacked her. There were too many bad memories. But today she wanted to see her friends and grab a cup of decaf. She climbed down from the Jeep with a little more effort than usual and made her way inside.

A new barista stood at the register. When Genny placed her order, she asked if Julie or Renee was working. The barista went to the back and returned a few moments later with Julie on her heels. Eyes wide, Julie held her hand over her mouth and darted from around the counter.

"Look at you! Katherine's getting so big."

"Tell me about it." Genny smiled and ran her hands over her belly.

"How much longer?"

"Ten weeks."

"Oh, wow. That's not long. Renee and I will be at the shower. I can't wait to hold my little niece." Julie's excitement amused Genny.

"Most people have said they are coming. Might have to have it somewhere else. I don't know if everyone will fit in my little house." Genny smiled and picked up her decaf coffee when a barista placed it on the pick-up counter. "I've got to run."

"Bye, girl. See you in two weeks!"

Genny looked around the parking lot and at the traffic passing by on the road as she stepped out the door. She surveyed the parking lot once more as she headed to the Jeep. Michael hadn't been seen since the assault almost seven months ago, but she couldn't stop herself from looking for him around every corner. The police had said that Michael was long gone, and she had to have faith that they were right. Climbing into the Jeep, she headed to Walmart to pick up a few items before heading home.

A tiny, pink, frilly dress complete with a matching headband caught Genny's eye. The baby section had been drawing her in the past few weeks. Paul had told her to wait until after the shower, but she couldn't help herself. Browsing up and down the aisles, everything brought a smile to Genny's face. Packs of onesies hung on pegs in front of her. She grabbed a pink pack and tossed it in the cart.

Time was slipping away, and Genny needed to get home and start dinner. Heading to the checkout, she stopped when a familiar blonde wearing scrubs was strolling down the aisle toward her. She held her breath and turned around, pretending to look at a rack of women's pajamas.

Genny listened to the squeak of Brianna's shoes until the sound faded. She pushed out her breath. Thank goodness Brianna didn't see her. She took in the area around her and found no evidence of Brianna except for her lingering perfume. Genny hurried to the checkout and went straight home.

Why did God insist on putting Brianna in Genny's life? It seemed every time she turned around, Brianna was there wearing a bright smile. At least she wasn't wearing a scowl like she did when they first met. She hadn't seen her since the day in the mall, but there was something different about Brianna. Even today she had a different air about her.

When Genny made her way up the front steps, the delicious aroma of spaghetti made her stomach growl. She loved it when Paul surprised her with dinner. Pushing the front door open, she walked in and sat the shopping bags on the counter. Paul stared at her and gave her a stern look.

"I see pink through that bag."

Genny smiled and raised her eyebrows.

"Let me guess. You couldn't help it."

"You know me so well." Genny waddled up to him and slipped her arms around his waist. "Is dinner ready?"

"Yep." Paul stepped back and grabbed two bowls from the cabinet.

"Two weeks until the baby shower." Genny grinned.

"I sure hope we get all we need so you will stop shopping."

Genny laughed. "Paul Thompson, you're so funny."

She stuck her fork in the middle of her bowl and twisted. "I saw Brianna at Walmart today." Opening her mouth, she inserted the fork, scraping her teeth on it as she pulled it out of her mouth. Paul looked at her and pressed his lips together. She held her hand over her mouth. "Sorry."

"What did she say?"

"She didn't see me, thank goodness." Genny ate another bite of spaghetti.

"There's a reason she was there."

Genny sighed. "Stop reminding me." Sitting her empty bowl on the coffee table, she stretched and flinched. "Either Katherine loves the spaghetti or hates it."

"Loves it." Paul grinned. He sat his bowl on the coffee table and they laid down on the couch. Paul rested his hand on Genny's belly.

"Do Mom and Dad have their flight reservations?"

"Yeah. They fly in on Friday and out on Monday."

"I can't wait to see them."

"Me either."

As much as Genny looked forward to holding Katherine in her arms, she worried how she would handle her crying, dirty diapers, and spit up. The Air Force allowed fathers two weeks of paternity leave and as far as she knew, that was the only time Paul was taking off. What would happen when it was her and Katherine? She could ask Tricia to stay but maybe not. She was Katherine's mother and responsible for her care.

October 8, 2013

Time is getting close. Ten more weeks until I can hold my baby girl. Paul is so excited. I've said it so many times and I'll say it again: Paul is going to be an awesome daddy. Life is strange sometimes. When I was twelve and infatuated with Paul, I'd never imagined that I'd be having his baby one day.

Paul turned the dial signaling the flame to race across the burner of the grill. Peter brought out a container of hamburger patties and placed them on the grill rack. He took a seat between Trevor and Brian.

Aaron Anderson looked at his watch. "It's almost noon. Are we the only guys here?" He laughed.

"In my day, women attended showers," Brian said.

"Yeah, Dad. I've never heard of both moms and dads being at a baby shower either."

The backdoor opened and Will Brown strolled onto the patio followed by Ryan Hammonds. They sat at the patio table with the other men.

"So, you ready Paul?" Aaron asked and smiled.

"I can't wait." Paul ran his hand over the top of his head.

"It never gets old. We have four and with each of my kids, it felt like the first time."

Paul smiled. He could already feel Katherine in his arms.

"Are you two going to have a house full?" Will asked.

"Katherine will be our only biological child. Genny's having a hysterectomy right after she's born. Any other children we may have will be adopted."

"That's awesome. Kind of like my sister and me. She was adopted," Will said.

The men talked for a while about fatherhood and Brian shared his thirty years of wisdom. Paul's face grew hot as Brian told stories of Paul's and Brandon's many escapades. Paul laughed along with the men but inside a heaviness settled in his chest. He missed his best friend and would have loved sharing this time with him. Brandon would have been a wonderful uncle to Katherine.

The backdoor opened and Paul's mom poked her head out. "Are the burgers ready?"

"I believe so," Brian said as he checked a patty. He pulled the patties off the grill and the men headed inside.

Paul raised his brow when he saw the number of women scattered around the house. Julie and Renee from The Roasted Bean, a few wives of his co-workers, Ryan's wife Ashley, and Melissa, Tamika, and Mrs. Baker. But no Genny.

Heading down the hall, he found her in the nursery rocking in the rocking chair his parents had given them as a shower gift. She smiled when he walked up to her.

"My love. You sure are rocking that chair. Better be careful or you'll knock a hole in the wall." He laughed and grabbed the arms to slow Genny down.

"I'm practicing rocking our baby." She grinned.

"Hopefully not that hard."

Genny giggled. "Eight more weeks."

"I can't wait to hold our miracle. Oh, the burgers are ready."

"Okay."

Paul took Genny's hands, pulled her to her feet, and kissed her.

After their friends left, Genny sat up in bed while Paul and his mom brought in the presents for a better look. Genny had been more tired recently, which according to the information he'd read, was normal.

"I think this is my favorite." Genny pulled the bedside bassinet to the edge of the bed. Paul walked over and visualized Katherine sleeping.

"I wish this was around when Paul was born." Tricia ran her hand along the edge.

Genny smiled when she held up a sleeper covered in pastel butterflies. Dropping the sleeper on her lap, she rummaged through the mound of clothes, linens, and blankets on Paul's side of the bed.

"Where is it?" She moved items around until she found it on the bottom. Sighing, she held the blanket to her chest and tears pooled in her eyes.

"That is so beautiful. Mrs. Baker is talented," Tricia said. Genny handed it to her, and she ran her fingers over the embroidered pastel butterflies scattered over the top.

"I changed my mind. This is my favorite gift. That goes in the hospital bag. I want to wrap Katherine in it at the hospital."

Paul smiled. "That's a wonderful idea, love."

He watched Genny and his mother gush over the tiny outfits that would clothe their daughter throughout her first year of life. God was good.

Two more weeks. Making it through thirty-eight weeks of pregnancy was surreal. Genny climbed into the Jeep and held the ultrasound picture of Katherine. Dr. Nichols had been keeping an eye on a lesion and considered moving the surgery up, but he said that it hadn't changed since her last ultrasound two weeks earlier. They'd take it day by day. If Genny went into labor before the seventeenth, there should be no problems.

Pulling out of the clinic parking lot, Genny drove toward the beach. Today was the second anniversary of Brandon's death. The Jeep console showed a temperature of fifty degrees, but it was warm enough for a short stroll on the beach to talk to Brandon.

Genny slipped on her jacket and tightened it as much as her middle would allow. A shiver ran down her arms. She didn't account for the wind. Trudging through the sand, she made it to the water's edge close enough that the water missed her shoes.

"Oh, Brandon." Tears spilled down Genny's cheeks. "I wish you were here. You would be the best uncle. Katherine looks a lot like us in the 4-D ultrasound. She has a dimple in her chin. Her cheeks and lips look like Paul's. I wonder if she will have our auburn hair or if it will be black like her daddy's." Genny rubbed her hands over her belly.

A gust of wind hit her, sending a chill deep into her bones. She made her way back to the Jeep and climbed inside. Wiping her cheeks, she drove out of the parking lot toward home. One of her favorite songs played as she pulled up to a traffic light. Glancing around for an audience, she began to sing when she didn't see anyone looking at her.

The light turned green, and Genny accelerated when the car in front of her moved. Screeching tires sounded behind followed by a deafening boom. Genny's body lunged forward, tightening the seat belt around her lower abdomen. A burning sensation filled her throat and eyes. She realized the airbag had deployed, but why? Searing pain shot through her middle.

"Ma'am?" A woman pulled on the door handle. Genny had enough wits about her to hit the unlock button. The woman gasped when she slung the door open. She turned her head and shouted, "She's pregnant!"

The ride in the ambulance went by in a blur. Paramedics scrambled by her side taking vitals. A nurse took over when they reached the emergency room, and she was whisked into an elevator. In what looked like an operating room, a nurse talking in a soothing voice started an IV.

Genny didn't know how long she'd laid on the table after the ultrasound, but she heard Dr. Nichols' voice and slowly exhaled.

"Well, Genevieve. When I said the baby could come early, I didn't mean like this." His smile eased her fears. "The ultrasound shows that the lesion ruptured. I suspect it was the seatbelt. The baby appears to be fine but when she's born, she will go to the NICU to be checked out, okay?"

Genny nodded. Where was Paul? Did he know what happened? Did she? Nothing made sense.

Dr. Nichols explained what would happen and the surgical and delivery teams introduced themselves, leaving Genny more confused. The medication she'd been given earlier must be affecting her.

"Genny?" The muffled voice sounded familiar.

Genny turned her head and widened her eyes. Although her hair and face were covered, the eyes belonged to Brianna.

"Oh my gosh Genny. I knew it was a car accident but had no idea it was you."

"My baby." Tears flooded down the sides of Genny's face. "I'm scared."

"I'm going to take care of her. I promise. I'm a neonatal nurse intern." Genny's heart raced.

"Intern?" Tremors violently shook her body.

"I'm Brianna's supervisor. Don't worry. Brianna is an excellent nurse and will take good care of your little one," the woman who stood next to Brianna said.

"Okay." Genny swallowed hard. She had no choice. A sense of calm floated over Genny when Brianna laid her hand on her shoulder. "I'll be praying."

The anesthesia team gathered by her side and the anesthesiologist explained his role and what he would be doing. A moment later, he placed a mask on her face.

"Breathe deep," he said.

As the room spun and the voices faded, Genny remembered it was the anniversary of Brandon's death. The birth of her daughter would give December first a different meaning—life. Darkness surrounded Genny when she filled her lungs with oxygen.

Chapter 31

P aul sat in the waiting room bouncing his leg. Ryan was trying to hold a conversation with him, but his mind wouldn't focus on anything but Genny and Katherine. Shortly after he arrived at the hospital and got an update on Genny, he called his parents. His mom said that they would be flying out the next morning.

A police officer was at the hospital for information on Genny and spoke to Paul. A truck had rear-ended Genny and pushed her into the car in front of her. The Jeep didn't sustain any major body damage due to the front grill guard and rear bumper guard. All the airbags deployed, the spare tire was damaged, and the tailgate was pushed in around the tire.

The officer had said that the truck was traveling around thirty-five miles per hour when it hit the Jeep. The driver was texting and cited for distracted driving. Anger had mixed with fear when he found out that someone's carelessness could have cost him his wife and daughter.

"Want a coffee?" Ryan asked.

Paul looked at his watch. Genny had been in surgery for at least an hour. He didn't know when the cesarean started, but his nerves were getting the best of him. "Sure."

Ryan rose and took a step then stopped when Paul's name was called. Paul looked up and raised his brows as he watched Brianna head his way. She was wearing scrubs and a surgical cap. He pulled himself to his feet and rubbed his hands on his uniform pants.

"I've got an update. The baby was delivered and is on her way to NICU to be checked out. Dr. Nichols feels there are no issues but wants the pediatrician to examine her. Genny is still in surgery for the hysterectomy. Once she's out and awake, you can see her. She'll be moved to a room, and I'll bring your baby to you."

Paul exhaled hard. "Okay, thank you, Brianna."

"Of course. I prayed for her and the baby during the delivery. I'll keep all of you in my prayers."

"I appreciate that."

"Sure," she said and walked back in the direction she came from.

Paul dropped to the seat and covered his face with his hands. Despite his will power, he broke down. Ryan sat down next to him and wrapped his arm around Paul's shoulders.

⇴⇴ ⇶

"You'll get to go to your room in a few minutes..." The voice came from across the room.

"Your baby boy is so precious. Wait until you see him...," someone said from one side of Genny.

"Everything went beautifully...," a voice said from the other side.

The voices blended together, and Genny opened her eyes. A curtain was pulled across the foot of the bed. Curtains on each side separated her from other patients. She realized she was in the post-op unit.

A man sat on the edge of the bed holding something in his arms. His face was blurred, but she presumed he was Paul. Squeezing her eyes shut and opening them, her heart rose to her throat when she saw Brandon's radiant smile.

"Hey sis." He looked down at the bundle in his arms. "She's beautiful."

Who was beautiful? Who was he holding? Surely not Katherine. "Don't worry, your baby girl is fine. I'm taking good care of her." Genny gasped. She had to be dreaming. Brandon tilted the bundle and Genny saw a beautiful baby with rosy skin and a head full of thick, black hair. Her features were a blend of her and Paul. Brandon was holding Katherine.

"She's got her daddy's hair." Brandon laughed. "I'm so glad you and Paul found love through your grief. If I could choose a husband for you, I'd choose Paul. He's a good man, Genny."

Brandon wrapped his fingers around her upper arm and squeezed. A smile spread across her face. Seeing Brandon filled her heart with love.

"Genevieve?"

Genny lifted her heavy lids and saw a nurse standing by the head of her bed.

"You look happy. I've never seen a patient coming out of anesthesia grinning."

"Where's my brother?"

"Brother? I thought he was your husband. He'll be here soon."

"No, my brother was here with my baby."

The nurse looked at the monitor and walked to a tall table and typed on a laptop. "No one besides you and me are here. I've been here since you were brought into recovery."

"Oh." The nurse probably thought she was crazy.

"Sometimes, patients do and say odd things coming out of anesthesia." She smiled and resumed typing. "Your baby is in the NICU. You'll see her as soon as you are in your room."

"NICU?" Genny's tongue stuck to the roof of her mouth.

"She's fine. The doctor checked her out. She's waiting for her mommy to get better. Your blood pressure is a little high but that can happen with general anesthesia. As soon as you are in the normal range, you'll be moved to your room."

"My husband?"

"I'll go get him. But try to take it easy so we can get that blood pressure down, okay?" Picking up a cup, the nurse held the straw to Genny's lips. The cool liquid quenched her parched mouth. The nurse sat the cup on a small table next to the bed and went behind the curtain.

Feeling as if she were crawling out of her skin, it was difficult for Genny to calm herself. She wanted Paul to hold her, and she wanted to hold their baby. She closed her eyes and took in a deep breath.

"Sweetheart?"

Genny's eyes flew open. "Paul!" Tears dampened her eyelashes. "Have you seen her?"

He leaned down and kissed her forehead. "Not yet."

The blood pressure cuff tightened around Genny's upper arm, and the nurse checked the monitor. "Your husband is good for you. You're back in the normal range. Let's give it another time or two then we'll get you to your room so you can see your baby."

"Okay." Paul leaned down and kissed her. Before he pulled away, she whispered, "Brandon was here."

"Was he?" He tilted his head.

"Yes, and he was holding Katherine. It seemed so real." Genny sighed. "I can't wait to see her."

He brushed his knuckles across her cheek. "Me either."

Traveling down the hall was strange. The lights overhead reminded Genny of a camera angle in a movie. Butterflies fluttered around in her stomach. They were about to see their daughter. Paul gently squeezed Genny's hand. He'd been holding her hand since the nurse pushed the bed into the hall. Slowing down, she pushed Genny into a room. Centering the bed between a set of wall lights, she locked the wheels and raised the head.

"A few more minutes." The nurse smiled.

Paul sat on the edge of the bed and took Genny's hands in his. "This is it." He smiled.

"I feel like I'm going to throw up."

Paul's smile fell.

"No, it's excitement. And probably the anesthesia." Genny breathed deeply and exhaled slowly.

The door creaked open, and Brianna rolled a bassinet up to the edge of Genny's bed. "Here's your beautiful daughter." She looked from Genny to Paul and smiled. Slipping her arms around Katherine, Brianna laid the infant in Genny's arms.

Brianna stood back and looked from Genny to Paul, rubbing her hands together. "I want to apologize to you two for how I acted…back then…last year." She sighed and bit her lip. "I wasn't a good person, but I've gotten my life together. I've rededicated my life to the Lord and Ethan is a godly man." She smiled slightly and took a step back.

Genny adjusted Katherine in her arms. Unexpected tears pooled in her eyes. "Thank you. You calmed my fears in the ER. I was so scared for her." Genny tilted her head down to Katherine.

"I was doing my j—"

"No. It was more than that. And…and it's my turn to apologize. I'm sorry for how I've treated you in the past." Genny gulped. She was amazed at how light her chest felt after letting go of her anger."

"I forgive you, Genny."

"I forgive you, too, Brianna," Paul added.

"I'm heading out so you can enjoy your daughter. Congratulations." Brianna gave a slight wave and walked out.

Genny looked at Paul. "She was good to me and helped me calm down." She kissed the top of Katherine's head, the baby's thick, black hair tickling her nose. "Anyway, life's too short."

"That it is."

Genny gazed at her daughter. She looked exactly like the ultrasounds. A dimpled chin like Genny, and lips and cheeks like her daddy. Katherine's face crinkled and red flooded her cheeks. Her loud wail filled the room.

"Shh, shh, sweet baby. I know it's scary out here." Genny ran a finger along Katherine's plump cheek. Her mouth closed and her green eyes studied Genny's face. "I love you so much." Genny lightly brushed her fingers through her daughter's hair. Katherine had enough hair to pull up for a barrette or tiny ponytail. She loosened the blanket and confirmed ten fingers and ten toes. Glancing at Paul, she held Katherine out to him. "Hold your daughter." She carefully laid Katherine in Paul's arms. She whimpered and flailed her arms. "What about her blanket from Mrs. Baker?"

"I'll call her." Paul held Katherine close to his chest.

"Okay, good." Genny noticed Katherine shift her eyes to Paul's face. "She feels the vibration of your voice like she did when you laid your head on my stomach and talked to her."

Paul held Katherine up to his face and kissed her cheek. As Genny watched her husband and daughter bond, a moment she doubted would happen had come true. They arrived at the hospital as husband and wife and would leave as a family of three.

December 5, 2013

Katherine was born on the anniversary of Brandon's death. It was like God wanted to turn a sad day into a happy day. After I was rear ended, I was so scared that my fears were coming true, but God gave us a healthy baby girl. She's so beautiful and a perfect mix of me and Paul.

"I bet you are ready to see your mommy. Say, 'I have a clean bottom and an empty tummy.'" Tricia laughed and handed a crying Katherine to Genny. She cradled her baby girl in her arms, and she began to nurse. "Okay, you two. Papa and I are going to go shopping for the day. I know you weren't expecting us for another few weeks. Dad and I will pick up groceries on the way home."

"Mom, you don't have to do that." Paul looked up as he brushed his finger over Katherine's cheek.

"I know." She smiled. "You three enjoy your time together. Dad and I will be home later. Let me know if you need anything while we're out."

"Okay, Mom." Tricia and Brian were a godsend. They had prepared the house for the baby's homecoming and now they were taking over kitchen duties. They were a blessing.

The house fell quiet not long after Brian and Tricia left. Paul slipped his finger under Katherine's fingers and brushed his thumb across her tiny knuckles. Lucy hopped up on the bed and laid at the foot, watching the trio intently. Paul patted the mattress between him and Genny and after a few moments of coaxing, she made her way to Paul and Genny and laid down between them close to Genny.

Wide-eyed, Genny watched Lucy sniff the back of Katherine's head. She raised up slightly and sniffed Katherine's ear. Genny looked at Paul and smiled.

"Thank you." Paul brushed his knuckles across Genny's cheek.

"What for?"

"Her." He looked down at Katherine.

"Well, we had help. I will be forever grateful that God trusted us with Katherine."

"Me, too."

Genny grimaced when Katherine's forehead crinkled, and her mouth stopped moving. Red filled Katherine's face. A moment later, her eyes drooped, and she continued nursing.

Once Katherine finished nursing, Paul took over so Genny could shower. He flung a burp cloth over his shoulder and brought Katherine up and began to softly pat her back.

"Motherhood looks good on you."

Genny looked down at herself. "Are you sure about that?"

"Yes." He winked.

"I've been thinking. I was so scared that I wouldn't know what to do. That I would disappoint you. And her. But I feel like I'm home. I've found my purpose. I mean, I'm not naive. I know there'll be a lot of sleepless nights and crying in my future. Our future." Genny raised her eyebrows. "I haven't been this happy in a long time. Well, besides marrying you." She leaned over to kiss him.

"I told you that you would be a wonderful mother."

A Genny looked at Katherine and smiled.

"I'm heading to the shower."

"Okay, love. We're going to hang out here."

Early in the evening, Brian and Tricia arrived home. They walked into the living room, looked at each other and smiled. "Dad and I were wondering if you two would like us to stay through Christmas. We know that's a few weeks. If not, let us know. We understand you are new parents, and this is an important time. With you still recovering, Genny. Well, we figured you could use some help."

Their expressions reminded Genny of children waiting to open presents on Christmas morning. Genny looked at Paul. She smiled and gave him a slight nod.

"Yeah?" he whispered.

"Yeah."

"We would love to have you. If you feel you can handle that bed for a few more weeks." Paul laughed and held Katherine up to his mother.

"Anything to be with our grandbaby." Tricia took Katherine from Paul and started singing to her.

Genny imagined her own mother singing to her granddaughter. Tricia passed Katherine to Brian and went to the kitchen to prepare dinner. Would Genny's father have held Katherine the way Brian was holding her? Genny had no doubt that her parents would have been wonderful grandparents.

"I wish they were here." Genny blew out her breath.

"I know, sweetheart. I do, too." Paul took her hand and gave it a gentle squeeze.

"Granny would be over the moon. I'm sure my parents would be too. And Brandon."

"You're right. They'd be in love with her."

Tears flowed down Genny's cheeks. Paul reached over and wiped them away. "I'm so glad we have your parents. And Mrs. Baker."

"Me, too. We are blessed."

Genny watched Brian head down the hall with Katherine in his arms. December first would forever be etched in her memory. Every year when they celebrated Katherine's birthday, the accident that brought her into the world two weeks early and Brandon's death would linger in the background.

$$Chapter\ 32$$

S tanding outside the guest room door with her hands on her hips, heat filled Genny's face. "Shh, you better not wake Katherine!" she whispered through clenched teeth.

"I'm sorry," Paul's muffled voice came through the door. "I found what I was looking for." He opened the door a crack and grinned.

"You look like Jack Nicholson in *The Shining*."

"Gee, thanks, Genevieve." Opening the door wide, he kissed her.

Genny went into the nursery to check on Katherine. She laid on her back with her arms and legs splayed. The blanket Mrs. Baker had made was pulled up to her waist. Genny brushed her fingers across the white onesie dotted with red and pink hearts.

Two days and Katherine would be eleven weeks old. Her first month of life went by in a whirlwind. Brian and Tricia had stayed until the day after Christmas. Having their help was a blessing, but Paul and Genny were glad to have their baby to themselves after they left.

The living room darkened as Genny made her way down the hall. Paul had closed the blinds on the back side of the house.

"What are you doing?" Genny crossed her arms.

"Preparing for your anniversary present." Paul turned on the lamp, pulled her into his arms and said, "Two years. It's hard to believe."

"Two years ago, could you have imagined that we'd have a baby?"

"No." He brushed her hair away from her face and kissed her.

"Are you doing something outside?" She smiled.

"Maybe." He rubbed his chin and winked. "I need you to stay in the house and not look out back."

"Why is that?" She wrinkled her brow.

"Just do what I ask, please." His eyes brightened.

"Okay." What was he up to? Being mysterious wasn't in Paul's nature.

Katherine cried out. Paul and Genny stood as still as statues for a few moments. She cried out again, and Genny made her way to the nursery.

Watching her daughter nurse as she rocked her, Genny thought about the accident. God had protected her baby girl. Life would have been over if anything would have happened to Katherine.

Genny laid Kathrine down in the bassinet in the living room. The backdoor opened and Paul squeezed through the crack. Genny rolled her eyes.

"What? I can't spoil the surprise, can I?" He grinned.

Someone knocked on the front door, and Lucy's ears raised. Paul strolled over to the door and invited Mrs. Baker inside. He followed her into the living room, where she reached into the bassinet to pick up Katherine. Paul was still wearing his grin when he looked at Genny. His behavior was downright confusing.

"Mrs. Baker is going to stay with Katherine while we are in the backyard."

"Oh." Genny watched Mrs. Baker sit down with Kathrine in her arms. Mrs. Baker loved Katherine like she was her own great granddaughter.

"Are you ready?" He held out his hand and led Genny out the backdoor. On the picnic table was a red tablecloth, two glasses of what she assumed was white grape juice and a bowl of chocolate-covered strawberries. When she sat down, Paul handed her a small red envelope. She opened it and pulled out a child's Valentine's Day card. She looked up at him.

"Since I never gave you a Valentine's Day card when we were kids, I thought I'd make up for it."

Moisture filled Genny's eyes.

"We have twenty-three more like it in the house." He laughed. Sitting on the picnic table, they spent a few minutes eating strawberries and drinking juice. Paul took the glass from Genny's hand. "Close your eyes."

"What?"

"Close your eyes, love."

Genny closed her eyes and sighed. She sensed his presence in front of her. *What is he doing?*

"Open your eyes," his tone was serious and a little mysterious. Genny braced herself for what she was about to see. "Genevieve."

"Sorry." Genny took a deep breath and opened her eyes. Paul was down on one knee holding a red velvet box that displayed a diamond engagement ring.

"Genevieve Marie Thompson, will you marry me again?" Paul asked.

Genny gasped and covered her mouth with her hands. Paul's face blurred through tears. Impulsively, she leaped off the table, dropped to her knees in front of him, and threw her arms around his neck.

"I guess that's a yes?" He lifted his brows.

"Yes! Yes! Yes!" Genny giggled and pressed her lips against his.

Paul slipped the ring on her finger. She focused on the marquise cut diamond solitaire with a row of small diamonds around the band. Turning her hand, she smiled as the diamonds sparkled in the sunlight. "This was your Christmas present when I was deployed. With every-thing that happened, it got pushed to the back burner. Our anniversary was the perfect time."

"Things like this are why I love you so much." She smiled and kissed him again.

"How about six months?"

"Can we pull it off in six months? Would the church even be avail-able?" Genny popped a small strawberry in her mouth.

"It's available. I already reserved it for August tenth."

"Paul Tyler!" Genny laughed. "It's perfect."

"The church was booked through the end of the year, but Ryan told me they'd had a cancellation for the tenth, so I took it."

"You'll be here, right?"

"What do you mean?"

"Any deployments coming up?" Genny held her breath.

"It's slowed down since troop withdrawals. I'll eventually deploy again. Maybe sometime in the next year or so."

"Okay. I hope you never have to deploy again after that. So does this mean a wedding with the white dress, bridesmaids, and the whole nine yards?"

"Of course."

They finished the strawberries and headed back inside. Katherine was asleep in Mrs. Baker's arms. Genny hadn't seen Mrs. Baker this happy in a long time. She had a feeling that Mrs. Baker was no longer lonely now that Katherine had come along. Several times, she'd watch Katherine while Genny went shopping or to an appointment. In some way, she'd involve Mrs. Baker in the wedding. She was Genny's adopted grandmother, after all.

⟫⟫⟩ ⟨⟨⟨⟵

Glancing at the mantel clock, Paul guessed Genny would be home in fifteen or twenty minutes. She and Melissa had signed up for a painting class and taken advantage of the church's Mother's Day Out program. Smiling, butterflies still fluttered in his stomach when she crossed his mind.

In the guest room, Paul had pulled a box out of the closet and one of his deployment bags hit the floor with a *thud*. Reaching inside, he found a book and pulled it out. It was the Journal Genny had given him to use during the deployment.

With everything that had happened, he hadn't had the chance to give the journal to Genny and forgot about it. He thumbed through the pages. The last entry was the day before he was sent home on emergency leave. When Genny returned home, he'd bring it to her attention.

"Hey Daddy," Genny said as she came in the door with Katherine in the car seat carrier.

"There's my family." Paul walked into the kitchen with the journal in his hand.

"What's that?" Genny made her way to the dining table and sat the carrier down.

"The deployment journal." Paul held it up.

"Oh, my gosh. I forgot all about it."

"Me, too. I found it in one of my deployment bags. Do you know where yours is?" Genny unbuckled Katherine and handed her to Paul. He followed her to the bedroom and watched her dig through a drawer, pulling items out and laying them on the floor.

"Hmm." Genny continued piling things onto the floor. "Here it is," she said and held it up. "So, what now?"

"Let's read." He smiled.

"Okay." Genny headed to the couch.

Paul laid Katherine in the portable crib and sat on the couch next to Genny. He thumbed through the pages and found an entry. He laughed.

"What?"

"What does that say?" He pointed to a word.

Genny groaned. "Cheeks. I had warm cheeks thinking about your strong arms around me." Pink brushed across her cheeks.

"Like now?" He reached over and she pulled away. "Standby for more translations. Your handwriting—"

"I know." She rolled her eyes. "And I know I can talk to you about anything. I love you, too," Genny said, holding up Paul's journal. She leaned over and kissed him.

Paul took the journal from her hand and laid both on the coffee table. He pulled her into his arms and held her for a while. Genny snuggled up against his shoulder. Resting his head against hers, deployments filled his mind.

Troops were returning home from the Middle East every day, but it would be a while longer until the bases were shut down. He prayed he wouldn't be called up to deploy, although he knew he was being unrealistic. Leaving Genny behind when he deployed last time was hard. He couldn't imagine how hard it would be to leave both Genny and Katherine.

⇒⇒⇒ ⇐⇐⇐

A slight breeze rustled the leaves on the oak tree. Genny heard Lucy sniffing and watched her sniff Katherine's head. She had become Katherine's protector. From the time they brought Katherine home from the hospital, Lucy had been by her side.

Katherine cooed and blew bubbles. Genny smiled and bounced Katherine on her knees. Her phone rang, and Melissa's name showed on the screen. As soon as Genny answered, she knew something was wrong.

"Melissa?"

"We're leaving." Melissa sniffled.

"Leaving?" Genny's mind flipped through the possibilities. They were going on vacation or to visit family? It wouldn't make sense. Why would she cry?

"We are moving." Melissa broke down.

"No! When?" Tears pooled in Genny's eyes.

"September."

It was May. They had four months.

"Where are you going?"

"Colorado."

"Oh, no. That's so far away." Something else to get used to.

Military members didn't stay at bases long. Paul had been stationed in Charleston for three and a half years. Peter had been transferred to Charleston the year before Paul. Did that mean that Paul would receive transfer orders soon? Tears welled in her eyes when she thought of who she'd miss in Charleston. At the top of the list was Mrs. Baker.

"I know. Why couldn't it be North Carolina?"

"We will visit as much as we can, Melissa. I promise."

Genny heard Melissa take a quick breath.

"We can wallow in our sorrow or take advantage of the time we have left. Let's sit down soon and come up with some ideas. Maybe we can do Painting with a Twist again. Or a spa day."

"Those sound fun." Asher cried in the background. "I need to go. It's time for Asher's feeding. I had to let you know."

"Okay, we'll talk soon."

Genny hung up and wiped the tears from her cheeks. Melissa was leaving. Her best friend from the time she'd moved to Charleston. What was she going to do now? It was time for Katherine's nap, and she headed inside.

Paul pulled into the driveway, and Genny grabbed a tissue to wipe her cheeks. When he came in and hung up his keys, he went straight to the living room and slipped his arms around Genny. Paul's attempt to explain military life was fruitless. Nothing he said could ease the pain of Peter and Melissa leaving.

"When will you get transferred?" Begging God, she held her breath waiting for his reply.

"I don't know, love. This is my fourth assignment."

"Soon?" Genny gulped.

"I've been here since two thousand nine. It's going to happen, sweetheart. I won't stay here until I retire."

Genny leaned her forehead against Paul's chest. "I wanted Katherine and Asher to spend more time together."

"I know." Paul kissed the side of her head.

May 14, 2013

Melissa and Peter are leaving. I can't believe it. Colorado is so far away. Now I'm scared that we will be leaving soon. Paul said it's possible that it may happen sooner than later. I've gotten used to living here. I love it. This is where our baby was born. Paul had been stationed in Colorado. He said it's beautiful. I don't want to leave Charleston.

Chapter 33

K atherine laid on her back in the middle of the bed. Genny rolled onto her side, watching her daughter sleep. She bit her bottom lip when she heard Paul pull into the driveway. Glancing between Katherine and the hall, Genny held her finger over her lips when Paul came into view. At the side of the bed, he leaned down and kissed her. Genny's eyes widened when he leaned over her.

"If you wake her…," she whispered.

Paul grinned and kissed Katherine's cheek.

Katherine's forehead creased, and crimson filled her cheeks. Genny's eyes narrowed, and she exhaled hard.

"I fed her half an hour ago, so she's not hungry."

"She wants to hang out with Daddy." With Katherine in his arms, Paul headed to the living room. Lucy jumped down from the couch when Paul sat down with Katherine wailing in his arms. Nothing he did calmed her. Grabbing a throw blanket off the back of the couch, he tossed it on the floor and Genny spread it out.

Katherine laid on her stomach and raised her head, looking around the room. Genny sat on the couch next to Paul and they watched her for a minute.

"Three more months until Peter and Melissa leave."

"I know. I still can't believe they're leaving. I'm glad they will be here for the wedding." Tears stung Genny's eyes. How was she going to make it after Melissa moved? Tamika worked full-time, and Zach was a teenager. It wasn't like they could get together for a play date.

"Me, too. It didn't take Peter and me long to become friends. And when Brandon died, he became my best friend."

"Do you think he still believes our marriage is fake?" Genny laughed.

"Um, I think Katherine proves it's not fake." He ran his hand down her arm and kissed her.

Genny glanced at Katherine and gasped. "She rolled over!" She sat up and held her hand over her mouth as she watched Katherine struggle to roll onto her back again.

"Good job, baby girl! You'll roll back over soon. Don't give up." He leaned over and took a hold of one of Katherine's feet. "Don't forget to put that in her book, Mommy. 'Rolled over at five months.'"

"I won't." Genny sat on the floor next to Katherine and tickled her tummy. She and Paul laughed when Katherine giggled.

"So, Mrs. Thompson, are you ready to become Mrs. Thompson?" Paul smiled.

Genny playfully swatted Paul's leg. Her phone buzzed, and she reached up and grabbed it off of the side table. She wrinkled her brow when she saw the name.

"Who is it?"

"Detective Carter." Genny's pulse raced.

"Wow, he hasn't called in a long time."

"No, he hasn't." Genny answered and walked into the kitchen.

"Hey, Genevieve. It's Dave Carter. I have some news."

Nausea burned her chest. "Yeah?"

"Michael Moretti was arrested yesterday in California."

Every muscle in her body went rigid. "California? He ran that far because of me?" Why would Michael flee to the west coast?

"Unfortunately, you aren't the only one. He attacked a total of four women."

"What?" Genny's voice was louder than she expected. Holding her hand over her mouth, ice flowed through Genny's veins. She turned toward the living room and saw Paul standing with Katherine in his arms.

"What is it?" he mouthed.

Genny held the phone to her chest for a second and whispered, "Michael's been arrested."

Relief soon turned into panic when Detective Carter mentioned court and testifying. That meant she would see Michael again. He nearly killed her, and the thought of seeing him would be like his hands slipping around her throat again. Tears filled her eyes, and she began to shake as the detective continued to talk about arraignment and the potential timeframe for trial.

Paul held out his hand. She took Katherine from his arms and handed him the phone. A few minutes later, Paul hung up and explained that court would likely take place in the next year. At most, she would be interviewed by the attorneys. She fought to keep the nausea down.

Hearing about Michael had brought one person to mind. She glanced at the wall clock and back at Paul.

"What?" He rubbed his finger over Katherine's cheek.

"There's someone I have to see." Paul read her mind and urged her to go. She kissed Katherine's head, handed her to Paul, and grabbed her keys.

She slowed down and turned into the neighborhood. As she approached the house, Trevor was in the driveway working on his Jeep. He ducked his head out from under the hood and straightened. His brows drew slightly together.

"Having problems?" Genny asked as she climbed down from the Jeep.

"Nah, changing the oil." He smiled, bringing out the wrinkles around his eyes.

"There's something I wanted to tell you in person." Genny strolled over to him.

He wiped his hands with a towel and shifted his weight. "Okay."

"Michael was arrested yesterday in California."

Trevor's eyes widened. "Are you sure?"

"I got a call from the detective. I had to tell you myself."

Moisture filled Trevor's eyes, and he rubbed them with the back of his hand. Genny stepped up to him and gave him a tight hug. "I don't blame you. If you knew what kind of person he was, I know you never would have let him join the club."

He looked away. Looking back at her, he took a deep breath. "I have to say this one last time, then I'll let it go."

"Okay." Genny had no doubt what he would say.

"I'm sorry, Genny." He wiped his eyes again.

"I forgive you."

May 29, 2013

Michael was arrested today. I'm scared about going to trial. I pray he accepts a plea deal, and they'll use my statement. I don't think I can face him again. I told Trevor in person. It's obvious that he has been carrying guilt since that night. I've always thought of Trevor as a father. My dad would be a little older than him if he had lived. I have a feeling he thinks of me as a daughter. I pray he is at peace about the situation now. I will be after Michael's sent to prison. And I'm sure he will be after assaulting four women.

A floor length white dupioni silk wedding gown hung on a hanger on the bathroom door. The gown was slightly fitted at the top with wide lace straps and an overlay of flowing chiffon covered the gathered skirt. Melissa removed the dress from the hanger and slipped it over Genny's head, careful to avoid the up do Tamika had spent the last hour curling and pinning. Melissa zipped up the zipper and walked around in front of Genny.

"Genny," Melissa covered her mouth with both hands. "You're beautiful."

Tamika stood next to Melissa. "Oh, my goodness. You are gorgeous."

Julie finished buckling the straps on Genny's shoes and joined the other bridesmaids.

"Oh, Gen. You are so beautiful."

"Thank you. Thank you for everything." Genny smiled and hugged her friends.

Katherine whimpered. Genny picked up her daughter and kissed her head. Standing in front of the floor length mirror, Genny watched eight-month-old Katherine shove her fingers into her mouth and stare at herself.

There was a knock at the door. Tamika pulled it open, and Mrs. Baker stood in the doorway. She approached Genny with a small velvet box in her hand. Genny saw tears in Mrs. Baker's eyes.

"I wore these when Stanley and I married." She held the box out to Genny and took Katherine into her arms.

Genny opened the box and gasped at the pear drop earrings. She looked up at Mrs. Baker. "These are beautiful."

"I don't know if you're participating in the old, new, borrowed, and blue tradition."

Genny shook her head. It never crossed her mind.

"This can be the old and new. They're not new, but new to you." Mrs. Baker smiled. "I want you to have them."

"Mrs. Baker—"

She held up her hand. "Don't say you can't. It would make me happy for you to have the earrings."

"Thank you." Genny hugged Mrs. Baker for a few moments.

Mrs. Baker kissed Genny's cheek. "The reception is all set up. That cake is breathtaking."

"Thank you for all your help. I can't wait to see it."

After Mrs. Baker left the room, Genny switched out her earrings. Tricia came in a few moments later and picked up Katherine to take her to the sanctuary. Ten minutes until the ceremony was scheduled to begin. One last check of her dress and makeup, and her bridesmaids took their place in the foyer.

Genny stared at herself in the mirror after her friends left the room. Tears gathered in her eyes. She was alone. No one to walk her down the aisle. She'd missed her father over the years, but especially now. Earlier in planning the wedding, Brian had come to mind, but Paul had already asked him to be his best man.

She pulled a tissue from the box. Standing close to the mirror, she blotted the mascara from under her eyes and blew out her breath. Five more minutes. Tremors shook her body. There was no reason to be nervous. She and Paul were already married. Walking down the aisle in front of everyone could be the reason. That wasn't it. She wanted to be on her father's arm. She drew in a quick breath and willed herself not to cry.

A knock at the door startled her. Ryan's wife was acting as their wedding planner and was probably checking on her. She pulled the door open and raised her eyebrows. Standing on the other side of the doorway was Brian. His smile reached his eyes.

"What are you doing here?"

"I'm walking my daughter down the aisle." He offered his arm.

"But you're the best man." Brian would sacrifice his position as best man to walk her down the aisle?

"I'm still the best man. I'll stand by my son after I give him your hand."

His expression softened. Taking a step toward her, he offered his arm again. "Genevieve, you are so beautiful. You are going to take Paul's breath away."

Brian had never called her Genevieve. She covered her mouth to hold back a sob, careful not to smudge her lipstick. Looping her arm around his, they made their way out of the room to the head of the aisle.

As the wedding march played, the crowd rose to their feet. Genny saw Paul standing next to Ryan. As she walked closer, the emotion that displayed on his face touched her heart. Soft pink teased his cheeks, and his eyes glistened. When Brian placed Genny's hand in Paul's, it was as if they were marrying for the first time. Brian took his place next to Paul, and Ryan began the ceremony.

In front of their family and friends, Paul and Genny pledged their love to each other and made a promise to keep God at the center of their lives and marriage. During Paul's vows, Genny thought about everything he had given her over the years since Brandon died. His protection, emotional support, and love meant the world to her. Soon, that love grew into the love that they shared standing at the altar.

Genny had struggled with how she and Paul had come to know each other. For years, she had been angry that God had taken her family from her. But she had finally come to a place where she understood that her family went beyond Paul and Katherine. She had parents, a grandmother, and many brothers and sisters. They may not be blood, but she loved them, and they loved her. That was all that mattered.

As the reception wound down, Paul stood and offered his arm. "Are you ready, Mrs. Thompson?" Genny rose and slipped her arm through his. The couple made their way to the doors of the reception hall, where their family and friends gathered to wish them well. They each kissed their baby girl and walked through hundreds of bubbles on the way to their new SUV.

As Paul pulled up to the exit of the parking lot, Genny's eyes found the Jeep and she smiled. She had driven it to the church with precious cargo in the back seat. It would be the last time she drove the Jeep for a while, except for special occasions. In a way, she felt that parking the Jeep would betray Brandon's memory. But Paul was right. It was hard to maneuver the height and running boards with a baby carrier. Paul squeezed her hand, and she looked his way.

"I love you, Genevieve." Paul kissed the back of her hand.

"I love you, too." She smiled at her husband.

The next morning, Genny walked out onto the beach and sat down on the cool sand. Digging her toes in deep, she watched the storm clouds gather above the ocean in the distance. She looked up at the house. Melissa's parents owned a beach house on a private beach and offered the house at a deep discount. Genny had never been on a private beach, but was quickly becoming a fan.

Sand squeaked behind Genny, and she turned to see Paul approaching. He lowered himself onto the sand behind her and she leaned back against his chest. They sat quietly, looking out over the ocean.

"I miss Katherine."

Paul leaned his head against Genny's. "Me, too, baby, but she's in good hands."

"I know." Genny breathed in. "The Outer Banks is so beautiful."

"Yes, it is."

Genny sighed.

"You okay, love?"

"Yeah. I was thinking about life and everything that's happened."

"Mmm. I think life's kind of like the weather. It's not always a bright and sunny day. Our lows are like a storm. Dark, ominous clouds weigh heavy on our shoulders, rain batters our face, and lightning slices through our hurting hearts. But, as God promises, the storms of life will end. And how does He show His promise?"

"A rainbow." Genny smiled to herself.

"Yes, we both have been through our share of storms, but He has always been faithful and has given us a rainbow."

"Yes, He has." Genny gasped. "Look." She pointed at distant rain falling into the ocean. "It looks like it's coming this way."

"Nah, it's going out."

Genny closed her eyes. After a few minutes, the smell of rain filled her senses. A minute later, large drops of rain began to fall. Genny squealed and jumped up. "I think you were mistaken!" She started giggling.

Paul grabbed her hand as they ran toward the house. Both laughed and didn't stop until they were inside. After toweling off, they walked over to the patio doors and watched the storm until it passed. Paul went into the kitchen to get a glass of water.

"Hey, babe. Come here."

Genny headed over and stood beside him. She smiled when she saw the rainbow stretched across the sky.

August 26, 2013

Paul and I have been "married" for a little over two weeks now. I have never been this happy. In the past, I would deny myself happiness because I was sure God would tear my happiness away. But now I put my trust in Him. That is the only way I will survive every day.

On our honeymoon, Paul said something that surprised me. When Katherine is a little older, he wants to look into foster to adopt. I wonder if God will lead us down that road. I have to admit that a small part of me hopes that God gives us a little boy one day. There's nothing like the love of a brother.

Playlists

I love listening to music while I write. I had a playlist for *A Heart's Journey* and added songs I felt Paul and Genny would listen to. I hope these playlists help you understand their personalities better.

Paul's Playlist:

"Animal" by Def Leppard

"Sweet Child O' Mine" by Guns N' Roses

"Where I Belong" by Building 429

"Awake" by Seventh Day Slumber

"Bring Me Down" by Pillar

"Hero" by Skillet

Genny's Playlist:

"Cold" by Crossfade

"Send the Pain Below" by Chevelle

"I Will Not Bow" by Breaking Benjamin

"Wish you were here" by Incubus

"Papercut" by Linkin Park

"Scars" by Papa Roach

Acknowledgments

T hank you to my husband, Rod, who provided invaluable information on the US Air Force, his job in the Air Force (which is Paul's job), and his knowledge of the Bible. He answered all my questions and listened to my endless excitement as I talked about different scenes and situations, but not too much. He didn't want me to spoil it for him because he wants to read the book himself. Thank you for believing in me, babe. I love you!

Thank you to my daughter, Rachel. Periodically, she read draft chapters. One day, she said that Genny's heart was on a journey, and I knew I'd found the title of the book.

Thank you, Gena, for reading many versions of the manuscript, brainstorming with me, and giving me honest feedback.

I want to thank my editor, Allison. You gave me invaluable feedback and encouragement. With your help, Paul and Genny came to life.

I am grateful to God for laying this story on my heart. I hope readers take comfort in God's love and know He is always with us, even when we feel forsaken or unworthy.

A Note to Readers

As with most authors, this novel was a labor of love. Paul and Genny's story began as a recurring dream years ago. One night in early April 2020, as I laid in bed trying to fall asleep, their story came to life and played through my mind like a vivid movie. I didn't fall asleep until after two in the morning and had to get up to take my daughter to school four hours later. When I returned home, I began writing the outline.

Paul and Genny became a part of my life as I worked to put their story on paper. I've learned so much about writing and myself through this experience. There's more to Paul and Genny's story. I hope to release *The Journey Home* by the end of 2022 or early 2023 at the latest. I hope you'll join them on their next journey.

Sign up for my newsletter to keep up to date on upcoming releases: http://eepurl.com/hVEPcH

Reviews are important to the success of a book. An <u>honest</u> review with retailers and social media is appreciated.

If any grammatical or continuity errors are found, please contact me at andieyoungwrites@gmail.com.

Thank you for your support!